NATURE'S PASSION

Colt was lost.

Never in his life had he known a woman like this one, real, unpretentious, and unafraid of ... sensuality. This was the woman with whom h... re his life.

He slipped hi... nd nuzzled at her hair as ... forth, watching as the ... he mare's neck.

He k... the smell of the mare, b... clean fresh smell of the wom... behind her, and slid his hands slo... berately down her hips, enjoying the seductive curves of her body. Unfastening her stocking, he rolled it slowly down . . .

Destiny moaned at Colt's touch and her head rolled from side to side as she watched the stallion in a frenzy to mate, nipping at the mare with bared teeth as he tried to mount her.

The mare trembled at his touch.

Destiny knew just how the mare felt.

* * *

On *One Shining Moment*

"Five stars! A great novel."   —*Affaire de Coeur*

"A story you'll read many times for the pure enjoyment of it. Excellent!"

—*Rendezvous*

On *Thorn of the Rose*

"Brimming with colorful characters, adventure, intrigue, and sultry escapades galore, *Thorn of the Rose* is a lively, emotionally intense, bawdy tale that will thrill readers."

—*Romantic Times*

TODAY'S HOTTEST READS
ARE TOMORROW'S SUPERSTARS

THE HEART REMEMBERS

SANDRA DAVIDSON

ZEBRA BOOKS
KENSINGTON PUBLISHING CORP.

ZEBRA BOOKS are published by

Kensington Publishing Corp.
850 Third Avenue
New York, NY 10022

First Printing: December, 1995

Printed in the United States of America

One

September 1995

"Young lady, I want to commend you on writing such an accurate book. . . ."

Destiny looked up at the ancient face with curiosity. Accurate? What a strange way to describe a work of fiction.

". . . about my ancestors," the old woman continued.

Destiny's eye flickered in surprise.

"You've done an excellent job. I only wish you hadn't exposed the intimate moments of their lives with such great detail. After all, what goes on between a man and a woman in the privacy of their bedroom should remain there."

Shifting her weight in the chair provided by the bookstore, Destiny wondered who this woman was and how she could possibly think *One Shining Moment* was a true story. Not only true, but about her ancestors? There was only one explanation. The poor old thing was senile. Perhaps, if she humored her, she'd go away happy.

Weary from signing her books in the mall bookstore for hours, Destiny was grateful her senile fan was the last one waiting in line for her autograph. Laying her pen on the table, she wiggled her stiff fingers to loosen them up. Tiny sparkles of light reflecting off the three huge cubic zirconia rings she wore danced across the black crepe dress of the old woman.

The image conjured up thoughts of fairy dust being

sprinkled by a magical being. She smiled, thinking about that. Obviously, her very active writer's imagination was working overtime.

Looking up at the timeworn face once again, her smile vanished, replaced by the oddest sensation of déjà vu as she gazed into vibrant blue eyes. "Do I know you?"

The woman's penetrating gaze was unwavering. "Do you?"

Shrugging off the strange feeling, Destiny took the paperback book from the woman's gnarled, liver-spotted hand. "I was mistaken. I'm sure we've never met."

Placing the historical romance on the table, she opened it to the title page to sign it, surprised by the worn, dog-eared condition it was in. Her book had been out only a matter of weeks, but obviously someone had read it several times already. "Who shall I autograph it to?"

The old lady looked at Destiny as if she were a simpleton. "Why, to Lydia McAmmon, of course, direct descendant of Shining Dawn and Blade McAmmon."

Destiny almost laughed out loud. "You can't be serious." Shining Dawn and Blade had been created from her imagination. In fact, all the characters in *One Shining Moment* had been invented except for the Indian leader Osceola, and a few other historical people. This woman wasn't senile, she was downright crazy.

"Indeed, I am very serious."

"A direct descendant? That's totally . . ." Remembering she was supposed to be humoring the old lady, Destiny signed her name with a flourish, saying, "Then that must mean Shining Dawn married Blade. That's nice to know. At the end of my book they hadn't married yet, you know."

"Exactly my point, young lady. You ended your book too soon. You should have continued the story until its logical conclusion. Seems to me a professional writer would do that."

That was it. She drew the line when people accused her

of being unprofessional. Sweet old lady or not, she wasn't going to stand for her reputation as a writer being besmirched. "I see. Well, I'm sorry you don't like the way I wrote my story, but since I made it up entirely from my imagination, I guess . . ."

"Made it up? How can you say that? Everything you wrote about is related most vividly in my ancestor's journal, except, of course, for your naughty little sex scenes."

Ignoring that last remark, Destiny asked, "You have a journal about the characters in my book? That's impossible."

"I beg to differ with you, child, but I do have Shining Dawn's journal."

It was obvious this woman was in need of a reality check. "Then I'm sure you won't mind showing it to me."

"My dear, the journal is over a hundred and fifty years old. I am not in the habit of carrying it around with me, but I would be most happy for you to come with me now, since you seem to doubt its existence, and see it for yourself."

Destiny wanted to say no and be done with this crazy conversation. She had made up her characters, and had nothing to prove, but she couldn't help being very curious. After all, she was a writer, and curiosity went with the territory.

The old woman spoke again, her voice becoming suddenly animated. "And when you're there, I shall be very happy to show you Blade McAmmon's Celtic cross, too."

The Celtic cross?

Blade's Celtic cross? That cinched it for her. Her curiosity was strong now. Her hero's cross had been an important part of her story. "You have the Celtic cross? But how . . ."

"How did I come by it?"

That wasn't what she meant. She was going to ask how Lydia could have it when it, too, was imaginary, but intrigued she just nodded her head.

"You'll find out how after you've read the journal."

Nothing could keep Destiny from going with Lydia now. "Thank you for your invitation, Mrs. McAmmon," Gathering up her remaining bookmarks and autographed by the author stickers, she swept them into her canvas book bag. "I'd be happy to go with you."

"It's *Miss* McAmmon, thank you very much, but you may call me Miss Lydia, everyone does. I never married, you see. Never had the inclination for such foolishness as romance."

"Then I'm amazed you ever picked up my book."

"I would never have known your book existed if not for the young lady my nephew is seeing. She told him about it, and he in turn told me that your book was written about our family. Naturally, I wanted to read it. I just wish . . ."

"I know. You wish I had left out the sex scenes." Destiny groaned inwardly, hoping she wouldn't live to regret humoring the old lady. Immediately her mind conjured up a dozen reasons why she shouldn't go with her, starting with her need to find a motel to stay in for the night.

Though St. Augustine was her hometown, she hadn't lived here for three years. She had moved to the solitude of the North Carolina mountains where her four published books were written with a speed that truly amazed her. She was in St. Augustine now only for the last of her book-signings before heading back to her beloved mountaintop home.

It wasn't like her to go traipsing off with a stranger, even if she were a feeble old woman. She was surprised to discover that her sense of adventure was stronger than her common sense.

In any case, perhaps she could clear up the mystery for Miss Lydia and her nephew. Set them straight. She didn't want them to go on thinking that the characters in her book were somehow related to them.

Saying her goodbyes to the store manager, and the clerks who had helped her with her book-signing, Destiny was amused at the curiosity they displayed toward the ancient woman waiting patiently for her, a contented smile upon her face.

In a matter of moments she was in her minivan, following Miss Lydia's ancient Oldsmobile down US1 to Moultrie Creek, then down the road that ran alongside the creek.

She turned onto a private road marked with a sign that read PRIVATE, KEEP OUT and a shiver of fear climbed up her spine. If it had been anyone but Miss Lydia leading the way she would have turned around and left by now, afraid she was being lured into a trap by some fanatical fan straight out of Stephen King's *Misery*.

The road led through a thick stand of woods that made her all the more uneasy, but remembering who she was with, she immediately felt foolish. If you can't trust a grandmotherly little old lady, who could you trust. Still, she couldn't help wondering why Miss Lydia was so eager for her to go to her house. Chastising herself, she decided her overactive imagination was at work again.

In a moment, when the beautiful old Victorian house came into view, she was very glad she had come.

The ornate gingerbread-trimmed home stood at the edge of a clearing, tall and stately against the backdrop of the shimmering blue of the Intercoastal waterway. Painted a creamy white with gingerbread trim frosted in a soft pastel peach, it took her breath away. She had always dreamed of living in a home like this.

Helping Miss Lydia up the wide stairs to the front door, Destiny basked in the beauty of the old home. It was so peaceful here, with the kind of privacy she craved. The same wonderful privacy she enjoyed in her mountain home. "What a beautiful house. Do you live here alone, Miss Lydia?"

"Most of the time I do, but I have a passel of great nieces and nephews who visit me every year, and of course, my nephew Drake lives right here in town. He comes out to check on me quite often. Perhaps, you'll get a chance to meet him."

Lydia opened the front door and ushered Destiny inside. "Make yourself right at home while I prepare lunch, and then I'll get out the journal and leave you alone to read it to your heart's content."

Darn it all, she wanted to get right to the journal, but knew it would be too impolite to insist on seeing it now. The old thing was probably very lonely and wanted a little company. What could it hurt? "Is there anything I can do to help?"

"Not a thing. Poke around if you like. I know how fascinating these old Victorian homes can be to romantic young women such as yourself."

Destiny didn't have to be asked twice. She had never been in an original Victorian home before. It would be great research if she ever decided to write a book about that era.

Starting in the parlor decorated with authentic period pieces, she made her way through the first floor, absorbing the details into her mind before climbing up the graceful curving staircase to the second floor.

The wide hallway upstairs was a pleasant change from the stark, narrow hallways of modern day homes, and the creaking of the floor as she walked upon it sounded cozy and friendly. She had always had a penchant for old homes.

Peeking into the first room on her left, she discovered what must surely be Lydia's own bedroom and hesitated only a second before walking in. After all, Miss Lydia did tell her she was free to poke around.

The room was elegantly appointed with dusty rose moire balloon curtains to accent the two large windows looking out over the water. And a huge tapestry of an English garden scene done in deep tones of burgundy, rose, and fern green decorated the wall opposite an ancient four-poster bed.

The bed was hung with hand-crocheted bed-curtains, and a cherry dressing table with a large oval mirror stood in the corner of the room reflecting the light from the windows.

A silvery object beckoned to her from atop the dressing table, and curious, Destiny walked over to it, her heart in her throat.

It couldn't be, but there it was . . .

. . . the Celtic cross.

She reached out to touch it, and crystal images bounced off her rings, raining the mirror with iridescent sparkles. She hardly noticed, absorbed in telling herself that the cross couldn't possibly be the one from her book.

But . . . as the ornate details of the pewter cross registered on her mind, so did the slight, perfectly round indentation on the otherwise unmarred surface. She caught her breath in astonishment.

She knew how the mark had come to be on the cross.

It was made by a bullet that had become embedded there when a soldier shot at Shining Dawn, hitting the cross that hung over her heart instead.

This was crazy and utterly impossible. She had made up that scene to add excitement to her story, and yet, here was the cross just as she had imagined it, and there was the mark made by the bullet.

She knew in her heart that it was no coincidence that the cross should be marked exactly as the one in her story. She had never believed in coincidence before and she wasn't going to start now. But if it wasn't a coincidence, then . . .

Shining Dawn and Blade really did exist.

But that couldn't be. Raking her brain for another more plausible explanation, she could come up with nothing that rang of truth. Her instincts had always been very powerful, bordering on the psychic even, and they were working overtime now, telling her to believe.

Believe.

Nothing could have stopped her from touching this relic of the past, this oh so real proof that the story she thought she had imagined had really happened.

Reaching down, she caressed the indentation with her finger and felt a slight tingling sensation. She blinked her eyes in surprise, and when she opened them, caught a movement in the oval mirror over the dressing table. Reflected there was a young man leaning casually against the wall.

Startled, she quickly composed herself, addressing his image in the glass, her hand still resting on the Celtic cross. "I wasn't being nosy. Miss Lydia told me I could look around."

The man continued to stare at her, but his gaze was cool and distant, as if he were looking right through her. Her heart quickened. He was without a doubt the sexiest man she had ever seen, and by his arrogant stance, it was obvious he knew it. He was tall, lanky, with short light brown hair and shoulders a woman could get lost in. He wore a white shirt and tight brown leather pants that caressed his slim hips and accentuated his long, long legs and she immediately envisioned them wrapped around her in the throes of lovemaking.

Silently, he continued to stare at her in the mirror, making her more acutely aware that she was alone with him and his blatant sexuality. Her face flamed remembering her erotic thoughts about him, but she steeled herself and turned around to face him, mumbling, "I'm sorry, let me introduce myself, I'm . . ."

The room was empty.

The man was gone. How odd and how rude.

Then, as reality hit her, she started shaking all over. It was impossible for him to make it out of the room without her seeing him in the short time it took for her to turn around. *The door had to be at least ten feet away.*

Did she imagine the whole thing?

Was she so desperate to find the man of her dreams she was actually seeing his reflection in mirrors now?

She ran to the door and peered down the hall, but he wasn't there. Somehow, she knew he wouldn't be.

Unnerved, she hurried down to the kitchen, hoping for her sanity's sake that he would be there, but Miss Lydia was alone, setting two plates on the kitchen table.

"Hope you don't mind eating in the kitchen, my dear, but it's much cozier here than in the dining room?"

That will be fine. Uh . . . Miss Lydia?"

"Yes?"

"Is there someone else here, in the house, I mean? Your nephew Drake, perhaps?"

"My nephew? My dear young lady, my nephew is exactly where he should be, at his law firm. Why do you ask?"

"It's just I could swear I saw a man reflected in the mirror over your dressing table."

"Probably just the play of light from the sun and water. I often see strange images in that mirror."

That couldn't be it. She had seen every detail of the man in living color, right down to the storm-cloud gray of his eyes. The only explanation was she had hallucinated him. But why? Was her mind trying to tell her something? Was it trying to tell her she needed a man?

Maybe so, but why him? He was too outrageously sexy, and way too young, only in his early twenties, she was sure. Why would she conjure up some one so young? She had never been attracted to younger men before. They offered no sense of security, emotional security that is, and that was what she needed most. She had all the financial security she needed now that her writing career was taking off.

Hmm, still, if she had to conjure up a man, she had certainly picked a good-looking one, and as long as he was imaginary it didn't matter if he were younger than she. What was that old saying? Oh yes, he could park his shoes under her bed anytime.

"My dear, are you all right? I was just telling you that the mirror belonged to Shining Dawn. In fact, everything in my bedroom belonged to her."

Destiny shook her head in astonishment. Shining Dawn. It was so strange to hear someone talk about her as if she were real, but then, she was, wasn't she? "You have no idea how confusing all this is to me."

"It is strange to think you had no knowledge of Shining Dawn's journal. I can't help wondering where you learned of her life."

"Not half as much as I wonder, believe me."

Destiny tried to brush off the eerie feeling that enveloped her, but too many strange things had already happened that day.

It suddenly occurred to her that Miss Lydia could have invented the journal to trick her into thinking it was real, but . . . there was no way she could have put that bullet indentation on the Celtic cross. Not unless she was adept at shooting guns. The idea of Miss Lydia shooting a bullet at the cross with her ancient, shaky hands was incongruous. No, Miss Lydia was telling the truth. The cross was genuine, and she'd bet her life that the journal was, too.

Feeling as though she was lost in the twilight zone she became all the more eager to start reading it. Perhaps it would reveal the answer to this bizarre mystery.

After a delicious lunch of cucumber sandwiches and tea, and thick rich brownies for dessert, Miss Lydia led her into the library and seated her at a lovely cherry reading table. Opening a drawer, she gently retrieved the journal. This was it. She would soon know which one of them was the crazy lady.

It didn't take her long to discover that the journal was authentic. No one could have possibly faked the delicate condition it was in. Bound in tan buckskin, the yellowed pages held faded indigo blue writing of perfect penmanship that was still legible. The name Shining Dawn jumped off the page at her, unexpectedly bringing tears to her eyes.

Shining Dawn *was* real.

She was real.

Her hand brushed lightly over the written page in awe, tracing the handwriting of a woman who had lived 125 years ago. Miss Lydia really was a descendant of Shining Dawn and Blade.

When she got past that enormous traumatic revelation, she settled in and absorbed herself in the story she knew so well. Time passed and the room became dimmer as she read on, totally unaware of anything but the true account of the characters in her book.

It was incredible, but it was all there. Shining Dawn, as a child of thirteen alone in the wilderness after her parents died of yellow fever. Sitting between their dead bodies, rifle in hand, trying to keep a panther from devouring the corpses. Now, knowing that had really happened, Destiny found herself crying over Shining Dawn's plight.

Blade McAmmon, the hero of her book, was in the journal, too. Blade was a half-breed soldier, ashamed of the Indian blood that flowed through his veins until Osceola and the grown-up Shining Dawn showed him that it was a proud heritage.

And there was Osceola in all his nobility and courage. His betrayal and capture at the parlay at Moultrie Creek. The dramatic scene where Shining Dawn was shot. The oversized Celtic cross over her heart saving her from death. It was all there. Truly incredible.

Each entry she read further increased her excitement. It was like finding long lost relatives, and in a way that's what she was doing, for she knew as much about their lives as she did her own. But how had she known? That was the truly amazing question.

She was three-quarters of a way through the journal when Miss Lydia came back into the room. Destiny was surprised to see that it was dark outside. How long had she been reading? "I'm sorry. I didn't realize it was so late. I won't impose on your time anymore, but I would like to come back, if I may, to finish reading the journal."

Lydia saw Destiny's tearstained face and said softly, "Are you expected anywhere tonight?"

"No."

"Then why not please an old lady and stay the night.

That way, you'll have plenty of time to finish the journal in the morning."

The offer was certainly tempting. When she left here she would have to find a motel for the night. And, too, she had just started reading the entries written in 1846, several years after the time period of her own book, and was very curious to see what had happened to Shining Dawn.

She still couldn't believe she wasn't dreaming all this. Had she somehow tuned in to an ancestor's memory? She had always believed that it was possible. If it were true, wouldn't that mean that she was related to one of the characters in her book? Perhaps even to Shining Dawn and Blade McAmmon?

Hmm, Destiny McAmmon. She liked the sound of that name. It pleased her to think that they could be her great, great, grandparents. But that was just wishful thinking on her part. Part of her need to have a family of her own. Chances are, she would never know just how she was able to create their true story so she might as well accept it. Better to leave now, and put the impossible out of her mind.

"I'd love to stay." The words came out of her mouth before she could stop them, causing her to blink in surprise.

"Wonderful. I have some lovely pot roast left over from last night. I'll just make a salad and we can have a nice little supper before retiring."

Smiling at Miss Lydia, Destiny said, "You are very kind to do this for a stranger."

"Stranger? Nothing of the kind. It seems obvious to me that we are related in some way, or you wouldn't know the intimate details of my family's life. Perhaps if you tell me about your family, I can find the connection."

Destiny got the strangest feeling that Miss Lydia had been waiting for this moment all day. What was so strange about that? It was natural for her to be curious about someone who knew so much about her ancestors. "I only wish I could, but you see, I have no memory at all of the first eight years of my life."

A strange smile flickered across Miss Lydia's face for an instant, and Destiny wondered if she just imagined it. Seated on white wicker furniture on the front porch, they ate their supper while Destiny told Lydia about her strange lack of memory.

"And you have no recollections at all?"

"None."

"How very odd. Then your name isn't really Davidson?"

"No. I took the last name of the doctor who saved my life the first day that I can remember. You see, someone, we have no idea who, left me on the steps of Flagler Hospital. I was near death."

"Oh, my poor child. And the name Destiny. How did you come by that unusual name?"

"I named myself that, although, thinking back, I have no idea why. The name just came to me. Dr. Davidson speculated that it was probably my real name. That it was the only thing about my past life that my mind dared remember. He thinks I must have gone through something very traumatic to block out everything that happened to me until the day he saved my life."

"How awful. And what happened to you after that?"

"The authorities tried to find my mother and father, but nothing came of it. It was as if they vanished from the face of the earth. I spent the rest of my childhood being shunted from one foster family to the next, never seeming to fit in anywhere."

"But you realize what that means . . . you could indeed be related to me."

A large lump formed in Destiny's throat and with eyes shining bright she answered, "Do you really think so? It just seems too good to be true."

The old woman reached over to pat Destiny's hand, then clutched it tight in her own gnarled hand. "Nothing of the sort. You named yourself most aptly, child, for it must surely have been destiny that drew me to your book-signing."

Was that it? Destiny wondered, looking into the ancient eyes of the woman who had changed her life so quickly. Was that the reason she had come to this house? To find her family?

A family. Was it possible that in all these years there was a family waiting for her, wondering what happened to her? She had given up hope of that a long time ago.

She had given up hope of ever marrying, too. Oh, there had been more than one man she could have married, but for some reason she couldn't explain she had always backed away from the relationship. Perhaps she was destined to be alone. Destined to achieve her dreams only between the covers of her romance novels.

Later that night, lying in bed in a pleasant, airy, white-washed room that looked out onto Spanish moss-draped oaks, Destiny lay awake, too elated to sleep. Miss Lydia had come into the room before going to her own, and placed the Celtic cross on the nightstand by the bed, the light shining in her eyes, rivaling the sparkle of Destiny's rings. "Dream on this. Perhaps it will help you believe that you do have a family."

Whooo. Whooo, uh whooo.

The soft call of the owl right outside the window broke through her reverie. Who? Who? Who? That was the question, wasn't it? Who was she?

She drifted off to sleep with that question on her mind, and awoke in the middle of the night, restlessly kicking off her covers in the sweltering heat. Reaching over to the nightstand, she picked up the Celtic cross, her fingers still weighted with star-bright rings and clasped it to her breast. Comforted by the coolness of the metal, she allowed sleep to take her once again.

She was dreaming. A wonderful dream of the sexy man in the mirror. But he wasn't leaning against the wall anymore. Now he was on the bed, leaning over her, whispering into her ear.

"I've been waiting a long time for this."

The sound of his soft, yet very masculine voice sent her heart soaring. She wanted to tell him she had been waiting for him, too, but his lips descended on hers, and he kissed her breath away.

Shocked at the impact of the passionate kiss, her body clamored for more and he was more than eager to give it to her. She felt the weight of his body as he lowered himself onto her and the electric touch of skin on skin almost made her faint from pleasure.

Her arms snaked around his neck eager to pull him closer, and his breath warmed her face with erotic little shivers. She looked into his eyes and drowned in their depths. She wanted him. More than she had ever wanted anyone before.

He kissed her again, grinding his mouth against hers, pushing her thighs apart with his leg, the touch of his manhood against her scorching her with desire.

Whooo. Whooo, uh whooo.

She awoke with a start still out of breath from the fervent kiss, still in the throes of passionate need. "Damn you, owl, did you have to wake me just when we were getting to the good part?"

The dream had been so real, so excruciatingly real that she could still smell the masculine fragrance of him on her body, the taste of him in her mouth. She wanted him, needed him, ached for him to complete the act of lovemaking they had been engaged in, and knowing the impossibility of that felt a terrible loneliness permeate her heart.

Two

She must have fallen back asleep for the next thing she knew sunshine was streaking through her window, filtered through the lush greenery outside. A residue of sexual need still clung to her as the memory of her dream came back to haunt her.

Her dream lover had filled her with exactly the kind of overpowering desire she had written about in her books, but never experienced in real life.

A light rapping on the door brought Destiny back to reality. "Come in."

Miss Lydia entered with a tray of food. "Still abed? My, my, but you young people do sleep the day away."

Destiny glanced at the ancient windup clock on the nightstand. Seven-thirty. She groaned inwardly. "You certainly get up bright and early, Miss Lydia."

"Five-thirty every morning, rain or shine. At my age, every second counts. Don't want to fritter away the time I have left."

Sitting up in bed while Miss Lydia placed the tray on her lap, Destiny commented, "I have a feeling you never frittered away a single day of your life."

"I wish that were true, but I was no different from you when I was young and pretty."

Destiny had no trouble picturing Miss Lydia as a young woman, for though her eyes were a faded blue, they still held a vibrant spark of life. It came to her then that Miss

Lydia might resemble her ancestor Shining Dawn and that thought sent a jolt of adrenaline through her that finished the job of waking her up.

Covering her excitement, she said, "Miss Lydia, really, you didn't have to bring me my breakfast in bed."

"And why not? A pretty thing like you deserves to be fussed over now and then, and I enjoy doing it."

Breathing in the fragrance of the steaming coffee and the delicious-looking crepes on the Fiesta plates, Destiny murmured, "Not half as much as I enjoy being the recipient. Your crepes look delicious."

Miss Lydia looked pleased with herself. "Thought you might enjoy them." Then, noticing the three oversized sparkling diamonds on Destiny's left hand, she commented, "Forgive my curiosity. I'm not usually so nosy, but I couldn't help but notice your rings at the book-signing yesterday, and I see you're still wearing them. Do you always wear your diamonds to bed? I must say, I don't blame you. They're really quite spectacular. You must be doing very well as a writer."

Destiny laughed. "I wear them all the time, but not because they're so valuable. Actually, they're only cubic zirconias. I bought myself one ring for each book I've had published, and I'm overdue to buy one for *One Shining Moment.*"

"What a nice way to reward yourself."

"Oh, they're not just for pleasure. They serve a very useful purpose. Everyone notices your hand when you're signing books, and my hands are not particularly beautiful. The rings add a glamorous focal point. That's why I wear them all on one hand. People are too overwhelmed by them to notice my large knuckles and too short nails."

"Well, my dear, that's very clever of you. And you say they're not genuine diamonds? Why, they sparkle so brilliantly, I could have sworn they were real."

"I have to admit, I love the sparkle, too. Until recently,

I couldn't afford real diamonds, and now that I can, you know what? I don't have any desire to buy them. I'm content with my CZs."

"CZs? Oh, yes, cubic zirconias. My, my, you learn something new every day, don't you? Well, your lovely CZs fooled me." Patting her hand, Lydia continued, "I'll leave you to your breakfast now. You'll find me working in my flower beds if you need me. The garden club will be meeting here on Thursday, and it wouldn't do for them to find any leaf mold or mites on my blossoms."

Watching the old woman walk to the door, Destiny couldn't help but admire how active she was for her age. She hoped that when she reached that age she would be just as spry.

After eating the delicious breakfast, she showered and dressed, then made a beeline for the journal. She could hardly wait to finish it, although she was still having a hard time with the concept that she was reading about people that really and truly existed.

In her novel, Blade had been offered the position as supervisor over all the Indian agents in Florida, and she discovered in the journal that was exactly what happened.

But the question was, how could she possibly have known that?

In all her research at the historical library in St. Augustine, she had never come across any mention of Blade and Shining Dawn. This was really crazy. Of course, there was one logical explanation for that, which just occurred to her. She had never investigated any records past 1838, because she had no reason to. Her story ended then. Perhaps, if she had looked up the years after that, she would have found them mentioned somewhere.

Opening the leather-bound journal very carefully, she turned to the page she left off at, reading the entries for 1846 with great interest. It seemed Little Bit Usina, Shining

Dawn's friend, had married Gary Mandrell, and the two couples remained close throughout the years.

Life was good for both families until September of that year when Blade left on a hunting trip with his young son, Johnny. Although it wasn't unusual for Shining Dawn to accompany him, she remained behind at their homestead near a small Indian reservation because she was pregnant with her third child.

Little Bit, pregnant with her second child, and about to give birth, was another compelling reason why she stayed behind. The diminutive woman trusted no one but Shining Dawn to be her midwife.

Destiny read what happened next with her heart in her throat.

September 15.

Blade has taken our son with him on a hunting trip, and will be gone for several days. He thinks I've been overprotective of Johnny, but I don't agree. He's only six, hardly more than a baby. However, I reluctantly gave in, knowing that it would be good for father and son to spend precious time together.

Little Bit insisted Gary join them. He has been so solicitous of her health that she cannot but sigh without him hovering over her. I thought it very brave of her to let him go, what with the birth of her baby only a week or two away, but she said she feared her nerves could not stand another day of his bothersome behavior. Little Susan was sent to her Aunt Celeste's until the laying-in period has ended.

Poor Dee Dee wanted to go hunting with her father, but I appeased her by promising her that she and I would have our own hunting trip when they returned. But, of course, we will be hunting for herbs and roots to make my special potent tea, instead of hunting for deer and bear.

September 18

Little Bit has been having pains for the past two nights and so the birth should be very soon. I pray that is so, for the heat and humidity are tremendous. I don't know how much longer she can bear it. I suffer too, but being only five months along, and barely showing at all, can better cope with it.

September 19

Terrible news has just reached us. Several Seminoles on the reservation have come down with the yellow fever. I am almost paralyzed with fear that I shall have to once again live through the terrible time when my parents died of that same horrific scourge.

Fate cannot be that cruel.

September 20

Today I took Little Bit and my daughter to the little cabin in the woods where Blade and I occasionally spent time before it got too run-down. I brought them there hoping the fever would not find us, but it was already too late. My own sweet little girl is burning up with fever.

September 21

Dee Dee's fever rages on and it is a terrible thing to behold. I fear for my sanity at having to go through this awful ordeal once again, and I thank the Great Spirit for sparing Blade and Johnny. Away on their hunting trip, they have no idea what is happening here.

Little Bit's labor goes on and on with only a short time between each pain, and I don't know how much more of it she can bear.

She cries for Gary, and her daughter Susan, and I wish for her sake they could be here, but for their

*own sake, I am glad that they are spared this awful
ordeal.*

September 24

*It is all over now, and weary and sick at heart
though I am, I need to put on paper the events of the
evening of September 21st.*

*It soon became obvious that Little Bit was in des-
perate trouble. She was overcome with the compulsion
to push out the child, but it would not come, just as
I feared. She grew weaker and weaker with each fruit-
less push and I knew I must do something quickly or
lose both her and her unborn child. The baby's head
was too large to be delivered in a normal fashion,
and unless I had the fortitude to cut her open and
take the child they would both surely die.*

*The howling began then. Wolves, attracted by Little
Bit's screams of pain, and my daughter's feverish
cries. The tiny, dilapidated cabin resounded with their
agonized voices till I feared I would go mad.*

*But I do not want to relate that terrible scene now,
it is too unbearable. For now, let it suffice to say that
at the moment I cut my dear friend's stomach open
to take the child from her, my daughter went into convulsions. I was then faced with the hardest decision
of my life: Whether to abandon Little Bit with her
gaping wound, and her poor little baby waiting to be
taken from her, or minister to my daughter in the
hopes of saving her.*

*By then, a terrible storm was raging outside and
the door to the cabin blew open. It was more than a
mortal woman could handle alone, and so I prayed
to the Great Spirit to keep my daughter safe. But it
seems even He had deserted me, for in terrible irony,
the moment Little Bit's son was born my little girl
was taken from me.*

But, I cannot write of that now, and I dare not even think of that awful night, for fear of losing my remaining sanity, for what happened was truly incomprehensible.

Perhaps one day, I'll be strong enough to write of it, but not now, my pain is too great.

September 25

Little Bit's son Colt is a huge, darling baby. I take comfort in holding him in my arms, and knowing that if not for me, he would not have been born. But, oh, when my arms are empty, they ache for my daughter, for my sweet little Dee Dee. I pray that I have the strength to go on for Blade and Johnny's sake. I know my husband will not mind when I tell him that I gave his Celtic cross to Little Bit for her son. I pray it will protect him, keep him safe as it once did for me, so many years ago.

That was the last passage written in Shining Dawn's journal. And no wonder. Shining Dawn and Little Bit had gone through hell that night, and neither of them probably ever wanted to be reminded of it.

The full impact of what she had read brought tears to Destiny's eyes and she let them flow freely, knowing from experience that to hold them back would have been impossible. Poor Shining Dawn. To have lost her daughter at the moment when Little Bit's son was being born was both ironic and tragic.

But, oh how she wished she had written more about her daughter's death. Obviously, the Celtic cross had not kept Shining Dawn's daughter safe. Did the little girl die from convulsions or did the wolves get her when the door blew open? Nothing in her report gave any clues.

It was frustrating not to know, for she felt such compassion for Shining Dawn and Blade at the loss of their daughter. She wanted to know that they had somehow overcome their grief and were able to live out the rest of their lives with some semblance of happiness.

She just had to know. And . . . it suddenly occurred to her how she might find out. She'd visit the St. Augustine Historical Library. Knowing what she did now would make her search fairly easy. If there was anything at all in the library on them, she'd find it.

It occurred to her that she could try to research someone else while she was at it.

Her dream lover.

She might find out that he was real, too.

She couldn't take her mind off of him. But then, she doubted any red-blooded American woman could. He had to be real. The aura of all that powerful masculinity was too dynamic to be imagined, and sexuality oozed from every pore of his beautiful body. Not even a prolific romance writer could have created a man like him.

She thought about what he had been wearing when she saw him reflected in the mirror, but knew it would be hard to pinpoint the time period he belonged to that way. The simple white shirt and leather pants he wore could have fit almost any time after the 1600s.

True. But they certainly didn't fit today's fashions.

His shirt had been yoked and the sleeves were much fuller than any worn today. So, unless he was one of the numerous reenactors from St. Augustine's historical district, he didn't belong to this century.

Too bad. Fabio would have had serious competition if her dream lover did belong to this time.

But it was wrong to compare the two, they were nothing alike. Where Fabio was hugely muscled, and longhaired, her dream lover had been tall and lean, exactly the way she liked her men. Her men? It had been a long time since she could call any man hers. But then, it was her own fault, wasn't it?

It seemed logical that the man in the mirror belonged to the same time period as the McAmmons' and the Mandrells'. That his appearance was connected to Blade McAmmon's Celtic cross. Ha! That was a laugh. There was nothing logical to any of this.

Glad to know her sense of humor was still intact, she sought out Miss Lydia in the garden and found her on her knees, slumped over a wheelbarrow.

"Miss Lydia!"

The old woman opened her eyes and looked up at her in confusion. "What is it? Did I drift off?"

Destiny could have sworn Miss Lydia had been unconscious, but now she wondered if she had just imagined it. How could she have recuperated so fast, if she had been unconscious?

"Are you all right?" she asked, running over to her and kneeling by her side. "You had me going there for a moment. I thought you had a heart attack or stroke."

"Perhaps you're right, my dear. I do have little strokes now and then, but they pass with no real damage. Once in a while my right arm goes numb on me, but it goes away in a few days, and I'm good as new. Don't worry about me. I'm a tough old bird."

Helping Miss Lydia to her feet, Destiny said, "I'm going to call your nephew. Someone should be staying here with you."

"Please . . . don't. He's much too busy to be wasting time baby-sitting for me. I have been thinking for some time now of advertising for a live-in companion, and I suppose this is the time to do so."

"That's a wonderful idea, but I'm not leaving until you do hire someone, if that's all right with you."

In the same light, lilting voice she had used at the bookstore, Miss Lydia exclaimed, "My dear, I'd like nothing better. But . . . I wouldn't want to take you away from your writing."

Her voice sounded so youthful, so healthy, it crossed Destiny's mind that Miss Lydia had faked her fainting spell to keep her there. No, that was ludicrous. What reason could she have for putting on such an act? Besides, it was beneath Lydia's dignity to do that.

"Don't worry about it. That's the beauty of being a writer. We can work at our craft anywhere. Now that everything's settled, let's get you inside and out of this heat. A glass of your lemonade would hit the spot right now."

Lydia's face was beaming. "I think you're right."

Later, when Miss Lydia was resting comfortably on the sofa in the parlor, Destiny called Drake McAmmon's office and reported to him what had happened and what she planned on doing about it. Drake was grateful, and told her he'd rearrange his schedule so he could be with his aunt tomorrow.

Relieved, she spent the rest of the day with Miss Lydia, watching her closely, but the spry old lady seemed to have no aftereffects from her fainting episode.

That made her feel considerably better. For selfishly, she thought that if Miss Lydia was a relative of hers, she couldn't bear the thought of losing her just when she was getting to know her.

To take her mind off such morbid thoughts, she turned her attention to the man of her dreams. She was hoping she'd dream about him again tonight, and went to bed much earlier than usual, eager for the dreaming to begin.

As she pulled the sheet up over her naked form, she remembered her conjecture that the Celtic cross was somehow connected to her dream lover. Each time he had appeared to her, she had been touching the cross.

Was there something supernatural about it?

Nonsense. It was just her powerful imagination working overtime again. Still . . . it wouldn't hurt to hold onto it, just as she had last night. If there was a chance of seeing him again, she'd be crazy not to take it.

Holding the cross in her hand, she felt a slight tingle when it rubbed against the gold bands of her rings, but she attributed it to the friction of metal against metal. Then something odd happened. A faint odor of whiskey suddenly permeated the air, then quickly dissipated, and she wondered if she had imagined that, too. Placing the cross on her chest, she held tight to it and closed her eyes.

Nothing. The room was silent and empty. So much for magical Celtic crosses.

Disappointed, and sheepish at her foolishness, she willed herself to sleep.

Sometime in the deepness of the night she dreamed of him again. He was in bed beside her, sleeping on his side as naturally as if he belonged there.

Sleeping?

This wasn't turning out to be a very sexy dream, but she didn't mind. Just looking at him was treat enough. Turning to face him, she studied his features, enjoying the view of his perfect nose and sensuous lips, the curve of his firm, masculine jaw.

He opened his mouth, and she held her breath in anticipation of his waking up and taking her in his arms. A loud grumbling sound emerged.

He was snoring.

Her dream lover was snoring.

Repressing the desire to laugh, she rested her head on her hands and stared contentedly at his wonderful face, committing it to memory. Even asleep, the power of his sexuality was so strong she had a hard time keeping her hands off him.

Then, suddenly, his eyes opened, as if startled by a noise.

She gasped in surprise.

The man let out a low, rumbling sound of approval when he saw her, and pulled her up against him as easily as if she were a rag doll. Before she had a chance to blink, he was kissing her fervently.

She responded immediately, captive to the desire that spiraled over her at the touch of his body against hers, nothing between them but the pewter cross around his neck. It occurred to her that the cross should be on her chest, not around his neck, but there was no time to worry about that now. She was aroused so quickly and with such great power, that she felt as if she were spinning through the universe.

His body turned to iron as his hands moved over her, exploring her, gently at first, then growing more demanding as want turned to need. And, oh, there was such need. Such desire to mate with him. But there was fear, too. Fear that they would once again be interrupted.

Please. No! She wanted this dream to go on forever.

She wanted to be with this man who had the power to make her feel so good, so womanly, so filled with life. She wanted to revel in the touch of his hands on her naked body.

He raised himself up and she feared he was leaving her. "Oh, no, don't go!" Her hands reached out to hold him. Seeing the hungry look in his eyes, she breathed a sigh of relief. He wasn't going anywhere. He just wanted to look at her, the way she had been looking at him when he was sleeping.

She smiled up at him, letting him know how much he pleased her, and he smiled back, filling her heart with warmth and light. If she hadn't been lost before, she was now.

This man was without a doubt a dream lover in every imaginable way. And she could think of a hundred ways she wanted to be loved by him.

If only he were real.

If only she could be with him always.

Then she felt the weight of his body again, and the thrill of his touch sent her soaring to a place she had never been before. It was as if they were meant to come together. As if their very existence depended on fulfilling the deep desire between them. And, believing that, she let it happen.

She couldn't have stopped it if she wanted to, for when he entered her, swiftly, surely, the world exploded and disappeared in the wake of the tremendous heat the touch of him inside her created. She was no longer capable of reason. No longer able to think of anything but the overpowering urgency of her need to be fulfilled. The frantic fear that their lovemaking would once more be interrupted.

She wrapped her legs around him, holding him tight, urging him on with little erotic sounds that escalated as the fever between them grew out of control.

They came together over and over again, moving with a frenzy that drove her out of her mind with desire. She had waited a long time for passion such as this. So very long that she wanted to laugh and cry at the same time, experiencing it at last. Overcome with feeling, she grabbed hold of the hair at the back of his head as if it were the mane of a bucking stallion and held on tight as he rode her hard.

Their bodies became slicked with sweat, but that only increased the pleasure between them. She reveled in the union of their bodies, the perfect union of their minds, both bent on the same happy conclusion—focusing on one intense thought—fulfillment of desire.

Too soon the heat of him, the wonderful soul-filling touch of him moving inside her brought her to the point of no return. Caught in the delirium of rapture her hands roamed down his head to his neck and would have gone further yet, but one of her rings got caught in the pewter chain of his Celtic cross. Too far gone to notice or care, her body shattered into a thousand molten pieces of sheer ecstasy.

When she was able to breathe again, she felt triumphant that she hadn't awakened in the midst of her fantasy. That would have been too unbearable. Their mating had been incredible. Too incredible, alas, to happen anywhere but in a dream. But if that's where she had to be to experience it, she was ready to dream her life away.

Untangling the heart-shaped stone still caught in the chain of the pewter cross, it occurred to her this would be a good place for her dream to end. But she was glad it hadn't.

Smiling up at him in anticipation of more wonderfully sensual kisses, she was surprised to see him gazing down at her with a puzzled expression.

"Where the hell did you come from? I thought I was dreaming. I know I was dreaming. Either I'm still drunk, still sleeping, or . . ."

The sound of his voice jarred her from the sweet haze of contentment. It sounded too real to be part of her dream. The smile slid from her face as her gaze strayed : . . over his shoulder . . . to the gaudy red-flowered wallpaper on the opposite wall.

Miss Lydia's walls were painted white.

Her heart began to race.

Wild-eyed, she took in the unfamiliar contents of the room surrounding her as the rising sun winked at her through a window that had not been there the night before.

Three

For a moment, it crossed Colt's mind that there was something decidedly strange about his being in bed with this woman, enticing though she may be. Then understanding hit him. He grinned and in a triumphant voice declared, "I get it. You're my birthday present from Daddy."

Destiny's dream was turning into a nightmare.

That was the answer. She had gone straight from her erotic dream into one of those mixed-up dreams that made no sense at all. None of this was really happening. How could it be? How could she have gone to sleep in Miss Lydia's beautiful Victorian home and awakened in what looked like a hotel room from the set of *Young Guns* or *Maverick,* or, or . . .

"Daddy told me he was going to get me a beautiful redhead for my birthday, but I thought he was just jokin'. But here you are, and Red, you've started my birthday off with a real bang." Taking her head in his hands, he licked lavishly at the tip of her nose.

The wet heat of his tongue, mingling with the sour aroma of whiskey on his breath broke through her shield of denial and she knew she wasn't dreaming.

This was real.

Very, very, real. If that wasn't enough to convince her, the sudden hardness poking against her thigh certainly was.

Trying hard to keep from panicking, she answered, "I

don't know what's happening, but whoever you are, please get off me before I scream for help."

"Aw, Red, why would you want to go and do that? I'm sure Daddy paid you real well for servicing me."

"Servicing you? *Servicing you?* How dare you! It was just a dream. That's all. A dream. I can't be held responsible for what happens in my dreams."

Her voice escalated into a frightened whimper as panic nibbled at the corners of her mind. If this was real, she had just made love to a perfect stranger and she didn't want to think about how that had been accomplished, or whose bed she was in now.

Colt laughed. "That's the lamest excuse I ever heard. About as bad as blaming it on being too drunk to know what you were doing."

Anger saved her from completely falling apart. "Get this straight. I've never met your daddy, and I'm not—repeat—not—and have never been a . . ." She tried to think of a word that didn't sound as harsh as hooker or prostitute, but all she could come up with was . . . "Scarlet Lady. I am a perfectly respectable romance writer who . . ."

Colt interrupted with a rowdy catcall. "Woow oooh! Scarlet Lady? That's not what they're called around these parts." Then seeing how angry she was getting, he figured he's better let up on her some. "Let me try and understand this. You weren't sent here by Daddy?"

"No!"

"Then tell me why a woman I've never met before, a *respectable lady* would hop into my bed in the middle of the night."

Tears stung at Destiny's eyes as she tried to hold onto her pride, not to mention what little was left of her dignity. But she couldn't blame him for thinking she was a hooker. How could he possibly conceive that she had somehow been magically transported to his bed in the midst of an erotic dream? It was hard enough for her to accept.

A loud rapping on the door kept her from trying to explain further. In astonishment, she watched as the man jumped out of bed and strode over to the door completely naked.

She started to turn her head away, but the flawless beauty of his masculine body was too much to resist. Hell, she was human wasn't she? If she had to end up in someone's bed she was darned glad it was his.

Tearing her gaze from him when he opened the door, she turned her attention to the giant man standing in the open doorway. Embarrassed that he might see her, she quickly pulled the covers over her head.

"Bo. Am I glad to see you. Maybe you can clear up the mystery of the beautiful redhead."

Bo looked at Colt in surprise. "So, you've seen her already, huh? Damn. Your daddy wanted me to come fetch you downstairs so he could surprise you. He's got her tied up right outside the hotel. What did ya do, peek out of the window while we were bringin' her around?"

"What in hell are you talkin' about? She's not outside, she's right there in my bed."

"Bed? Hey, I know you got drunk last night, but I didn't think you'd start to seeing horses in your bed."

"Horse? Horse?" Then, as the truth dawned on him, Colt ran to the window and looked out. Tied to a post in front of the hotel was a beautiful chestnut horse. Letting out a war whoop, he strode over to Bo and slapped his shoulder. "Seems I got me two beautiful redheads for my birthday, and right this minute, I couldn't tell you which of them pleases me most. Hot damn. That's the mare I've been trying to pry loose from Tom Langford for two months. She'll be the perfect broodmare for Big Red."

"I thought so, too. Now, tell me about this other redhead. Did you go and get yourself a new girl? Your ma will be pleased to hear that."

Colt turned to look at the sheet-draped curvaceous form

lying in his bed. "She's not exactly the kind of girl you bring home to your mama."

Bo whistled out loud as he took in the sight of the tousled-haired beauty who suddenly thrust her head out of the covers and sat up with fire in her eyes.

"How many times do I have to tell you I'm not that kind of woman? You'd better stop telling people I am or I'll take you to court and sue your ass for slander."

"Whew eeee!" Bo hooted, staring at the wildcat in Colt's bed. "She's got a mouth on her, too. Guess I'll get out of your way. You got your hands full with that one. I'll just tell your daddy you're busy right now."

"No. Tell him I'll be right down. No need for him to be disappointed after all the trouble he went through to surprise me."

"Good idea." Bo peeked around Colt's tall frame for one last peek at the redhead, then pushed his hat back on his head and rolled his eyes at Colt as he walked out the door. "Might be, you'll want to put some clothes on 'fore you go down."

Realizing for the first time he was naked as a newborn pup, Colt grinned sheepishly at Bo. "Might be you're right." Closing the door, he turned and said, "Yup, this is turning out to be one hell of a birthday for me, and the day has only just begun."

Dazed and still disoriented, Destiny watched as Colt searched the room for his clothing, putting on each piece as he found it. He made quite a spectacle walking around wearing a shirt, hat, but no pants. If she hadn't been in such a bad way, she knew she would have found him very endearing, if not downright sexy. But at the moment, she couldn't think about anything but getting herself out of this incomprehensible situation.

He approached the bed, and her heart stood still. "Don't you go getting any ideas. I've got a black belt in karate and I'm not afraid to use it."

Reaching under the covers at the foot of the bed, Colt pulled out his pants and stepped into them saying, "Lady, I can't make head nor tail of what you're saying, and right now, I don't have the time to figure it out. I've got a rendezvous with another redhead, but don't be getting jealous, there's still room in my heart for you. I've got some interesting ideas about you—me—and that there bed."

Destiny shouted after him as he left the room. "Come back here. You can't leave me here like this. I don't have any clothes to wear. What am I supposed to do?"

Colt poked his head back in the door. "Reddddd, you don't need clothes for what I have in mind." With that, he slammed the door shut, and Destiny felt the full impact of the strange situation she was in.

This couldn't really be happening to her. She had to be dreaming. Nothing else made any sense.

She lay there for a time, hoping that her topsy-turvy world would right itself, but it soon dawned on her that nothing was going to change.

All right. The first thing she had to do was to figure out just exactly where she was and there was only one way to do that. *Get out of bed and look out the window.* But, suddenly, she didn't want to do that.

This was crazy. Why was she afraid to look out the window?

A tiny voice inside her answered, *because you're afraid of what you'll see.*

A shiver made its way up her spine and she clutched at the blanket, wrapping it tightly around her, her mind thinking about another thing that frightened her even more. Thinking about how she came to be in this bed in the first place. Had someone drugged her and carried her here? Terrible as that idea was, it was less frightening than other possibilities.

But if she believed that, she'd have to believe that Miss Lydia was somehow involved. That was just plain ludicrous.

It would be easier for her to believe she had traveled through time than to believe that sweet old lady would do something like that. What reason would she have?

Then the answer hit her. She had sleepwalked. That was it. She had sleepwalked into another room in Miss Lydia's house and climbed into bed with, with, who . . . Drake McAmmon? Lydia's nephew?

That had to be it. Anything else bordered on the insane.

Feeling more confident, she slid over to the edge of the bed and placed one foot gingerly on the wooden floor. Nothing happened. Of course nothing happened. Why in the world would she think something would?

Unless . . . unless . . . her subconscious was keeping some vital information from her.

Why not? Hadn't it been keeping the first eight years of her life locked up somewhere in her brain where she couldn't get to it?

She placed the other foot on the floor, but still nothing happened. *Okay, here goes.* Standing up, she clutched the blanket tightly around her. It was the only security she had at the moment.

Everything was the same. What had she expected? That the room would disappear, leaving her in a vacuum? With nothing left to lose, she gathered her courage and walked over to the window, steeling herself before daring to look out.

One quick glance, and the blood rushed to her head. Gripping the windowsill for support, she took in the alien scene laid out below. Alien, because, although she recognized the landscape as part of St. Augustine, it was not the St. Augustine she had grown up in.

Where once there had been black asphalt road, now there was dirt. Where once there were cars, now there were horses and buggies and people dressed in nineteenth-century clothing and . . . It was as if she were looking at the set of a period movie, only this was the real thing. The real thing.

The—real—thing.

Deep within her heart she knew it was true. She had somehow managed to travel through time. Either that, or she was completely out of her mind.

That knowledge brought her close to panic and she breathed in and out deeply, trying to calm herself. What in God's name was she going to do now?

Her gaze swept over the 1800's setting for something, anything, familiar, in need to at least know where she was, and there it was, staring her in the face. The town plaza. It looked much like it did in the twentieth century, only now there were period-costumed people playing croquet upon the green.

The familiar sight of it gave her some semblance of stability for at least she knew where she was, if not when she was there.

A reddish-brown horse, obviously the birthday gift to her dream lover, munched peacefully on the grass at the edge of the green, while a cluster of people looked on, admiring the beautiful animal. It was a perfect postcard scene that made her predicament all the more difficult to take, for by their peaceful continence, Destiny knew that the townspeople were completely unaware of anything supernatural in their midst.

What a lonely feeling it was.

A sudden shiver made its way up her spine, and her eyes sought the one familiar figure in the scene below. The man she had been making love to just a few minutes ago.

He looked up at the window just then, and waved, a wide grin on his face, and she quickly stepped out of view, pressing her back against the wall. She remembered what he had said about having ideas about her and there was no doubt in her mind what he meant. Her heart suddenly raced out of control from fear and from sexual excitement.

Damn. Damn. Damn.

Not only was she naked and alone, but she would have

to deal with her sexy dream lover when he returned. It was one thing to have uninhibited hot sex in a dream, but knowing it had been the real thing was just a little too much to cope with.

Sliding slowly down the wall, she slumped to the floor, too weak to support her own weight. A large, hard lump came to her throat as she struggled to hold back the tears. She knew if she didn't control her emotions immediately, she would fall apart completely. She had to take back control of her life, and the first step was to try and figure out why this had happened to her and what she could do about it.

Was it because she had written a novel about this time period? That couldn't be the answer, otherwise the past would be inundated with writers. She almost smiled at the thought of Judith McNaught, Janelle Taylor, Jude Deveraux, and a host of other very famous authors bumping into one another as they scurried through the streets of St. Augustine in a panic.

Well, as long as she still had her sense of humor, she wasn't defeated. If her time travel had nothing to do with writing about nineteenth-century St. Augustine, then what? But then, she knew the answer all along, didn't she? It had to do with her uncanny knowledge of Shining Dawn's life.

What other reason could there be? But if that was the answer, it was all beyond her comprehension. Well, that was too bad. She had better figure it out, and soon, if she was ever going to go back to her own time.

But that was easier said than done, for at this particular moment in time, her brain wasn't exactly working too clearly. More than that, a terrible sense of insecurity suddenly caught her in its grip, constricting her chest so tight she had a hard time breathing. She shook it off, making herself relax, knowing if she didn't, she'd have a panic attack.

In a few moments her breathing was normal again, and her sense of survival strong.

It just wasn't fair.

Anger rose quickly, starting in her stomach and working its way up to her throat and she let it out in a frustrated little scream. She couldn't let her promising career end like this, alone, naked, without one single thing to call her own but the fake diamonds she wore on her hand.

This was really great. If there was a God, He sure was a villainous one to leave her in this awful fix.

She knew what Shining Dawn must have felt when she prayed in vain to her God to save her parents' life. And to the Great Spirit to save her daughter's life, years later. That gave her strength. She would be as strong as Shining Dawn had been and she would get out of this mess somehow.

A light rapping sounded, and she wrapped the blanket even tighter and opened the door. She had no idea who was out there, but she didn't care, anything was better than being so alone. The sight of the Indian woman standing there dressed in the bright clothing of the Seminoles was the last thing she expected to see.

"Missy hungry? Lily Tiger bring you food. Mister Colt, he asked me to."

For the first time Destiny noticed that the woman carried a wooden tray of food. "Please . . . come in. I need your help."

Lily Tiger hesitated for a moment, her large brown eyes enormous as she stepped inside the room. "What you want, Missy?"

Destiny closed the door quickly, hearing someone walking down the hall, then sweeping her hand over the blanket she wore, said, "I desperately need something to wear. I, I have no clothing at all."

The large brown eyes suddenly narrowed.

"Please, you must believe me. I am not a scarlet lady, or whatever you call hookers. I don't know how I came to be in this room." That was certainly no lie. Fearing to scare off her only lifeline at the moment, she knew she had better not tell her any crazy story about time traveling. "Perhaps, I blacked out. When I awoke I was in that bed, without a stitch of clothing on."

The young Indian woman shook her head sympathetically. "Poor Missy, you not the first woman to be swept off feet by Colt Mandrell, I think."

"Mandrell? He's a Mandrell? Oh, great. Of all the people to be caught in bed with, why did it have to be a Mandrell?" She immediately regretted blurting that out, knowing the Indian woman would think the worst, but she just couldn't help herself. In her book, Gordon Mandrell had been an evil man and his stepdaughter Celeste was his equal. "Don't tell me Colt Mandrell is Gordon's son?"

"Not son, grandson. He son of Little Bit and Gary Mandrell. The old master been dead now many years."

Grandson? Colt? But . . . that would mean that he was the baby Shining Dawn delivered at the moment of her daughter's death. That would mean it wasn't 1838.

She had naturally assumed she had been swept back to the time her book took place, or even possibly to 1846, the year Shining Dawn's journal ended. But if Colt was Little Bit and Gary Mandrell's son, it had to be much later in time than that.

This was getting more confusing all the time. "Lily, will you tell me what today's date is."

Lily looked at her funny. "It September twenty-first."

"I mean the year. I need to know what year it is."

Lily started to back away from Destiny, then changed her mind and patted her arm instead. "You poor lady. You been through terrible time, I think."

"I have. Believe me, I have."

"It 1870."

Seventy? But why that year? she wondered. There was no rhyme or reason for why she was here now. And yet, the only thing that made any kind of sense at all, was that she had been transported to 1870 for some very compelling reason. This was getting crazier and crazier.

"Lily? I need your help desperately. Will you be my friend?"

Gazing at the beautiful young woman in trouble, Lily's heart went out to her. Only a truly troubled lady would forget what year it was. "I don't understand why lady of your wealth should need my help. I have nothing to give you."

"My wealth? I stand here before you without a thing to call my own. How can you possibly think I am wealthy?"

Lily's gaze traveled to the fake diamond rings on Destiny's fingers. "You have great wealth on your hand. Enough, I think, to buy half of town."

Destiny stared at Lily in amazement, then gazing down at the three large-stoned rings on her left hand, she said, "But these are . . ."

Are what? Even in her own time it was very difficult to tell a true diamond from a cubic zirconia. It would take an expert to do that.

Her spirit soared. The people of this time would have no way of knowing about them.

Perhaps she wasn't as helpless and destitute as she thought.

"Lily, thank you, thank you, thank you. Lend me something to wear. Point me in the direction of a jeweler, and I'll buy you the prettiest dress this ancient, time-shifting, little town has to offer."

"You crazy lady, but I like you and will be your friend. I be back in little while with something for you to wear."

Drawing in her first breath of air without fear constricting her throat, Destiny decided she was going to be all right. Kissing each ring in turn, she danced around the room. She had gained back some control of her life.

A loud knocking on the door halted her dance, and she ran over to open it, smiling joyously.

Colt Mandrell stood there, filling the doorway, sexuality oozing from every pore.

She slammed the door on him, but he deftly caught it with his foot, and pushed his way in, grinning at her in a very sensual way. She knew what he had on his mind.

"Now, Red, is that any way to greet me? It is my room, you know."

"Don't call me Red. I hate it when people call me that." Holding out a lock of her hair, she said, "My hair is much closer to brown than to red, so if you must call me something call me by my proper . . ."

"Proper? Hell, Red, I can't find one bitty little thing that's proper about you. But I don't mind. I like my women a little on the wild side." With that, he pulled her up against his body, holding her captive with strong arms.

Pushing at his chest, she cried, "I am not your woman and get your hands off me."

"You sure do change your mind a lot. Even for a female. You were a lot friendlier a little while ago. I liked you much better when you were climbing all over me like a wildcat in heat."

Destiny's face flamed. His description was just a little too close for comfort. "I thought I was dreaming. And, I'll just bet you did, too. Admit it."

A puzzled expression crossed Colt's face, but it disappeared immediately. "I was in no condition to know what was going on, but obviously it wasn't a dream or you wouldn't be here. And honey, I'm mighty glad you are. I just wish I could stay and renew our acquaintance, but my mama's expecting me for breakfast, it being my birthday and all. But don't you go worrying over it, I'll be back before you know it and we can take up where we left off."

He nuzzled at her ear, whispering, "I just paid another night's rent on this room."

Destiny was too incensed to think of anything to say. Colt was without a doubt the most exasperating man she had ever met. How dare he think he could just parade in here and she'd melt in his arms.

"But before I go . . ." His lips came down on hers before she knew what was happening and she felt herself growing weak in the knees as her body responded all too eagerly to his touch.

His kisses should be declared illegal.

She knew if he didn't stop soon she would indeed be climbing all over him again. And after what he said about a wildcat in heat she'd be damned if she'd give him that satisfaction.

Using all her strength she pushed him away, but he grabbed at her catching a hold of the blanket wound around her instead. The next thing she knew, she was standing before him naked.

Colt felt as if he'd been hit by a two by four and he knew his expression must surely reflect that. He couldn't stop staring at her. She stood there, a frozen forest nymph of voluptuous proportions, with a body designed for loving. And he was all too willing to oblige. Recuperating, he let his gaze travel over her body, inch by delectable inch, committing her round, curvaceous and very luscious body to memory.

This is what a woman was supposed to look like.

Soft, sensuous, full-bodied like Venus, or Eve in the Garden of Eden.

She moved her hand and light shimmered magically from it, but he was too intent on the rest of her to turn his attention to her hand. "Sorry, I didn't intend to . . . Hell, that's a lie. No red-blooded man this side of the grave would ever be sorry to see you in all your redheaded, glory. Honey, believe me, whoever paid you for being here, didn't pay half of what you're worth. Why, I do believe a man would give up just about everything he owned to fu . . ."

The sound of her hand meeting his cheek resounded through the room. "Get out of here, you, you . . ." Tears stung her eyes as she lowered her head so he couldn't see how much he hurt her.

Retrieving the wayward blanket, she wrapped herself in it once again and wiped her eyes before facing him. "I believe your mother is waiting for you?"

Colt's grin turned to a quizzical gaze, then melted into a look of sympathy when he saw her quivering chin. "Red, I'm sorry. I guess I still don't understand how you got here, or why you chose me to bed."

"You wouldn't believe me if I told you."

In a quiet voice, he said, "Try me."

"All right. I'll tell you, but I'm warning you, you better not laugh. I fell asleep and dreamt of you two nights in a row. The first night an owl woke me before we could finish making love, but the second night we were able to go all the way. When I awoke, I found myself in your bed."

Colt shook his head slowly, saying, "I know this is crazy, but I think I believe you."

"You do?"

"I dreamt about you two nights ago, too. And I swear to you I heard that same owl. I don't mind admitting I woke up in a bad way. What the hell is going on here?"

"I don't have any answers for you. I only know that somehow I was transported from the twentieth century to the nineteenth century, and . . ."

Staggering back a couple of steps, Colt said, "Whoa! Hold on there. I wasn't drunk two nights ago, and I know for a fact that I dreamt about you then. But that's as far as I'm willing to travel down your garden path. Don't expect me to believe some crazy story about coming from the future. 'Cause, honey, that's where our paths meander in different directions."

"I can't blame you for that. If I wasn't the one who did the time traveling, I wouldn't believe it either. But honestly, you've got to believe me. It did happen. And if it happened once it can happen again. I'm going to find out how to do it."

"Don't be so all fired anxious to leave me. We've hardly had a chance to get acquainted. Though, come to think of it, our introduction was the sweetest . . ."

"I'm trying to have a serious discussion with you, and all you can think about is sex?"

"After seeing you looking so deliciously . . ." Groaning, he took a step toward her, and she quickly backed away. He responded by raising his hands in surrender. "I'm not going to touch you. Look. I have to go now. But I promise you, I'll be back as soon as I can, then, if you like, we can talk this out."

"Mr. Mandrell, until you understand that I did come here from another time, we have nothing at all to talk about."

Colt stood staring at the lovely face before him a long time. "You really believe that, I can see it in your eyes. Maybe you got kicked in the head by a horse. I once saw that happen. It can knock all the sense out of you for a while, but . . ."

Destiny shoved him hard in the chest, frustrated and close to tears. "Damn you. I wish a horse would kick you in the head. Maybe then you'd wake up and realize the truth."

Colt backed out of the door, making a hasty retreat. He almost stumbled over Lily Tiger who was standing right behind him. "Sorry." Tipping his hat to her, and then to the redhead, he turned and made a quick exit.

When he walked outside the hotel, he looked up at the window and saw her gazing down at him. Grinning, he blew her an exuberant kiss as a wild thought flooded his brain, jolting him with surprise.

That's the woman I'm going to marry.

Where the hell had that come from?

It hadn't even entered his mind before this morning that

he might want to be married. In fact, he was pretty sure that was the very last thing on his mind.

Another equally astonishing thought hit him. He had explored every inch of her luscious, womanly body, had touched her, tasted her, and thoroughly bedded her, but he didn't have any idea what her name was.

Four

Destiny turned away from the window too late. Darn it. He caught her looking at him again. The man seemed to have a sixth sense when it came to her. As if he could read her mind, or maybe her heart. That wouldn't surprise her a bit. If he was powerful enough to draw her here from the twentieth century, he was powerful enough to do just about anything.

Her knees started to shake as she thought about the all too real power he had over her. He had to be the catalyst for her traveling through time. But why? That was the question.

If she didn't start getting some answers soon, she was going to go out of her mind. Ha! That was a laugh. She probably already had. She wasn't feeling very stable at the moment.

"Missy?"

Destiny jumped. She had forgotten all about Lily Tiger. Proof enough that she was indeed losing her mind. Turning to face her, she tried to compose her frazzled nerves. But, since that seemed impossible in the heightened state she was in, she tried covering the condition she was in with an air of stability, pretending to be the calm, sane person she used to be.

Seeing the sudden fright on Lily's face, she knew she hadn't succeeded.

"Please, Lily, don't be frightened of me. I'm really very harmless. And don't worry. I didn't escape from an insane asylum." A deranged giggle escaped her mouth, blowing the credibility of that statement, and she started to cry like a baby.

Lily led the blanket-clad woman over to the bed. "You sit. You need rest, I think. All will be better soon. You want me get doctor for you?"

Feeling ashamed of herself for falling apart, Destiny wiped the tears from her eyes and said in a very quiet voice, "No. I'm fine, really. Or at least I will be when I get dressed."

"Here," Lily said, shoving her bundle of clothing into Destiny's lap.

Destiny smiled. The poor little thing was trying so hard not to be afraid of her. If she couldn't be composed for herself, then she would do it for Lily. "Thank you. It will only take a moment to pull myself together, then you can show me the way to the jewelers, and I'll make good my promise to buy you a new dress."

"No jeweler in town."

That sobered Destiny considerably. If she couldn't sell one of her rings, she would be back to square one.

"But the banker, Mr. Raiford, he buy jewelry from folks all the time. He some kind of collector. He like jewelry very much. I think he buy your pretty rings."

Exhaling deeply in a deep sigh of relief, Destiny pulled the white cotton blouse over her head, tugging it into place. She grimaced, discovering that her ample breasts strained against the too tight material.

Stepping into the calico skirt bordered with colorful Seminole patchwork, she struggled to button the waistband. Damn. She could hardly breathe. Lily Tiger's waist was much smaller than her own. That was really depressing. Her waist was the only part of her body she could proudly call small. But not anymore it seemed. Of course, she had read that the people of this century were smaller. "How do I look?"

A sweet little tittering escaped Lily's mouth. "I think you look plenty funny. I never seen white woman wear Indian clothes before, but I think men will like."

Destiny ran to the small mirror over the washstand and gazed at her reflection. A crazy woman stared back. "Ohh, how am I ever going to convince your Mr. Raiford looking like this. He'll take one look at me and slam the door in my face."

"Not him. He love pretty woman. He love diamonds even more. He will bargain with you but he will try to give you less than they worth."

That would be pretty hard to do Destiny thought, a mischievous smile crossing her face. Pretty hard to do.

In a matter of moments they were walking into the bank and Destiny's knees were in serious danger of giving out on her. The short walk from the hotel had been tremendously exciting. Seeing the men and women of 1870 up close, dressed in the wonderful clothing of this era was extraordinary. Especially so for her, a writer, who made her living off the past. She was so intrigued by it all she found herself enjoying it in a nervous, otherworldly sort of way.

But her fears returned as soon as they stepped inside the one-story building made of coquina shell. Her survival depended on her pulling this off, convincing the banker that her cubic zirconias were real. At least the bands of the rings were real gold. That made her feel a little less like a criminal.

Realizing that if the banker saw all three rings he might not believe in their authenticity so readily she removed two of them and asked Lily to hold them for her.

Lily gave her a strange look, but took the rings, smiling up at Destiny uneasily. Destiny smiled back reassuringly and together they made their way over to Brent Raiford.

He wasn't hard to spot. He was standing by his desk, his head bent over some papers held by a rough-looking man with a scar on his cheek. Destiny shivered, thinking what a nightmare it would have been if she had awakened in that man's bed instead of Colt Mandrell's.

But Brent Raiford's looks were as handsome as the rough-looking man's were sinister. In fact, he looked so much like a young James Garner playing the part of Maverick, she had to blink and look again. Gathering her courage she said, "Mr. Raiford?"

Preoccupied with his figures, Brent looked up slowly, letting his yessss slide out of his mouth lazily, but it slid to a premature stop when he beheld the very exotic, very beautiful woman before him.

Jumping to his feet, he said, "What can I do for y'all today?" His gaze acknowledged Lily Tiger then swept back to feast on the enticing white woman with the deliciously large breasts. Instantly, a part of his anatomy stood at attention. He was grateful the long jacket he wore kept his condition undetected.

"I understand you buy diamonds from time to time."

His eyes opened wide as he gazed at her finger and the enormous ring that shimmered with light as she pulled it off and handed it to him. Beautiful *and* rich. A potent combination.

The diamond was exquisite, the clarity of it, superior, but what took his breath away was the size of it. It had to be at least five carats. A rare beauty, unseen by him in all his years of searching for just such a treasure.

"Hmm, interesting," he said, sounding bored. "I suppose I could be persuaded to buy a ring like this, but uh . . ."

Prepared for just that reaction, Destiny took the ring back from him without hesitation. "I'm sorry, sir, I've changed my mind. I've decided I'm much too attached to the ring, for sentimental reasons, you understand. I'm sorry to have bothered you."

Brent watched as the ring disappeared from his hand, reappearing on the woman's finger. "Uh, perhaps you could be persuaded if the price was right. It has just come to me that I know someone who might be very interested in a stone like that."

Very sweetly, Destiny replied, "Oh, I just don't know. If I didn't find myself short of funds, I wouldn't even consider it, but . . . what is a poor girl to do when's she's alone in this big ol' world." Destiny cringed inside at her corny words, but she had to admit she was happy with the results of her poor little female act. James Garner, Jr. was practically falling all over himself to be the big strong protector.

Taking her by the arm, he escorted her to a chair by his desk, at the same time dismissing with a wave of his hand the man he had been conferring with. "Darlin', sit right here while I take a closer look at your diamond. I'm sure we can come to an agreement on price. Why, I wouldn't feel right if I let a charming young lady such as yourself leave here the least bit unhappy."

"Why, thank you, kind sir. Please take your time. I want you to study the stone very carefully. I would feel just awful if you weren't completely satisfied with the quality." There. She felt better now. She had warned him to look at it closely. If he bought it now, she would have no qualms about accepting the money.

She held her breath while Brent turned the ring over and over, scrutinizing it with one of those little glasses Destiny recognized as being part of the jeweler's trade. Uh, oh! It hadn't occurred to her that people of the 1800s would have such technology.

"Hmm, I do believe we can come to an agreement, say three thousand dollars?"

Destiny practically wet her pants. Three thousand dollars had to be a lot of money in 1870. "Oh, dear. I was so hoping it would be worth a little more. Say five thousand dollars?"

Brent couldn't believe his luck. A stone of this flawless condition and rarity had to be worth a king's fortune.

"Umm, for the sake of southern womanhood, I suppose I could say, split the difference? Four thousand."

She had him.

"Make it four thousand five hundred and you've got yourself a diamond."

Smiling triumphantly, Brent answered, "And you've got yourself a small fortune, young lady."

"Thank you, Mr. Raiford. You can put three thousand of it into a savings account for me, and I'll take the rest in cash."

At the last moment, she remembered she was supposed to be a poor little thing and batted her eyelashes at him. "I'm sure you'll understand my urgency. I, I haven't had a decent meal since . . . I can't remember when." That was no lie. She was starving, but first on her list of things to spend money on was a new dress for Lily.

Wondering why someone with such wealth would be in need of a decent meal, Brent decided she had probably been some rich man's mistress, who had fallen on hard times. How else could she have gotten her hands on such a gem as that. His hardness became very uncomfortable as he thought about how talented she must be in bed to warrant such an expensive reward.

Kissing her hand, he said, "I quite understand. But I must caution you not to carry so large a sum around town. I urge you to keep no more than a hundred or two in greenbacks and put the rest in your account. It would be much safer there."

"That won't be necessary, Mr. Raiford. I don't plan on holding onto it for very long."

"I see, in that case, please call on me again if I can be of further assistance."

"Oh, but you can. I'll be needing a place to stay. Would you know offhand of any rooming house where I might rent a small room?"

"My dear young woman. With three thousand dollars in

the bank you could buy yourself a home and still have enough money left to live off quite comfortably for a matter of time."

That hadn't occurred to Destiny. She wondered how much homes cost now. Obviously, not very much, but then people didn't make very much now either. "I suppose that would be smart."

"I just happen to know of a home that will be available very soon. It will be foreclosed on tomorrow at noon if the woman doesn't come up with the balance of her mortgage by then. She has been in arrears for over a year and the bank has lost its patience."

"A woman?" That shouldn't have surprised her. This snake oil salesman would probably throw his own mother out on the street without a moment's thought. And it wouldn't surprise her if the woman turned out to be a widow with a flock of children.

"That's right. Mrs. Penelope Peabody."

"How much does the poor creature owe?"

"More than she will have the ability to pay."

The crud. "Hmm, that sounds very tempting, and I would like to see this house, but not right now. I have something important I must do. Shall I meet you there, say six o'clock this evening?"

"Sounds right to me. You can ask Lily Tiger to show you the way. She knows the Peabody house very well."

Destiny looked at Lily curiously, then said her goodbyes to the banker and left. As soon as she got outside, she wiped the hand he kissed on her skirt. Ugh. What a slimy man.

"Lily, do you know the house he's talking about?"

"I know very well. I stay there with Miss Penelope a while. She very kind to take me in when no one else would. I hope you not think of taking her home from her."

"Trust me, Lily. And tell me about Miss Penelope. She wouldn't happen to be a widow, would she?"

"How you know?"

Destiny smiled to herself. "I'd like to talk to her before Mr. Raiford gets there, but first, I promised you a dress and you're going to get it. Right now."

Lily's eyes became shiny and large. "I think maybe you better take rings back. It make me scared to carry such a fortune. I never knew pretty rocks could be so valuable."

Laughing, Destiny held her hand out to receive the rings. "I think I know how you feel. I never expected to get more than a thousand or two for the ring. Evidently diamonds that size must be very rare. I better keep them safely out of sight from now on."

Slipping the rings on her fingers, she turned the stones to face the palm of her hand, deciding that one of the purchases she'd make today would be an extra-long chain. She would string the rings on it and wear it around her neck where they would be safe and out of sight of curious eyes. "What a relief. I was afraid I was going to have to resort to begging on the street to survive."

Lily gasped in shock.

"I'm only jesting you, Lily."

It dawned on Destiny that she was feeling a little more like her old self and she credited her newfound wealth with that. Things could never be really bad if you had money enough to ride out the bad times. She just hoped her money would last long enough for her to figure out how to get back to her own time.

Sighing deeply, she felt suddenly morose at the knowledge that the only people who would miss her if she never returned were her agent and her editor, and then only until the next inventive writer came along. She vowed, right there and then that if she ever made it back, she'd make it a point to cultivate new friends.

Lily's bright orange dress was their first purchase. It was almost their last purchase, too, for Lily insisted over the protests of the store clerk to change into it immediately. Since the store's only dressing room was currently being used as a storage space, piled high with unopened boxes, that presented a problem. But the insistent Lily finally got her way, and was escorted to the living quarters of the owner right behind the store.

While Destiny waited for Lily to emerge from the store, she waited outside, absorbing the sight, smell, and sound of Victorian St. Augustine. Although she thought she knew what to expect to see, it surpassed anything she could ever have imagined.

The town was more crude than she expected, more barren of buildings and people, but at the same time it was a visual delight to her eyes and to her mind, if you could overlook the hordes of flies and the stench of garbage laying too long in the sun. There was a lot to be said for curbside trash pickup.

For the most part, the people of St. Augustine seemed as intelligent and civilized as those of her own time, but she sensed that just underneath the surface beat the heart of primitive man. Of course, the only thing she had to base that on was Colt Mandrell. He was certainly a lot wilder than the men of the twentieth century and a lot sexier, too.

Why did it always come back to sex when she thought of him? The answer to that was pretty clear. Because she had enjoyed such extraordinary lovemaking with him. She could hardly be expected to forget that.

"Missy?"

Destiny pulled herself reluctantly from provocative thoughts of Colt and turned to gaze at the bedazzling Lily. The orange complimented her Indian looks tremendously. "You look very beautiful, Lily."

Lily beamed. "I very happy. Thank you. This first store-bought dress I own."

"Well, stick with me, and it will be the first of many."

Continuing down King Road, Lily and Destiny weaved their way toward the bayfront, stopping at every likely store to see what kind of merchandise they could find. Shop till you drop took on a whole new meaning to her as she walked the length of the dirt street, carrying a growing bundle of purchases.

She was very glad Lily was with her for it was hard to tell the retail stores from private residences, since many of the places they went into bore no sign at all. In fact, many of the establishments were in the private residences of the stores' owners.

After a while, she became aware that she and Lily were being followed by a growing number of people. Turning around, she saw a small parade of men, women, children, and even a couple of dogs, just a few feet behind. Her newfound self-assurance vanished. "Lily, why are those people following us?"

"Perhaps because you dressed so strangely for a white woman? Or perhaps because you so beautiful. Or . . . perhaps because you buy so many things. St. Augustine still hurting plenty from the long war."

For a moment, Destiny wondered which war she was talking about, then it dawned on her it was the civil war. That floored her for a moment. *The Civil War.* It was hard to believe that in this time, the war was just a few years past. "I get the picture, Lily. Obviously, I'm just a curiosity." Relieved that her followers had no hostile intentions, she remarked, "Well, I might as well let it work to my advantage."

Gesturing to three boys of about nine or ten, she said, "How would you boys like to earn some money."

The boys stepped forward eagerly.

"If you carry these packages back to the St. Augustine Hotel for me, I'll give you each a silver dollar."

The boys seemed stunned at that news, making Destiny sure she was about to overpay them considerably. "It will be your responsibility to see that they get to Colt Mandrell's room. Do you think you can manage that?"

Three small heads nodded solemnly.

"Good." Piling the packages in their arms, she sent them on their way. Looking around her, she discovered the parade of people was still growing. She frowned, wondering what they were thinking. Did they think she was a crazy woman or just an eccentric rich woman buying out the town? Neither image was one she cared to cultivate.

"Okay, Lily, lead me to a decent place to eat. I'm starved. Then we'll go back to the hotel so I can change my clothes before we go over to the Widow Peabody's house. I've got an offer she can't refuse."

It occurred to Destiny that her twentieth-century jargon must sound pretty strange to Lily, but the little woman didn't seem fazed by it at all. Perhaps because she, too, sounded different from the white folks in town. From the rudimentary way Lily spoke, she got the impression that the young Seminole woman had not been raised among white men. She probably came from one of the Indian reservations in Florida.

Eager to get a chance to hear about Lily's life, she decided it might not be so bad having to stay in this era for a little while. Think of all the research she would have for her next book. Taking a deep breath, Destiny felt her body relax and realized she was adjusting to her new life already.

They entered the restaurant, and were immediately seated at a small, clay-colored tile-topped table. Destiny ran her fingers over the cool, hard surface, while she waited to be served, then focused her attention on Lily. Poor thing, having to accompany a crazy woman all over town.

She smiled and said, "Have I told you how grateful I am for your help? I couldn't have made it through this terrible day without you."

Lily smiled back and Destiny saw a black hole where her two front teeth should have been. But, surprisingly, even without her front teeth, the Indian woman was very attractive.

"I think you are strong woman. You will do fine without me."

A shiver of fear climbed up Destiny's spine. "Without you? Does that mean you don't want to be my friend?"

Tilting her head from one side to the other, Lily looked at Destiny quizzically. "I thought . . . now that you a woman of means, you have no more use for me."

"Oh, Lily, I'll need you all the more, unless, of course, you have a family. I didn't stop to think you had other obligations. I'm sorry, I've been completely selfish. Forgive me."

Lily reached over to grasp Destiny's hand. "I know. I see it on your face. It must have been a bad thing that happened to you. But it is over, yes?"

"No. It's not over. But don't worry about me, I'll be all right."

"I know this. But I will stay with you, if you wish. I will be your friend as long as you want me."

"Thank you, Lily."

Famished, Destiny devoured her lunch, while Lily picked at hers, spending most of the time telling Destiny about her life. "And when I eight winters old, Mother and Father died. I sent to Indian reservation near here to live with Grandmother. It was good time for me. Grandmother blood aunt to the great Coacoochie. You whites call him Wild Cat."

"I know. I have written about him in a book, Lily. He was a great man. Just like Osceola."

"You knew Osceola?"

"In a way. I read about his life, then wrote about him in my book."

"This book. Will you teach me to read it?"

"I wish I could, but it . . ." How in the world was she supposed to tell Lily that the book existed only in the distant future. "It's out of print."

"What that mean?"

"It means that the men who make up books have not made any more of this one. It cannot be found anywhere."

"Oh."

Seeing how disappointed she was, Destiny continued, "But if you like, I'll teach you to read from another book."

"I would like. Thank you."

"You've got a deal. Now, tell me more about your life, I'm sorry for interrupting you."

"As I was saying, Grandmother very wise woman. She taught me much. She taught me not to fear all whites. She friends with white sister to Osceola, you know."

"Shining Dawn? Are you talking about Shining Dawn?"

"But how you know this?"

"Because I have written about her, too. What do you know of her? Where can I find her? I want to meet her so much."

"Ohh. You cannot. She gone."

Destiny's heart sank. "Gone? Oh, no, when did she die?"

"No. She gone. You understand? Far away, with husband Blade." Seeing the sudden sadness on Destiny's face, Lily continued. "But she return soon, I think. That what Miz Peabody say."

Shining Dawn. Returning soon. It seemed so unreal. She might actually have a chance to meet Shining Dawn before she went back to her own time. Hardly able to contain her excitement, she thought it must truly be fate that brought her and Lily together. However, knowing that St. Augustine was a very small town, everyone here probably knows one another.

No wonder she stuck out like a sore thumb. The townsfolk weren't used to seeing strangers, especially strange women wearing Indian clothing. Come to think of it, that would be just as unusual in the St. Augustine of the twentieth century, too. It looked like she was destined to be a celebrity of some kind no matter where or when she lived.

"Then, when I twelve winters, Grandmother die. I sent

to wicked lady's home to live there as servant. I did not like that. When I fourteen I run away back to reservation and Miz Shining Dawn took me in."

"She sounds like a very nice lady. I'm glad she was your friend, but I'm curious. Who was this wicked lady you lived with? I can think of someone who fits that title and she probably still lives in this town. It wouldn't happen to be Celeste Mandrell, would it?"

"Miz Celeste! You right. How you know this?"

Destiny laughed out loud. "Because I wrote about her in my book, too."

After lunch, Destiny and Lily walked back to the hotel so that she could change into one of her new outfits. She and Lily had fun opening the boxes and bags, and strewing their contents all over the floor. Destiny chose a rust-colored dress trimmed with black and white-striped satin ruffles and Lily helped her into it.

Before she dressed, she placed the sterling silver chain she had remembered to buy around her neck, with her two remaining rings attached. It dangled cozily between her breasts, giving her a feeling of security. As long as she had her fake diamonds she would never be poor.

Thanks to the corset that Lily insisted she wear underneath the dress, it fit perfectly. In fact, the bodice was designed to fit like a glove. Destiny couldn't believe how small her waist looked now, tightly trapped in the corset. Unfortunately, it also made her breasts seem even larger. That was discouraging. They received too much attention already.

A loud rapping on the door had Lily and Destiny scurrying around to pick up the mess they had made. When everything was shoved under the bed, Destiny smoothed down her new dress with her hands and opened the door. The desk clerk stood there, package in hand.

This came for you a few minutes ago."

Curious, Destiny took the box, tied with a giant polka-dotted pink bow, and closed the door. She was curious to know what was inside. She knew it couldn't have been one of her purchases, because she had accounted for every one of them. Hastily tearing it open, she cried excitedly, "I can't imagine what this is."

A pile of pink fluff assailed her eyes and she lifted out the beautiful feminine pink dress. A card nestled in the voluminous material tumbled out on the floor and she bent over to pick it up. It was addressed to Red. She knew immediately who it was from. With her heart in her throat she read the message written in a bold hand. "Sorry I left you without anything to wear. Hope this makes up for it. Something has come up. I won't be back till late afternoon. Colt."

Lily tittered, the musical sound filling the air. "I think Mr. Colt like you very much."

Destiny didn't hear her. She stood holding the dress to her chest, her mind filled with warm thoughts of the man who had bought her such a completely feminine dress. She was sure it didn't cost nearly as much as the clothing she had just purchased, but she loved it so much more.

Why had Colt chosen such a sweet dress for her?

Is that the way he pictured her, soft, feminine?

If so, then it must have finally got through his thick skull that she wasn't a scarlet lady. The pink dress with tiny pink bows running down the front of it, and delicate cream-colored lace on the collar was certainly not the kind of dress a man would buy that kind of woman.

Suddenly she felt younger, prettier, seeing herself through Colt's young—yes—young—masculine eyes. For without a doubt, he was younger than she. It thrilled her to think that he looked at her as if she, too, were very young.

Since he had never seen her with clothes on, he had nothing to influence his judgment, and yet he decided she should look soft and feminine and youthful. For some reason that she couldn't fathom, that made her feel very good.

But it was wrong to let herself get carried away on a

cloud of pink fluff. After all, she wasn't going to stay around long enough to get to know Colt. She was going to go back to her own time just as soon as she could, and it just wouldn't do getting hung up on a nineteenth-century man, even if he was the sexiest man alive.

And he was.

Five

Pushing all thought of Colt out of her mind, Destiny left the hotel with Lily Tiger, strolling past the town plaza where people were still playing croquet. The sound of wooden mallets striking wooden balls split the air as she turned left onto the waterfront. "The Peabody house is on the bay front?"

"Yes, why you surprised?"

How could she tell Lily that in the twentieth century a waterfront home was worth mucho bucks. "No reason."

Lily looked at her solemnly. "It would be bad to make friend move from home."

Destiny smiled reassuringly at her, and they continued on to the house. It was a two-story, wood-framed home with a large porch overlooking the water and a Spanish-style overhanging balcony on the second floor. She had seen many such homes in her own time, both restored and original and that made her feel a little easier knowing that not everything in the 1800s would be foreign to her.

In fact, she thought, as they drew closer to the house, it seemed vaguely familiar to her. Gazing over at the waterfront, she decided it was the same house she had once tried to buy several years ago. But that was before she was a writer. She had noticed it just yesterday, before her book-signing and had been surprised to find it had been turned into a bed and breakfast inn.

Yesterday?

Yesterday had been a hundred and twenty-five years from now. Would she ever get used to that?

Knocking on the door, Destiny became startled when it was immediately flung open. A tall, thin, snow white-haired woman of indeterminate years stood framed in the doorway, wielding a large iron skillet in her hand.

Seeing them standing there, the woman lowered her unusual weapon saying, "I'm sorry, you gave me a start. I thought it was that awful Raiford man here to foreclose on my home a day early." Then seeing the crowd of people standing outside her home, she asked, "What are those people doing here? I don't like folks hanging about my place. Danged nosy, if you ask me."

Keeping her eye on the skillet, Destiny smiled graciously, "They're here, I expect, because they're curious about me. You see, I'm new in town."

Penelope was still not quite sure whether this strange young woman was friend or foe. Spreading her legs apart in a defensive stance, she ordered, "And just who in blue blazes are you?"

Smiling sheepishly, Destiny held her hand out to the woman. "I'm Destiny Davidson, a friend of Lily Tiger's."

Grasping the outstretched hand, Penelope yanked Destiny through the door. "Well, don't just stand there. Come in before you let in all the blasted flies."

So much for Destiny's picture of a sweet, helpless old widow woman. Penelope Peabody was far from that.

In a moment, Destiny found herself standing in the front parlor, and decided to get right to the point. "Mrs. Peabody, I know it's impolite to ask, but we don't have much time before Mr. Raiford comes. He'll be meeting me here at six. How much money do you need to pay off your mortgage?"

Laying the heavy skillet face down on a tapestry-covered table, Penelope answered, "I'd like to tell you to mind your own damn business, but you don't strike me as a busybody. Why do you want to know?"

"Because I'm prepared to pay off the mortgage for you, and in exchange, all I ask is that you give me a room in your home for as long as I need it."

Penelope stared at her as if she was looking at a crazy woman, and of course, she was, but that was beside the point. "What do you say?"

It didn't take Penelope long to size up Miss Destiny Davidson and come to the conclusion that she was the genuine thing. "I owe seven hundred and forty-seven dollars, and twenty-two cents—exactly."

"Is that all?"

"Is that all? My dear young woman, that is considered a great deal of money in these parts."

"Well, the offer is still open. I can afford that much. It would really be doing me an enormous favor if you would agree to it."

Penelope's face took on a strange look, startling Destiny. Then, without warning, she covered her face with her apron and began to sob into it. That was the last thing Destiny expected from this assertive widow.

Gazing over at Lily, they exchanged concerned looks, but held their ground, knowing that Penelope was not the kind of woman to brook any sympathetic gestures.

In a moment, the widow composed herself and wiping tears from her eyes spoke with great dignity. "I accept your offer."

"Good. Would first thing in the morning be too soon to move in?"

"You can move in tonight, if you wish."

"Oh, that's a relief. I wasn't looking forward to spending another night in Colt Mandrell's hotel room." As soon as the words were out of her mouth she knew how bad they must sound.

Penelope stared at Destiny as if sizing her up with her eyes. "I expect you're the woman the whole town is talkin' about. Now, I don't hold with gossip, never have, but if it's true you and the Mandrell boy shared a room last night, I don't want to know about it."

"Mrs. Peabody, you don't have to worry about my conduct in your home. I won't do anything to jeopardize your good name."

Looking very relieved, Penelope answered, "I think we're going to get along just fine. Come on, let me show you to your room. Used to be me and my husband's, before he passed on. I moved out 'cause I couldn't bear the loneliness. You'll like it fine. It's the best room in the house." Turning to Lily, she said, "You go out there and tell them people they can go home now. I swan, I don't understand why some people can be so nosy."

"They not leave till they know what Destiny doing here."

"Then tell them that she will be residing here." Without further ado, Penelope headed up the stairs.

Destiny followed after her, and was entranced with her new room. She ran to the window and looked out at the bay front directly across the dirt road. Gazing to the left she could see Fort Marion where Blade McAmmon had been stationed, and where Osceola had been held captive.

For a moment, she forgot what time period she was in, for the fort, called Fort Marion now, and the Castillo de San Marcos in the twentieth century, looked as she had always remembered it. She had spent many happy hours there, exploring it, when she researched her book.

"I love it. Just as soon as we finish our business with Raiford, I'll go to the hotel and get my things." Reaching into the deep side pocket of her dress, she drew out a roll of bills and counted off eight hundred dollars' worth of greenbacks. Penelope took them with a shaky hand.

"Oh, Lordy. I can't believe this is really happening. Young lady, are you sure you're not an angel? If you hadn't come to town at this exact time, I would have found myself out on the street tomorrow, thanks to that snake Brent Raiford."

The tinkling of a bell sounded, and Penelope's expression turned stern. "Speaking of the devil . . ."

The two women hurried down the stairs, then composed themselves before opening the door to Brent Raiford. Lily entered right behind him, and Penelope gave her a warning look to keep her mouth shut. That wasn't going to be easy for Lily. Her nervous titter escaped into a burst of tinkling laughter.

Penelope's sharp glance finally quieted Lily. She wanted the satisfaction of catching Mr. high and mighty Raiford by complete surprise.

Brent's gaze traveled from one woman to the next, lighting on Destiny. He almost didn't recognize her in her stylish new clothing, but the snug bodice of her dress was very familiar. The woman had the best set of tits he'd ever seen. "Ah, I see you've arrived already, Miss Davidson. I like punctuality in a woman. I hope Miz Peabody has been civil to you."

Working hard to keep her face composed, Destiny answered, "Under the circumstances, I would say she has been very civil."

"Of course, of course." Putting the sympathetic smile of an undertaker on his face, he addressed Penelope. "I regret having to do this, but as I've explained numerous times, the bank cannot afford to become a house of charity. So, if you'll be so kind, I'd like to show Miss Davidson around the house."

Penelope fanned herself with the money. "My, my, but it's hot in here. Don't you think so, Mistuh Raiford?"

Brent eyed the bills and his sympathetic smile widened. "I'm afraid a few miserly one-dollar notes won't make a difference to the bank, my dear."

"These happen to be one-hundred-dollar greenbacks, suh. And I do believe there are exactly eight of them. So, if you'll just hand over my deed, I'll lay these here beauties in your hand."

Speaking to her as if he were addressing a simpleton, he said, "My dear woman, you couldn't possibly have come up with all the money you owe, so it's useless to pretend."

Taking him by the hand, Penelope slapped the eight bills in his palm. "Count them, and be sure to give me the exact change. I cannot afford to become a house of charity."

Brent's eyes widened as he did just that. "What fool would lend that kind of money to you?"

"It's none of your damn business. Write me a receipt and I guess I can let you take the money right now."

Turning to Destiny, Brent said, "I'm sorry. It seems I've sent you over here for nothing. But, if you'll trust me again, I'm sure I can find another suitable home for you to buy."

"I don't doubt that. But there's no need. Penelope has graciously consented to renting me a room."

"I see. Since our business is concluded, then I'd like very much to take you to dinner."

Destiny started to say no, but his next words stayed her tongue.

"I thought it would be a good opportunity to talk to you about your diamond."

Feeling the color drain from her face, she answered, "Is there anything wrong?"

"Come to dinner, and we'll discuss it."

Uh, oh! Did he know? Did he suspect it was a fake? Poor Penelope could be out on the street tomorrow if he discovered the truth. "To tell you the truth, I'm famished. Lead the way."

Colt Mandrell rode back to town on his new mare, Scarlet Lady, named after his redheaded bed partner. Of course, he wouldn't tell her how the mare got her name, she packed too mean a wallop.

Tying the horse to a hitching post in front of the hotel, he made his way over to a young girl peddling carnations and bought every one she had. He was feeling mighty good, and could hardly wait to see Red again. He hadn't been able to take his mind off her for a moment, the whole day. But after the great time they had in bed, that was hardly surprising.

Taking the stairs to his room two at a time, he was stopped in his tracks by the voice of the desk clerk saying, "If you're lookin' for the, uh, young lady, she's gone."

"Gone?" Tracing his footsteps, he strode up to the clerk. "Where in hell is she?"

"Moved in with Miz Peabody, or so I hear tell. You know how fast news travels around here."

Before he could finish the sentence, Colt was out the door, flowers in hand. Mounting Scarlet Lady, he cantered down the road and around the corner to the Peabody house in time to see the redhead emerging from the house accompanied by a man. It didn't take him long to recognize his brother-in-law.

It figured. Brent wasn't one to pass up any new attractive woman who came to town. He'd been a skirt chaser as long as he'd known him, and he'd warned Susan about marrying him to no avail. His sister had a mind of her own, and had told him in no uncertain terms to mind his own business.

Well, now it was his business.

Reining in his horse, he watched from a distance as Brent bent over Red's hand. Colt realized he was kissing it, and his first reaction was to ride up to them and smash Brent in the mouth. But he composed himself, wanting to see what the redhead would do. See if she was too intelligent to fall for Brent's sleazy charm.

Nudging his horse, he rode over to the side of the road and hid out of sight behind a large horse and carriage. In a few moments, they passed by, and he watched as the redhead smiled up at Brent's face as if he were the most fascinating man alive.

Disappointment was too mild a word for what he was

feeling. He'd been a fool to think she was anything more than a shallow little opportunist, looking for a free ride. Well, she would soon be in for a big disappointment when she found out that Brent was married.

Looking down at the colorful bouquet of flowers, he felt like a damn fool. She had really done a job on his heart. He had even believed that she was the girl he was going to marry. But, obviously, it must have been his lust for her that threw him off kilter.

A sad-faced elderly woman passed by just then, and he leapt from his horse and handed her the flowers, doffing his hat to her without saying a word. The woman accepted them the same way, but the expression on her face was no longer sad.

Mounting his horse, Colt rode to his favorite tavern, and proceeded to get drunk.

Six

Paul Proudhorse rode slowly down King Street, his narrowed eyes scrutinizing both sides of the road, searching for Colt Mandrell. This wouldn't be the first time he had to look for his friend and employer when he was on a drinking spree, and he was sure it wouldn't be the last. Colt was a man of enormous physical energy, and sometimes that energy just plain spilled over and had to be dissipated through a wild, drunken orgy.

Fact was, he had some growing up to do. Still sowing his wild oats. He would have envied Colt his wildness if it wasn't for Faith. Since the moment he saw her, he had no interest in anything but making her his wife, raising a family.

Funny how two friends, raised together, could be so different. Well, maybe not. He was Seminole, Colt was white. They looked at life very differently.

Colt's family had taken him in when his father was found dead on the side of the road near Picolatta. As for his mother, no one knew what happened to her. He certainly didn't know.

The only recollection he had of her was her soft voice as she sang to him in the language of the Creeks, a language he no longer understood after so many years of living with the whites.

It hurt a little, even now, to think of his lost family. No one had ever told him, but he knew his father had drunk himself to death. Whiskey. The curse of his people. He hoped it wouldn't become a curse to Colt.

Spying the chestnut mare tied outside a tavern, Paul reined in beside it, dismounted, and tied his horse to a post. Rolling up his sleeves in anticipation of a fight, he gritted his teeth and strode in.

The boisterous voices of the tavern's clientele hushed to a low murmur at his appearance. They knew why he was there. He knew every man in that tavern, and they knew him. They wouldn't interfere.

A loud rumbling suddenly filled the quieted room and Paul followed the sound to the back of the tavern. Immediately, the crowd parted, making way for him, giving him a clear view of Colt sitting at the table, his head lolling to one side, passed out and snoring loudly.

He was also bound with rope from head to foot.

Paul frowned, but said nothing. He knew how rambunctious Colt could get when he was drunk.

" 'Bout time you came," Billy Capo said, walking up to Paul. "He was getting ready to go find Brent Raiford and challenge him to a gun duel. Somethin' about a redhead. Must be that purty woman who just came to town. I thought it best to keep him out of trouble. This were the only way I knew how. Took three of us to hold him down."

Paul nodded his head slightly to acknowledge the barkeeper, then began to untie Colt.

"Yup, he fought hard, but once he figured out he warn't goin' anywhere, he settled down. 'Course, Rita May feeding him one whiskey after another had somethin' to do with that."

Leaning over Colt, Paul spoke in a low, but demanding voice, "Colt. Wake up."

Colt's eyes opened slowly. Gazing bleary-eyed at his friend who was weaving in and out of his vision, he replied, "Hold on there, Paul, you're makin' me dizzy."

Paul continued to untie Colt.

"Ahh, Chief, don't be mad at me. I'm jusss fine. Want me to prove it? Let me shoot your hat off your head." When Paul didn't respond, Colt laughed at his own joke. Freed of his bonds, he struggled to his feet, and fell against Paul. "It was jusss a joke, Chief. Jusss a joke. Don't be an old poop. Sit down and have a drink with me."

By this time, Paul was supporting all Colt's weight with his arms. Taking advantage of the situation, Paul moved Colt toward the door. "Let's just get a little fresh air first."

"Good idea. Good idea. Ishh starting to get a little stale in here."

Walking him outside, Paul decided his friend was too drunk to ride his horse out to the ranch. The best thing to do was to take him to his mama's house. Colt would be mighty mad with him for that when he sobered up, but there was nothing to be done about that. Like a good southern boy, he'd behave at his mama's. That's all that mattered.

Destiny sat across the table from Brent trying to hide her growing apprehension. If he knew her diamond was a fake, poor Penelope would be out on the street tomorrow, not to mention herself.

Trying to appear unconcerned, she gazed around the restaurant and was surprised at how elegant it looked. Decked out with lavender tablecloths in a soft nubby fabric and tall silver candelabra on each table, it looked quite elegant. Against the rather rough-hewn background of stark pale coquina walls the effect was quite lovely. She was glad to know that even in nineteenth-century St. Augustine, refinement could be found.

The only thing that marred her enjoyment of the room was the stifling heat. She longed for the modern convenience of air-conditioning, or at the very least, a ceiling fan to disperse the cloying humidity. And then there was the matter of the flies. They were everywhere. Funny thing though, no one else in the restaurant seemed to mind them. Obviously, they were used to them. Well, she didn't want to have to get used to them. She wanted out of this era and back to her own.

Once their orders had been taken, Destiny watched as Brent settled back in his chair and began to speak. She waited anxiously for him to broach the subject, afraid of what he was going to say, but he was in no hurry. He started chatting about himself and his life as a banker and realtor.

"Yes, I've got big plans for St. Augustine's future. This place attracts people here during the winter months, but not enough to make it worth the trouble. Tell me, Destiny, do you have any idea what keeps people away?"

Tired of all the boring small talk, Destiny tried to hide her irritation. "I'm sure you're going to tell me."

"Transportation, or I should say the lack of it. Think for a moment about how you got here, and you'll understand what I mean."

The image of her and Colt locked in a passionate embrace presented itself before her eyes, and she almost choked on her wine.

"That's just it, isn't it? There is no easy way to get here. Certainly not by ocean where the conditions off our coast are too treacherous for ships. What does that leave? Traveling by steamer down the St. John's River until you get to Picolatta, and then boarding a stagecoach to travel over seventeen miles of the worst roads in the territory."

Destiny had no idea what he was leading up to, but she was sure he was mentioning all this for a reason.

"Sure, the St. John's Railroad will eventually have decent rail service, but that's still a few years away."

"What point are you trying to make Mr. Raiford?"

"Just this. I want to start a sophisticated transportation system. One that encompasses steamer service up the St. John's River and rail service luxurious enough to attract the wealthy to our healthy winter climes. Then I want to build hotels the likes of which have never been seen before. I need land for that, and a partner willing to invest. I, uh, couldn't help but think of you."

"Mr. Raiford, it seems you got me here under false pretenses. I thought you wanted to talk to me about my diamond?"

"I do. I do."

"Then please tell me what it is you want to know, because I have no intention of becoming your partner."

"My, my, you're very blunt for a woman. But I find it very refreshing. Surely, you don't come from the South? Southern women would die before telling anyone what they really think."

Destiny wasn't about to walk into that one. The less he knew about her the better. "The diamond?"

"Don't be so quick to say no. You'll be mighty sorry you passed up such a great opportunity. I want you to take this copy of my proposal home with you. Read it over carefully before you make up your mind. Will you do that much for me?"

"All right, I will. Now, will you tell me what it is you wanted to know about the diamond?"

"The diamond? Oh, yes. I was interested in its origin."

Uh, oh, here it comes. "It's origin?"

"Yes. You see, I've had a chance to study it closer, and there's something quite unusual about it."

She was afraid of that. Now what was she going to do? Fluttering her eyelashes, she said, "I don't know what you mean."

"I mean, that I am in awe of how flawless it is."

Destiny took a large swallow of wine to hide the unexpected triumph she felt.

"Is it one of them South African diamonds that I've been hearing about lately? They were imported only a year or two ago, so I haven't had a chance to see one yet. You'd think Florida was at the ends of the earth for the great time it takes for anything new to find its way here."

"Why, yes, I do believe it is. How very clever of you to know that, Mr. Raiford."

Reaching across the table, Brent took her hand in his, rubbing her palm intimately with his thumb. "Please, I insist that you call me Brent."

Destiny yanked her hand away. It was obvious Brent was as much in the dark about the diamond as ever. In fact, it seemed the only reason he wanted to see her was to talk her out of the wealth he supposed her to have. That, and to hit on her. The lech. She should have known. If she hadn't had such a guilty conscience about the cubic zirconia she would have picked up on what he really wanted a lot sooner. That would have spared her having to suffer his company.

"I'm so glad you're pleased with the diamond. Have you had a chance to show it to your . . . wife?"

A frown creased Brent's handsome face.

"So that's what this is all about. Your treating me so cold because you found out I'm married. Well, darlin', you don't have to worry your pretty little head about that. My wife is a very understanding woman."

Patting his hand very affectionately, she answered sweetly, "Unfortunately, Brent, I'm not."

After that, he didn't have much to say. Relieved that her secret was still safe, Destiny made short work of her supper, then returned to Penelope's house. She had given Lily instructions to enlist the aid of the boys again, this time to pick up her belongings and bring them to her new home. They had done so already.

That was a relief, for the last thing she wanted was to go back to the hotel and bump into the amorous cowboy again. The farther away she was from him, the better. When she was with him she couldn't think straight.

Penelope and Lily helped her put her new clothes away,

then the three women sat in Penelope's parlor and talked. Destiny steered the conversation to the Mandrells, hoping to find out more about Little Bit and Gary. If she couldn't meet Shining Dawn and Blade, she wanted to at least meet other characters from her book before she went back to her own time. The thought of that sent an excited ripple through her body. "Do the Mandrells live here in town?"

"The elders do. Elizabeth and Gary. Used to live out on the stud farm, don't you know, but Elizabeth took kind of sickly, so Gary bought them a house here in town and handed over the working of the farm to Colt."

"Stud farm? You can't mean . . . No, of course you don't mean a breeding farm for slaves."

Penelope gazed at Destiny with a perplexed look on her face. "Child, where have you been the past five years? The war ended in sixty-five. The slaves were set free then. More to the point, how could you think that nice people like Elizabeth and Gary Mandrell would have anything to do with the kind of farm you're talkin' about? I meant a stud farm for the breeding of horses. Colt has the finest one south of Kentucky and Tennessee."

"Of course. I don't know what I was thinking." That wasn't true. She knew just what made her think of that. In her book, two of her important characters were slaves who had lived on just such a stud farm. And it was Gary Mandrell's father, the evil Gordon Mandrell, who had owned it. She sure hoped Colt was nothing like his notorious grandfather.

"If you'd like, we can go calling on Miz Little Bit. That's what everyone in St. Augustine calls Elizabeth Mandrell. When you see her you'll understand why. I'm sure she'd love to meet the young lady her son . . . On second thought, that might not be such a good idea."

Destiny had the good grace to blush. "Please . . . I'd really like to go calling on her. I know so much about her and yet I've never met her. Would you take me to see her?"

Penelope thought some on that subject, then came to the conclusion that it might be just the medicine Miz Little Bit needed. Destiny was a mighty sweet young lady. Perhaps once Little Bit got to know her, she'd overlook her indiscretion. She had to have heard about it by now, since every dang person in town was talking about it.

"Very well. I was planning on going over there in the morning anyway. I don't see why you couldn't come along."

Next morning, a very excited Destiny accompanied by a very curious Penelope, was ushered into the Mandrell home, a pretty little cottage on Water Street. The tranquil, oak-lined, narrow road that edged Matanzas Bay was off the beaten track, giving it a great deal of privacy from the busy section of town.

The two women waited in the parlor while a maid summoned the mistress of the house. Destiny had a hard time containing her excitement. She would finally be meeting one of the characters from her book.

Little Bit entered the room in a flurry of violet cotton, and Destiny could hardly contain her delight. The woman she had dubbed Little Bit in her book because of her small stature, was indeed as tiny as she had imagined. However, she looked a lot older than she pictured her. She had to remind herself that it wasn't 1837, but 1870. And she couldn't help wondering once again why she had been sent to this particular year. If she had to end up in the past, she would have preferred to have ended up in 1837 the time her book had been set in.

"Why, Penelope. I didn't expect to see you today. I heard you had a new boarder, and thought you'd be too busy to lollygag around with me today." Little Bit's gaze moved slowly, but very deliberately to the young woman standing next to Penelope. Taking in her very womanly form, she said, "I take it this is she?"

The ice in Little Bit's voice sent a chill through Destiny's heart. Gathering her courage, she extended her hand and said softly, "Hello, Miss Elizabeth. I'm Destiny Davidson."

Little Bit stonily stared down at Destiny's lace-gloved hand.

Embarrassed and feeling very awkward standing there, Destiny said, "I'm sorry, perhaps it was a mistake to come."

For the first time, Little Bit stared directly into Destiny's eyes, and the eyes that stared back looked oddly familiar. A strange shiver went up her spine, although she had no idea why. "Have . . . Have we met before?"

Destiny's hand retreated to her side. "No, we haven't."

"But, surely we have met. Not here. Not in this town, but somewhere . . . somewhere. . . ." An image floated through Little Bit's mind, but she couldn't accept it and pushed it out of her consciousness. "It will come to me, I'm sure."

Then, before Destiny could reply, Colt was standing in the doorway. He was barefooted and bare chested, except for the Celtic cross around his neck, and so damnably sexy with rumpled hair and tight pants, she felt her heart calling out to him, along with other parts of her anatomy. Damn. Every time she looked at him she felt like crawling into bed with him.

Colt's heart was in danger of coming right out of his chest, it was beating so fast when he saw her standing there. She was dressed in the gown he had sent to the hotel, and looked so demure, so completely feminine that he wondered if he could bear the sweet agonizing ache of seeing her, but not touching her.

He wanted to stay angry at her. Life would be easier that way, and he tried to conjure up the image of her and Brent together, but it didn't work. His crazy thought of marrying her was sounding even louder today, seeing her dressed in the clothing he had picked out for her.

There was no doubt about it, this was the woman he

wanted, and he'd be damned if he'd let Brent Raiford, or any other man, for that matter, stand in his way.

"I heard your voice, Red, and thought I must still be dreaming," he said, running his fingers through his hair nervously. "You look mighty pretty in pink."

Destiny blushed furiously. She had deliberately worn the dress he had given her, hoping she would see him, but thinking she would not. The sight of him completely unnerved her.

It should be against the law for a man to look that good.

Little Bit's gaze traveled from her son to Destiny and then back to her son again. She knew now that what was between them was powerful. That took her by surprise, for she knew she would have to reassess her opinion of Miss Destiny Davidson.

This was no wanton woman out for a good time. Destiny was very obviously genuinely attracted to her son, and he to her. If she wasn't mistaken the emotion that crackled in the air between them was more than just animal lust. Could it be possible that her son and Destiny were falling in love? If that were true, she could find it in her heart to forgive their little indiscretion.

"I never expected to see you here at my mother's, Red. I didn't even know the two of you were acquainted."

Little Bit answered for her. "Well, son, you don't know everything, or you wouldn't have been squandering your time and your health drinking last night. You could have been keeping company with this delightful young lady."

Penelope and Destiny exchanged surprised looks.

Speaking to Destiny, Little Bit continued, "But perhaps I've misspoken. I suddenly realize that you may already be betrothed, or even married, Miss Davidson."

"No, Miss Elizabeth. There is no man in my life . . . yet." It was obvious to Destiny that Little Bit had a change of heart concerning her, and no doubt now was hearing wedding bells. This was so like the Little Bit she had written about.

Davidson, Colt thought to himself. So that was her name. "Uh, Miss Davidson . . ."

"Colt, I doubt your young lady would be offended if you called her by her given name. After all, I understand you two are thoroughly acquainted."

Colt groaned under his breath. Obviously, his mother had heard all about Red and him in the hotel room. Now how was he supposed to tell her he didn't even know her first name? She'd be scandalized by that, for sure. "Umm, uhh, Mother, why don't you make the introductions. I'm sure you'll feel much better knowing we've been properly introduced."

Seeing the astonishment on his mother's face, Colt knew he hadn't fooled her.

"Colt Mandrell, don't tell me you don't even know her given name? Why, surely you are jesting?"

"I'd never jest about something like that to you, Mother, knowing how serious you take such matters."

Destiny could see that Little Bit was having trouble digesting that news. She was having a hard time staying composed, and Destiny didn't blame her. It would have been scandalous even in her time to know that a man and woman had slept together without even knowing each other's names.

Knowing it was probably past Little Bit's capacity to speak right now, Destiny answered for her. "Colt, my name is Destiny."

"Destiny." Colt savored the name with his tongue. "That's a very unusual name, but it suits you well."

"I'm very glad you approve." Destiny's gaze traveled over Colt's broad shoulders and chest, resting on the very familiar Celtic cross.

The Celtic cross.

That was it.

Colt had appeared to her in the mirror when she touched the cross. Then, in a dream when she held the cross. and, yes, when they were making love, he had been wearing the cross.

The pewter cross was her means of traveling through time.

It had to be the answer.

But, exciting as that thought was, it was muted by the knowledge that she would be leaving her sexy dream lover.

Why did life have to be so complicated?

Why couldn't Colt have lived in her own time?

Seeing Destiny's interest in her son's bare chest, Little Bit scolded him saying, "Colt, where are your manners? Please go put a shirt on. Then you may join us for tea."

Oh, no, Destiny thought in a panic. Don't put your shirt on, or I won't be able to touch the cross. But too late, Colt was leaving the room. Well, no matter. He wasn't going anywhere. She'd have another chance to touch it soon enough.

"Please forgive his manners, Miss Davidson. He was raised much better than that. I certainly taught him better than to greet a young lady half dressed, but yesterday was his birthday, and I'm afraid his celebration of it became too . . . exuberant."

"His birthday? How old is your son, Miss Elizabeth?"

"Please call me Little Bit. It's hard to believe that it's been twenty-four years since that awful night when he was born."

Twenty-four? Their age difference was much greater than she suspected. It was just as well that she would be leaving, because she had no intention of getting involved with someone still wet behind the ears. She wanted a seasoned man, not one still trying to figure out what being a man was all about. She had to admit though, in bed, he sure knew how to act like a man.

But twenty-four? She had made love to a man seven, no, eight years younger than she.

Of course, at the time, his age was the very last thing on her mind. But now, it was taking on considerable importance. She had always believed a man should be older, old-fashioned though that notion might be. She also believed that the man should love the woman more than she loved him if the relationship was going to last a lifetime.

Boy, she never realized till now just how opinionated she was. No wonder she had never married. What man would want someone so set in her ways?

Yes, the sooner she left, the better. She doubted she'd have the strength to resist Colt if she stayed in close proximity to him. And she was sure that her feelings for him were much stronger than his for her. Why? Because she couldn't imagine anyone being more strongly attracted to someone than she was to him. She was devastated every time she so much as glanced his way.

Colt walked back into the room just then, and one look at him confirmed everything she thought. He now wore a blue chambray shirt that set off his tanned face most becomingly. And he looked more manly than ever. Their eyes met, and electricity danced between them.

Destiny had a hard time concentrating on the women's conversation as they sat drinking tea at a little table in the parlor. Colt didn't touch his, but spent the entire time just staring at her, making her stumble over her words, and her hand tremble as she drank from the little bone china cup.

He had to know it was his presence that caused her to act that way, and that bothered her even more. She didn't want him to know the power he had over her. She wanted to appear cool and distant.

That was a laugh. Inside she felt like a volcano about to erupt. The sooner she touched the cross and left, the safer she would be.

"And now, children, Penelope and I will leave you alone

for a short while. If what you tell me is true, that you don't really know each other at all, then I think it's about time you got acquainted."

Colt and Destiny barely knew when the two older women left. Lost in a world of their own, they derived great satisfaction just gazing at each other, absorbing the image of the other into their brains, and into their hearts. They talked, but as quickly as words were spoken, they were forgotten. The only thing that mattered was being in the same room together.

When even that was no longer enough, Colt stood, and taking her hand, drew her to her feet. As lithe and natural as a panther, his arm slipped around her waist. She knew what he was going to do, and her heart began to race.

Tilting her head up, her lips met his in a soft, tender kiss so miraculously sweet she felt the urge to cry.

"Can you possibly be feeling what I am?" he said in a husky voice.

Destiny's eyes fluttered open. At the sight of his wonderful face, she took in a deep, shuddering breath. "I don't know. What do you feel, Colt?"

"Like devouring you."

Laughing nervously, she answered, "But then there'd be nothing left of me."

"I know. That's the only thing that stops me. I'd hate never being able to see you, or touch you, again."

A sudden sadness washed over Destiny as she thought about what she was going to do. She deeply regretted having to leave him. But she must. Her life as a successful writer was waiting for her. She couldn't give that up. Not even for the sexiest man in the universe.

With a trembling hand, she fingered the lapel of his shirt, moving her hands in a caress so he wouldn't know what her true motive was.

She needn't have worried. In the state he was in, she was sure anything she did would seem erotic to him. Seeking the opening of his shirt, her fingers brushed the material, and his hastily buttoned shirt became undone. This was it.

Suddenly, it really hit her hard that she would never see him again. Swallowing hard, she gazed up into his eyes for one last heartrending look that would have to last her a lifetime. Then . . . almost reluctantly, her fingers moved inside his shirt . . .

. . . to touch the Celtic cross.

Seven

"Ow!" Destiny's eyes squeezed shut in pain as a jolt of electricity zapped her hand. Opening them again she stared up at Colt's face in disbelief.

He was still there.

More to the point, she was still in the past. Nothing had happened. But why not? She had been so sure, so damn sure. Why didn't it work?

And why had she felt such a strong electric shock? She had felt only a tingle the first time she touched the cross. It didn't make any sense.

Colt seemed oblivious to the jolt, but how could that be? If she felt it, he had to feel it. The cross was nestled against his skin.

"Didn't you feel anything?" she cried in bewilderment.

It seemed strange to Colt that she should be worried about the amount of sexual arousement he felt. But then, he decided she was just being typically female, trying to get him to express how much he cared. "I'd have to be dead not to feel anything when you touch me, Red."

Taking her by the arm with a firm grip, he said, "Let's get out of here before I get so carried away I'm tempted to make love to you right here on my mother's floor."

Things were getting crazier for Destiny all the time. Colt was acting like a typical male. Didn't he understand what was going on? What a ridiculous question. Of course he didn't understand. How could he when she still couldn't?

It looked like she was going to be stuck here forever. She might as well make the most of it. After all, how hard could it be living in the same time as Colt Mandrell?

No. Damn it all. She couldn't give up so easily.

If she could travel back in time, then she could travel forward in time. There had to be a way. One thing was certain: Colt Mandrell was a part of the solution. The cross was just a part of it. If she had been thinking clearly she would have realized that. Nothing had happened when she touched it that first time, aside from the tingle she felt.

Actually, something had happened. Colt had appeared to her then. But he hadn't really been there physically. It was more like a psychic experience that time.

It must have been the combination of touching the cross and making love at the same time that propelled her through time. That meant she didn't dare let her sexy dream man out of her sight. Without his cooperation, she'd be stranded for sure.

Well, judging by the look in Colt's eyes, she'd have a chance to test her new theory real soon. It wasn't going to take much to get him into bed.

It sounded so cold and calculating, even to her own mind, but what she was feeling was far from that. She didn't need an excuse for being with Colt. The very thought of making love to him made her weak in the knees. Struggling for composure, she said in a breathless little voice that betrayed her, "Where would you like to go?"

Colt could hardly believe what Destiny was saying. Running his hands up her curvaceous form, he murmured, "To my farm. We can have all the privacy we want there."

Afraid of appearing too eager, Destiny tried acting coy to disguise her true emotions. "It's very . . . tempting, but . . ."

She didn't have a chance to answer further for the door opened then and a pretty, young brunette walked in.

"Oh, I'm sorry. I didn't know I'd be interrupting anything. I was hoping to find Paul. Have you seen my reluctant bridegroom?"

"Not since he brought me here last night. Something I didn't fully appreciate at the time. Wouldn't be surprised if he's hiding out in the stables. In fact, my guess is, he spent the night there with Scarlet Lady."

"Scarlet Lady?" Faith wailed, her gaze traveling to the beautiful redhead, standing intimately close to Colt.

Realizing what Faith was thinking, Colt laughed heartily. "Scarlet Lady is the name of the new mare Daddy gave me for my birthday."

Feeling reassured that he hadn't been referring to the voluptuous redhead in his arms, Faith murmured, "Aren't you going to introduce me to your new friend? It's just a formality, mind you, since the whole town knows who she is by now."

It was obvious to Destiny from the natural ease they had with each other, that Colt and this pretty young woman were well acquainted. That bothered her more than she wanted to admit. But, at the same time, she found herself strangely drawn to the girl.

Something about her seemed oddly familiar.

Perhaps she was one of the characters in her book. No, that couldn't be it. No one in her story fit the description of this young woman.

"Destiny, I want you to meet Faith McAmmon. She's been staying with my folks while her family is out of town."

Destiny's mouth flew open in surprise. That was the last thing she expected to hear.

Faith was Shining Dawn and Blade McAmmon's daughter?

But, no, that couldn't be. Shining Dawn's little girl had died in 1846, and, her other child had been a boy named Johnny. She remembered that from the journal. Ah, yes, but Shining Dawn had been pregnant when she helped Little Bit give birth to Colt. What had she written? That she had been five months along. Yes, that was it. Faith had to be the child she was carrying then.

So, that's what it was. This camaraderie so evident between Colt and Faith. They had known each other since birth.

Feeling decidedly better after figuring out that their relationship was platonic, she answered sincerely, "It's nice to meet you, Faith."

Faith looked Destiny over from her head to her feet with a deliberation she didn't try to hide. But Destiny didn't mind. The girl had a delightful twinkle in her eyes that told her she was just being playful.

"Mmm, so you're the mysterious lady who has the whole town agog. I don't wonder. You're very beautiful in an odd sort of way. Hold onto her, Colt, every unattached man in town will be after her."

"And some who aren't so unattached, too," Colt said under his breath.

"I heard that," Faith exclaimed. "You're talking about Brent aren't you? Lily Tiger told me all about his showing up at Miz Penelope's yesterday after Destiny's shopping spree."

Turning to Destiny, she continued, "That was awfully kind of you, Destiny, paying off Penelope's mortgage. You could have bought the house right out from under the poor thing and had it all to yourself."

Colt listened in stunned silence. Where in hell did Destiny get the money to pay off Mrs. Peabody's mortgage? How could she have been naked, without so much as a pair of shoes one moment, then paying off a mortgage and going on a shopping spree the next?

He didn't have to think very hard about that answer. Brent had given her the money.

And there was only one reason why the bastard would be that generous to a total stranger. She had given him something valuable in return, and it didn't take a lot of brains to figure out just what that was.

Unaware of what Colt was thinking, Destiny was in awe
of how much Faith knew about her. Small town gossip traveled at the speed of light in the nineteenth century. And
that was totally without telephones or fax machines. Amazing. "What else does everyone in town know about me,
Faith?"

An angry Colt answered, "They know that you have the
morals of a she cat."

His words hit Destiny like a blow to the heart. She had
no idea what she had done to deserve them, but he soon
let her know.

"I gave you the benefit of a doubt when I saw you cozy-
ing up to Brent Raiford. I didn't want to believe you could
be taken in by his slick charm. And I was right. He didn't
take you in. You took him, for all you could get. But your
beautiful ass is worth it, baby. I'm sorry I didn't think of
making you my mistress before my dear brother-in-law
did."

Destiny stared at Colt as if he were speaking a foreign
language, then understanding spread over her, along with
the flush of red that covered her face and neck. "Is that
what you think?"

Colt didn't answer. He didn't have to. It was obvious
what he believed.

"Is that what you really think? I can see you're never
going to forget about the way we met. Well, I'll be darned
if I'm going to lower myself to try and explain any further.
Think what you want, Colt Mandrell."

Turning on her heels, Destiny quickly exited the room,
leaving Colt to face yet another irate female.

"You're the biggest fool this town ever had," Faith
scolded. "How could you believe for a moment that Destiny
is capable of selling herself for money? And besides that,
she's independently wealthy. She doesn't need any man to
take care of her."

"What are you talking about?"

"I'm talking about the gigantic diamond ring she sold to your brother-in-law for a small fortune. And guess what, Lily Tiger told me she has two more of them."

Colt struggled with the answer to that one, and came up with, "That just means she used her body to get them from some other man."

"Ohh, Colt Tyler Mandrell, you've got a lot of growing up to do. Just because all you can think of when you look at her is her body, doesn't mean that she's nothing but a plaything. If I were you, I'd hightail it out of here and catch up to her before she's had a chance to figure out just what a fool you are."

Faith's words hit home. Just because she had made love to him, didn't mean she jumped into bed with every man who wanted her. Hell, he couldn't imagine any man not wanting her. She was so damned desirable.

He suddenly felt something akin to pride, knowing she had chosen him to take to her bed. Well, it had actually been his bed, and the circumstances of their getting together were very peculiar, to say the least, but there was something to what she had said about them meeting in a dream. He just didn't care to try and figure it out. There were some things in this world better left to the fates.

Taking Faith by the shoulders, he kissed her forehead, then headed for the door. "Some day soon I want to have a talk with you, young lady. About how you know so much about what a man thinks when he looks at a woman. But right now, I'm in a hurry. Make my excuses to my mother, all right?"

"Where are you going?"

"Back to the farm, and I won't be alone. Find Paul and tell him to saddle a horse for Destiny and meet me at the crossroads. Then, sweetheart, spend the rest of the day with your reluctant bridegroom. Maybe you can break him down and get him to agree to marrying you now, instead of wasting any more precious time. Marriage to someone very special is a rare gift."

Destiny strode down the road to Penelope's house in a whirl of pink and lace. How dare he think she was capable of selling her body for money! If he knew her, he'd . . . But that was just it, he didn't know her. He may have known her body, but he had no idea what she was like inside. And, if she had anything to say about it, he never would.

She never wanted to see him again. Even if that meant she had to stay in this primitive, mosquito-infested, hot as hell, air-conditionerless time forever.

If she had to stay, why, she would just . . .

Just what?

The only thing she knew how to do was write books and St. Augustine of 1870 wasn't exactly the mecca of the publishing world. She doubted they even had a bookstore. She wanted, no, craved everything she had in the twentieth century. Central air, television, her trendy little minivan, not to mention all the perks she had enjoyed being a published author. She wanted fame, she wanted wealth, and most of all she wanted respect.

Well, she had one of the three already. Fame. Everyone in town knew who she was, but it wasn't the kind of fame she had in mind. She hadn't worked hard all this time to become notorious for having sex in a hotel room with a perfect stranger.

Ohh! Why had she lost her temper that way? She was only punishing herself. She would have to make up to him sooner or later if she was ever going to get him into bed again. She was determined to accomplish that because it was the only way she knew out of this dilemma.

Her reverie was rudely broken as she felt herself being jerked violently into the air. Colt had a firm grasp on her under her arms and was lifting her up onto his saddle.

Letting out a startled shriek, she cried, "Let me go."

"Settle down, Red. We're going for a ride."

Before she knew it, she was lying face down over Colt's lap, and he was keeping her there with a firm hand on her rump.

"What do you think you're doing? Put me down!"

"Not until we get out of town. The folks here know too much about us already. I'm going to find us some privacy."

Suddenly, they were galloping down the road and Destiny didn't have the time to talk. She was too intent on keeping from sliding off as her body pounded against Colt's, knocking the wind out of her lungs. Winding her hands around Colt's leg, she closed her eyes to the upside-down blur of the passing landscape.

"If I ever get off this horse alive, I'll . . ."

And then the horse was pulling to a stop and she was sliding down its body, landing miraculously on her feet. Out of breath from the grueling ride, short though it may have been, her chest heaved as she took in a large hurting breath. By then Colt was off the horse, too.

Mortified, and very angry, she kicked his shin just as hard as she could and got great satisfaction out of the shout of pain that burst from his mouth. "Who the hell do you think you are, Conan the Barbarian?"

Tugging her dress into shape, she finger-combed her tousled hair back into place, while Colt hopped around on one foot, deliberately overdramatizing his injury.

How dare he make fun of her like that. She was about to kick his other shin, when out of the corner of her eye she saw a man riding toward her on a horse, towing a riderless one behind him. Looking up at his face, she almost fainted with fear. Though he was dressed like the white men in town, she could tell by his face he was a real live Indian.

Suppressing a cry, she ran behind Colt, holding tight to

his waist as she used his body as a shield. "Don't just stand there like an idiot. Do something!"

Colt saw the fear in her eyes and turned to see Paul sitting calmly in his saddle, staring down at the redhead as if she were a crazy woman.

It astonished Colt that she should be afraid of Paul. Seminoles hadn't been hostile for quite a while now. But obviously, she didn't know that.

Hiding his amusement, he reached for his gun holstered at his side and shouted to Paul. "Halt there, Injun. Don't come any closer or I'll have to shoot you down like a dawg."

Destiny wasn't prepared for that. She didn't want anyone to die because of her. Grasping at his arm, she shouted, "No. Don't."

Paul laughed out loud. "Don't worry 'bout me, little lady. I can outdraw the likes of Colt Mandrell any day of the week."

Wide-eyed, Destiny's gaze traveled from the Indian to Colt and then back again, seeing the amusement in both sets of eyes.

Colt burst out laughing. "Red, meet Paul Proudhorse, my foreman, and, I might add, my best friend."

Feeling very foolish, Destiny folded her arms over her chest. "Why didn't you let me know that before I made a fool out of myself?" Tilting her chin up defiantly, she said in a frosty voice, "Please take me back to town now. I've got more important things to do than be the source of amusement for little boys playing cowboys and Indians."

Her comment hit Colt unexpectedly hard. He didn't like being compared to a little boy. Not when he suspected she was older than he, not when it was very important to him that she look up to him as a man.

Covering his hurt, he drawled, "Hell, Red, I'd rather play with you. I can think of some games that would be quite stimulating. Do you know how to ride a horse?"

She couldn't help imagining what kind of games he would play with her, and she felt herself grow wet just thinking about them. Damn. He was so sexy, she couldn't even stay mad at him. "What do you want to know for?"

" 'Cause we're riding out to my farm."

Destiny lowered her head so Colt couldn't see her embarrassment. He really wanted to know if she could ride a horse. Oh, great. She was so darned horny, she thought he was talking about some sex game. And she had been more than willing to play. However, she wasn't about to let him know that. "And if I say no?"

"Then there'll be no need for the extra horse. I'll carry you on Scarlet Lady like a sack of wheat. I just figured you'd be more comfortable on a mount of your own."

Something thrilled inside her at the assertiveness of Colt Mandrell, and she chided herself for feeling that way. She was a '90s woman, equal to any man, yet here she was feeling sexual excitement at the caveman antics of a man eight years her junior.

Good thing there were no women-libbers around to see this. It went against everything she believed in to let a man order her around like that.

But this wasn't just any man. This was the man who had the power to send her through 125 years of time. And she'd better not forget it.

Trying hard to hide her joy, she decided to antagonize him further. He deserved it after carrying her off like that. "Mr. Proudhorse, will you accompany us? I don't want to be alone with Mr. Mandrell, if I can help it. After all, I have my reputation to consider."

Reputation? Colt bit his tongue to keep from laughing at that one. But he didn't dare laugh, or she'd start walking back to town for sure, and that would put a definite crimp in the plans he had for her. "Paul can't join us. You see, there's a pretty little thing back in town waiting for him to set the date for their wedding."

Paul frowned. "I told you not to butt into my business. I'm not marrying Faith until I can afford a spread of my own, and that won't be any time soon. Stop putting ideas in her head."

"Forget about your damn pride, man. Faith loves you. She always has. She don't care spit about material positions. The only thing she wants is you. Don't turn her into a dried-up old spinster who'll never know the joys of a man-woman relationship."

Dried-up old spinster? Was he serious? Destiny thought. Why, Faith couldn't be any older than twenty-four. What did that make her at thirty-two? She didn't want to think about that. But it did make her realize all the more, the difference in ages between her and Colt.

The next thing she knew, Paul was riding off, and she was mounting the horse he left behind. Excitement began to build inside her at the thought of being alone with Colt. Not just because there was a good chance that she could finally go back to her own time, but because she wanted more than anything to be with him one last time.

One last time.

One time to last a lifetime. Suddenly, the thought of leaving didn't fill her with great joy. She wouldn't just be leaving nineteenth-century Florida, she would be leaving Colt Mandrell.

That thought sobered her considerably, and she rode alongside of him in silence, conflicting thoughts at war in her head and in her heart.

Colt was responsible for kidnapping her from the twentieth century, but he was also responsible for making her feel alive, sexually and every other way, too. He was the most exciting man she had ever known, and the thought of never seeing him again was even more unbearable than the thought of never being in the twentieth century. What was she to do?

When in doubt, go with the flow.

Oh, sure, go with the flow. That's what got her into this mess in the first place. If she hadn't been so darn eager to make love to Colt she would still be enjoying the amenities and privileges as one of America's up-and-coming romance authors.

Colt's sexy voice broke through her reverie, exclaiming huskily, "We're home."

Riding around a bend in the narrow road carved through deep woods, she saw green and spacious paddocks dotting the landscape. Whitewashed three rail fences delineated them, while beautiful sleek horses grazed peacefully on lush grass. And beyond a formidable arched gate stood a gracious, two-story home nestled between stately oaks draped with Spanish moss.

A lump formed in her throat as she stared at the lovely setting. "Oh, Colt, it's beautiful."

Colt sat straighter in his saddle. He felt an unexpected joy over her admiration of his home. "It is, isn't it? Put a lot of work into making it look this good. My daddy started it a long time ago, but during the war, when food was scarce, my mother got sickly. They turned the farm over to me and I've been working it, adding onto it, ever since."

Hearing the pride in his voice, Destiny said, "I can tell how much you love this place. It shows. The place sparkles with life."

"I'm glad you like it, 'cause that's one of the things I wanted to talk to you about. I didn't want to rush this, but hell, Red, when I'm around you all I can think of is . . ."

Destiny suddenly stiffened, afraid he was going to spoil everything by asking her to be his mistress. She should have known it would come to this. It always came to this with men. But then what else could she expect from a wild, young stud?

"How would you like to live here with me?"

It was true. He still thought she was a woman of little virtue. She was surprised at how much that bothered her, even though reason told her it was only natural for him to feel that way after the hot sex they had enjoyed in his bed. It was just as much her fault as his, but that still didn't keep her from feeling hurt. "Colt, damn you, when are you going to realize that I am not, and will never be, any man's mistress. That goes for you as well as your lecherous brother-in-law."

Colt swallowed his hurt. He had to. He couldn't blame her for thinking that. Not after the way he had behaved. Stopping in front of his home, he jumped down from the horse and walked over to Destiny's mount. Helping her down, he circled her waist with his arms and looked into her eyes, saying solemnly, "I wasn't thinking of having you as my mistress. I'm asking you to be my wife."

Blinking back her surprise, Destiny saw that he was serious. Her eyes grew moist. This wonderful, exciting young man had opened his heart to her, and she had carelessly trounced on it.

The last thing she ever wanted to do was to hurt Colt Mandrell, but still, how could she lie to him? How could she tell him she'd marry him when she had every intention of going back to her own life? Wouldn't that be harder on him in the long run? Better to say the words now, than later when the hurt would be too much.

"Oh, Colt. You've only known me a few hours. How can you possibly know that I'm the one you want to marry? You don't know anything about me."

"I know all I need to know. Surely you know it, too? You didn't come to me in a dream on some stupid fluke of nature. It had to be something pretty powerful to draw you here to me. Don't you see, it was destiny. Surely *you* believe in its existence."

"Colt, I do believe in destiny, fate, whatever you want to call it, and I can't deny that I'm very attracted to you. There *is* a powerful bond between us, but . . ."

"But nothing. We were meant to be together. Don't deny

it. Marry me. Let's not waste one precious moment of time."

Time. Ah, yes, time. Her enemy. Time was the best reason she could think of for not marrying him. At any moment, she could be swept back to her own time. Never see Colt again. How could she commit to him knowing that?

And if for some reason she still couldn't go back when they made love this time, why then, it might happen the next time, or the time after that. She might discover the right way to do it at any moment.

It might even happen by accident.

What if she married him? Loved him with all her heart, had his children, and then was swept through time again? She couldn't do that to him, and she damn well couldn't do it to herself.

But how was she supposed to make him understand that? She had tried to tell him once before that she came from another time and like any intelligent human being, he hadn't believed her.

And there was another form of time that was her enemy, as well. The time between their ages. Eight years. He was young, wild, and impulsive. Kidnapping her today was a good example of that. As for her, she was too set in her ways. How could she ever adjust to such an impulsive man?

"Colt, you speak like a man who's running out of time. But you're so very young. Time is on your side. You've got a long life ahead of you. Why are you in such a hurry to marry?"

"Don't think I haven't asked myself that a dozen times? I honestly don't know the answer to that. Hell, before I met you marriage was the last thing on my mind. But something happened to me when we met in that dream. I can't explain it. I only know that I have to be with you."

"I feel the same way, but it's not as simple as all that. Please don't ask me to commit to you right now. Give me time."

There was that word again. She was starting to hate it with all her heart

"You win. I won't press it, but Red, remember this, you said it yourself. Time is on my side. I'll use it to win you over."

Pulling her into his arms, Colt kissed her, igniting the flame between them. She would belong to him body and mind. He'd make sure of that.

Colt's words made her feel incredibly sad. Time wasn't really on Colt's side. In just a little while she'd be gone.

This was going to be much harder than she ever imagined.

Seeing the sadness in her eyes, Colt kissed her lightly. "Let me show you around. When you truly see this place the way I do, maybe you won't be so quick to dismiss my proposal."

In a hurry to get her inside where he could persuade her with his body, instead of with inadequate words, he hastily unsaddled the horses, then took her by the hand and led her into the house.

"Everyone's at church, or out in the stables, except for the housekeeper and a couple of my men. We'll have the place to ourselves."

Destiny's heart fluttered with anticipation.

Alone with Colt.

She knew what that meant, They would soon be making love. She suddenly realized how much she wanted that. Not just so she could go back to her former life, but because the need to be in his arms once again was becoming over-powering. The longer she was in his presence the more she hungered for him. If he didn't initiate the first move, and soon, she would forget her pride and approach him.

Colt walked her through the first floor of the house, and she had a hard time concentrating on her surroundings. She couldn't have said what color the walls were, or what the furniture looked like if her life depended on it.

He held tight to her hand as they moved from room to room, his thumb rubbing against her palm unconsciously, she thought, but the effect was having a very conscious result on her body.

Colt stopped speaking about the merits of his new, modern water pump in the kitchen in midsentence. He was having too hard a time focusing on anything but his desire to bed her.

Tilting her chin up, he kissed her. "Mmm, I think we've seen enough down here. I'd rather show you the view from my bedroom."

A booming voice sounded from the stairs, and they jumped apart.

It was Bo, the giant man Destiny had met in Colt's hotel room. A bright blush spread across her face. She had been caught once again in a compromising situation. What must the man think of her?

"Sorry, Colt, ma'am, didn't expect to see you here."

"Something came up. I have something important I want to discuss with Miss Davidson upstairs, and I don't want to be interrupted by anyone, understand?"

A wide grin spread across Bo's face. "I understand. Don't worry 'bout nothin', I'll guard the way."

Destiny's blush deepened until she rationalized it to herself. What did it matter what Bo thought? In a few moments she would be back in the twentieth century, and she'd never see him again. Let him think what he wants.

Colt took her by the arm and ushered her up the stairs, and when he closed the door behind them, she forgot a world existed anywhere but in his presence.

This was where they would make love.

Her knees almost buckled at that thought.

Trying to hide her excitement, she looked around casually. The room was much larger than she expected, and surprisingly cool and dark.

The walls were papered in a paisley print of dark, vibrant shades of rust, and brown, and fern green. They accentuated the dark mahogany of the luxurious-looking four-poster bed, which curiously was placed predominately in front of the bay window.

The room reeked of maleness. Of Colt Mandrell. Being there, amidst all that masculinity added to her sexual excitement, added to the anticipation of what was to come.

"Come. See the view." With his arms around her waist, he led her around the bed to stand before the window that ran almost from floor to ceiling. There was just a foot or two of space between the bed and the window and she suddenly realized that the bed had been placed there to take advantage of the view.

Looking out the window, she was immediately mesmerized. The scene below was of a small private paddock with an oasis of trees in the very center. It was lovely, but even lovelier was the magnificent large reddish brown stallion tossing his head and rearing on his hind legs.

"Oh, Colt, he's wonderful. The perfect match for Scarlet Lady. But what is he so excited about?"

Colt frowned. "I don't know what has him so agitated."

Then suddenly a blur of chestnut red sailed over the fence and Destiny gasped as she realized that Scarlet Lady had jumped the fence and was now in the paddock with the stallion.

"Damn!" Colt said. "No wonder he's all stirred up. Scarlet Lady must have gone into season. I've got to get her out of there before . . ."

Destiny stayed him with a hand on his arm. "Oh, Colt, don't. Let them have their time together. They look so right together, so magnificent."

"Honey, you don't understand. If I don't stop them, the stallion will mount her."

Gazing deep into Colt's eyes, she answered breathlessly, "I know."

Eight

Colt was lost.

Never in his life had he known a woman like this one. It astounded him to know that she wanted to observe the stallion and mare mating. She was real, unpretentious, and unafraid of her sensuality. She didn't hide it behind a facade of feigned shock at nature's earthy ways, and it made him realize his instincts about her were correct. This was the woman with whom he wanted to share his life.

He envisioned them working the farm together, breeding generations of superior chestnut thoroughbreds and breeding their own beautiful children with hair the same reddish brown hue. They would be partners in every sense of the word.

Gazing down at her as she watched the stallion and mare prancing around each other, eager and ready to mate, he was overwhelmed with a feeling of pure joy, and pure love. He wanted to share with her everything he had, but more than anything, right this moment he wanted to share his bed with her. Wanted, in the best way he knew how, to show her how much he cared for her.

Moving behind her, he slipped his arms around her waist and nuzzled at her hair as together they swayed slowly back and forth, watching as the stallion rubbed his sleek head over the mare's neck.

He knew the stallion was enraptured by the smell of the mare, but not as much as he was at the clean fresh smell of the woman in his arms. He savored her fragrance, and the touch of her silken hair on his cheek, the wonderful sensation of holding her in his arms.

Moving his hands slowly up her sides, he journeyed to the exquisite breasts that peeked alluringly from the top of her low-cut dress. He could no more keep from touching them than he could live without food or sleep. Reaching inside her bodice, he pulled them free of their fabric prison. Cupping them with his hands, his teeth ground together, tormented by the intense desire the touch of her created.

Looking over her shoulder at the lovely breasts captive in his grasp, he saw the silver chain that had been pulled free from its nest between her breasts and his eyes opened wide at the giant diamond rings that dangled there. Removing the chain from her neck, he placed it in his pocket for safekeeping, then continued his exploration of her delicious breasts, rubbing her nipples beneath his thumbs.

Destiny gave out a little moan, the soft, sweetness of her voice telling him she was ready for him. Telling him she wanted him as much as he wanted her. That nothing would keep them from mating.

Down in the paddock, the stallion was moving into position to mount the mare, and the sound of the mare's excited whinny carried to the lovers who had met in the fantasy of a midnight dream.

Colt's fingers dug into her flesh possessively, reveling in the knowledge that she was his for the taking. That soon they would be in paradise once more.

Impatient for it to begin he unlaced the back of her dress and in a moment it was a pool of pink fluff on the floor at their feet.

Destiny was naked now, except for the shoes on her feet and the erotic bondage of the corset and silken stockings that molded her shape so seductively. Her attention was still on the horses, but he knew she was keenly aware of him, waiting for his touch.

He quickly removed his own clothing and the Celtic cross around his neck, wanting nothing between his skin and hers, while Destiny still gazed at the two highly excited animals about to mate. He could see a faint image of her in the window glass and it excited him to see the sensual expression on her face.

When he was finished undressing, he knelt behind her, and slid his hands slowly and deliberately down her hips, enjoying the seductive curves of her body under his fingers. Unfastening her stocking, he rolled it down her leg, his excitement growing by leaps and bounds. At her ankle, he removed her shoe and slipped the stocking off, then started all over with her other shapely leg.

When the second stocking had been removed, his hands started up her leg, leaving shivers in their wake, and he knew she was not immune to his touch. His searching fingers shook a little, knowing what they would find at journey's end.

She was breathing erratically now, and that gave him the courage to be bold. As he grew close to the source of her womanhood, the heat between her thighs fueled his desire for her, and he sent one urgent finger searching for the part of her that he most needed now.

Destiny moaned a little at Colt's touch and her head rolled from side to side as she watched the stallion in a frenzy to mate, nipping at the mare with bared teeth as he tried to mount her.

The mare trembled at his touch.

Destiny knew just how the mare felt.

The touch of Colt's fingers between her legs left her weak and wanting and when his finger found her—open and welcoming—she felt it slip inside her, almost fainting from the pleasure of it. He stood up slowly, sliding his body up the sleek curves of her back, and she drew in her breath sharply, startled to discover he was naked.

The stallion was mounting the mare now, his gigantic, engorged shaft searching urgently over the mare's rump.

Destiny gasped, feeling Colt's hardness against her.

Colt heard her gasp and turned her around to face him. His mouth came down on hers in a kiss that took away her breath. She answered it with a little moan, and her arms circled his neck, cradling the back of his head with her hands.

The touch of skin on skin was exciting, but something was different. Something nagged the corners of her mind. Her hands moved to the nape of his neck, seeking the chain of the Celtic cross, but it wasn't there.

He wasn't wearing it.

She wouldn't be going anywhere right now, except to heaven when they made love. Tears formed in her eyes as she felt enormous relief roll over her. She would enjoy this time with him to the fullest without worrying about being torn from his arms, and at this moment her need for him was all she could think of.

"Oh, Colt, I want you so."

That was all Colt needed to hear. She was ready for him and he was more than ready for her. Reaching around to her back, he tried to concentrate on unlacing her corset, but the touch of her was driving him insane. His fingers fumbled countless times and he cursed under his breath as each endless second passed.

Wasted moments that could be better spent inside her.

When he was finally able to finish the task, he dropped the corset to the floor with great satisfaction.

She stood before him now, a vision of such feminine loveliness a hard lump formed in his throat. He couldn't take his eyes from her, needing to absorb every detail as she stood before the window staring into his eyes.

She was framed in the scene below, a scene that encompassed the magnificent stallion and graceful mare now joined together in powerful, fluid motion. For the rest of his life, he would remember this erotic, and oh so beautiful image of chestnut-red horses, and chestnut-haired woman, and he counted himself blessed to have experienced this wonderful moment.

Overcome with the urgent need to complete what had been started, he lifted her high into his arms with strength he didn't know he possessed, and laid her on the bed a few steps behind him.

She had come to him in a dream, but he wasn't dreaming now.

Somewhere deep within, he suddenly feared she would be swept away as she had on the night they first met, but he brushed the feeling off.

Lowering himself onto her, his eyes closed with pleasure at the exquisite, naked touch of her, he parted her mouth with his tongue, delving in to give her a taste of what was to come.

Destiny's mouth ground against his, circling his tongue with her own as her mouth opened wider to take all she could of him.

That was enough to send him out of control and his hands moved over her breasts as he pushed his leg between hers, opening them to receive him.

Moaning softly, Destiny urged him on, ready, oh so ready, to take him inside her. The need for him had come on so swiftly she knew that the passion between them was a fierce and wonderful thing.

Colt entered her swiftly, deeply, overwhelmed with desire at the same moment the stallion let out a loud shriek in the paddock, releasing his sperm into the mare. The sound of it filled the bedroom, and the two lovers paused for just a moment to stare into each other's eyes, passion's flame bright between them. And then their deep need for each other made them oblivious to everything as they entered a world where only they could dwell.

The image of their joined bodies was reflected on the

window glass, a misty, heavenly picture of two bodies, two mated beings, fulfilling a prophecy, giving themselves up to the beauty and majesty of love.

The strength and endurance of Colt's young body perfectly complemented the utter womanliness of Destiny's. It was as if they were designed for each other, as if some mystical force had brought them together because no one else, either in the past, or in the present, or in the future years to come could ever make love as superbly as these two.

So perfect was their lovemaking, that when the moment of ecstasy came, it was with such tremendous force, such tremendous feeling that the two lovers seemed to merge into one entity of molten diamond, sparkling with light.

When it was done, they clung to each other, knowing that what they had experienced defied any need of explanation.

Taking a deep, shuddering breath to compose himself, Colt suddenly pinned Destiny's arms over her head, his heart still filled with such powerful feelings he couldn't dissipate them in any other way. "I'll never let you go."

The image on the windowpane began to fade away as the sky darkened and rain began to spatter against it, like giant teardrops falling from the eyes of the goddess of unfulfilled wishes, matching the tears that fell onto Destiny's cheeks.

Staring into his eyes shining with light and with love, she whispered sadly, "Nothing lasts . . . forever."

Colt couldn't believe she still doubted that they were meant to be together. "Surely, what we shared was as important to you as it was to me. My God, tell me it's true. You'd have to be made of stone not to have felt what I did."

"Oh, Colt, how can you even ask? You mean more to me than I can ever say. But this is only a fluke. Don't you understand? Some terrible cosmic mistake that will rectify itself sooner or later and send me back where I came from. I was unsure of that until now, afraid I was condemned to stay here forever, but now I fear even more that I will go. That I am condemned to be parted from you."

Colt took her head in his hands and stared into her eyes. "My God, you still believe you traveled through time to be here with me! Don't you know how crazy that sounds? How can you believe that what we have together is some kind of temporary Sunday horse-and-buggy ride through time? Well, I can't believe that. What we have is more important than that."

"That doesn't change the fact that it's true. If you were wearing the Celtic cross when we made love, I really believe I would have been thrown back to my own time. Don't you see? You were wearing it the night we made love in our dream."

Frustrated and impatient at her stubbornness, Colt climbed out of bed, dragging her with him. "Well, there's one sure way to test that theory?"

"What do you mean? What are you going to do?"

Bending down, Colt picked up the cross where it lay with his clothing and waved it in her face. "Prove that you're wrong. Or, maybe you'll prove I'm wrong. Either way, we're going to make love again while I wear the cross. Then we'll be done with your crazy notion once and for all."

"Oh, Colt, you don't know what you're doing. If we do this, you'll never see me again."

"I'm willing to take that chance. How about you?"

Seeing the determination in his eyes, Destiny knew she would give in to him. Besides, it was what she wanted, wasn't it? To leave the past where she was nothing more than an obscure woman who would leave no mark on the world when she left. To go back to a time where she had achieved success in a career that many craved, but few attained. Wasn't that worth going back for?

Yes, but what about your personal life? What about that? What did she have to show for that after thirty-two years?

But that—wasn't—her—fault.

It hadn't been her choice to be deserted by her family.

Wasn't that the real reason she had never gotten close to anyone before?

Because she never wanted to risk abandonment again?

No. That was just psychobabble nonsense. She was a strong woman, she never needed anyone in her life before now.

Before now.

Gazing into Colt's angry storm-cloud eyes, Destiny felt an enormous rush of love. She loved him despite the difference in their ages, despite his wild, unpredictable ways. How cruel life could be. For in loving him would be their end.

With a heavy heart, she said, "All right, Colt, let's settle it before we're both so deeply entangled, so deeply in love that it would be a terrible tragedy if we were separated."

Destiny seemed so sincere, she almost had him believing her story. But how could it be possible that she came from another time? And yet, was it any harder to believe than the fact they had met in a dream? Perhaps not. If he made love to her while wearing the cross would he be in danger of losing her?

"You've got me so damn crazy, I don't know what's real anymore." Pulling her into his arms, he crushed her against his chest. "I'm not taking any chances. I couldn't bear to lose you."

Tears welled in Destiny's eyes. "I don't want to lose you either, but it will happen. Sooner or later, it will happen. I can't live that way. Waiting. Wondering when I'll be torn from your arms. What if we had a child? Don't you understand how impossible our situation is? I would die if I was swept away from my child.

"I was separated from my own parents when I was only eight. Don't ask me to risk going through that again with my own child."

For the first time Colt understood the seriousness of their situation.

He was in real danger of losing her.

Not to time, or to the winds of fate, but to her own overwhelming, irrational fear.

He had to show her there was nothing to worry about. That they could be together without fear, or what they had between them would be destroyed.

Placing the pewter cross around his neck, he reached out to take her hand. "Red . . . trust in our love. Come back to bed with me and let me show you that you have nothing to fear."

Nine

Destiny felt herself weaken.

Go to him. Be with him.

Believe in him.

She took a tentative step toward him, and then another. A loud pounding sound startled her, and she came to a halt.

"I told you not to disturb me," Colt shouted through the door, watching in frustration as Destiny retreated from him both physically and mentally.

Bo's voice boomed back, "Sorry, Colt, thought you'd want to know your ma's here. Climbing out of Susan's buggy as we speak."

Colt groaned. His mother here? Whatever possessed her to travel out here in her condition? "I'll be right down. See that she's comfortable . . . and Bo, get her something to drink. She's going to need it after that long hot trip."

Colt was shocked that his mother had made the trip from town. She hadn't been out to the farm since she had taken sick. Why had she chosen this crucial moment to come? When he had seen her this morning, she had given him no indication that she was going to visit.

"Red . . . my mother is the only person in this world I'd let interrupt us now. Forgive me, but I've got to make sure she's all right."

"Oh, Colt, I have a feeling I'm the reason she's here."

Taking her into his arms, he nuzzled his nose in her neck. "I'm sure you're dead right about that, but it's nothin' to be concerned about. Come down with me and you'll see."

"I can't. I don't want to face her now. Besides, it would take me too long to get back into my clothes."

"I'll help you dress."

"No, please, you go. Before she comes up here and finds us together."

Colt laughed, seeing how scared Red was of his tiny mother. "I wouldn't put it past her. All right, I'll go, but Red, be prepared to continue where we left off when I get back. We're going to settle this time travel business today."

Pulling on his pants and boots, Colt started for the door.

"Your shirt, Colt. You know she doesn't like to see you without a shirt."

Smiling sheepishly, Colt slipped into his shirt, then remembering he had placed her valuable diamond rings in his pocket, reached in to retrieve the chain. He handed it to her saying, "Honey, some day you're going to have to tell me how you come to own such costly gems." Then, tweaking her nose, he grinned and left the room.

Destiny placed the chain around her neck thinking about how she was going to explain the rings. Then the thought of a more immediate problem hit her. If Little Bit had traveled all the way out to the farm in ill health just to see what was going on between her and Colt, she wasn't about to leave before she accomplished her mission.

Gazing down at the clothing at her feet, she decided it would be impossible to get into them without help. Especially the darn corset. Unfortunately, without the corset on she wouldn't be able to button her form-fitting dress.

Making her way over to the large chifforobe in the corner of the room, she opened the doors and searched for something to wear. The last thing she wanted was for Little Bit to catch her with no clothes on. Pulling one of Colt's shirts off a wooden hanger, she slipped it on. As she expected, the sleeves were way too long. Rolling them up, she buttoned the front of the shirt, then rummaged back in the chifforobe for a pair of Colt's pants. Recognizing the leather pants he had worn the day she saw him in the mirror, she pulled them out and struggled into them. The pants fit like a second skin. She rolled up the long pants legs, then tied the tails of the shirt at her waist.

Giving herself a quick perusal in the chifforobe mirror, she finger-combed her hair into place and made her way downstairs with butterflies dancing in her stomach. The last thing she wanted to do was face Little Bit after she had just been making love with her son.

Little Bit attacked Colt as soon as he entered the parlor. "Where is she? What have you done to the poor girl?"

Feigning innocence, he answered, "What are you talking about, Mother."

"You know very well what I'm talking about. The whole town knows what I'm talking about. You were seen scooping that poor child up on your horse and riding off with her, and I want to know what you've done with her. You can't treat her like she's a plaything, a, a . . ."

He knew his mother would find out about his impulsive abduction, but he hadn't expected her to act on it so quickly. "Mother, she's just fine. Really. She came with me of her own volition. Ask Paul if you don't believe me."

"Paul? So, you've got him involved in this, too. I should have known. Shame on you. Well, mark my word, I'm going to speak to your father about this as soon as he returns from Georgia. Oh, why did he have to leave today of all days?"

Colt tried hard to keep from laughing. She was treating him as if he were a child again. "By the time he returns, I'll be married to Destiny, and there'll be nothing anyone can say about it."

Little Bit struggled for breath, her hands searching frantically behind her. Finding the solidity of a chair, she sat in it with a large thud for such a small body. "Married?

Oh, my! You mean it? You and Destiny are betrothed? Why, that's wonderful. Just wonderful. Where is the dear girl? I want to give her a great big hug and welcome her to the family."

Destiny walked into the room in time to hear she was going to be married. Did he have to tell her that? Damn it all, her life was getting increasingly complicated.

Peeking around her son's tall frame, Little Bit saw the woman in question walk into the room. She let out a delighted shriek and rose from the chair very quickly for a woman of frail health. "Oh, my dear, dear girl."

Colt turned around, surprised that Destiny was brave enough to come down, and gave a long, drawn-out whistle. She was unbelievably sensuous in his clothing. Lustful thoughts whirled around in his head, and he could hardly wait to put them into action.

When it finally registered on Little Bit how strangely Destiny was dressed, she cried, "My dear, whatever possessed you to dress in my son's clothing?"

Thinking fast, Destiny answered, "I wanted to go for a ride with Colt, but I don't have a riding outfit. I didn't think my pretty new dress was suitable."

"Indeed, you're right. The first thing we'll do when we return to town is to buy you a proper riding habit. I won't have my daughter-in-law traipsing around dressed like a man."

Smiling more confidently than she felt, Destiny said, "Miss Little Bit, that's sweet of you, but really . . ."

Unexpectedly, Little Bit burst into tears and Destiny stared at her in shock. What had she done to upset her?

Colt was at his mother's side immediately. "What is it? Are you feeling sick? You shouldn't have come all the way out here against your doctor's orders."

Destiny was touched by the powerful love Colt felt for his mother. Every time she saw him with her it came through loud and clear. Although she had no memory of her own mother, she understood the bond between mother and child, even if that child was a grown-up, beautiful hunk of a man.

Her love for him kept growing stronger and stronger, and that scared her.

Wiping her tears away, Little Bit took her son's rugged hand in one of hers and Destiny's much smaller one in her other hand. "They're tears of joy, children. You've made me so happy. You'll never know how many nights I've lain awake worrying about my son. He's always been a handful. I've been afraid he would turn out like his grandfather Gordon, or his wicked aunt Celeste, but now, my dear, knowing he is about to marry you, my cup runneth over. If anyone can tame this wild stallion, it will certainly be you."

Little Bit was making it very hard for Destiny to tell the woman the truth. "I don't know about that, Miz Little Bit. I don't think anyone can tame your son. And please, I haven't really agreed to marry Colt. Not just yet, anyway. I'm afraid he's rushing things a bit. So, if you don't mind, I'd rather not discuss marriage. I need time to think about it."

Just then, Brent Raiford walked into the room, followed by a woman Destiny knew must be Colt's sister, Susan. There was a strong family resemblance. She was grateful for the interruption, even if it was from the likes of Brent.

"Did I hear someone mention marriage?" Brent said in a mocking voice. "Surely, you jest. Who would be foolish enough to marry you, Colt?"

Colt ignored the remark, saying, "My, my, the whole family's here. Bo didn't tell me you two rode out with Mother. What's the occasion, Sue? I thought you hated coming out here?"

"I do. But Mother wants Brent to ride out to the McAmmon place to see if they've returned yet. I'm going to keep him company."

Frowning, Colt addressed his mother. "No need for Brent

to do that. I promised you I'd look after their property, and I've been doing just that."

"Well, son, you've been so preoccupied of late, I didn't think of asking you, but if you insist, then I agree that you should go. That is, if you can tear yourself away from Destiny."

Seeing the chance to get Destiny alone, he answered, "No need. She's coming with me. If the McAmmons are back, it will be the perfect time for her to meet them."

"No need to drag Destiny out in that heat," Brent interjected, "when she can stay here cool and comfortable and keep us company while you're gone."

Susan didn't miss the interest in her husband's eyes when he looked at Destiny. She was glad the seductive little minx would soon be married to Colt.

She was sure Colt would keep Destiny so busy in bed she'd have no time to think of straying. "Brent, darling, leave the lovers be. Can't you see they want to be alone? Surely, you must have a vague memory of how that feels?"

Bo cleared his throat, letting his presence be known. "Uh, Colt, do you think it's wise to go over there unescorted? Whoever it was that killed Miz Langford could still be around."

The room became suddenly silent.

Looking from one face to the other, Destiny waited for some kind of explanation. When none was forthcoming, she asked, "Colt, is there a killer on the loose?"

"Yeah, unfortunately. Someone assaulted and murdered Tom Langford's wife while she was working in their orange grove. Happened just a week ago. That's why I was at the hotel in town. Helping Tom any way I could to get through the funeral and all. But there's nothing to worry about, honey, I won't take any chances with you along."

Turning to Bo, he said, "I'm going by the old stagecoach road that runs behind the Langford place. It goes straight through to the McAmmon property. Not many people are even aware of its existence anymore."

"Good idea," Bo answered. "I'll feel a mite easier knowing that. We don't need no more good folks slaughtered like that."

"The whole town is buzzing about it," Susan said. "At least, they were until you came along, Destiny."

Susan sounded almost callous. It surprised Destiny how much she looked like Colt physically, but how little she was like him where it counted, in her heart. "How terrible. Were you good friends with her and her husband, Colt?"

"We've always been very close. That's the way it is out here away from town. We look out for one another."

Colt's expression took on a fervency that made Destiny realize how much the woman's death had affected him.

"I want to get my hands on the bastard who did that. I'd make sure he didn't die an easy death, I can promise you that."

Riding down the narrow, overgrown road on the back of a buckskin gelding, Destiny drew in a deep, satisfying breath. She was happy to be away from Susan and Brent and had no idea which one of them she disliked the most. They certainly deserved each other. She wondered again how Susan and Colt could come from the same family.

Gazing at Colt, riding tall in the saddle, she felt an enormous surge of love. She would be safe with him. He'd protect her with his life, if it came down to it. She didn't know how she knew that, but she felt great confidence that it was true. He was an extraordinary man, no matter the time he lived in.

Brent was right though, it was unusually hot and though they were riding down a tree-shaded road, there was no breeze to cool her. After two hours in the saddle, the humidity was taking its toll. Braiding her hair into one long length at the back of her head as she rode, the reins clenched between her teeth, she felt a little cooler, but not enough to make a difference.

Oh, for a glass of ice-cold lemonade in an air-conditioned room.

Trying to take her mind off the heat, she thought about the delicious picnic lunch, Maybelle, Colt's housekeeper had packed for them to take along. Maybelle was a plump and pretty former slave who Colt explained had shown up on his doorstep shortly after the war ended. Close to starvation, he had taken her in and given her the position of housekeeper.

She smiled to herself thinking that she was yet another stray he had taken in.

Her stomach grumbled, reminding her she was hungry and thirsty, mostly thirsty, but she couldn't remember if Maybelle had packed anything for them to drink. Oh, please, let there be something to drink. And please, let them get there before she collapsed from the heat.

Colt turned in his saddle from time to time to check on her, and she smiled at him each time, not wanting him to know what a wimp she was turning out to be. And then, to make matters worse, the trees grew sparse as they rode through a clearing, with only occasional protection from the sun's heat and blinding glare.

It burned into her scalp unmercifully, making her increasingly light-headed. She wanted to call out to Colt to stop and rest, but her pride wouldn't let her. Perhaps they were nearing the end of the ride. She could hold out for just a little longer.

The next thing she knew, Colt was pulling her off the saddle, and into his arms. Her head lolled back, too weak to hold it up while he carried her over to the shade of a giant moss-covered oak.

Laying her down, he handed her a canteen of water.

"Red, why didn't you tell me the heat was too much for you? I would have stopped long ago. Here, drink this."

Sitting up only long enough to take a long drink, she laid her head back down. She closed her eyes and was surprised to find her strength was already starting to return.

"When was the last time you had anything to drink or eat?"

She had to think about that. Her life had been so intense and exciting, she hadn't had time to think about food. "I had a cup of tea at your mother's."

"That's all you've had today? One cup of tea? No wonder you collapsed. Your body needs a lot of liquids on hot days like this."

"I'll be fine. Just give me a moment to rest." Destiny turned her head to the side, her eyes still closed to the bright sunlight. Instantly, from out of the corner of her eye, she saw the face of a Seminole warrior flying at her. It honed in on her, moving directly in front of her, until it stared into her eyes just a few inches from her face.

Her body jerked with surprise as she snapped open her eyes. "What the . . ."

The image disappeared.

"What is it?" Colt asked, seeing the shock registered on her face.

"Oh, my, you're not going to believe this, but I swear to you I just saw an Indian warrior staring into my eyes. It was just his face. No body. I know how weird that sounds, but I did see it."

Colt laughed. "That's a good trick, considering that you had your eyes closed. You must be so dehydrated, you're delirious."

"No. Really. This was no hallucination. I saw every detail of his face in full Technicolor. He wore a colorful turban of orange and turquoise, like the Seminoles wear. But it wasn't Paul Proudhorse, and I know it couldn't be Osceola, this Indian was too young and healthy. And yet, even so, there was something vaguely familiar about him."

Colt held out the canteen. "I think you'd better take another drink. You're not making any sense. Of course, you didn't see Osceola. The man's been dead a long time now. And what the hell is this tek knee color you were talking about?"

"Never mind. You wouldn't believe me if I told you."

Lifting her hand from her side, Colt placed the canteen in it. "Here. Drink." Then spying something where her hand had been, he reached down and picked it up. "What is this? It was lying under your hand."

Destiny looked at the small leather pouch on a long leather thong necklace with curiosity. "I have no idea where that came from. It belongs to a Seminole though. Oh, Colt, maybe I wasn't hallucinating."

"You're jumping to conclusions now. What makes you think the pouch belongs to a Seminole?"

"I can tell by the beaded design. It's a Seminole warrior's medicine bag."

"And just how would you know that?"

"I'm not really sure. I just do." Seeing Colt start to open the pouch, she shouted, "Don't. It would be bad luck for anyone but the person who owns it to open it."

Colt laughed again. But hearing the sincerity in her voice, he placed the bag on the ground unopened.

Destiny picked it up and placed it around her neck.

In a feigned mocking voice, he said, "Isn't it bad luck for you to wear it? It doesn't belong to you."

"Colt, I can't explain it, but somehow I feel it's all right for me to have this. What the heck is going on here?"

"Honey, it's not so hard to figure out. There's nothing mysterious about it. We're close to an Indian reservation. It's not unusual to find things like that. As for the face that you imagined. I can't explain that, unless you're gifted with second sight."

"Well, I have always been kind of psychic. Perhaps the owner of the pouch is, too. Did you know that Native Americans and Celtic people both are considered to be highly gifted that way? Shining Dawn certainly was. At least when it came to her adopted brother, Osceola. She had visions that helped him become the great Seminole leader he was."

"What is this word, sigh kick? I've never heard it before."

"Psychic is sort of the same thing you call second sight. Shining Dawn and Osceola had a psychic connection between them. A very special bond that lasted all their lives. Don't you see? It's possible I have that same kind of bond with the owner of this medicine bag."

Colt kissed the tip of her cute little nose. "I'm beginning to think anything's possible where you're concerned. But don't expect me to like this bonding with another man. Even if he lives only in your dreams."

Speaking softly, Destiny answered, "Colt, not too long ago, you lived only in my dreams."

Kissing her hand, Colt said, "Don't go getting any ideas about your Seminole friend. You belong to me, and honey, I'm selfish. I don't plan on sharing you with anyone."

Destiny beamed. She was really glad he hadn't dismissed her vision as nonsense. "Did you say the Indian reservation was near here?"

Colt nodded his head.

"Then we must be near the McAmmon homestead. I know they live on a reservation."

"Honey, we crossed their property line just before you collapsed. But where did you get the idea they lived on a reservation? They haven't lived there for years. Their land does abut the reservation though. On the west side of their property. Abuts the Langford property, too, but it's not part of the reservation. The McAmmons own it."

"Oh, well, I'm just relieved to hear we're almost there."

Destiny took another long drink from the canteen and handed it back to Colt. "I think I'll be all right now. If I can take my mind off my sore bottom, that is. I'm not used to sitting in a saddle for such a long ride. How much farther do we have to go?"

Pointing his finger, he answered. "Look through that stand of woods over there. You can see the chimney of the cabin."

Helping her to her feet, Colt took the opportunity to take her in his arms and kiss her. "Privacy. Pure, unblemished privacy, at last. No one will interrupt us here. The McAmmons built their cabin out here on the St. John's River to get away from civilization, and it worked. The only visitors they get are their close friends, and an occasional visit from riverboat travelers."

Destiny stared up into his eyes. "I wouldn't be so sure about our privacy. After all, I've already had one visitor."

Colt looked puzzled until he remembered her imaginary Indian friend. Laughing, he took her by the hand and led her to her horse. "Long as he stays away from the bedroom, I guess I can tolerate him."

In a very short time, they arrived at the small cabin situated in the middle of a clearing, an orange glow from the setting sun bathing it in soft light. Destiny devoured it with her eyes. So, this was where Shining Dawn and Blade lived.

She took in everything. From the stable and corral, to the well made of coquina shell, to the giant wooden tub under a large tree. She smiled, realizing that it must be where they bathed. Saddle sore, dusty, and tired, the thought of soaking her aching muscles in the tub was very appealing.

The cabin itself was made from palm logs, and had sturdy shuttered windows painted a verdant green. On the western side of the cabin was a pretty fenced-in garden bursting with color, vegetables and flowers growing side by side. From the look of it, someone had been taking good care of it. "Colt, have you been tending the garden while the McAmmons are gone?"

"Yeah. Shining Dawn takes great pleasure in her garden. I wanted to make sure it was still here when she got back."

Knowing how much he cared for his neighbors gave Destiny a warm feeling. No doubt about it, Colt Mandrell was an extraordinary man. "I hope it's soon. Shining Dawn and Blade are very special to me. They're the hero and heroine in one of my books."

Colt shook his head. "Red, you're always taking me by surprise. I think it's time you told me about your life."

"It's about time you asked. All right. Just as soon as I've had time to recuperate from the ride, I'll tell you my sad story."

With dark coming on, Colt immediately set about unsaddling the horses. Before going into the cabin, Destiny helped water and feed them. The horses would spend the night in the small corral.

In a way, she was almost afraid to go inside the cabin. She had written about the people who lived here, had entered their world inside her head, and now . . . Now, she would be entering their world in a physical way. The thought of that spooked her.

Seeing her hesitation at the door, Colt took her by the hand and led her inside. He was surprised at how tightly she held onto him. There was so much about this exciting woman that was still a mystery to him. But then, if he had his say, he'd have the rest of his life to unravel it all. Life would never be boring with Destiny at his side.

Walking over to the nearest window, he unlatched the shutters and opened them wide to let in some light.

The first thing Destiny noticed about the cabin was the smell of palm logs that permeated the air. She had been in many cabins made from cedar logs, but this smell was very different.

Then next thing she noticed was the coziness of the place,

even though it was pretty dark inside, with all but one of the windows still shuttered. The living room and kitchen were combined in one large room, and there were two doors that most likely led to bedrooms, and another that led outside to the back of the cabin. It was a simple home, but one she could be very comfortable living in.

When Colt lit a lantern, the warmth of the light made the room seem even cozier. "I love it."

Colt looked at her closely and saw that she truly meant it. He had thought, knowing of her wealth—at least, the wealth he supposed her to have because of her large diamonds—that she wouldn't be happy without the trappings of luxury around her. He was glad that wasn't true.

It seemed he had a lot to learn about her, and he was damn eager to begin.

Spying a painting of a man and woman hanging over the fireplace, Destiny sucked in her breath in anticipation. Was it Shining Dawn and Blade?

Making her way over to it, she stared up at the image of a lovely tawny-haired woman dressed in a beautiful ball gown of gold. A lump came to her throat when she saw the beaded Indian belt around the woman's waist. It belonged to Osceola. Shining Dawn had worn it around her waist as an act of defiance against her uncle General Jesup. At least, in her book that was the reason Shining Dawn had worn it to the ball at the government house.

Every detail in her book was turning out to be true.

Gazing up at the portrait, she said, "She's beautiful."

Nodding his head slowly, Colt stared at the portrait intently. "She is—was. That picture must have been painted a long time ago. I don't ever remember her looking so young. She must be just about your age here."

Destiny felt a thrill go up her spine. "Such a friendly face. I almost feel I know her. She looks exactly as I pictured her. And Blade, he's just as handsome as I pictured him. Isn't that strange?"

"Yeah . . . Strange. Red . . . seeing you here side by side with the picture, I can see a resemblance between the two of you. Different colored hair, but same shaped eyes, and nose, and even your mouth. You must be related to her somehow."

"I think I must be, too. It's beginning to make sense now. My knowledge of her and Blade, of your mother and father. The story I wrote about them must have come to me from ancient memory."

"Ancient memory? Isn't that something like second sight? I've been told that it's memory handed down from one generation to the next. Memory collected in the brain and passed on to descendants."

"Not their brains, Colt, but their hearts and their souls. The brain is too cold an organ. I believe it's the heart that remembers."

"The heart remembers." Colt mulled that over in his head. "Could be you're right. I hope you are, because that would mean that whatever happens between us, you'll never forget what we have together."

Destiny's eyes glistened with light. Looking at Colt in the lantern-lit room, she said, "I'll always remember you."

Ten

A subdued ambience overtook the cabin as the world outside grew dark. Colt lit another lantern and set it on the table while they ate their supper, washing it down with a bottle of wine he had found in the pantry.

The effects of the wine soon added to the sadness Destiny was feeling, knowing in just a short while she would be leaving the man she wanted above all others.

Colt sensed her mood and tried to draw her out of her quiet misery by asking her questions about her life, and she responded, wanting him to know everything before she had to leave him. Maybe then he'd understand the futility of their love.

Her answers left Colt stunned and shocked, but he didn't question them. Everything she told him had a ring of truth about it. The amount of detail she furnished was too much to be made up. Too *incredible* to have been made up. His mind was overwhelmed with awareness of things he had never even imagined before. Things like television, and telephones, and airplanes.

Machines that cooled foods and cooled rooms, and even pulled horseless buggies. He could understand that much better than the invisible beams that transported pictures into a box, or transported voices across great distances. And yet, if those incredible things were possible, then wasn't it also possible to transport people from one century to another?

Just as astounding to him was the knowledge that she, a

female, had written four novels. That one of them had been about the people he knew and loved.

He was compelled to believe her, for she knew too much about the Mandrells and McAmmons. Knew things that no one but family members had any knowledge of. Things that even he hadn't known until a year or two ago when his mother confided them to him.

"I still can't get over the fact you actually wrote a book about Shining Dawn and Blade, and even my mother and father. That's amazing, considering that you'd never met them."

"Colt, it's all starting to make sense to me now, after seeing my resemblance to Shining Dawn. I must be related to her and Blade. Wouldn't it be something if they turned out to be my great, great grandparents? Ohh, I'd give anything to meet them before I . . ."

Colt knew what she meant to say and the nerve in his cheek jumped. "You'll meet them all right."

He seemed so sure of himself, Destiny didn't have the heart to argue with him. Circling his waist with her arms, she leaned her head against his chest. They had such little time left.

A pall came over him as he kissed the top of her head. For the first time he realized that what she feared might actually happen. If everything else she said was true, then wasn't it possible that she was right about being separated from him when they made love? Yet, even knowing that, he had to take the risk. Their very future together depended on it. "Red . . . it's time."

Time. She knew what he meant. Time had become Colt's enemy, too, now that he believed her. "Can we wait just a little while longer? I saw a tub outside. I'd like to wash away the dust and dirt. I want to come to you fresh and clean. I want to make the memory of this night all you could ever hope it to be."

Trying to hide the emotion he felt, Colt strode outside

to fill the tub with water from the well, while Destiny searched for towels and soap. She found them in a cedar trunk, then went outside to join Colt.

Watching him as he worked at filling the tub, her heart ached with love. She couldn't stand the thought of losing him, but she knew that she would. She would be swept away from him, as easily as a dry leaf in the wind. . . . Just as easily as she had been swept away from her mother and father.

Why did she think that? What an odd way of putting it.

She hadn't left her parents. They had left her.

She hadn't abandoned them. They had abandoned her.

Wasn't that the real reason she had never married? Because she was afraid of being abandoned once again by someone she loved?

How ironic to find that her fears were genuine.

She would be abandoned once again through no fault of Colt's, no fault of her own.

If it had to happen, then let it be now and be done with it once and for all. It would be too cruel for it to happen any other time. *I'm ready for it now. I can bear it now, but never after today. Please, not after today.*

Colt finished filling the tub, then beckoned her to him. Swallowing her fears, she walked over to him and began to undress. A gentle hand on her shoulder stayed her movements. "Let me undress you."

She nodded her head, and a sudden shyness enveloped her. Gazing up at the heavens while he removed her clothing, she felt reassured, seeing the stars twinkling down at her. How many times had this same scene been played out across the continents of mother earth? She and Colt were a part of it all, and that gave her the comfort and the confidence she needed to let it happen.

He unbuttoned her shirt, his head bending close to the material to see what he was doing in the dim light, and she thought it so endearing she wanted to hug him, but knew it would spoil his concentration.

When he was done, he slipped the shirt off her shoulders and let it fall to the ground, a smile of satisfaction on his wonderful face.

She stood there naked from the waist up, except for the rings on the silver chain around her neck. But they too, were soon gone, falling to the ground to join the shirt. Feeling a prickle of excitement on her skin as the heat of his gaze moved over her breasts, she watched with sweet anticipation as his hands moved slowly to cup them with great gentleness.

Closing her eyes as his hands moved over her, exploring every curve of her breasts with intense concentration, she gave herself up to the moment. It felt so wonderful, so good, so incredibly right that they should be here together, alone, with nothing but the great dark sky and the creatures of the night to keep them company.

The world became hushed as Colt's hands moved over her so lovingly, and she imagined all the animals in the woods pausing to take note of their presence among them, watching from the cover of the trees the beautiful union of man and woman fulfilling the purpose of their existence.

Standing before him, naked and vulnerable, her head soared with emotion, seeing the love shining in his eyes. She must truly be the most beloved of women to have such a man as he looking at her that way. She wanted to remember this moment, that wonderful look, always.

Always.

And then, he had the leather pants unbuttoned, and was pulling them down around her feet. She stepped out of them, and stood before him naked.

"Oh, God, I could cry from the sheer joy of looking at you."

His words were so unexpected, so beautiful, she couldn't answer. Instead, she reached out to touch his cheek, gazing at him with such love in her heart, she felt overwhelmed with emotion.

Instinctively, she knew that he wanted her to undress him, too, and her hands moved to his waist, unbuckling his leather holster belt. The heavy weight of it surprised her when she held it in her hands before letting it fall to the ground.

Turning her attention to unbuttoning his shirt, her gaze never wavered from his. Seeing the shudder of excitement that rippled across his chest as she slipped it off, she smiled to herself, and began to unbutton his pants.

His arms reached out twice to touch her, but retreated, and she knew he was waiting for the moment when they would stand before each other equal in their nakedness.

With deliberation, she removed the Celtic cross from his neck. He didn't protest, knowing this was not the time to test her theory. That would come all too soon, when they were in bed. Letting the cross slip from her fingers, it landed on the soft pile of clothing. For just a second, out of the corner of her eye, she thought she saw a flash of light as it clinked gently against the rings on her silver chain.

But she didn't have time to think about that, for Colt was stepping out of his pants, scooping her up in his arms, and carrying her to the huge wooden tub designed for two.

He set her in the water and climbed in beside her while visions of Shining Dawn and Blade using the tub as she and Colt were now danced in her head. A smile played across her face at that thought.

He drew her down into the water with him, maneuvering her to sit on his lap facing him and she felt his hardness. She kept it from penetrating her, thinking, not yet. Oh, no, not yet. She wanted this night to last forever.

Colt soaped his hands with the fragrant herbal soap until they were well lathered, then proceeded to caress her breasts. The silky, slippery sensation drove her wild, and her nipples quickly hardened, jutting out to greet his fingers.

Her eyes closed in pleasure, her head rolling slowly back and forth in time to the rhythm of his movements, thinking, yes, let this night go on forever.

But Colt had other plans. He slid his hands down her abdomen to her waist, then to her hips, lifting her buttocks up to move his hands boldly between her legs.

She almost lost it then. Circling his neck with her arms, she braced herself as both his hands explored her most intimate parts, moving back and forth as if he were trying to memorize everything that he felt.

The effect on her was twofold. It was, oh so soothing to have her saddle-sore bottom massaged, but at the same time, his hands worked a different kind of magic. Desire for him grew stronger with each masterful stroke, and she let him know how much it pleasured her, urging him on with her voice.

She could tell by the dreamy expression on his face that he was enjoying it, too, and she wanted him to enjoy it even more. Soaping her own hands, she explored his body as his stroking continued between her legs. Starting with his chest, she worked her way down with circling motions of her slippery hands, moving in time to the rhythm of his hands.

When she came to his iron-hard shaft, she circled it with one soapy hand. Nothing in the world felt as good as touching him there. She reveled at the wondrous feeling, knowing for the first time in her life that lovemaking between a man and a woman in love was the most precious of gifts.

The touch of her hand on his manhood was more than Colt could stand. Scooping up water with his hands, he washed the soap from Destiny and himself, then lifted her in his arms.

Towels and clothing lay forgotten on the grass as he carried her inside the cabin into the darkness of the bedroom, sitting her on the bed. "I'll be right back," he said in a husky voice.

Destiny's heart thrilled knowing that in a moment they would consummate the love and desire between them. Waiting for his return, she stared impatiently at the doorway. When she saw it grow brighter and brighter, she knew where he had gone. To fetch the lantern.

He walked through the door, and she saw that he had also fetched their pile of clothing, his revolver, and something else as well.

The Celtic cross was around his neck once more.

Her heart constricted.

This was it.

The last time they would ever make love.

Isn't that what she wanted? Wasn't that the only way she could protect her heart?

"You don't mind, do you?" Colt said, placing the lantern and clothing on a chest of drawers. "I want to see what I'm getting."

Her troubled thoughts flew away as she concentrated on his words. She understood what he meant. She felt the same way. Part of the enjoyment of their lovemaking was seeing the pleasure on Colt's face.

But that wasn't exactly what he had in mind, she soon discovered as he knelt at the side of the bed.

Taking her hand in his, he kissed it fervently. "Honey, sit at the edge of the bed."

Wondering what he wanted, she obliged, her eyelashes fluttering in surprise when he unexpectedly nudged her legs apart. "I want to see all of you."

She held her breath, feeling the gentle touch of his fingers as they parted the delicate tissue that protected her opening. It felt so good, so right that he should know all of her, that she let it continue. Her eyes closed from the pleasure of his touch, while at the same time her mouth opened in anticipation of being plundered, too.

"Red . . . I want to know what you taste like . . . here."
One finger caressed her opening.

She started to protest, but changed her mind, remembering how much she wanted him to enjoy this precious time they had together.

A shock of pleasure jolted her body as she felt the heat of his tongue on her. Without thinking, she reacted by opening her legs wider and thrusting her pelvis closer. Nothing, absolutely nothing in the world compared to the deep sensual pleasure that rolled over her body.

Colt's tongue explored where his finger had before, reveling in the sweet taste of this woman he adored, and when he felt her undulate closer to his mouth, he knew she was enjoying it as much as he was. That was all he needed to know to free him. He could enjoy her to the fullest knowing she welcomed him.

Stiffening his tongue, he sent it inside her, using it as he would his shaft, thrusting it in and out, then retreating to circle her opening again. Every time he came to a certain spot, she reacted so strongly he knew it must be where she derived her greatest pleasure. Concentrating on that part of her, he used his mouth and tongue in every way he could think of to bring her to a climax.

Destiny cried out, knowing that if he didn't stop immediately she would have no control over what happened. "Colt, stop, or I'll come . . . now."

He answered by stepping up the intensity of his loving, nuzzling her with his mouth and tongue and nose, until she could do nothing but hold onto his head. She cried out as wave after wave of ecstasy washed over her.

Listening to her passion-filled cries broke the last vestige of control Colt had over his willpower. His hands moved up to her waist, lifting her, moving her up to lie on the bed.

Covering her with his body, his mouth came down on hers in a crushing kiss as he entered her with one great push.

Destiny's eyes blinked in surprise at the powerful thrust,

and still on the edge of rapture felt herself heading into yet another wave. She tried to hold it back, but she was too far gone. She held tight to him as he sensed her need and began to ride her hard.

For one small moment, before rapture swept her away, she tried to remove the cross from his neck, but Colt took her hand away. By then, she was past caring about anything but the exquisite pleasure that engulfed her as they moved in perfect harmony of body and mind.

They were reaching for the stars. Adrift in the universe of love and emotion, of need and fulfillment. Of white, hot heat that drew them closer and closer to the sun until they exploded, shattering the borders between their bodies as they blended into one living, breathing entity.

Breathing raggedly, eyes closed tight to the world around her, she tried to prepare herself for leaving him, for the time travel that she was sure was imminent. What would she see when she opened her eyes? Deep in her heart she was unsure of what she wanted to see most, the man she loved so profoundly, or the familiar world where she had status and respect.

His body was still pressed to hers, but were they still joined together in reality or in a dream? Would she wake up and find herself back at Lydia McAmmon's?

Opening her eyes, she peered through the darkness and saw the small beacon of light flickering in the lantern.

She was still in the past.

Colt felt the trembling of her body, and turned her head to face his. She was crying silent tears. Wiping away the wetness with his fingers, he said, "Tell me those are tears of joy—that you're glad you're still here with me. That you're happy your theory was wrong."

"Is it? I don't know that, and neither do you. It could still happen the next time we make love, or the time after that. Maybe there was just one little thing that we did that made it work before. When we do it again, it will happen."

Colt had no answer for that. If she wasn't convinced now, then what could he say that would make her believe that she was here to stay? Kissing her lightly, he held her in his arms until she drifted off to sleep.

In a few moments he heard her breathing become deeper and he envied her. He couldn't sleep. His mind was too filled with trying to think of a solution to their predicament. He had to find one. Destiny was the woman he loved, and he wouldn't let her go without a fight.

He lay awake a long time thinking, until his brain refused to function any longer. Yawning, he rolled over on his side, facing the outside of the bed.

Destiny stirred, making little whimpering noises as she tossed and turned.

Knowing she must be having a bad dream, he rolled back over to comfort her. She suddenly jerked violently, startling him, then sat upright in bed, staring at the dim lantern light. "The wolves. The wolves. Make them stop howling."

Her words tore a hole in his gut. This was no ordinary nightmare. Sitting up, he touched her shoulder lightly, speaking softly. "Honey, you're dreaming. There are no wolves here. You're safe here in the cabin with . . ."

She screamed out in fright, and attacked him, scratching his face with a fingernail. Blood streamed down his cheek.

Reaching for her flailing hands, he pinned them to the mattress, pressing his weight on her, until she lay flat on the bed. In a moment, she became calm and fell into a deep sleep once more.

Still shaken by her unexpected outburst, he wondered what had provoked it. Why was she dreaming about wolves?

The last thought he had before falling asleep was, that there was something he should remember about wolves.

Eleven

Destiny awoke in Colt's arms, but rather than feeling content, she felt restless, edgy, and had to resist the compulsion to push him away. It didn't make any sense. She loved him, adored being in his arms, and yet, for some reason she couldn't fathom, she felt uneasy. It was as if . . . as if . . .

She couldn't think any further than that.

A black curtain was drawn across her memory. It always happened when she tried to remember her childhood, but why now? She wasn't thinking about her childhood now. What had triggered that response?

Feeling the tension in her body, Colt caressed her back, moving his hands down her spinal cord. "Still thinking about your nightmare?"

Colt watched as she rolled over to face him, drawing the covers up around her neck to cover her nakedness, her eyes large with fright.

"I don't know what you're talking about."

Surprised by her response, he answered, "I'm talking about the nightmare you had last night . . . about wolves."

"Wolves? Don't be silly. I slept like a baby."

"Honey, you had a terrible nightmare. You must remember. Look, you scratched my face when I tried to calm you."

Destiny gazed at the raw-looking scratch on Colt's face and winced. She couldn't have done that to him. "You must have been the one having the nightmare, scratched yourself in the process, because I'm telling you I did not have a nightmare."

Her voice was getting irritable, and Colt realized that talking about it any further would be useless. He couldn't help wondering about it, though. How could she have such a violent dream and not remember it at all?

Something very important was troubling her.

Something so bad she refused to remember it. But what? And then, a surprising thought came to him. It had something to do with him.

He was involved in whatever troubling secret her mind was keeping from her. He had to be. Nothing else made any sense. But he was damned sure it also had something to do with her traveling through time. It made sense to think that there was a powerful reason why she had come to him, of all men, past, present, or distant future. Now if he could just figure out what that reason was, he'd have the answer to their dilemma.

Seeing the disturbed look on Colt's face, Destiny was instantly sorry for the way she was acting. None of this was Colt's fault. But damn it all, it wasn't her fault either. They were caught up in something beyond their understanding, beyond their ability to change any of it. They were doomed to go along for the ride and see where fate would take them.

Suddenly, the sound of a horse whinnying nervously pulled Colt from his reverie. Instantly, he became alert. Touching Destiny's arm, he whispered, "Be still. There's someone out there."

Climbing out of bed, he searched through their clothing for his gun belt, then finding it, pulled his revolver out of the holster. Destiny looked at him wide-eyed.

"Who's there, Colt? Why do you need a gun?"

"If it were a friend out there, he'd've been knocking on the door by now. Get dressed. As quietly as you can." Pulling on his pants, Colt said softly, "I'm going out the back door. See who our visitor is. If we're lucky, it's just a panther, or some other four-legged predator."

"And if we're not lucky?"

He didn't answer.

"Colt, you're scaring me. Don't leave me here alone. Stay with me, please."

"Honey, I can't. The element of surprise is important. I don't want them waiting around out there for us to come out. They could pick us off like ducks in a pond."

Pulling on his boots, he thought about the layout of the cabin and decided there was only one vulnerable spot. The window he had unshuttered. He was glad he hadn't opened the window in the bedroom, or they might be lying dead on the bed by now, their bodies undiscovered until Shining Dawn and Blade returned home.

Pushing that unpleasant picture from his thought, he handed Destiny his revolver. "Do you know how to use a gun?"

She shook her head nervously, anxiety embracing her in a tight hold.

"Nothing to it. When you want to fire, just cock back this lever here and pull the trigger."

Her hands shook when she took it from him.

Smiling grimly, he said, "Red, you're holding a *Colt* revolver in your hand. I was named after Samuel Colt, the man who invented this gun. It's been lucky for me and it will be for you, too. I'm not going to let anything happen to you, understand?"

Destiny nodded her head solemnly.

"Good. Keep that thought in your head, and anyone comes in this room but me, you shoot first and shake hands second."

Taking in a deep breath, she watched as Colt took a rifle mounted over a chest of drawers, and loaded it with ammunition from a small wooden box. Giving her one long look, as if he wanted to commit her to memory, he left.

Knowing it would be impossible for her to just sit in a corner and wait, she walked into the living room in time to see Colt slip out the back door.

When he disappeared, her courage disappeared with him. Making her way to an old wooden rocking chair in the large open room, she turned it to face the door Colt had left through. The only source of light was right next to it. The unshuttered window.

Restless and nervously awaiting his return, she held tight to the gun, replaying over and over in her head the disturbing conversation she had heard about the murder of Colt's neighbor.

She knew why Colt was so worried.

He was afraid their visitor was the man who raped and murdered Tom Langford's wife.

Thinking about Colt out there alone, so determined to protect her, she loved him all the more. *Oh Colt, come back to me safely.*

Suddenly, she sensed movement as the room became dimmer. Looking over at the window, she saw the shadow of a man slowly creeping by.

Before the image disappeared from view she saw the unmistakable outline of a man's hat. Cold fear engulfed her.

Colt wasn't wearing a hat.

Gripping the revolver tighter, she cocked it, then found the trigger just as a loud explosion rent the air.

She jumped violently, her finger jerking on the trigger, and another explosion rocked her, while at the same moment she saw a hole appear through the door. Somewhere inside her brain she realized she was responsible for it.

Two more shots rang out in succession, the sound of them brutal. Cold. Frightening.

She visualized Colt lying dead.

No. That couldn't happen. It mustn't happen.

But she knew it could.

Knew that it was her fate to lose everyone she loved.

Hearing a dull thud against the door, she raised the gun, aiming it with both hands, and watched . . .

. . . as the door latch lifted very slowly.

Twelve

Let it be Colt. Oh, please, let it be Colt.

The door opened violently, revealing a scar-faced man with a gun in his hand.

Too frightened and shocked to move, she stared at him in horror. Suddenly, the man's expression changed from grim to pleading and he reached out for her, his hand groping as if trying to see through murky darkness. Toppling forward, he fell on the floor at her feet.

She screamed, then sprang from her chair, the sound of her voice freeing her from her paralysis, her weapon still clenched tight in her grip.

And then Colt was rushing through the door, and she never saw a more welcome sight in her life. He stepped over the stranger's body, then kneeled over him to see if he was still breathing.

Destiny's voice quaked with fear. "Is he still alive?"

Colt turned his head to gaze at her, and she gasped, seeing the bright ribbon of blood dripping down his cheek.

In the blink of all eye, she was in his arms, and he was soothing her with a soft voice. "Honey, it's all right. He can't hurt you. He's dead."

Her fingers touched his cheek. "Oh, Colt, I'm not worried about myself. You're hurt. Is it bad? Are you going to die?"

Colt laughed. "No, I'm not going to die. The blood isn't from a bullet wound. For an assassin, the man wasn't a very good shot. I scraped my face on the corner of the well when I ducked behind it."

"Thank heavens. I was so afraid for you."

"And I was afraid for you, until you shot him right through the door. I didn't think you'd have the nerve."

"Shoot him? I didn't shoot him. No, I couldn't have. I must have been you."

Seeing the agitated state she was in, Colt caressed her chestnut hair, brushing long strands out of her eyes. "Honey, no need to talk of it now. We're both safe. That's all that matters." Uncurling her fingers from her grip on the revolver, he took it from her.

Destiny gave out a long, shuddering breath, happy to be free of it. She tried to relax her body, knowing they were safe, but when she looked down at the dead man on the floor, the image of his face came back to haunt her.

She had seen that scarred face before.

But where? When? Maybe when she had a chance to think clearly it would come to her.

Colt led her over to the settee and sat her down. "Red, you sit here and rest while I take care of him."

"What are you going to do with him?"

"Honey, I'm just going to take him outside so you don't have to look at him. I'll be right back, all right?"

She nodded her head solemnly.

Moved by the sight of her looking so small and vulnerable, Colt kissed her forehead, then braced himself for the chore ahead.

Dragging the dead man outside, he closed the door behind him, then searched the man's clothing for some clue to his identity. It was hard to believe that someone he had never met wanted to kill him. Why? What possible motive could he have?

The man's clothing revealed some loose coins, a folded piece of paper, and a thick wad of greenbacks. He counted the money, whistling low when he added it all up. Five hundred dollars! That was a lot of money for anyone to be carrying, let alone someone who looked like a drifter. It was looking more and more like the man might be a hired gun.

That was bad news, if it were true, because it would mean the man who hired this thug was still out there somewhere, and still a threat.

Unfolding the piece of paper, he discovered it was a rent receipt made out to a Mr. George Dunn for the month of September. At least, that was a start. The man had paid for a full month's rent, and since this was almost October, he could have lived there for weeks, if not months. That meant someone in St. Augustine knew something about him. No one who came to St. Augustine stayed unknown for very long.

His gaze traveled down to the signature on the receipt. Brent Raiford. It was signed by Brent Raiford.

Of course the fact his brother-in-law knew the man wasn't enough to prove it had been Brent who hired the assassin. After all, Brent owned two boardinghouses in St. Augustine, and couldn't be responsible for the caliber of person that resided at them.

But his gut was telling him otherwise.

He had always had an uneasy feeling around Brent, and now he was beginning to think he had good reason. But the question was, why would Brent want him dead? What could he hope to gain? The answer to that came to him in a wave of nausea.

Everything.

Everything Colt owned.

Colt's sister Susan was his heir if anything should happen to him, and since Brent was married to his sister . . . If he died, Brent would get his hands on his lucrative horse farm. That was motivation enough for a greedy man.

The thought of Brent claiming the animals he adored, Big Red and Scarlet Lady, and all his other exquisite thoroughbreds made him sick to his stomach. Unfortunately, until he had more substantial proof, he would have to keep his thoughts to himself.

Going to the water pump, he primed it, then worked the handle until the water started flowing and washed his hands to rid himself of the touch of the dead man. Afraid of leaving Destiny alone too long, he made his way back inside. She had been through a lot today and he was afraid she was ready to break down.

But it seemed he had underestimated her, for when he entered, she was washing blood from the floor with a rag. "I don't want Shining Dawn to see this when she comes home."

A surge of admiration coursed through him. "I'll just burn that rag when you're done, then you can wash up."

When she was ready, Colt pumped water for her while she washed, and despite the trauma she had experienced she smiled, thinking about the length one had to go through to obtain water in the nineteenth century.

The sudden pounding of hooves on the road sent her into a panic. Shading her eyes with her hand, she looked out to the road and saw a group of men riding toward her. "Colt."

"Honey, it's just Tom Langford and his men. Nothing to worry about. He must have heard the shots and come over to investigate."

Destiny immediately relaxed when she saw the friendly, weather-beaten face of the older man seated on a giant horse. Tom was soft-spoken and fatherly, two attributes that put her right at ease. After introductions were made, she went inside to see about getting them all something to drink, while the men took care of the body, loading it onto the back of a wagon.

When they came inside, she served them homemade beer from Blade's tapped barrel, and sat down next to Colt on the settee to hear what they had to say.

"I was checking my fences when I heard those shots. Since I knew Blade and his wife weren't back yet, and weren't likely to be doing target practice, I thought I'd better see what was going on."

"Do you have any idea who he is, Mr. Langford?" Destiny was hoping he could put a name on the familiar face of the dead man.

Tom shook his head. "Nope, I surely don't. But I'm mighty interested in finding out. Could be, he's the same man what killed my wife."

Destiny had been thinking the same thing. She racked her brain, trying to remember where she had seen the dead man before, but came up with a blank. She had met so many people since she had been swept back in time that she knew she might never think of exactly where she had seen him. And for that reason, she would keep it to herself. What use in building up Tom's hopes if she could never come up with the answer?

Tom offered to escort them back to Colt's farm with his men riding shotgun, and Colt took him up on it. They traveled by the main road, since the wagon was too wide to travel on the back road, and Destiny was happy to see other travelers passing by. She had begun to think Shining Dawn lived at the ends of the earth.

A stagecoach rumbled by, traveling very fast, but it slowed, then came to a halt when the driver saw the dead man in the back of the wagon. Getting down from his perch atop the coach, the driver started conversing with Tom in a low voice.

The door to the coach opened and an attractive young woman emerged, curious to see what was going on. Colt recognized her immediately and shouted, "Angel!"

Destiny's heart lurched. He called her Angel?

The young woman smiled radiantly and ran over to Colt. Jumping from his horse, he took her in his arms, twirling her round and round.

Jealousy ate at Destiny. Who was this beautiful young

thing Colt so affectionately called Angel? He had never called her that.

Aware of Destiny's eyes on him, Colt took the girl by the hand and led her over to Destiny. On close view, Destiny saw that she was very young, no older than eighteen or nineteen. The perfect age for Colt, she thought bitterly.

"Red, I want you to meet a very special young lady, Angel Peabody, Penelope's daughter."

A rush of pure happiness rolled over Destiny. "Angel? Is that your name?"

"Yes, ma'am."

Ma'am? It made her feel like an old lady to be called that. "I would never have believed Penelope Peabody would name a daughter Angel."

"I know. That's what everyone thinks. She's so practical, so brusque, but believe me, Miss. ."

"Destiny. Destiny Davidson."

"Destiny. If you knew my mother as well as I do, you'd know that she has a much gentler side with folks she loves."

Turning to Colt, Angel asked, "What's goin' on here, Colt? Who's the man in the wagon?"

"We have no idea, Angel. He tried to kill me, and instead was killed in self-defense. You have any idea who he is?"

Angel stepped forward without any trepidation and looked down at the still countenance of the man now lying on his back in the wagon, arms folded across the bloody spot on his chest.

"Sorry, don't recognize him. But then, I've been away at school almost three months. Someone in town is bound to know, though."

The wagon started moving down the road and Colt declared, "Well, we'd better be on our way. How long you going to be home?"

Giving him a warm smile, she cooed, "I'm home for good, Colt. Whether Mother agrees or not. I am not going back to school. I've had my fill of readin', and writin' and figurin'. All I'm interested in right now is finding me a husband." Looking up at him with adoring eyes, she murmured. "Just thought you'd like to know."

Colt stuck his thumbs in his front pockets and gazed down at Angel with a grin on his face. He never looked more sexy, Destiny thought, watching in disapproving silence.

"I wouldn't go announcing your plans too casually, Angel, or you'll be stampeded. Enough single men around here to start an army."

Twirling her long black curls around her finger, she said, "I'm just telling my closest friends, Colt. My very closest friends."

Destiny wanted to slap the silly grin off Colt's face. He was a typical male, taken in by an inviting smile on a pretty face. She remembered then that Lily Tiger had told her he was very popular with all the young ladies of St. Augustine, and practically had to fight them off. From the looks of it, that wasn't exactly an exaggeration.

Feeling suddenly insecure, she mounted her horse again and started riding to catch up to Tom Langford and his men who had started down the road again.

Avoiding looking at the grim sight in the wagon, she passed it and rode up to Tom Langford.

"Don't let it get you down, Miz Destiny. Whoever the man is, he deserved what he got. Colt tells me he tried to kill him. You would have been next, but I'm afraid your death wouldn't have been so swift."

A jagged grimace of pain crossed Tom's face, and she knew he was thinking about his wife's death. "I know." Then, in a soft voice, she asked, "Mr. Langford, do you think he's the same man who killed your wife?"

"I hope not. I want the pleasure of killing him myself."

"I can't blame you for that."

"Like as not, I'll never know who killed Judith. That's going to be real hard to live with. One thing's for certain:

I'm selling my place and moving to town. I can't stand being there without her. Everything I see reminds me of her."

"Is that what you really want to do?"

"Yup. Should have done it long before this. Little Bit and Gary had the right idea moving into town. My wife would still be alive if I had."

"Mr. Langford, fate has a way of catching up to you, no matter where you are."

Tom smiled sadly. "Perhaps you're right."

"Have you told Colt you wanted to sell?"

"He were the first one to know, but he's not in any position to buy. He's recently spent a lot of money in building up his stock of thoroughbred horses. They don't come cheap. Sure wish he could though. You see, I had made up my mind to sell only to a Mandrell or McAmmon, so's my land could be put to good use adding on to a good neighbor's place. Besides, I know it would be well taken care of in their hands."

Destiny thought about that for a few moments. "If Colt can't buy, that leaves only Shining Dawn and Blade. Do they have enough money to buy it?"

"Not hardly. Not many folks around here do. Still struggling to recuperate from the war. It nearly wiped out a lot of folks. 'Course there's Johnny, Shining Dawn and Blade's son, but the boy don't believe in owning land."

"Really? Why is that?"

" 'Cause he's Injun through and through. Hell, he even dresses like a Seminole. Believe me, he could pass for one, too, though he's only one-quarter Injun."

What a revelation. Johnny McAmmon looked like his father but acted like his mother. She knew Shining Dawn had lived with the Seminoles since she was thirteen, although she didn't have a drop of Native American blood. But that didn't stop her from completely embracing their way of life, to the consternation of Blade, when he was trying to court her.

It pleased her to think of Shining Dawn's son following in his mother's footsteps. And why not? His mother and father had dedicated their lives to helping the Seminoles. It was only natural for him to relate to the people he saw most while growing up.

"It don't look like I'll be selling to a neighbor, but one thing's certain, I won't sell to the likes of Brent Raiford, even if he is married to a Mandrell. He's got plans for making some kind of transportation mecca for travelers. The fool thinks he can get the rich Northerners to come down here to spend their money. Dangdest thing I ever heard, but I tell you what, if he does, it won't be on my property."

Destiny smiled to herself thinking about Disneyworld and all the other mega tourist attractions in twentieth-century Florida. Just as well he didn't know what the future held. She liked Tom, liked the fact that he cared enough about his land to see that it went to the right people and she wished there was a way to help him.

Then an idea hit her. She thought of a way she could help him, help herself, and help a certain young couple who needed a chance to start their lives together. Faith and Paul Proudhorse.

Why not? She herself would probably benefit the most. If she had to stay in this time, she would have need of her own place. What better location for her than smack dab between Colt's and Shining Dawn's properties?

She could be close to her ancestors, and close to Colt, but still maintain her own independence. That was becoming more and more important to her, because unless she could be certain she wouldn't be traveling through time again, she would never be free to marry him.

How could she? How could she ever be free to live a normal life, have Colt's children, and be sure that she would always be there for them. She couldn't. Not as long as she was in danger of being swept away at any moment. Oh, why had she been put in this terrible position? It would have been better never knowing Colt existed than to love him but never feel secure in that love. "Mr. Langford, would you consider selling your land to me?"

Tom looked at her with a puzzled expression. "You got that kind of wealth?"

"Yes, I do." Two more cubic zirconias worth, she thought to herself. "And I can work it so that you can get your wish, too. Half the land can belong to a McAmmon."

"Oh? Just how do you propose to do that?"

She wished that she could proudly proclaim that she was a McAmmon, but then how could she possibly explain that she was their great-great-granddaughter? Besides, she wasn't absolutely sure she was. Lots of people look alike who aren't related at all.

"Well, you caught me by surprise and I haven't had time to work this through, but when you said you wanted it to go to a Mandrell or a McAmmon, I thought of Faith McAmmon. She wants to marry Paul Proudhorse, but he's too stubborn and wants to wait until he's more financially stable.

"It occurred to me that I could make Paul my partner. God knows, I'll need all the help I can get. Paul could manage the place for me. What do you think?"

"Young lady, that sounds mighty fine to me. Mighty fine. I just can't help wondering why you're being so generous. Not too many people would do what you're doing."

How could she tell him she had ulterior motives? That once again she hoped to buy the family she could never have any other way. "Well, I'm almost certain Faith is a distant relative. Isn't that reason enough?"

"It's reason enough for me, young lady."

"Good, then I'd like to settle it as soon as possible. I could ride back to town with you. I just have to stop at the bank. See Brent Raiford, and hope he's interested in buying another diamond ring."

"Raiford? I wouldn't be telling him what you want the money for, if I was you. He wants my land real bad. Colt's and the McAmmon place, too. If he finds out you're buying my place, well . . ."

"I'm no fool, Mr. Langford. He won't find out from me. Is it a deal then?"

"It's a deal."

As they rode along, Tom told her his price, and she was amazed at how cheap land was in this century. It came as a relief to find that the sale of one more fake diamond added to the amount she still had in the bank would be enough. That would leave only her favorite ring, a three-carat heart-shaped stone. It was smaller than the other two, but the symbol of the heart had always been special to her, even before she had become an author.

Colt rode up in time to see Destiny shaking hands with Tom and he wondered what in hell Destiny was up to now. He thought she had ridden off in a huff because she was jealous of his attention to Angel, but now realized he must have been mistaken. She wasn't acting like a jealous woman anymore. In fact, she was acting like a woman with a purpose, and he couldn't help wondering what that purpose was.

"Looks like y'all have settled something between you. I'm wondering what that could be."

Destiny gave Tom a warning glance to let him know she wanted to keep their deal a secret from Colt. Tom obliged. He wasn't one for keeping secrets from friends, but he knew it wouldn't be long before Colt found out on his own. It wasn't exactly the kind of information you could keep secret for very long in this close-knit community.

That was a fact. Like everyone else in the county, he'd heard about Destiny and Colt sharing a bed in the hotel. Seems that was all anyone had to talk about. Hard to blame them though considering the strange circumstances, what with her not having so much as a stitch of clothing anywhere in the room. Had Colt tossed them out the window to keep her captive in the room?

Wouldn't put it past that rambunctious young whippersnapper to hold onto the woman he wanted any way he could.

Yup, he had no doubt Colt Mandrell was in love with the pretty redhead. He could see it written all over his face whenever he so much as caught a glimpse of her. Wouldn't be surprised to find she loved him, too. Didn't strike him as the kind of woman who'd be free with her virtue for any other reason.

No. It was a pretty safe bet that his land would be occupied by Mandrells as well as McAmmons, for if Colt had any sense at all, he'd marry the girl.

He couldn't help wondering, though, why Miss Davidson felt it necessary to keep her acquisition secret from Colt. He had a good idea things was going to get mighty interesting around these parts, real soon.

Colt watched as Destiny rode alongside Tom Langford, smiling at him in a conspiratorial way, and he wondered what it was she had to say to a man she had never met before. But then, she had never met him before she made love to him.

Not that he was worried about her hopping into bed with Tom. He trusted Tom, Hell, he was beginning to trust her, too. She wasn't the loose-moraled woman he had believed her to be when he found her in his bed. He hoped, believed, that she really did love him. What he couldn't understand was why she had become so cold and distant to him ever since this morning.

Don't try to understand a woman's mind.

His daddy had told him that a long time ago. He said, enjoy them, admire them, but don't try and understand them because it would make you crazy trying to figure them out.

Daddy was right. Destiny was, without a doubt, one unpredictable, and unreasonable woman. Last night she had been so warm and loving, and now, since her dream about wolves, she was growing more and more distant from him.

As she conversed with Tom he could see her growing even more distant from him. It was as if Tom was offering her some kind of security that he himself could not. But that didn't make any sense. He had offered her the security of marriage, what more could she ask for? There was no understanding women.

By the time they arrived back at the farm, Destiny had completely shut herself off from him. She wouldn't even look in his direction and that made him very angry. Why didn't she have faith that everything would work out between them? Why couldn't she see that she had traveled through time because she was meant to be with him?

Riding over to the stable, Colt saw Bo standing there grim-faced, and a cold fear swept through him. "What is it, Bo? Is it Mother?"

"Your mother's fine. Brent and Susan took her back to town a couple of hours ago."

Dismounting, he said, "Damn. You had me scared there. If it's not my mother, what is it?"

"It's Scarlet Lady. Something's wrong with her. Paul is with her now. He suspects she's been poisoned."

"Poisoned? How?"

"That's just it. We can't figure out who would want to poison a sweet animal like that. It don't make sense."

The muscle in Colt's cheek began to twitch. "Maybe it does." Making his way to Scarlet Lady's stall, he said, "Did Brent go anywhere near her today?"

"Yeah. He heard all about your daddy's gift and wanted to see her. I took him to the stable. Thought it was funny though, at the time. He's never cared a tinker's dam about horses. But damn, I never suspected he might want to harm one. You telling me he's the one who poisoned the mare?"

Colt's tight-lipped silence spoke volumes.

Tom helped Destiny down from her horse and they both made their way into the stable. Destiny's heart constricted when she saw Colt kneeling beside the mare, his hand stroking her mane. Paul was standing by the animal's head maneuvering a long rubber tube thrust down her throat. Destiny could see that it was connected to a pail of soapy-looking liquid standing beside him.

"Is she going to be all right, Colt?"

Colt didn't answer. Watching him as he turned his attention back to the sick animal, she felt like an intruder. More than that, she felt as if she didn't know him at all, and perhaps she didn't. She knew him as a wild and sexy young man and never dreamed there was another, more serious side to him. Responsible, capable of handling such a terrible thing with cold, hard maturity.

Tom patted her shoulder. "Honey, Colt loves those animals more than most men love their womenfolk. Leave him be, for now. He don't even know we're here anymore. Every ounce of his being is concentrating on that there animal. Let's go up to the house. You must be tired after that long ride."

Smiling gratefully, Destiny let Tom escort her out into the bright sunlight. Tom was right. There was nothing she could do to help. Colt didn't need her now. He'd do just fine without her.

She tried to convince herself that was true, hoping to assuage the guilt she felt at buying Tom's property. But deep within her heart she knew the truth. Having a place of her own would not keep her or Colt safe from heartbreak. Sooner or later, there would be a reckoning.

Thirteen

Maybelle took one look at the bedraggled woman before her, and pressed a glass of brandy into her hand. "Here, Miz Destiny, I be thinking you need this."

Emotionally and physically drained from the events of the day, Destiny had no objection. Taking a deep drink of the liquid heat, she let Colt's kindly housekeeper lead her to a chair.

Sinking into a thick cushion, she realized how totally drained she felt. She was on an emotional roller coaster, loving Colt, wanting to be with him, but fearful that she would be swept away from him. And then there was the shooting, and the dead man, and the wolves and Scarlet Lady being poisoned, and . . .

Wolves?

Where had that come from?

Oh, yes. Colt had told her that she had been dreaming about them. But she had no conscious memory of that. How could she have forgotten a dream so violent she had lashed out and scratched Colt?

What was the matter with her anyway? Why was her memory so flawed? What could have happened to her that was too terrible for her brain to cope with? She took another large sip of brandy and closed her eyes, as the warmth of the liquor spread down her throat.

"Miss Destiny?"

Realizing her mind had been drifting, she forced herself

back to the present and opened her eyes. Tom and Bo were standing over her. "Forgive me. I'm just a little tired and . . ."

"Ma'am?" Bo said. "You got a right to be tired. Tom has just been telling me what you and Colt went through out at the McAmmon place."

"I'm fine, really. I'm just concerned about Colt. How is Scarlet Lady?"

"Too early to tell. But my feeling is if she lasts the night, she'll be all right. The poison will be out of her system by then. Why don't you take your mind off Scarlet Lady and go to bed? Colt will be spending the night at her side, and I'm sure he'll be relieved to know you're resting up."

Maybelle filled Destiny's brandy glass again. "Child, you drink this and you'll sleep like a baby. I'll help you get ready for bed."

It felt so good to Destiny to have someone make decisions for her. Taking another deep drink, she let the liquor do its work and felt herself relax. "Tom, will you be staying the night?"

Tom knew what she meant. "Of course. First thing in the morning I'll take you to town and we can conclude our business."

Taking a deep breath, Destiny stood up, her body sore and aching from so many hours in the saddle. "Good, then if you all will excuse me . . ."

That was the last thing she remembered.

Wavering streams of light tickled her eyes and she awoke feeling unsettled and nervous. She was in Colt's bed. Alone.

An image came to her of someone carrying her up the stairs. Tom, she thought. Everything that had happened the day before swept over her like a shroud. Scarlet Lady. She had to find out if she survived the night. Pushing back the covers, she swung her legs over the side of the bed when a light rapping sounded on the door, and Maybelle entered the room.

Draped over her arm was Destiny's pink dress, newly cleaned and pressed. "Maybelle! How sweet of you!"

"Hmph, caint have you traipsing around in Master Colt's clothin'. It ain't decent."

Suppressing a smile, Destiny answered, "Yes, ma'am. Now if you'll help me dress real quick, I have to check on Scarlet Lady. Have you heard anything, Maybelle?"

"Heard from Master Colt himself. She be jus' fine. Jus' fine. Caint nobody beat the young master when it comes to doctorin' horses."

Jubilant, Destiny ran down the stairs, looking for Colt the moment Maybelle was done dressing her. But he was nowhere to be found. She decided he must still be with Scarlet Lady and made her way out to the stable. The mare greeted her with a very healthy-sounding whicker from the corral outside the building.

Stroking her velvet nose, Destiny's gaze took in the interior of the stable and she saw Colt asleep on a cot outside the mare's stall. Making her way inside, she stared down at his face. A rush of feeling swept over her. Scraped and scratched though he may be, he still looked wonderful to her. Would she ever get over the thrill of just gazing at him? Not likely, she loved him more each time she saw him.

If only she could write a happy ending to this love story.

If only Colt could save her as swiftly and effectively as he had Scarlet Lady. But she wasn't creating a novel now, this was real life.

Feeling a hand on her shoulder, Destiny turned her head to see Paul Proudhorse standing there. Motioning with his finger for her to be quiet, he took her by the arm and led her outside.

"Let him sleep, Miss Destiny. He was up all night with the mare."

"How is she?"

"She's just fine now, but it was touch and go for a while there. I'd surely like to get my hands on the person who did this. It would have been a terrible waste of horseflesh if we had lost her."

"Paul, do you think it was Brent Raiford?"

"I wish I knew. Let me just say I hope for Colt's sake it wasn't. For Miz Little Bit's, too."

"I don't understand what motive he could possibly have. I can understand him wanting Colt's property, but how would it benefit him to kill a helpless animal?"

"Who knows the workings of an evil man's mind?"

"You're right about that."

"Well, if you'll excuse me, I want to finish my chores."

"Paul . . ."

"Yes, Miss Destiny."

"I have something I want to talk to you about, and it has to be right now. I'll be leaving for town in a little while."

"Leaving? I thought . . ."

"I know what you thought, Paul, but you're wrong. It can't be. I won't be staying here with Colt. Believe me, I wish I could, but circumstances prevent that from happening. In a way, that's what I wanted to talk to you about."

Paul looked puzzled. Destiny couldn't blame him for that. "Paul, I'm buying the Langford property and I'd like to make you my partner."

Paul never so much as blinked, but inside his heart was beating like a tom-tom. "Your partner?"

"Yes, I have the money to buy the property, but not the expertise to manage it right. That's where you come in. We would split any profit we made right down the middle. What do you say?"

"Did Faith talk you into this? 'Cuz if she did, I want you to know I don't accept charity."

"Charity? There's no charity involved here."

Visibly relieved, Paul answered, "If you're telling the truth, then you won't mind accepting the money I've saved so far. It's only eleven hundred, but . . ."

"Oh, Paul. That would be marvelous. I'm sure we'll need it to make improvements."

Paul's face broke out in a wide grin. "That's for certain." Then, remembering something, he suddenly became subdued. "But I can't just go off and leave Colt like that."

"Seems to me, Bo could take your place as foreman. He strikes me as a very capable man."

"He is, no doubt about that. And if it weren't for my friendship with Colt, Bo would have had my position long ago."

"Then there's no reason to turn me down, is there?"

"If you put it like that, I guess not. All right, you've got yourself a new partner. But I'll need some time to put things in order here first."

"Take all the time you need. I'll be going in to town to finalize the sale today, and then Tom is going to take me back to his place, or I should say, our new place after that. I expect the first piece of mail I get will be an invitation to your wedding."

"What's this about a wedding?"

Paul beamed at Tom as he made his way over to them. "I have a feeling you and Destiny knew about it before I did."

"Hmm, I believe you're right. But seems to me there's one important person here that's still left in the dark. If I was you, I'd hightail it to town and ask her before she accepts an offer from some other eager young man."

Paul laughed the assertive laughter of a man who had no doubts about his powers of persuasion. "I'll ride in with the two of you, if you don't mind."

"Welcome the company. By the way, thanks for finding room in your bunkhouse for my men last night. Hope they behaved themselves."

"They were no trouble at all. I was wondering if they planned on staying on after the sale?"

"Yup. All four of them. They've been with me ever since they became free men. Funny. it's hard to believe they were ever slaves. You won't find harder-working men, and loyal to a fault."

"That's good news. We'll be off to a good start then." Light at heart, Paul went back to his chores, proud in his new position as landowner. He could marry Faith now and start the family he had always wanted. Surely the Great Spirit had sent Destiny to him.

Colt hadn't awakened by the time Destiny left for town with Paul and Tom and two of his men. She was glad of that. The last thing she wanted was a confrontation. She didn't know if she had the strength, or the willpower to resist him. But she had to try. The alternative would bring her a few moments of bliss and a lifetime of regret.

But how could she be so sure of that? Perhaps her traveling through time had been a fluke that would never be repeated. Perhaps she could live out her days with Colt in contentment.

But deep in her heart she didn't really believe that. How could she, when she had already been separated from her mother and father.

What did that have to do with Colt?

That question nagged at her all the way to town. What *did* it have to do with Colt?

Colt . . . Colt . . . Something was nudging at the corners of her mind, trying to break through the wall she had put up to keep from feeling the hurt. Fingering the huge cubic zirconia on her finger, she pushed her haunting thoughts back and turned in her saddle to address Tom. "I'll go directly to the bank, then meet you at your lawyer's office. What did you say his name was?"

"Cedric Farley. You can't miss his office. It's on the corner of Cuna and Saint George Street. I'll have my men waiting for you outside the bank with weapons in hand, just in case anyone gets any ideas. Don't mind telling you, I'll be glad when the money is safe and secure in my own bank."

"My sentiments exactly. The sooner we get this over with, the happier I'll be."

Tom looked into Destiny's eyes. She didn't look like a woman who would soon be feeling happier. "You sure you want to go through with this? It's not too late to change your mind."

"I'm sure."

"I can't help but worry about your safety. If that man you shot isn't the man who murdered my wife, your life could be in danger, too."

"Don't worry about me. Your wife was alone when she was killed. I won't make that mistake, Tom, believe me."

"I don't think you understand. Judith was alone, but she was armed, and she knew how to use her gun. It's even possible she knew her attacker. He could have taken her when her defenses were down. I don't want that to happen to you."

Hearing the pain behind his softspoken words, she said, "It won't happen, Tom."

"Sweetheart, you're an innocent. You have no idea what you're up against. Colt would surely kill me if he knew I was telling you this, but for your own protection I think you should know just how gruesome her death was. It's not easy telling you this, and I ask for your forgiveness in advance, but . . ."

Tom's face took on a look of incredible grief, and Destiny ached for him. "Tom, you don't have to tell me this."

"God almighty, I do have to tell you, hon, You have to know so's you can protect yourself. That bastard pistol-whipped her around the head until he had her on the ground. Then he raped her, slit her throat, and left her to die."

Lowering his head, Tom swallowed hard, trying to keep control of his emotions. "Before he left, he dragged her body up against a tree, and wrapped her legs around the trunk in an obscene position." Raising his head, he gazed at her with tortured eyes. "You understand what I'm saying?"

Destiny blanched at Tom's graphic description. Her heart went out to him, knowing how difficult it must have been for him to tell her that. Doubly hard, for not only was he talking about his beloved wife, but he was a Victorian gentleman who she was sure had never spoken to a woman in such a blunt way before.

"I understand, Tom. Thank you for telling me. Obviously, the man is some kind of monster. I can see that now, and I'll be very cautious. In fact, if it will make you feel any better, I'll hire someone to be a bodyguard for Faith and me. We won't go anywhere without him. Will that make you feel any better?

"A whole lot better."

Tom rode off then, since they were too close to town to take any chances of being seen together. She didn't want Brent to get word of the sale until it was legal. After all, if he refused to buy her ring, there would be no deal.

Worried that he was no longer interested in purchasing any more of her rings, she walked into the bank with trepidation, trying hard to keep from showing how nervous she felt.

Brent was at his desk, just as he had been the first time she met him. His eyes lit up when he saw her, and she knew he must be hoping she had changed her mind about investing in his project.

Taking the ring from her finger, she handed it to him saying, "I'm selling another ring, and out of courtesy, wanted you to have first option to buy it."

Brent stared at the huge ring in surprise. "My dear young lady, how many of those rare beauties do you have?"

Taken aback by his bluntness she blurted out the truth. "Just one more, but I hope it never becomes necessary for me to sell it."

"I can only wonder why you want to sell this one," he said, peering at the stone closely. "It is without a doubt, a superior stone."

"It is, isn't it? It should bring even more than my last one, wouldn't you say?"

"Ahh, but unfortunately, I cannot afford to pay as much as I did for the last one. Circumstances forbid it. Since I couldn't convince you, or anyone else for that matter, to invest in my vision for St. Augustine's future, I'll have to use more of my own funds. That leaves very little to splurge on frivolous things like diamond rings."

She had been afraid of that. Now what was she to do? "Then could you recommend someone else who might be interested?"

"Hold on there, I didn't say I wasn't interested. I am very interested. It would be the perfect piece to finish a collection of a lifetime. If you'll accept the same price as the last stone, I'll be glad to take if off your hands."

Relieved, Destiny opened her mouth to accept when suddenly the image of the man she had killed flashed through her head. This is where she had seen him before. Right here. In the bank. He was talking to Brent the time she sold her first ring. Could Brent Raiford be a part of the plot to kill Colt?

"Well, what do you say, my dear? Are we in agreement?"

Pulling herself together, Destiny forced a smile to her face. "Agreed. I'll take the money in greenbacks, and will be withdrawing everything but two hundred from my savings account, thank you."

Brent's eyes narrowed. "That's a mighty large sum to be carrying around. You must have something big in the works. Are you planning on saving more widows from me, Destiny?"

Destiny laughed nervously. She should have known he'd find out. "No more widows, Mr. Raiford. But if you think there's someone else who needs saving from you, I'll gladly consider it."

"You are a formidable woman, Destiny Davidson. I'd hate to count you among my enemies."

Putting on her southern belle accent, she cooed, "Why, Mr. Raiford, do you have so many enemies they must be counted?"

Brent smiled warmly.

But the warmth didn't reach his rattlesnake eyes.

Fourteen

The next two weeks were a blur of activity for Destiny. She accomplished a lot, deliberately concentrating all her energy on her new home. It was the only way she could keep from going to Colt. The only way she could forget for a while the last time they had been together.

Throwing herself into her work helped, but there were always moments when she was caught off guard and the terrible hunger for him would take over.

Watching the sun set over the St. John's River as she sat upon the deck, she thought about everything that had happened since she moved to her new home.

It was wearisome just thinking about it.

Tom had shown her around the property as soon as they returned from town with her few belongings, and he introduced her to the four loyal ex-slaves who would continue to work the farm and lush fruit-bearing orange grove. It was a bittersweet moment when Tom finally left with a wagon load of belongings, promising to return and show her and Paul everything they needed to know to run the place.

Lily Tiger had been at Penelope's when they picked up Destiny's clothing, and it wasn't hard to talk the sweet little woman into becoming her housekeeper.

Faith arrived a few days later, and proceeded to make herself right at home. She fell in love with the farm on first sight. That was fine with Destiny, for from the moment she first saw the enormous gazebo Tom had built for his wife right on the banks of the river, she had claimed it for her own.

She had started working on it right away, having walls constructed so that she could turn it into her very own place which would consist of nothing more than a bedroom and a small writing room. She would take her meals in the main house with the rest of her new little family.

Lily had been happy to claim the kitchen and the small room off it for her own, leaving the large master bedroom for Paul and Faith. Each woman knew her duties and her place in the family, and the only ones with any misgivings over the arrangement were Paul and Tom. It was obvious the men thought it would be impossible for three women to live amicably together.

But they hadn't reckoned on the immediate friendship among the women, a friendship that grew stronger with each new day. Faith adored Destiny and looked up to her, almost as she would an older sister, and as for Lily, the Seminole woman felt content for the first time in her life.

Only one awkward moment marred the homecoming for Destiny and her new family: preparing them for the time when she might no longer be there. But it was something she felt compelled to do. It would be callous of her to just leave them wondering, worrying about what happened to her. Walking over to the deck railing, she leaned against it, staring out at the water as she replayed the scene in her head.

It was the end of an evening meal, when they were all still sitting at the table. "I want you all to know how happy I am that we're together like this. I can already see that we work together wonderfully, and I look forward to the future of River's Edge. But . . . darn it all, this is going to be harder to say than I ever imagined."

Standing up, she looked in turn at each of the people sitting at the table. Paul, Faith, Lily Tiger, and the four dark faces of Hank, Jim, Dogie, and Joseph. "You all need to know that the day may come when I might no longer be here. When I might just suddenly disappear."

The room suddenly erupted into worried murmuring.

"Please . . . Understand this. It won't be because of foul play. No one will be responsible for my disappearance, not even myself. I know how odd that must sound, but trust me, it's true."

Hank, never one to tiptoe around issues, said, "Ma'am, why would you want to go and do dat? We'll be here fo' you if things get too tough."

"I know you will, Hank. But that's not the problem. I won't disappear on my own volition because I couldn't face my responsibilities. Don't think that for a moment. It will be because of forces beyond my control. Beyond anyone's control."

A sob interrupted Destiny's speech and everyone turned to look at Faith.

"You're scaring me, Destiny."

"Honey, please don't be scared. If I do disappear, nothing bad will happen to me other than I'll miss all of you. But it may never happen and that will be fine with me. I've come to believe that I'm here for a reason. I just want you all to be prepared in case it does happen."

Turning to Paul, sitting at the head of the table, she said, "That's why I made you a partner in River's Edge. If you'll check the deed, you'll discover that you and Faith will inherit the farm if anything happens to me."

Paul rose from his seat. "Destiny, there isn't anyone in this room who would ever wish you anything but the best. Surely you can trust us with the truth, whatever it might be."

Destiny smiled bitterly. "I know you think that, but believe me, the truth is too, too hard to believe. Let me just say that in the eventuality of my sudden disappearance, I've written a letter addressed to all of you. Cedric Farley has it in his safe. It will explain everything, and you'll understand then what it's impossible to understand now. I know how cryptic that sounds, but that's all I'm prepared to say."

"Well, then, ma'am," Hank interjected, "seeing as how ya told us dis disappearing act might never happen, do you s'pose we can put it right out of our minds, till the need arises?"

"Please, it would make me feel a lot better. I just needed to tell you that so I could take my mind off it, and concentrate of happier thoughts. Like Faith and Paul's wedding plans."

Yes, it had been a hectic, not to mention heart-wrenching two weeks. Now, hot, tired, and dirty from working on her gazebo home, it felt good to just sit and stare at the pink marbled sky at the end of a busy day.

Brushing sweat and sawdust from her face, she stared out at the wonderful view, completely absorbed in the beauty of it. She wished with all her heart that she could share the sunset with the man she loved. Sighing, she decided maybe it wasn't such a good idea to be here alone after all. She'd join the others and let their happy chatter take her mind from Colt.

Hearing the creaking of the floor behind her, she smiled, expecting it to be Faith or Lily wanting to visit. Turning, she felt her face drain of color as she stared into penetrating gray eyes.

"Colt!"

He stared back, his eyes boring into hers, accusing her without words.

"I was just thinking about how much I missed you, Colt, and here you are. I guess my psychic abilities are getting stronger." She smiled at him, but it faded away in the silent accusation of his solemn gaze.

A lump formed in her throat as she drank in his beautiful, but oh so masculine tanned face. The red of the setting sun glowed in his eyes, turning them from cool silver to panther gold.

"So, now you know," she said in a resigned voice that echoed regret.

"Now, I know."

She swallowed hard, aching to run into his arms, but knowing she must not. "How is Scarlet Lady?"

"In a lot better condition than I am right now."

His words penetrated her heart with deep sorrow. "I'm sorry.

"Are you?"

You know I am. Oh, Colt, I wish it didn't have to be this way, but—"

"Don't. I don't want to hear about your fears, your regrets," he said holding up his hand as if to stop her words from reaching him. "I just wanted to see for myself that it was really true. I called Paul a liar when he told me you had bought this place. Can you believe that? I called my best friend a liar. That's how much I believed in our love. Our future together. So, imagine my surprise when I found out it was true. It took quite a few days for me to come to grips with that. Well, I'm straight now. Now that I've seen it for myself, I won't bother you anymore."

He turned to go, setting Destiny in motion. She couldn't let him leave like that. "Colt . . . wait. You don't understand. It doesn't have to end. There's no reason why we can't go on seeing each other."

Colt turned around to face her, his expression bitter, incredulous. "What did you have in mind, honey? How did you want to handle it? Would you like us to have weekly rendezvous in bed? Is that what you want? Would that satisfy you?"

"Stop it. You make it sound so crude."

Colt laughed harshly. "Crude? Cruel is more like it. Cruel and heartless and childish. Grow up, Red. Life doesn't come with any guarantees. There isn't a man or woman alive who doesn't take risks when they fall in love, but they're not cowardly little children like you. You're so afraid of being hurt you're willing to give up the only thing that really matters. Well, you've made your bed, now lie in it—alone!"

Tears streamed down Destiny's face as she watched the man she loved walk away.

The sun was sinking below the river, and the cool night air claimed the surrounding landscape. She shivered and hugged herself, trying to tell herself that this was the way it had to be, but it was cold comfort. If she were trying to save herself from hurt, it was just a little too late.

Fifteen

December 1870

Destiny's gaze took in the finishing touches of her gazebo house with great satisfaction. Her new home had turned out even better than she had hoped.

She stood by proudly as Lily and Faith oohed and ahed over everything, although when she had first told them of her plans for the gazebo, they had looked at her like she was losing her mind.

Now their enthusiasm knew no bounds. Faith was fascinated with the cheerful floral print balloon curtains hanging from the oversized windows on the circular walls. Destiny had made them herself, designing them so that they could be lowered for privacy in the evening, and raised to let in the fabulous panoramic view in the morning.

There was something very satisfying about working with your hands, she had discovered. The result made it all worth while. She had planned and executed every little detail of her home by herself, right down to personally mixing the colors for the walls, and was happy with the delicate pale shade of pink she created. It was a peaceful color, a tranquil color, the perfect one to accent the light, airy ambience of the room.

But her pride and joy was the bed she had decorated with an abundance of colorful pillows piled against the headboard. Some were covered with the same floral print as her curtains, others done in white crochet or dusty rose moire.

For the final touch she had hung frothy white mosquito netting from the ceiling over the bed, draping it luxuriously down to the floor on either side of the bed. It looked frivolous and feminine, but would serve a useful function in an era that had no screened windows.

In keeping with the summer house theme, she had chosen white wicker furniture. Everything from the table that held her oil lamp, to the settee and chairs in her tiny writing room area, to the dresser that held her belongings was made from it.

Faith immediately proclaimed she wanted her bed to look exactly like Destiny's and Lily decided that she wanted a gazebo home of her own.

When the women were done admiring the bed they opened the door facing the river and the oohs and ahhs started all over again.

Destiny was proud of her deck. It hung over the river and afforded a great view of the setting sun. She could sit out here and enjoy the peace and quiet to her heart's content.

Heart's content.

That certainly wasn't the right phrase. Her heart would never be content without Colt, but she was beginning to wonder if he felt the same way. Through Faith, she had learned that he was seeing a lot of Angel Peabody.

She could have guessed that would happen. Angel was an attractive girl, and she had let it be known that she was looking for a husband. But it bothered her that he had so quickly turned to another woman. Had he ever truly loved her?

Deep in her heart she knew the answer. He was turning to Angel on the rebound. He couldn't have stopped loving her so easily.

"Destiny?"

Destiny pulled herself from her reverie and answered Faith with a "Hmm?"

"I want your full attention when I tell you this, you hear?"

Wondering what was on Faith's mind, Destiny sat on the bed and folded her hands in her lap. "All right. What is it?"

"I just wanted you to know that Paul and I decided we want to get married as soon as possible. You have no idea how hard it is living in the same house as him, but not being able to, you know, express our love for each other."

"I can understand that, but, honey, don't you think you should wait until your mother and father return? I know if I were Shining Dawn, I'd want to see my one and only daughter's wedding."

Faith plopped down on the bed beside her in a pout. "I don't care. I'm not waiting for her one minute longer. And besides, she won't mind missing my wedding one tiny little bit. In fact, it'll probably be a relief to her."

Shocked, Destiny looked at Lily Tiger, wondering what she would have to say about it, but the little Seminole woman kept her thoughts to herself. Well, she couldn't. Someone had to defend Shining Dawn. "How can you say that?"

"It's easy. You don't know my mother. She has never given me much mind since the day I was born. She's devoted her life to my father and my brother. I sometimes think she wishes she never had a daughter."

Destiny was astounded by what she heard. That didn't sound like the Shining Dawn she had written about, unless . . . "Do you suppose the death of her first daughter was so painful that she shut up a part of herself to keep from being hurt?"

A funny look came over Faith's face. "Where did you get the idea I had an older sister?"

"Why . . . I . . . . have no idea, I guess I thought you

mentioned it to me before. Are you trying to tell me it's not true?"

"Destiny, believe me, I'm the only daughter."

Destiny was so completely confused by now she didn't know what to believe. "I could have sworn . . . I thought Shining Dawn had a little girl who died the night that Colt was born."

"Why, wherever did you get an idea like that?"

"I don't know. I must have heard it somewhere. Are you telling me it's not true?"

Faith laughed nervously. "Of course, it's not true. Don't you suppose I'd know if I had a sister? Oh, I did hear rumors to that effect when I was a child, but my father assured me that no sister of mine had ever died. You know, it's funny though, he forbade me ever to bring up that subject to my mother."

"Why was that?"

"He said it was too hard for my mother to talk about because of the terrible things that went on that night. Did you know she had to cut open Little Bit's stomach to take Colt or he and Miz Little Bit would have died? I don't know where she got the courage to do that. I don't know whether I could have done it."

Destiny didn't know what to believe now. Had there been another daughter or not?

If there was no other daughter why had Shining Dawn written about her in her journal, and if she really did exist, why would Blade and Shining Dawn keep it from Faith? It didn't make any sense.

A light knocking on the door brought an end to the conversation. Destiny opened the front door, surprised to see Tom standing there with a stranger.

"Tom! Please come in."

Grinning from ear to ear, Tom stepped inside, and removed his hat, holding it to his chest. "Sweetheart, you have no idea how happy I am that you've put this place to such wonderful use. My wife would have loved the sweet little house you've turned it into."

"I'm glad to hear that. I was worried you might think I was desecrating the beautiful gazebo you built for your wife."

"Well, now you know better." Seeing Faith and Lily, Tom nodded at each of them, saying, "I'm glad all three of you women are here. This concerns you all. A while back, Destiny and I discussed getting a bodyguard for you women, but since she didn't do anything about it, I did. I won't rest easy until I know y'all are being properly protected out here."

Stepping aside, he ushered in the man half hidden behind him. "Ladies, this here is Hunt Farley. He'll look after you real good."

All three women gazed at the man in awe. Tall, broad-shouldered, and tanned, he had dark brown hair and green eyes narrowed to a permanent squint. Destiny was sure, though, that narrowed though they may be, they didn't miss a thing.

Hunt nodded his head at the women, taking each of them in one at a time as Tom introduced them to him, but he said nothing. Destiny got the feeling that Mister Hunt Farley was a man of few words.

"Farley, you say? Are you related to the lawyer Cedric Farley?"

"He's my brother, ma'am."

Destiny mulled that information over. "Hunt, you sure you want to do this? Watching over three women can be quite a daunting chore for some men, I imagine."

Hunt's penetrating gaze locked onto her face. "Ma'am, I ain't complainin'."

"Well then . . ." Destiny held out her hand to Hunt. "Welcome to River's Edge Farm."

Looking into his eyes as he shook her hand, Destiny felt something stir within her. The hand that grasped hers was sandpaper rough, but it felt strong and good to hold. This man was no professional hired gun. No one got rough hands like that just toting a gun. That made her feel a whole lot better. She didn't want a cold-eyed hired killer anywhere near Faith or Lily, not to mention herself.

"River's Edge? So, it even has a new name," Tom said cheerfully. "I'm glad. I can see the farm is in good hands now. Caring hands. Won't surprise me a bit if you make your River's Edge a big success."

Hunt was still holding her hand. Curious, she turned her attention back to him, making him aware of what he was doing and he released his hold on her. He had held her so tight, she still felt the pressure of his hand on hers.

"Would you gentlemen care for some tea? I was just about to serve Lily and Faith."

"None for me, honey," Tom said. "Can't stay. I've got to get back to town. Just wanted to make sure you were situated right with Hunt first."

"What about you, Mr. Farley? Will you join us for tea?"

"Name's Hunt, ma'am. Only name I answer to."

"Hunt it is. Will you have tea?"

Hunt declined with a slight movement of his head, then his gaze took in the contents of the feminine little house with repressed curiosity. At least, Destiny thought it was curiosity. It seemed she was going to have a hard time figuring out exactly what this quiet man was thinking, but she decided she was up to the challenge.

"I'm going to go speak with Paul before I head back to town," Tom said, placing a hand on Hunt's shoulder. "And I'll make sure Hunt here has a place to bunk, too."

"Mr. Langford, I'll be seeing you at my wedding, I hope. Paul and I will be getting married in two weeks. You'll be getting an invitation real soon."

"I wouldn't miss that for the world, Faith, honey. See ya all then."

Tom walked out the door, but Hunt still stood there. Feeling awkward, Destiny said, "Hunt, we can decide later to what extent you'll be guarding us women. I certainly don't expect you to be dogging my every step."

"Then you'd be wrong, ma'am."

Hunt hadn't moved from the spot he stood on, but Destiny felt as if he were looming over her. "What? What do you mean?"

"Ma'am, only one way to protect you right and that's to stay within protecting distance. My way of thinkin', that's mighty close."

Destiny's mouth opened in surprise. "Well, that's all well and good, Hunt, but as you can see my home is very small. I'm afraid we'd be tripping over each other if you stayed here."

"Here?" Hunt came close to losing his low-key demeanor. "Didn't mean for you to get the impression I was staying here."

Destiny immediately relaxed, amused that she had elicited some emotion in the inscrutable Mr. Hunt Farley.

"I won't be quite that close, ma'am, but don't worry, I'll be at your side in a twinkling of an eye, if you should need me." Turning on his heels, Hunt walked out the door.

Flying to the nearest window, Destiny peered out in time to see Hunt walk over to the nearest tree. He stood up against it, staring at the house. Seeing her, he acknowledged her with a nodding of his head, and with two fingers, he flicked his hat down farther until it almost covered his squinty eyes.

Almost.

Her eyes large with wonder, Destiny turned to face the other women. "Oh, my."

Lily began to titter.

Faith said, "I know what you mean. If I wasn't so much in love with Paul I do believe I would be making a fool of myself over him. He's the most mysterious, most heavenly, most manly man I ever did meet."

Destiny had to agree. In all of her life in the twentieth century she had never met two such masculine men as Colt Mandrell and Hunt Farley.

River's Edge Farm was a flurry of activity as the time grew closer to Faith and Paul's wedding day. Destiny didn't have much time to think about Colt, but she couldn't keep from thinking about Hunt because he was always there. Whatever she was doing, she had only to look up and he'd be there.

She had no idea when he slept, or even where he slept. When she went to bed at night, she sensed his presence somewhere outside, and when she awoke in the morning, the first thing she'd do is peer out the window, and there he'd be. He obviously was a man of his word. He did take his job seriously.

Too darn seriously.

When the wedding was over and she had a chance to take a deep breath, she would have to have a talk with him. It was too disconcerting to be scrutinized so closely all the time.

Then, on the day before the wedding, Destiny had a surprise visitor. Opening the door, she saw Little Bit Mandrell standing there.

"Miss Little Bit! Is anything wrong? Has something happened to Colt?"

Pushing past her, Little Bit entered the room. "You are in a better position to answer that question, young lady."

Uh oh! Destiny turned to face Little Bit. "What do you mean?"

"What do I mean? My son is back to his old ways. Going to town every night. Getting drunk, picking fights with men twice his size. And he refuses to talk about you. Obviously somethin' has happened between the two of you and I want to know what it is."

Destiny felt a twinge of guilt. "I'm sorry, I don't want to talk about it either."

With a quivering voice, Little Bit answered, "I was afraid of that. I don't understand. You two were so happy, so right for each other, and then you up and buy the Langford place and all that is changed. I'm so worried about his future, I don't know what to do."

Destiny softened, seeing how close to tears Little Bit was. "Please don't be upset. Your son is a good man. A hard-working man. You don't have to worry about him ending up as the town drunk, believe me."

Little Bit dabbed at her eyes with a lavender-scented handkerchief tucked in the cuff of her sleeve. "I know you're right. It's just . . . I had such high hopes for the two of you. The love between you is so strong. I thought you had a chance for the kind of happiness very few people ever experience."

Now it was time for Destiny to cry. Turning her face away to hide her shiny eyes, she said, "Come, sit out on the deck while I make us some tea, then we can talk."

In a few moments the two women were sitting across from each other, enjoying the ritual of taking tea.

"Miss Little Bit, this special kind of love you were talking about. Did you . . . do you have it with your husband?"

Little Bit's eyes glistened like the sun rays bouncing off the water just a few feet away. "Oh, yes, Gary and I are still very deeply in love, but it wasn't love at first sight, the way it is between you and Colt. We started off as good friends."

Smiling at the remembrance, she continued, "You see, I was seeing John Graham at the time, who by the way ended up marrying the governor's daughter, and Gary was smitten with Shining Dawn. Who could blame him, she was such a vibrant, exciting young woman. But even before we were over the heartbreak of our first loves, we were drawn to each other."

Feeling great warmth for the woman who had given birth to Colt, she said softly, "I'm so glad Colt came from a home with such great love."

Little Bit looked up just then, sensing before seeing the tall, handsome man who was walking around the gazebo house toward them on the deck. She smiled radiantly, and Destiny turned to see who she was looking at.

At first, she thought it was Colt, and her heart did flip-flops, but as the figure drew closer, she saw it was an older version of Colt.

"Gary, come meet the young lady who has won our son's heart."

Gary Mandrell. Colt's father. So much like him that she immediately felt affection for this man she had never seen before. Gary was much better looking than she had pictured him when she wrote her book, and so charismatic that he deserved to be the hero of his own book, rather than just a secondary character.

She had to remind herself this wasn't a book she was writing, this was real life. She took his offered hand, and smiled when he raised it to his lips, kissing it. Yes, he definitely could have been the hero in her book.

"I understand you were away in Georgia. When did you get back?"

"Last night. I don't know if I dare leave again. I can't believe how many exciting events occurred while I was gone. And you, my dear young lady, are responsible for most of them."

Destiny smiled up at him shyly, but said nothing.

"Are you sure you're not a fairy godmother in disguise?"

"What do you mean?"

"Paying off Penelope's mortgage for her, making Paul a partner here so that he could marry Faith. If you were a fairy godmother, then there would be one wish left. I hope it will be to make my son a very happy man."

Destiny fingered the last remaining cubic zirconia on her

hand. One more wish. She had given up one of her rings for each of the things Gary mentioned. One beautiful heart-shaped ring remained. Could she somehow use it to grant that one wonderful wish? Had she overlooked some way that she could use her ring to make her own life end like a romantic fairy tale?

Sixteen

The distant beating of drums had been sounding since high noon. It wasn't the first time Destiny had heard them. When the west wind swept over her property, she occasionally heard the faraway rhythmic music emanating from the nearby reservation. But that didn't mean she was used to the drumming, or the fact that the Seminoles were her neighbors. They were a constant reminder that she lived in a different time.

She thought about that as she changed out of the simple dress she had worn all morning while helping Lily and Penelope prepare for the wedding. Slipping into her new pale peach satin gown, she struggled to fasten the pumpkin-colored sash around her waist. Tying it behind her in a large bow that billowed out like a bustle, she looked at herself in the full-length mirror that Penelope had given her as a housewarming present.

She liked the image reflected there, and had to admit it was fun to dress up now and then. Still, she missed dressing in the comfy T-shirts and shorts of her own era.

Giving the bow one more tug, and her cheeks one last tweak to make them rosy, à la Scarlet O'Hara, she headed for the door, with a decided lack of enthusiasm.

Much as she was happy for Paul and Faith, she wasn't looking forward to the wedding. She was a private person, uncomfortable in large groups of people, especially people she had never met before, and in about one minute she would be facing a whole slew of strangers.

However, for Faith and Paul's sake, she would smile at everyone and pretend to enjoy herself. Bracing herself for the ordeal, she opened the door and found Paul with his hand raised to knock. Dressed in his Sunday best, he looked every inch the handsome bridegroom. But what in the world was he doing here?

"Paul . . . what is it? Is something wrong?"

The grin that quickly appeared on his face assured her that all was right. "Wrong? Nothin' can go wrong today. I won't allow it. Lily Tiger sent me here to make sure you understood that the ceremony will start at four promptly."

"Why would she do that? She knows very well I am aware of the time. The time and everything else concerning this day. Haven't I had to listen to her lament about all the things that could go wrong? First she was afraid it would be too hot, then she was afraid it would be too cold. But it's turned out just lovely for a December day. Warm enough to enjoy without shawls to hide our pretty dresses."

"I suspect the real reason she sent me was to get me out of the way. Faith's acting as skittish as a colt. Won't hear of me seein' her in her wedding dress, and Lily hinted very loudly that there was no place for menfolk in the bride's home on her weddin' day, so . . . here I am."

"So you are." Destiny smiled to herself, seeing how nervous Paul was. She wouldn't have thought him the type. "Now, what am I going to do with you?"

The drums sounded louder than before, and Destiny looked up at Paul quizzically. "Is it my imagination or are the drums louder today?

"You're not imagining it. They are louder, or perhaps I should say, closer. The Seminole are on their way here from the reservation. They honor me by attending my weddin'. Seminoles and Creeks are closely related, you know."

"They're coming here?" Destiny said with a sinking heart. "Oh, no, how will we ever feed them all?"

"From the way Lily Tiger has been cookin', I don't expect we have to worry. Besides, folks have been stoppin' in with platters and bowls of food enough to feed the cavalry."

Glancing over at the main house, Destiny couldn't believe her eyes. A crowd of people was milling around. "Where in the world did they all come from? Faith told me she only sent out invitations to the Mandrells, the Peabodys, and Farleys, and of course, to Tom Langford."

"Folks around here don't need no invitation. Long as they show up with food, they feel they're welcome."

It seemed Destiny had a lot to learn about nineteenth-century life in rural Florida. Well, there was nothing to do but smile and hope for the best.

Fortifying herself with a deep, cleansing breath of air, she accompanied Paul back to the main house, nodding and smiling at all the curious folk. Inside she was a bundle of nerves. What did one say to perfect strangers, anyway?

Drawing closer to the house, she spotted a few familiar faces and began to feel a little better. There was Tom Langford decked out in boots, jacket, and wide-brimmed hat, and Penelope Peabody in a flower print dress and a ridiculous hat with a stuffed bird topping it. It seemed there was a lot to learn about Penelope, too. She certainly wasn't the stern, no-nonsense person she had seemed the first time she met her.

Destiny quickly recognized Gary and Little Bit, though they had their backs turned to her. They were busily chatting with Hunt and his brother Cedric Farley, the lawyer.

Seeing the brothers together for the first time, she could see the family resemblance. It seemed strange, though, that a worldly lawyer and a rustic cowboy could be related. But then, she knew very little about Hunt, other than he was a man of few words and a definite loner. But he did strike her as being an intelligent man. At least the two brothers had that much in common.

Paul joined in conversation with Hunt and Cedric, and Destiny continued to the house alone. But she felt Hunt's eyes on her as she made her way through the throng of people, and knew that even today, he was mindful of his job of protecting her. She'd talk to him later about that. Urge him to relax a little and enjoy himself. After all, what could happen to her on a joyous occasion like this?

"Afternoon, Destiny."

Destiny recognized the overly friendly voice of Brent Raiford and a little shiver went up her spine. She nodded her head at him politely, hoping he wouldn't take it as an invitation to chat. Dressed in black like a riverboat gambler, he looked all the more like a young James Garner. Funny thing, she had always liked James Garner, but she detested Brent at first sight.

For the first time, Destiny noticed Susan by his side and her gaze swept over the very beautiful, very expensive midnight blue velvet gown Susan was wearing. Curious, her gaze lowered to Susan's hand, wondering if she wore one of Destiny's dearly departed fake diamonds to complete her costly outfit. Susan's hands were covered with black lace gloves. Her ring could never have fit under the tight material.

That was interesting to know. Susan was not the beneficiary of either of her rings and it occurred to her that Susan might not be aware of their existence. Raising her eyes, Destiny nodded a hello to Susan and felt butterflies dance in her stomach. Beneath the stylish velvet hat that matched her dress hung a veil that covered her face but didn't quite hide the nasty bruise on Susan's cheek.

Did Brent do that to her? Who else could be responsible? Was it possible that beneath his sleek handsome exterior lay the cold heart of a wife beater?

Hearing someone call out Colt's name, Destiny looked

past Hunt and Cedric to see Angel Peabody smile and wave to someone who must be standing directly behind her.

Destiny stiffened, knowing Colt was approaching her from the back, but she needn't have worried about having to talk to him. Angel, dressed in a pink creation that made her look every inch an angel was determined to claim him as her own.

She had the sudden urge to trip the all too eager young thing when she walked by her, but restrained herself. If Colt wanted to make a fool of himself over an eighteen-year-old, there was nothing she could do about it. Was there?

Forcing a smile, she turned to face them, but her smile froze when she saw Angel's arm wrapped tightly around Colt's. She remembered how wonderful it felt to hold him that way, and a slice of pain ripped through her heart.

Damn you, Colt, why did I have to fall in love with you?

The last thing she wanted to do was to talk to Colt now, but Angel wasn't about to leave her in peace. Tugging on his arm, she dragged Colt up to Destiny, spouting an enthusiastic greeting.

Forcing a smile, Destiny said, "Hello, Angel. You look lovely today. You could be the bride yourself."

"Oh, pooh, I wish it were true. I just can't wait until my wedding day."

Angel smiled up at Colt, and the smile he returned was genuinely warm. Destiny's heart sank. Had he asked Angel to marry him when she had turned him down? Was he that fickle?

Why not? He was young. It went with the territory. He probably didn't have the slightest idea of what a long-term relationship meant.

She tried very hard to convince herself it was true, but she knew she was just lying to herself. Colt didn't have a fickle bone in his beautiful body.

Ashamed of herself, she smiled in Colt's general direction, trying, but failing, to avoid his gaze. Damn, he looked so sexy today. "Nice to see you again, Colt. I'm glad you decided to come."

Colt's face was impassive as he said, "Why wouldn't I be here, Destiny? Paul and Faith are my best friends. I'd never let them down."

It was obvious to Destiny that he was telling her that she had let him down. That the wedding was the only reason he was there. That he had ended their relationship and had no intentions of renewing it.

Swallowing her pride, Destiny said, "Well, if you two will excuse me, I've got some things to do before the ceremony." Flashing one last look at Colt's rigid face, she entered the house.

Seeing Faith in her beautiful gown of pale blue batiste, Destiny pushed all thoughts of Colt from her mind. This was Faith's day, and she wouldn't let any gloominess on her part spoil it for her.

"Oh, Faith, you look beautiful."

Faith blushed prettily, then turned with a warm smile to the man standing beside her. "Destiny, this is Reverend Skinner. He'll be saying the words over Paul and me." Then glancing out the window, she spied Paul heading for the door and gave out a little shriek. "Oh, dear, he mustn't see me." Lifting her skirts, she flew into the bedroom.

Destiny laughed merrily until she saw that Paul wasn't alone. Colt and Angel were with him. Close to panic herself, she looked around for a safe refuge and saw Hunt Farley. He must have followed her to the house. For the first time since he started guarding her, she was grateful for his presence.

Walking swiftly to his side, she looped her arm through his, and said, "Hunt, don't leave me. I need you."

An odd feeling came over Hunt, hearing Destiny's soft plea.

It was a strange letting go of something inside, a loosening of the rigid control he had always had on his heart.

She needed him.

Warmth spread through his body as he gazed down at her lovely face. He opened his mouth to answer her when he saw Colt come through the door with Angel on his arm. He should have guessed. Destiny didn't want or need him. She was upset about seeing Colt and Angel together.

When Colt entered the house, something came over Destiny. She wanted him to feel the pangs of jealousy the same way that she did. Without thinking of the consequences, she began to flirt outrageously with Hunt, smiling up to his face as if he were the most fascinating man alive. Well, maybe he was. Next to Colt.

Colt watched Destiny cozy up to Hunt and had to control the urge to throttle her. Hunt was only human. If she didn't turn down the heat real soon, the poor guy would be in a bad way. Gazing at Hunt's face to see how he was holding up, Colt knew he wasn't enjoying Destiny's flirtatious manner one bit. He knew, because whenever Hunt got angry, the nerve in his cheek twitched a warning.

It was twitching now.

Smiling to himself, he decided to stand back and enjoy the scene. Destiny didn't know what she was getting into taking on the likes of Hunt Farley. Wouldn't surprise him a bit if Hunt took her over his knee and spanked her as she deserved.

The Seminoles arrived then, and reluctantly, Colt went out to greet them, leaving Destiny alone with Hunt.

Hunt waited for Colt and the others to leave, then spoke his mind. "Don't ever do that again unless you mean it."

Staring at Hunt in surprise, Destiny realized for the first time that she had been playing with Hunt's feelings as well as Colt's. What surprised her even more was the fact that he seemed to care for her.

"I'm sorry, Hunt. I wasn't thinking . . ."

Hunt squinted his eyes down to a narrow slit, but that didn't hide the heat that generated from them. "I don't like being used to fuel another man's passion."

Guilt-ridden, she lashed back at him, "I said I was sorry."

Jutting his face just inches from hers, he said in a low, threatening voice, "Woman, I'm a man like any other. Don't underestimate your power to seduce me. You might get what you asked for." With that he went outside to join Colt in greeting the Seminoles.

Colt and Hunt and Paul acted as hosts to the Seminole, escorting them around the grounds to make sure there were no misunderstandings between them and the townsfolk. Everyone was on their best behavior, it seemed, except Brent, who was getting slowly sloshed, as usual.

Colt had to suppress more than one chuckle when he saw the way some of the more timid white women reacted to the Indians. You would have thought they were afraid of being scalped. He was surprised and pleased to find that Destiny responded to the Seminole in a positive way. In fact, it was strange, but she seemed more comfortable with them than she did with the white folks.

Could there be something to what she said about having a bond with the Seminole warrior she had visualized? If Shining Dawn was her great-great-grandmother, which seemed very likely, then it certainly could be true. Shining Dawn had always had a special bond with her adopted brother, Osceola.

He noticed that Destiny unobtrusively studied every warrior's face, but if one of them was the one in her vision, she did a good job of keeping that information to herself.

Leaning against a tree, he watched her progress around the grounds, admiring her graceful form, her lovely smile, and he wanted all the more to have her as his wife. What pride he would feel, knowing she belonged to him, knowing that she would be at his side through good times and . . .

Damn, that was just it.

Would she be by his side? Or would she go hurtling through time again?

For the first time, he began to appreciate what was troubling her. It was a real dilemma.

He was glad when Penelope announced it was time for the wedding and everyone moved down to the banks of the river. The trees had been draped with strips of Seminole patchwork banners and pale blue satin ribbons blew gently in the faint breeze coming off the water.

A hush came over the crowd when one of the Indians drew out a wooden flute pipe and began to play. It transformed the setting into a magical landscape and gave just the right touch to the wedding ceremony.

Colt turned to look at Destiny and was surprised to see tears streaming down her face. His heart melted with love knowing she was as affected by the beautiful scene as he.

Destiny's concentration on the wedding was broken as she became more and more aware of Colt's eyes on her. His powerful aura compelled her to look at him, and when she did her heart filled to the brim with overwhelming love for him. Oh, how she wished it were she being married now to this man who held her heart so effortlessly in the curl of his lips, the penetrating depth of his gaze.

Wiping her eyes with the tip of her fingers, she stared back at him, unable to break the invisible hold he had on her, the sweet joy that filled her at the sight of his male beauty. Of all the men she had known in times past and times future, none looked so wonderful as he.

But at the same time just looking at him brought an ache to her heart. She wished with all her heart that she was free to love him without fear of being separated from him. Instead, she was finding that the more she grew to love him the greater her fear became.

Happy shouts and applause jolted her from her solemn reverie, and she glanced back at Faith and Paul in time to see them kiss. The ceremony was over, their lives together beginning.

She envied them.

Leaving the happy couple surrounded by well-wishers, Destiny walked back to the house to help Lily Tiger prepare for the reception. Hunt caught up to her, and she was grateful, but she was beginning to feel very melancholy. Smiling up at him, she hooked her arm around his, and leaned her head against his shoulder. They strolled across the lawn, looking every bit like a couple to anyone who should see them.

But they weren't, and it was obvious to Destiny that Hunt was still upset with her. She could feel the stiffness in his arm, and in the way he carried himself. Coming to a stop, she looked up at him, pleading softly, "Hunt, don't be angry with me. If I didn't already love Colt, you'd be on the top of my list of potential beaus."

Hunt stared down at her with a fathomless expression and she wished she knew what was in his heart.

Hearing Angel Peabody's voice right behind her, murmuring sweet talk to Colt, she panicked. She wasn't ready to face her youthful exuberance again, and she certainly didn't want Colt to see how much his presence was affecting her.

Without thinking, she stepped into Hunt's arms, regretting it as soon as she did it. What in the world had gotten into her? If she couldn't handle seeing Colt and Angel together she was much worse off than she had supposed.

She quickly glanced up at Hunt's face and begged him with her eyes to go along with her foolishness one more time. If he abandoned her now, she'd be completely humiliated. To her surprise, Hunt gave out a little moan and folded his arms around her, his hold on her much tighter than necessary.

Looking up at him with a questioning look, she was shocked when his lips came down on hers in a fervent kiss.

She hadn't been expecting that. Her mouth opened against his in a little gasp and he took advantage of that and pushed his tongue into her mouth.

She would have gasped again, but Colt was tearing her from Hunt's arms and slamming into his jaw with his fist. Hunt staggered backward, then righted himself. Cursing under his breath, he cupped his aching chin with the palm of his hand and glared at Colt.

"Colt!" Destiny shouted angrily at him, afraid he was going to hit Hunt again. She needn't have worried, Colt was nursing his hurt hand and apologizing to Hunt at the same time.

"Damn. I'm sorry about that. Shouldn't have taken it out on you, but I'm not allowed to hit a lady." The scowl on his face when he looked at her left no doubt who he was talking about.

Infuriated that he could actually blame her for Hunt's sock to the jaw, she countered with, "Well, there's no law that says I can't hit you, and I will, Colt Mandrell, if you ever lay a hand on Hunt again."

Grabbing her firmly by the arm, Colt started walking her toward her house, while she protested all the way.

"What do you think you're doing?"

"Taking you someplace where we can have a private talk. We've stirred up enough curiosity here without airing any more of our life before every blasted person in St. Augustine."

"Oh, no you don't. I have no intentions of ruining my reputation any further by being alone with you."

"Ha! What reputation? Everyone here knows we're lovers, have been since the first time we met, I don't think being alone with me for a few private minutes is going to further jeopardize your sparkling reputation."

Turning to a group of older men watching them with great interest, he addressed them. "Am I right?"

A round of applause, followed by hearty shouts of affirmation cheered him on and he marched her to her home in righteous indignation.

"Colt Mandrell, I'll never forgive you for making a fool of me like that. Why did you have to hit Hunt, anyway?"

Shoving her gently through her door, he closed it behind him and slammed the bolt shut, locking them in. "Why? I'll tell you why, because his cheek wasn't twitching anymore."

Destiny looked at him as if he were insane. "What in the world are you talking about?"

Poking at his own cheek, he answered, "His cheek. It twitches when he's mad. It was twitching the first time you flirted with him, so naturally I couldn't be mad at him. But just now, when he kissed you, it wasn't twitching anymore, and I figured he was enjoying it too much. But I can't blame him for that. Pretty hard to ignore a woman ripe for loving when she throws herself at you."

"Oh?" she said, hands on hips. "Tell me about it. Is that why you spend so much time with Angel Peabody, 'cause you can't resist her when she throws herself at you?"

"Red. Is that what's eating you? You afraid I'll be wanting to bed other women?" With his face just inches from hers, he said, "You know how to prevent that from happening, don't you?"

"I know. Marry you." Destiny's heart thrilled hearing that. Even in his anger at her, it was clear he hadn't made love to another woman yet. Her voice became very soft as she tried to reason with him. "Oh, Colt, you know I can't. Don't torture me with that."

Filled with anguish, Colt raised his hands in surrender. "All right, Red, you win. I give up. I want you on whatever terms I can get you. I can't go on like this, seeing you, wanting you, but having to keep my hands off you. I'd rather chop them off, then go without ever touching you again."

Tears sparkled in Destiny's eyes as she reached out for him, circling his neck with her hands. Colt pulled her up against him and buried his face in her neck, tears glistening in his eyes as he held tight to her. She was all he ever wanted in this world, and he would have her at any cost.

"Do you mean it? Oh, Colt, I love you so much. It's been so terrible being without you, but you have to understand, I can't marry you, not until I know we can always be together. Can you accept that?"

Gazing at her with a solemn expression, he answered, "I don't like it, but I guess I'll have to accept it. I don't want to lose you."

"Oh, Colt, I'm willing to try. If I had my way, we'd never be parted. I just don't know if that's possible. But I see no reason why we can't compromise. Be together often enough to satisfy our need to see each other, but still live in separate homes. I need to keep some distance from you. It's the only way I know to protect my heart."

"Honey, I understand more than you know. I know you could be taken from me, but I swear, there must be some way to fight this. To stop it from happening. I'll find a way—we'll find a way."

She didn't believe that for a moment, but she kept her feelings to herself. They were together now, and she wasn't going to do anything to jeopardize that.

Overwhelmed with feelings too long ignored, Colt ground his mouth into hers, reeling at the strong emotion it brought forth. "I need you, Red, I need you bad." Reaching behind her, his impatient fingers worked at the lacing of her bodice.

She pushed him away. "Oh, Colt, I want you, too, but we can't. Not now. Not with all those people out there knowing we're in here. If we don't go out pretty soon, they'll be talking about us, wondering what we're doing."

"Honey," he pleaded, "it won't take long if we don't undress. No one need know. Don't make me wait for you. It's been too damn long."

Destiny smiled up at him. "For me, too. But we . . ."

Her eyes grew big with wonder as she watched Colt unbutton his pants, freeing his manhood. She knew what he
had in mind when he sat down on the armless wooden rocking chair Paul had made for her.

With quickening breath, and no need of any instruction,
she removed her pantaloons, then lifted her skirts, and maneuvered herself onto his lap. Slowly descending on his
hardness, she closed her eyes as the piercing began, holding
her breath at the wonderful sensation of him penetrating to
her very depths.

It felt so good.

So very, very, good, she wanted him to know. Taking his
head in her hands, she kissed him deeply.

Immediately, the chair started rocking, and Destiny realized he was deliberately setting it into motion. Holding her
waist, he used his forward thrusting to move the chair, and
soon it set up a natural rhythm that was pleasing to them.

It was a strange way to make love. Fully clothed. No
touching of skin on skin anywhere but the one area of their
full concentration. But oh, the intensity was so much greater
with no honey-touched caresses of breasts or buttocks or
other delicious parts to distract them from their goal.

Although it was accomplishing the satisfaction of their
most immediate need, it was far from the wonderful full
bodied, hands exploring ways they had previously made
love. But it would do in an emergency.

And this was an emergency.

Colt was right though, it wasn't going to take long. As
their need for gratification escalated the chair stopped rocking and their combined movements now became an upward,
downward thrusting, with Destiny's feet braced against the
floor for full impact.

She wanted to cry out, so intense was her feeling, but
she knew her voice would carry, so she stifled her cries
into Colt's mouth.

Colt felt her breathy cries, and knew she was close to

the end. Grasping her by the buttocks, he ground into her, capturing her tight against him.

The explosion came, rocketing them with life's greatest force in one blissful wave after another, and for that miraculous moment, two bodies became one, two minds joined in perfect harmony as Colt's seed flooded her, uniting with a waiting egg that pulsated with promised life.

Seventeen

Emerging from her tiny home a few minutes later, Destiny was sure everyone knew what had gone on between her and Colt, and she felt very self-conscious. Colt had given her a little pep talk before leaving, telling her that no one would suspect they had made love in so short a time, but she wasn't too sure about that.

Still, she couldn't stay in her little house all night. It would be too impolite. So gathering her courage, she walked outside. She was sure everyone would be staring at her, but found, much to her surprise, that she wasn't the center of attention, after all.

Everyone seemed to be absorbed in having a good time. The fiddler was about to start playing, and in anticipation, women were scurrying to find their husbands.

Most of the men were clustered near the boathouse, absorbed in conversation with the Seminole men, and Destiny was happy to see that their intense conversation seemed to be very friendly.

She tried to pick out Colt's tall frame in the group, but couldn't find him. Then she looked for Hunt's face among the men, but he didn't seem to be there either. Hmm, he was being derelict in his duty, she'd have to tease him about that.

Then it came to her that he might be a little upset because she had gone into the house with Colt. He was an astute man, he'd have to know what they had been doing. She wondered how he felt about that, but decided she didn't want to know. She had enough to worry about with Colt.

Would their truce work? Would they be able to see each other without getting totally involved in each other's lives? Now, in the hard light of day, she had her doubts.

Joining the women around the fiddler, Destiny clapped in time to the lively music, enjoying the easy camaraderie amongst the women. Perhaps, if she had to stay in this time, she would be able to make friends. Their cheerful demeanor gave her hope of that.

After a while some of the men were drawn by the music and the women applauded loudly when they stepped around the circle of women, dancing as their ancestors from Scotland and Ireland had for centuries past.

Faith joined the men, lifting the skirts to her beautiful dress, and dancing like some magical fairy sprite let loose to enthrall the spectators. Paul watched his bride dance, a look of pure joy on his face, and a feeling of pride came over Destiny as she thought about the part she had played to get these two together.

Feeling a tug on her skirt, Destiny looked down to see a small boy standing there, holding a folded note. She took it from him, and opened it to read, *Come to me now. I'll be waiting for you at the orange grove. I want you to myself for a little while longer. CM*

A flood of happiness washed over her. Colt wanted to be with her again, and there was no doubt in her mind that she wanted to be with him. Speaking to the boy, she said, "Did the man who gave you this expect an answer?"

The boy shook his head solemnly.

"Do you know where he is right now?"

"Ma'am, he rode off. That way." The boy pointed in the direction of the orange grove. Destiny's heart thrilled. Colt was so eager for their secret rendezvous, he had left already. Destiny started for the stable, then remembering her loyal bodyguard, looked around to see if he was watching. He was nowhere to be seen. That was strange, or . . . maybe it wasn't. This was such a happy occasion, what could possibly happen to her tonight?

Walking to the stable, she was surprised to see Big Red, saddled and waiting for her outside the stable door. How thoughtful. Colt had saddled his own horse for her. My, my, he was eager for her to come. She had been told that he never let anyone near his prized stallion.

She had never ridden a stallion before and knew that they could be difficult to handle, but if Colt wasn't worried, then it must be all right. Gathering up her voluminous skirt, she grasped hold of the saddle horn and pulled herself up. Big Red acted like a perfect gentleman. Nudging him with her knees, she steered him around behind the stable out of sight of curious eyes.

Bo rounded the corner of the stable in time to see her. "Where do you think you're going, young lady?"

"Oh, Bo, you needn't worry about me. I won't be alone. Colt is waiting for me in the orange grove. Promise you won't tell anyone, especially Hunt. Colt and I need this time alone to work out our problems."

Bo laughed with delight. "Glad to hear that. If ever two people needed to be together it's you and Colt. Go ahead then, I won't tell anyone."

Blowing him a kiss, Destiny rode off, eager to meet her lover. It felt good to ride free and fast like the wind that blew through her hair. Good to get away from civilization and all the complications it entailed. She rode on and on, enjoying the ride, gaining confidence in her ability to handle the powerful animal underneath her, and arrived at the orange grove just as the sun disappeared over the horizon.

Slowing to a canter, she rode through the wide rows of trees feeling a little uneasy. Where was Colt? Why wasn't he riding out to greet her? Was he playing games with her? She smiled to herself, thinking that was exactly what he was doing. He was probably going to jump out at her from behind one of the orange trees.

When that didn't happen, her uneasiness returned even stronger. Had something happened to keep him away? Maybe she should head back to the reception.

It was becoming increasingly dark, and harder and harder to see her surroundings. To make matters worse, the stallion suddenly started acting skittish, and she wondered again at her ability to handle such a powerful animal.

Dismounting, she guided him to a patch of tall grass between two immature orange trees, holding the reins in her hand as he grazed. There, that was better. He was much calmer now. Relaxing a little, she waited for Colt to appear. He was probably at a different part of the orange grove and would find his way to her very soon.

Believing that, she took a deep breath of the fragrant air and decided she enjoyed the peace and quiet of the grove. The only thing that disturbed the tranquil night was the loud grinding of Big Red's massive teeth as he chomped on the grass and the faint murmur of the breeze blowing through the orderly rows of orange trees.

Then, somewhere in the darkness, the sharp sound of a twig breaking startled her. Spinning around, she peered through the gray haze to the twisted shadows of the trees that suddenly seemed to take on human forms. "Colt? Is that you?"

Something wasn't right. Colt wouldn't leave her alone for this long.

No. He wouldn't.

Her heart started to race as an awful thought hit her. What if it wasn't Colt who had written that note? She had no idea what his handwriting looked like. It could have been anyone. But that was foolish. Why would anyone want to get her out here . . .

. . . alone?

Her imagination was getting the best of her. She had nothing to fear, she . . .

Big Red whinnied nervously, startling her even more. He began to prance in place, and she was a little afraid of him. She had to admit, she felt more secure on his back than off where she could be kicked by one of his powerful hooves. It had been a mistake to get off him.

One mistake among many.

She shouldn't have come out here. She'd mount Big Red and ride back to the safety of the reception.

Soothing him with her voice, she grabbed the horn of the saddle and was about to climb up when he raised his head and flattened his ears. Did he hear something that she didn't? Looking around her uneasily, she thought, was someone out here . . . watching? One thing for sure, it wasn't Colt. The stallion wouldn't flatten his ears to his master.

Suddenly, an eerie howling filled the air, and the stallion reared, knocking Destiny backward, then bolted off, thundering down the lane between the orange trees.

Destiny listened to the hollow, lonely sound of his hooves pounding on the ground growing fainter and fainter, until he was out of sight.

Frozen with fear she stared at the lonely landscape, knowing . . . deep within . . . that the howling she had heard did not come from a wolf. But how did she know that?

Because . . . somewhere in the deep recesses of her mind she knew what a real wolf sounded like.

Because . . . dear God, the howling had sounded . . . *human*.

Her heart raced out of control. She didn't know which thought was worse, that it was really a wolf or that it wasn't. If it wasn't a wolf, then what was it? Who was it? Why would anyone try to frighten her in such an unearthly way?

She tried to tell herself she was being silly, that whoever was out there meant her no harm, but the shiver that climbed up her spine was telling her differently.

Another twig snapped, and she jumped. The sound had been closer, but was it to her left or to her right? She took

a step backward, backing into something solid, and stifled
a scream. It was only a tree, only a . . . tree.

She remembered then that Tom's wife had been murdered
in this very orange grove, her legs wrapped around a . . .
But she didn't want to remember about *that* tree.

Wild with fear, she looked around for something to use
as a weapon, but there was nothing. Why had she ridden
off alone like that. Why . . .

She could feel his presence now and her skin crawled at
the thought of evil, malevolent eyes gazing at her through
the dark as if she were the prey, and they the cold deadly
eyes of the hunter.

*The dark-clad man moved slowly, deliberately, stalking
the delicious woman he craved. He could see her now, and
it excited him to feel her fear, see the sense of helplessness
emanating from her sweet body. That's the way he liked it.
Her terror hardened him, giving him great power, and it
made his desire to spill her blood in the throes of sexual
fulfillment all the more compelling.*

*He had been waiting for this moment for days, knowing it
would come, knowing she would be his to do with as he
wanted.*

*He would take her, then kill her, then leave her at the
very same tree he had left the other one. His hardness
throbbed just thinking about it. They would find her, just
as they found the other one, and they would know his om
nipotent power.*

*Pleased at that thought, delighted laughter burst from
his throat.*

Destiny heard the deranged laughter and became instantly
paralyzed with fear. She tried to run but her legs were too
heavy, too wooden.

She was going to die.

She had conquered time, had found the man she loved only to be slaughtered like a sheep by some nineteenth-century serial killer. It wasn't fair. Life wasn't fair.

But she knew that already, didn't she? She had lost her parents, lost the career she had worked so hard to achieve, lost the man she desired above all others, and now she would lose her life.

Eighteen

The reception was in full swing when Colt moved among his friends and neighbors smiling, nodding, exchanging small talk. The area near the river was lit with bright torches giving a festive ambience over the gathering of friends and neighbors.

Approaching the long trestle table dotted with lanterns and heaped with tempting food, he passed by without sampling any of it. His mind was on one thing only, finding Destiny. He'd been searching for her everywhere, but no one had seen her for a while.

He had even gone back to her house, thinking she was too bashful to come out after their lovemaking session, but she wasn't there either. He was in a quandary of where to look next.

Walking by the stable, fear prickled the back of his neck when he discovered that Big Red was missing, too. No one but Destiny would dare go near his stallion. They knew better.

Spying Bo emerging from the stable, he called out to him. "Have you seen Destiny anywhere?" The shock that registered on Bo's face gave Colt a sinking feeling in his stomach. Something was wrong.

"Colt, what are you doing here? Destiny told me you were meeting her at the orange grove. She was happy as a lark about it. Don't tell me you two had another fight?"

The color drained from Colt's face.

Something was very, very wrong. "What the hell are you talking about, Bo? I never made any arrangement to meet her there. Why would she tell you that?"

"Colt, I swear, she really did think she was meeting you. She was happy about it. Damn, what's going on? Did someone trick her into thinking . . ."

Colt didn't want to think of that possibility. "Damn it all, where's Hunt, he's supposed to be watching out for her. I don't understand how she slipped away without him seeing her."

Hearing the nervous high-pitched whinnying of a horse, Colt looked up and was jolted by the sight of Big Red, trotting over to the barn, riderless.

His blood turned to ice.

Where was Destiny?

He tried to tell himself the empty saddle didn't have to mean that she was hurt, or worse. It could mean that she took a little spill or that the stallion had somehow got away from her. But while his mind tried to soothe his fears, his heart sent him into instant action.

Running over to Big Red, he captured him by the bridle and mounted him, shouting to Bo, "I'm going after her. If I'm not back in fifteen minutes, round up some men and come looking."

"The hell with that, I'm going with you."

Colt had no time to argue with him. He kneed the horse and took off at a gallop. Destiny. Dear God, don't let anything happen to her. I can't lose her. I won't lose her.

But, in his heart, he knew it could happen. Knew someone had deliberately lured her out to the orange grove. Someone who wanted her to be alone, helpless. But who? There were so many people here today, it could have been anyone.

It could be the man who murdered Tom's wife.

Spurring his horse on, he rode toward the grove, fearing the worst, hoping for the best. If anything happened to her . . . He couldn't finish his thought. Nothing could happen to her. He wouldn't allow it.

No sooner had Big Red galloped out of sight than another long, drawn out unearthly howl penetrated Destiny's ears, sending shivers up her spine. She started to shake uncontrollably.

The sound was closer now.

Cold panic rolled over her as once again her eyes searched frantically for a weapon of some kind. In desperation, she yanked on a branch of the tree she was under, but it was unyielding. The only branches flimsy enough to break off afforded her no protection at all.

She was helpless.

There was nothing left to do but run.

But how could she do that when she didn't know in which direction it was safe to run? She couldn't tell where the howling was coming from, it seemed to assault her from every direction.

Pressing her back into the tree for security, she turned her head slowly, surveying the landscape, but that frightened her all the more.

Shadows swayed like ghostly figures let loose from hell.

Was the madman one of the ghostly shadows?

Was he moving closer to her with every breath of the night wind blowing against her in the darkness?

A sudden prickling sensation climbed up her spine and she knew . . . somehow she knew . . .

. . . someone was behind her.

Before she could react, rough hands grabbed her by the wrists, pulling her arms painfully behind the tree she stood against. She screamed in pain and in fear, feeling like a helpless rabbit caught in the jaws of a wolf.

No. She couldn't accept that. She couldn't die so easily. She struggled wildly to get loose, but it was too late, rope

was biting into her wrists—pulling at her—binding her—
holding her captive to the tree.

And then . . .

. . . the whispered voice of her attacker swept over her
as softly as the breeze that fluttered the leaves of the trees.

"Destiny . . . My sweet . . . sweet . . . destiny. It's useless to fight your fate. You're mine now. To do with as I
want."

Fighting her desire to sink into oblivion, to faint so that
she would not have to face her fate, she cried, "Who are
you? What kind of monster are you? Why are you doing
this to me?" Her words came out in a small quivering voice
she had never heard before.

And then the black-clad form of her attacker slipped into
view, standing before her like some evil apparition seen
only in the darkest, deepest nightmare, and her awful fear
turned to unbearable terror.

She looked at his face, hoping to see something human
about it, something that would let her know she had a
chance to survive, but all she saw was a black cloth with
slits cut out for eyes, tied around his head.

There was nothing human that she could relate to except
for the tight-lipped mouth that spoke to her so softly she
could barely hear the words it uttered.

"You call me a monster? You, who have taunted and tortured me? You who had the power to make me beg for what
I wanted from you? But where is your power now?"

A glint of metal flashed in the night, and she knew the
man had drawn some kind of long-bladed knife. She sucked
in her breath, and waited for the first slash.

"Where is your power? Here? Between your legs?" The
blade of the knife slashed through her skirt, causing her to
spread her legs apart to keep from being stabbed. The delicate fabric was torn asunder, exposing her legs to the terrible weapon.

She felt the swish of air as the blade jabbed between her

legs again, heard the grating sound of it scraping against rough bark, but she felt no pain. He wasn't trying to stab her, not yet anyway. He was playing with her as a cat played with a mouse before its lethal claws and teeth finished it off.

"Yes, that's where your power was. But it belongs to me now, doesn't it? I can take you as I please. I can make you beg for mercy, beg for release. I can make . . ."

Destiny heard no more. Retreating deep within herself, she sought refuge from the monster before her, sought solace in a prayer wrenched free from the protective cover of her subconscious. "Dear God, don't let me die like this. Great Spirit, help me as you once helped me before." But even as she uttered the words, she thought, no, not as before, please don't take me from Colt.

Instantly, the wavering image of an Indian appeared directly behind the hulking monster who still jabbed his knife between her legs as if it were some metal phallus in the midst of sexual intercourse. She willed herself to tune out the monster and concentrate on the soul-warming image of the translucent figure behind him.

It was the Seminole she had seen in her vision.

He was trying to tell her something, gesturing with his hands, and she suddenly felt a spark of hope.

Taking in a deep, ragged breath, she began to hope that she could survive. With strength and courage she didn't know she possessed, she shouted to her attacker in a manner that astounded even her. "Look behind you, madman, before you talk any more of power. See the kind of power I wield."

Taken aback by the strength of her voice, he ceased his frenzied slashing, and his hand came to a rest at his side. It was no trick on her part. He was sure of that. She sounded too strong, too sure of herself. There had to be someone behind him.

Very slowly he turned to face her rescuer, blinking in

confusion when all he saw was the misty darkness and the muted images of the orange trees. Where was he? Was it all a clever ploy to stop his attack, to stall for time, hoping someone would come?

She would pay dearly for that. For in the time it had taken him to turn around he had lost his hardness, his power. But it would return.

Oh, yes, it would return and when it did he would use his power to strip her of all humanity. He would use her body as he liked and she would know how godlike he truly was.

But, wait . . . what was that?

He cursed, as the now familiar sound of pounding hooves grew louder. He had waited too long. It was too late. Too late to retrieve his power once again. Too late to fulfill his bloodlust.

For the faintest moment, he thought about thrusting the blade into her, to extract some kind of revenge, but to what end? He wanted her to experience his full power, and for that she had to be alive.

Sheathing his knife, he delayed his leaving long enough to release some of his frustration. Taking her by the head, he ground his mouth into hers. This small taste would have to be enough for now.

Destiny's world began to fade to black as she endured the awful kiss, the pull of his mouth as he sucked on her lips. She could take no more.

No . . . more . . . Then suddenly, it was over and she heard him murmur "Till we meet again."

In the blink of her eyes he was gone, and she heard Colt's voice shouting her name. Looking up, she saw him riding through the trees, the most beautiful sight in all the world.

She was safe. Nothing could hurt her now.

As Colt drew to a halt before her, Destiny stared up at her savior mounted on the giant stallion, her heart in her throat. He looked so virile, so heartbreakingly wonderful, it brought tears to her eyes that even her terrible ordeal had not. She had thought just a heartbeat ago that she would never see him again. She had really thought she would die at the hands of the howling maniac, but she hadn't. God had heard her plea.

Or was it the Great Spirit, for she remembered praying to him, too. Now that she was safe, it seemed strange that she had done that, even stranger the remembered words of her prayer that echoed now through her head. "Help me as you once did before." Why had she said that? And, why had she amended her prayer, asking the Great Spirit not to take her from Colt.

That was the moment the image of the Seminole had appeared. She was certain now that she had the same mystical bond with him that Shining Dawn had with Osceola until his death.

But what had prompted the words to that prayer? Was it part of the forgotten memory of her childhood? But there was no time to think of that now, Colt was jumping from his horse, raining kisses on her face while Bo struggled to untie the ropes that bound her. The look Colt gave her was of such strong relief it touched her deeply.

As soon as she was free of her bonds, Colt enfolded her into his arms, the solid touch of her more wonderful than anything he had ever felt before. She was shaking like a rabbit caught in the clutches of a hawk, but he couldn't think of that now. His only thought was to get her to safety. Perhaps the man who had attacked her still lingered close by.

He shuddered to think of the monster who had come so close to making her another of his victims, for it was clear to him that the madman had used this peaceful orchard as a killing ground once before. Destiny had come close to suffering the same fate as Judith Langford.

The thought of that enraged him. Holding her at arm's

distance, he cried fervently, "Who was it, Destiny? Who was the bastard that did this to you?"

"Oh, Colt, it was awful. I didn't think I'd ever see you again and . . ."

"Who was it? Who did this to you?" he snapped, his nerves on edge seeing for the first time the shredded remains of her skirt. "Did he violate you?" Gathering her into his arms once more, he cried, "Dear God, tell me he didn't touch you."

"Colt, I'm all right. He didn't touch me, but he would have if you hadn't come. He would have killed me if you hadn't come. I wish I could tell you who it was, but I couldn't see his face. He wore a mask of some sort. It was awful, everything was so awful. The howling and the—"

"Howling?"

"I know it sounds strange, but it's true. He stalked me like an animal, howled at me like a wolf. Oh, dear God, he was going to kill me, he was going . . ."

Knowing she was close to losing it all, he caressed her back with his hands, and soothed her with his voice. "It's all right, honey. The danger is over. Whoever or whatever was out there has gone." He kissed her tenderly on the forehead, then turned to Bo. "Take her back to the house. I'm going to have a look around."

Destiny swallowed her disappointment. She wanted to be with Colt. She had so much she wanted to tell him, if only he would let her. "Colt, I'm afraid. Please come with us. I couldn't stand it if something happened to you."

Colt walked her over to Bo. "Go with him. Nothing will happen to me." How could he tell her that he had to stay. Had to search for a clue to the killer's identity. How could he sleep again, not knowing who wanted her dead?

With eyes shining bright with unfallen tears, Destiny mounted Bo's horse, the ribboned remnants of her skirt fanning around her. Bo climbed up behind her, encircling her body to hold the reins. Exhausted and in need of comfort, she leaned up against his chest, staring down at Colt as they rode off.

He stared back at her with a solemn face, but Destiny saw the concern that he tried to hide but couldn't. For just a moment, she thought he looked older, and she realized it was because she no longer looked at him as just a sexy cowboy. He was so much more.

He was a man. In every sense of the word.

A man who she could look to not just for the wonderful physical security his strong young body offered her, but for the emotional security she had been looking for all her life.

She just prayed she'd have a chance to tell him how much he meant to her.

Nineteen

Huddling behind one of the largest trees in the grove, he watched as Colt Mandrell rode to Destiny's side like some revolting medieval knight in shining armor. Cursing his luck, he retreated, moving deeper into the cover of the trees.

In sullen resentment, he watched as Colt took her in his arms while the other one freed her from the sacred bondage of the tree.

He heard her call out her lover's name as if he were almighty God and it infuriated him to hear it.

He had been so close, so close, but it wasn't over yet. Soon she would cry out his name. Soon, he would be her god, if just for one blood-sweet, enraptured moment.

Frustrated, and bitterly disappointed, a powerful ache throbbed through his engorged member, and he unbuttoned his pants to stroke it, in need of release from the terrible agony of unfulfillment.

Release was a long time in coming. But the fear of being discovered as he watched Colt walking slowly through the trees, his searching gaze taking in everything he surveyed helped build the excitement he needed to finish.

A tremendous jolt of pain spiked through him just before he came, and he had to stifle the cry that formed in his throat. And then it was over, his seed ejaculating against the rough bark of the tree that shielded him from Colt's view.

It was a pale imitation of what he would have experi-

enced with Destiny's young, vital body under him, and it left him still hungering for her, but he didn't doubt for a moment that she would be his for the taking. After all, when he was in a state of excitement, he was masterful, invincible, omnipotent.

He waited patiently until Colt turned his back to his position then in furtive silence, made his way to the other side of the grove where he had hidden his horse. As he rode away it came to him that he had passed up a chance to kill Colt, but he quickly dismissed it.

No, it would compound his pleasure to see the expression on Colt's face when he saw Destiny's broken body. In fact, the more he thought of it, the more he wanted Colt to be present when he took her life.

He could wait.

Colt wandered through the trees, knowing in advance how futile it was to search after dark. But as long as he could see at all, he had to try. He was desperate to find something, anything that would give him a clue as to who had lured her out to this lonely place. He'd never rest again until he found the man who had come so close to taking her from him.

Her mention of the howling had rocked him. He thought about her disturbing dream about howling wolves and wondered if it had been a premonition of today's events. Knowing her proclivity for the supernatural, it seemed likely.

The thought of her having to endure being stalked by a howling madman filled him with anger. Did the monster get pleasure from scaring helpless women before he killed them? Is that how it had been with Judith Langford before her death?

Rage began to build inside him as he thought about the brutal way his friend's wife had died. He had no doubt that Destiny would have been killed the same horrible way.

Thinking about that made him more determined than ever to find some clue to the man's identity.

Knowing the impossibility of searching the whole grove, he concentrated on the area where the larger, older trees grew, the most likely place a man would hide. The younger trees were not thick enough to hide a man.

But first, he would search around the tree where Destiny had been tied. There was a chance the stalker had left something behind. Walking over to the tree, he was immediately attracted to the large scrapes on the surface of the bark. It reminded him of the marks made by deer antlers or bear claws, but he knew they represented something much more sinister than that.

Bending down, he traced the deep scratches with his finger. It chilled him to think that any one of the knife strikes could have killed her. His fingers encountered a piece of torn fabric stuck to the bark and a shiver went up his spine. It was from Destiny's gown.

He plucked it off, then brushing his lips over it, placed it in his pocket for good luck. The thought of her looking so impeccably groomed and innocent just a few hours ago, drove him crazy. She had taken his breath away when he saw her in her pretty peach-colored gown. Why hadn't he told her that?

Standing up, he moved on to another tree, noticing that he could see much better now. He attributed it to the bright rising moon, and clear winter night, but knew also that his night vision had always been superior.

Trying to think like the stalker, he headed for a tree large enough to hide the monster. When he rounded it, his finger holding steady on the trigger of his revolver, he knew he had found something. The grass here was tamped down. Someone had been standing here.

Kneeling down on one knee, he patted the grass, feeling for something the bastard might have dropped, but there was nothing but the scratchy damp vegetation. He was about to rise, when his attention was suddenly drawn to something moving slowly down the trunk of the tree.

At first he thought it was some crawling insect, but on closer inspection he saw that it was a wet and glistening substance dribbling down the rough surface of the bark.

He started to poke at it with his finger, but stopped.

He knew what it was.

Bile rose in his throat as he rose to his feet and stumbled backward.

Blind with rage, he rode back to the house, conjuring up one image after another of all the men he knew. Which one of them was capable of raping and murdering? Which one? But not one man came to mind. He knew some pretty rough characters, having frequented every tavern in St. Augustine, but they weren't the kind of men who would stalk a female.

The trill of happy revelers drifted to his ears when he returned, and for a moment it seemed unreal. He had just been to a site where a murderer had waited to carry out a bloodlust, and now here, people cavorted unaware of what had transpired. He thought he knew how Destiny must have felt traveling to a different world from the one she knew, for he felt otherworldly now, too.

Unfortunately, it was the same world that held a madman who wanted the woman he loved.

His rage became stronger as he approached the house and saw Destiny looking so sweet and innocent in her pretty peach . . . His stomach lurched as he remembered the front of her skirt slashed to ribbons.

As soon as she spotted him she ran down the steps holding the front of her gown closed. "Oh, Colt, thank heaven you're back. I was so worried."

Colt gritted his teeth as he jumped from his horse, tying it to the hitching post before facing her. "You were worried? How about me? How about the way I worried about you knowing you had set off by yourself? Any fool would know how dangerous that was, but not you. No, not you!"

Destiny drew back from him, surprised at his outburst. He had been fine when he found her. Why was he angry now? "Colt, please . . . keep your voice down. I haven't told anyone what happened yet. I didn't want to spoil Faith and Paul's wedding."

Hunt walked up to Colt then, and placed his hands on his shoulders. "Colt, Destiny's right. This isn't the time or place to have one of your love spats with Destiny. This is a wedding celebration after all."

Colt knocked his hands away, shouting, "Love spat? Is that what you think this is about? Do you have any idea how close Destiny came to being killed by Judith's murderer? Where the hell were you? You're being paid to protect Destiny. Why weren't you doing your job?"

Hunt retreated a few steps. "What are you talkin' about? What happened? I thought she was . . . I saw you two go into her house and thought . . . Well, never mind what I thought. The point is, I thought she was safe with you."

Close to losing control, Colt said, "You really don't know what happened, do you? Well, ask Bo. He'll tell you. And the rest of you. You have a right to know, too. Your women are in danger. Watch over them. Protect them, for God's sake! Protect them."

Overcome with emotion, Colt grasped Destiny by the arm and led her to her home, walking her through the gauntlet of his shocked neighbors, who were murmuring nervously in confusion.

Too restless from rage and from frustration to be constricted in the tiny space in her house, he led her around to the deck where the orange sphere in the sky peered down at the young couple.

Pacing back and forth across the deck, Colt tried to keep his voice down so it wouldn't travel to the reception area, but it wasn't easy. "Do you have any idea how close you came to being killed today?"

Ironic laughter tumbled from her throat, while tears suddenly glistened in her eyes. "I know, oh, how I know. I'm the one who had to listen to the howling of a madman. I'm the one who had a knife blade thrust between her thighs."

Colt stopped in his tracks. "That bastard, that sick bastard. Did he hurt you? Tell me he didn't hurt you! I don't know if I could take it if he hurt you."

"Colt, calm down. He didn't touch me. He could have. He could have slashed me to pieces by the time you got there, but he didn't. He seemed to want to play with me first. Frighten me beyond reason. I think that's how he got his kicks."

"Oh, great. Not only are we dealing with a killer, he just happens to be a sadistic one as well. Lady, when you get in trouble, you really get into trouble." Angry, and frustrated, he took her by the arms, digging his fingers into her as he jerked her body closer to his.

"Don't you see, none of this would have happened if you had married me, lived with me on my farm where you'd be safe! But no, Little Miss Independence had to get her own place. A place frequented by mad killers."

Letting go of her suddenly, Colt stared up at the sky, shaking his head in resignation. "Damn it. You've made me all too aware of how quickly life can change. How fast things can go awry. I should have known that already. Since the moment I laid eyes on you such an unbelievably short time ago, you've wreaked havoc with my life."

That was the last straw for Destiny. Through heart-wrenching sobs, she cried, "Well, I'm sorry. But my life isn't exactly peachy keen either, you know. I'm the one who almost got killed. I'm the one who was sent hurtling through space. I'm the one who is so in love with you that I can't think straight."

The last of Colt's anger melted away. "Red, honey, it's all right. You're safe with me now. He'll never get near you again. I promise you."

In an instant she was in Colt's arms and he was soothing

her with his voice and hands and lips. "It's all right, Red, it's all right."

And it was. It had never been so right in her life. In his arms she felt a wonderful sense of contentment, security, the indescribable feeling of being cherished, and she knew she would never need anything more than she had at this moment. The sobbing stopped as quickly as it had begun as she rested her head against his chest, listening to the strong beat of his heart.

"Colt?" She looked up at his face, the face that she loved so much, and his mouth came down slowly to meet hers. He kissed her long and deep, and she melted into his arms.

"I went out there to be with you, so happy that you wanted me again. We were so rushed earlier, it wasn't enough to satisfy my craving for your touch."

Little Bit and Susan rounded the corner then, brushing past Hunt who had posted himself at the corner of her house. Seeing them, Destiny quickly wiped her eyes with her fingers. She didn't want Little Bit to get upset seeing her crying.

"Destiny. Colt. There you are. Oh, my dear, dear child, I just heard about the terrible ordeal you went through, and I thank heaven Colt and Bo found you in the nick of time. I wish I could stay and comfort you, but my husband insists on taking me and Susan home this very minute. He wants to join a band of vigilantes that will hunt for that awful monster."

Embracing Destiny, she held onto her a long time, saying, "It's just too terrible to think of, isn't it, dear. I'm so very glad you have Colt to watch over you."

Colt leaned over to kiss his diminutive mother, patting her on the back. "I'll walk you over to your carriage. There's something I need to talk to Daddy about."

Glancing curiously over at Destiny, Little Bit couldn't help wondering if it had anything to do with her. "Why don't you call it a night. You look exhausted."

"I will. And you drive home safely."

Suddenly reluctant to leave, Little Bit inquired, "Will I see you soon, Colt? This terrible business has me so upset, I'm afraid something terrible will happen and I'll never see you again."

Smiling reassuringly at his mother, he answered, "I'll stop by tomorrow afternoon. I have to go to town anyway, to see my lawyer in the morning."

Curious, Susan took her brother's arm as they walked toward the waiting carriage. "Lawyer? What do you need to see Farley about? I didn't know your affairs were so complicated you needed a lawyer."

"They've suddenly become that complicated. I'll stop by your house after I see Farley. You'll need to know what I'm doing, since it has to do with your husband. Speaking of which, where is he? Why isn't he taking you home?"

"I have no idea where he is. He deserted me as soon as we got here. But that's nothing new. I'd be shocked if he acted any different."

A sudden prickling sensation climbed up Colt's spine and he stopped, and looked around him. Walking over to Hunt, he spoke to him in a low voice so no one else could hear, alerting Hunt to his concern. Then speaking louder, said, "I'll be back, soon as I see my mother off."

Hunt answered in his usual manner, tilting his hat farther down on his face with a flick of his finger.

Destiny watched Hunt and Colt talking and wondered what they had to say to each other. They seemed to be on best of terms once again. She'd never understand men if she lived to be a hundred.

After Colt walked away, she made her way over to Hunt. "Don't go getting trigger happy if you see someone walking into my house later. Lily Tiger is going to spend the night with me so Faith and Paul can have the big house to themselves."

"I know."

"Oh. Good. I forgot to mention that to Colt. I think he plans on spending the night, too. It will be interesting to see which one of them gets the bed and which one gets the floor to sleep on."

"I'm putting my bet on Colt to get the bed."

Destiny blushed. Then, hearing Angel Peabody's voice once again calling out Colt's name, she frowned. Couldn't that man-crazy girl ever leave him alone?

She watched to see what Colt would do, and was very happy to see him lead her over to Bo who was standing with Angel's mother, Penelope. She relaxed completely when the three of them climbed into a gig and rode off. Evidently it was Bo who would be bringing Angel and her mother home.

They weren't the only ones leaving. It seemed the party was over. Word had spread of her ordeal in the orange grove. Men were protectively holding on to their women as they helped them into their carriages and she was glad of that. It was important for everyone to know that Mrs. Langford's murder was not a random act.

Standing by Hunt's side, she watched as the crowd thinned out. Saw Faith and Paul walking toward their new home, saw Tom Langford busily engaged in talking to the sheriff

She could go inside now. All was safe.

Hunt was here. Colt was here. The sheriff, too. They would be taking turns to watch over her through the night.

Yawning, she reached up to kiss Hunt's cheek. " 'Night." Hunt stared down at her as if he wanted to say something to her, but then changed his mind. Instead, he nodded a tight-lipped good night to her as she opened the door to her cozy little home.

The moon cast a dim, shadowy light inside as she stepped into her home, closing the door behind her. Because of the abundance of windows there was enough light to see by without lighting a lantern. She was glad of that, because she hated the greasy, oily smell they made.

Walking over to her bed, she turned down the covers and

reached around her back to unfasten the laces that held her bodice together, cursing at the difficult chore. If she had to stay in this time, the first thing she would do is invent the zipper. She didn't care a whit if it did change history.

When at last she was free of her too-tight dress, she stepped out of it, and started all over again on the corset. Yes, inventing the zipper was starting to look like a great idea.

Suddenly, all thoughts of zippers disappeared as she felt a sudden awareness.

She was not alone.

Picking up her silk duster, she slipped into it, trying to act natural, and slowly started toward the door, following the faint streak of light that beckoned to her from the deck-side windows.

Catching a movement to her left, she stopped, knowing she had no choice but to face her intruder.

A dark figure was sitting in the reading chair in the corner of the room.

If the angels were with her, it would be Lily Tiger sitting there. Perhaps Lily had come when she was out back talking to Colt. Perhaps . . .

But she knew she was fooling herself. Lily wouldn't have left the party until the last guest had left. "Who's there?"

The figure in the chair gave out a little grunt and rose. When it stepped into the faint light wafting through the windows, her heart stopped.

It wasn't Lily.

Of course it wasn't Lily.

She knew it wouldn't be Lily.

Brent Raiford leered at her scantily clad body, visible through the untied opening of her duster, and she quickly drew it tight.

"Don't cover up on my account, bitch."

Twenty

Destiny stared at Brent in shock.

She couldn't believe this was really happening. But isn't that the way every woman feels when she finds herself in a situation like this?

Brent stood there with a lecherous grin on his face, and shock turned quickly to anger. How dare he call her that. How dare he enter her home uninvited. Hadn't she been through enough tonight, having to deal with a howling madman?

Well, she didn't have to put up with a drunken lech, too. "Get out—now—or I'll have Hunt Farley throw your ass out."

"Tsk, tsk, such filthy language from such a pretty little mouth. You don't want to call Farley, it would spoil our fun. You like to have fun, don't you, Destiny? Like today, taking Colt Mandrell into your bed."

Destiny took a deep breath. So that's what prompted this visit. Brent was all worked up knowing she had been with Colt. Softening her voice, she said, "Brent, it's been a tough day. Do you suppose we could have this conversation another time? Having fun is not on my agenda tonight. I'd really like to get some sleep."

Brent took a step toward her. "You'd really like to get some sleep," he mimicked in a scornful voice. "Well, I'd really like to fuck you."

The words stabbed at Destiny's heart like a knife. "That's it. I'm calling . . ."

Destiny never got a chance to finish her sentence. Moving unexpectedly fast for a drunk man, Brent grasped her around the waist with one hand and cut off her scream with his other, clamping her tight over the mouth and nose. Destiny struggled against him, but he was too strong.

"There. That's more like it. Now we won't have to worry about being interrupted. I snuck in here when I saw you were busily engaged in an argument with Colt on your deck. I waited for you here, planning the fun we can have in your little house all pink and pretty and shaped just like the part of you men have given up priceless diamonds to explore."

Destiny's heart sank. She knew it wasn't just his drunkenness that had prompted his sick words. This man clearly hated women.

"Isn't that why you moved out here all by yourself? So you'd be free to entertain men in your cunt-shaped house? Admit it, sweetheart, you don't really want me to leave. I can do things for you that you never dreamed of. I can bring you to your knees in awe, I can make you beg for it, I can . . ."

Desperate to be free, Destiny's hand groped behind her, searching for his most vulnerable spot. Finding what she was looking for, she squeezed it hard. Brent let go of her with a shout of pain, and she ran for the door and flung it open.

Hunt and Colt were there in an instant, rushing past her, revolvers drawn. Destiny followed them back into the house.

Brent almost seemed to expect them, for he chuckled evilly, and said, "Sorry, boys, have I been sniffing too close to your territory?"

The next thing Destiny knew, Colt's fist was pounding into Brent's face, and he was toppling over. Hunt had to pull Colt off him or he would have beat him to a pulp.

Hearing the commotion, Tom Langford and the sheriff ran to the house and Hunt explained what had happened.

The sheriff raised the lantern he was carrying to Brent's face. "Drunk as a skunk. Think I'll just let ol' Brent sleep it off in the jail house. His wife can come collect him in the mornin'. I wouldn't want to be in his shoes when she does."

"Before you go," Colt said, "I've got one thing to say to my brother-in-law here." Walking over to Brent, he took him by the lapels of his jacket, yanking him close to his face. "Just want you to know I've written Susan out of my will. I'm going to the lawyers in the morning to sign the papers. She'll inherit nothing. You hear. Nothing! So there's no reason for you to lust after my land anymore. And you'd damn well better never lust after my woman again. You got that straight, or are you too drunk to remember?"

The hatred emanating from Brent's eyes was stone cold. "I won't forget."

Destiny felt a chill go up her spine at his words, and was glad when the sheriff and Tom left with Brent walking between them. They passed Lily Tiger as she came through the door carrying a candle. "You all right, Destiny?"

"I'm fine, Lily. I was never in any danger. Not with my two heros here on the job."

Destiny smiled at Hunt, and then Colt, but they didn't smile back. They were looking at each other with a serious expression on their faces, and she realized their minds were still on Brent Raiford.

"Well, thank you both. I'm sure we don't have to worry about Brent anymore."

"That's where you're wrong, honey," Hunt said, "I'm thinking we better start worrying a whole lot about him."

She would have thought Hunt's worries ridiculous, but for one small thing . . . When she had looked into Brent's eyes in the light of the lantern she could have sworn he was sober. Why would he pretend to be drunk?

Suddenly too tired to think, she was glad when Lily Tiger suggested that the men leave. Slipping into a cotton nightgown and then into bed, she was fast asleep before Lily had a chance to blow out the lantern.

The howling of wolves woke Destiny with a start. Opening her eyes in the pink paleness of the new day, her gaze took in the sleeping form of Lily beside her in bed and the pounding of her heart slowed to a normal, steady beat. Everything was all right.

It was just a dream.

Just another dream of wolves.

No need to wonder why she dreamt of them now, it was all too obvious. Her encounter with the howler in the orange grove. Where was he now? Waiting for her to make a fatal mistake? Remembering that Colt had been sleeping in the chair by the window, she glanced over there and found he was gone.

Feeling suddenly vulnerable, she climbed out of bed and walked over to the windows that circled the room, peering out of each of them as she searched for any sign of Hunt or Colt. She needed the reassurance of knowing someone was watching over her.

Through the window overlooking the deck, she saw a figure slouched in a chair and became alarmed. Whoever it was was asleep, or . . .

No. The possibility of the killer creeping up on Hunt or Colt seemed too remote. Hunt had eyes in the back of his head, and she wouldn't be surprised if he could see through the dark, like a cat, or a panther.

Opening the door, she stepped out onto the deck and the faint morning breeze from the river caught at her nightgown causing it to billow out around her.

But what if it wasn't Hunt out there? What if it was Colt? He had promised to take turns watching over her, too. Could the killer have taken him by surprise when he was distracted by his worry over her?

She took a few steps toward the still figure, still unable to make out who it was, but thinking it was a strange place for a guard to be. He was an easy target sitting in the open like that.

She took another, cautious step forward, then stopped dead as she felt rather than heard the tread of another's heavier footsteps on the wooden planks under her bare feet.

Spinning around, she stared into the furtive eyes of Hunt Farley.

"Oh, Hunt, you frightened me. I thought . . . I thought that was you or Colt sitting over there. Who is it?"

"Stuffed my clothes with leaves to look like a man. I wanted to be prepared in case we had visitors last night."

"Well, you fooled me, only I thought maybe you were injured or, or, dead. Where's Colt? Is he all right?"

"He's fine. Left a few minutes ago. Had urgent business in town. Told me to let you know, he'd be back as soon as he could."

Seeing the disappointment on her face, Hunt felt a stab of pain to his heart. Why couldn't it be him that had seen her first. Maybe he would have had a chance then.

Staring down at her, so soft and feminine looking in her nightgown, he felt a deep sense of loss, mingled with desire. "I think you'd better go back inside."

Destiny was surprised by the husky, urgent way he spoke and reached out to touch his arm. "Are you all right?"

"I will be when you go back inside."

Destiny was puzzled by his coolness until she saw the way he was looking at her, his eyes grazing over her body.

Suddenly conscious that she wore only a thin cotton gown, she wondered how much of her body he could see through it in the pale dawn light. She remembered him telling her once before that he was only a man, that he could be seduced like any other. That's the last thing she wanted to do to this man who she admired so much. "I'm sorry . . . I'll go in now."

She started for her door, but stopped at the sound of his voice, low and urgent. "Whatever it is that's keeping you from marrying Colt—settle it soon, before you have every man from here to Tallahassee trying to claim you as their own . . . and Destiny . . . I'll be one of them."

Destiny turned to face Hunt. Smiling softly, she said, "Any woman would be proud to be courted by you, and I'm no exception. But, Hunt, believe me, I'm not the right woman for you. Right now, I'm not the right woman for any man."

"You may believe that, but that don't change the facts. This is a rough society we live in. A man's society where women living on their own just can't fit in. You need a man, or a bodyguard; I'm thinking you'll be happier with a man."

Staring at the lean, masculine form before her, she answered, "Thank you for your advice, Hunt. I'll think about what you had to say." With that, she went inside and closed the door behind her. Sighing deeply, she climbed back in bed beside the now snoring Lily Tiger.

Between the snoring, the trauma she had been through, and her fear of dreaming about howling wolves again, she decided it was useless to try and sleep again.

Things were going from bad to worse very rapidly. And now, she not only had to worry about Colt's feelings but Hunt's as well. What a mess she was making of her life.

Hunt was right, though. It was time to stop trying to keep Colt on a shelf like some little wooden doll she could take down and play with when she had a mind. He was a man in need of a wife, and she was a woman in need of him. The love they shared was too powerful to be denied. She would tell him that as soon as he returned. She would tell him she was ready to put her fears behind her and be his wife.

And if that meant that some day in the future she was swept back to her own time, then, she would just have to face up to it. She wasn't going to waste one more moment worrying about something that might never be. After her close call with death last night, she knew life was too, too short to deny one moment of happiness.

But just as quickly as she decided on that, she changed her mind again. There was one powerful reason why she couldn't marry him. The most powerful reason of all.

Children.

How could she marry him when she wasn't prepared to give him a family? That was the one sacrifice she was unwilling to make. It would break her heart too much to have a child and then lose it when she was swept back in time.

Thank God, she hadn't gotten pregnant already. Considering the free and easy way she had been having sex with Colt, it could have happened all too easily.

Then, unexpectedly, a strange feeling crept over her, from deep within the center of her being, and she turned her head to look at the wooden rocking chair where she and Colt had made love a few hours earlier.

Had her body been so eager to make love then because it had been the time she was most fertile?

Time. Was it once again her enemy?

Had it trapped her into getting pregnant?

Deep in her heart she knew the answer. Time had always been her enemy. First, the valuable time of her childhood, lost somewhere in the murky recesses of her mind. Then when it had swept her from the world where she was revered and admired as a writer to a place where she had to struggle to achieve a life all over again.

Not to mention the eight years' time difference between Colt's youthful age and her more mature age. Time was her enemy there, too. But this, this was the most terrible trick of all time had played on her. Making sure that she made love at the only time that she was fertile.

She had named herself well. For she was destined to be a pawn of time, helpless to change what it had ordained for her.

From somewhere deep within her, she fought that idea. For her sanity's sake she could not accept it. For the love that she shared with Colt and for the child she was so certain she carried within her, she must fight it.

She would not be separated from her child as she had been from her own parents.

That was the one thing she would not stand for. It was the compelling force that gave her the will, the determination to fight hard to win.

She would conquer time.

She would discover the secret of traveling through time so that she would never have to fear it again.

Twenty-one

Riding into town at first light, Colt thought about the sleeping beauty he had so very reluctantly left behind. He hated leaving her, but it was important that he see the lawyer and sign the papers that would free him and Destiny from Brent's grasp. After today, Brent would have no more reason to poison his horses or send hired guns after him. With Susan written out of his will, there was no way Brent could ever claim his land.

He wished there were more he could do. Brent was becoming out of control, and one night in jail wasn't going to do much good. But the sheriff had no choice but to let him go. What could he charge him with? Drunk and disorderly conduct? Suspicion of poisoning an animal?

He sure as hell couldn't charge him with hiring George Dunn to kill him. He needed tangible proof for that. That's why it was imperative that he change his will immediately. If he couldn't keep Brent behind bars, at least he could prevent him from going after anything that belonged to him.

That included Destiny.

The thought of Brent's hands on her made him crazy. What had possessed the man to try and get her into bed last night? Was he so drunk he didn't realize what he was doing? It was hard to fathom the mind of someone like him, and that worried him. It wasn't hard to figure out what made most men tick, but Brent was a different sort of animal.

Animal? The word left an icy feeling in his gut. Isn't that what he had called Destiny's stalker? Was it possible Brent was more than a lecherous cad? No. That was too ridiculous to think of, and yet . . . who's to say a murderer couldn't also be a lech? Brent was complicated enough to be both those things.

Spurring his horse on, he rode faster, eager to get his business done so he could be with Destiny. He wasn't going to let her out of his sight so long as Judith's killer still roamed the countryside, and vowed he'd spend every night in her bed, or she in his, from this day onward. Even if he had to hog-tie her to accomplish that.

She could be a mighty stubborn woman when she wanted. A far cry from soft, pliable Angel. But he wasn't complaining. He loved Destiny's iron will, her fierce determination, and her feeling of self-worth. No weakhearted little female for him. This wild country needed strong women. *He needed a strong woman.*

A woman who would be his partner in every sense of the word. In work, and in play. A woman strong enough to bear his children.

Funny, before he met Destiny the thought of having children never entered his mind, but now it was as natural for him to think of having them as it was to love Destiny.

That's what life was all about, wasn't it? Family? Living together, loving together, making the most of what this beautiful land of his had to offer.

But it didn't make any sense to think of children now. He knew he didn't dare bring that particular subject up to Destiny. He was afraid it might frighten her back to the stage where she wouldn't want anything to do with him. He'd have to be patient, take everything one step at a time.

Arriving in town, he discovered it was too early for the lawyer's office to open. Hell, nothing was open yet. He forgot that city folk didn't work on the same schedule as people who worked the land, or cared for the animals.

Pondering what he should do to pass the time, he thought about the visit he promised his mother, but decided against it. She was probably still wrought up over everything that happened last night. Better to let his daddy handle her.

Besides, it was more important to see Susan right now. She had a right to know what he had decided. He just hoped she'd understand.

Meeting with his sister turned out to be easier than he expected. She was in a very subdued mood having heard from one of the sheriff's men that her husband was sleeping off a drunk in jail.

Colt tried to talk to Sue about Brent, but she changed the subject, offering to cook him breakfast. He took her up on it and was surprised to find that she actually knew how to cook.

When he told her about changing his will, rather than be upset, she seemed relieved that she wouldn't be inheriting his property. He couldn't help wondering if she suspected that Brent wanted the land at any cost, including murder.

After breakfast, they sat on the back veranda overlooking the wide expanse of the Matanzas River. "Susan, I've never understood why you put up with Brent. Why don't you leave? It's not as if you ever loved him."

"Dear boy, you never will understand, will you? No, I don't love Brent, but I happen to love being Mrs. Brent Raiford, the wealthiest woman in town." Gesturing with her hands, she said, "Look at this magnificent view. I adore giving garden parties here, seeing the envy in everyone's eyes when they see how I live."

"But you pay a heavy price for that. Living with a man who doesn't love you, who flaunts other women in your face."

"Oh, Colt, what a little innocent you are underneath that manly exterior. Don't you understand that his not giving a damn about me has given me untold freedom to do just as

I please? Do you think he's the only one who's taken a lover?"

Seeing his shocked expression, Susan regretted telling him. "But it's more than that. I'm not going to give up my place in this community to a new Mrs. Raiford. Some simple-headed twit with a wasp waist a pair of . . . Well, you know what I mean."

Colt laughed, relieved that his decision to write her out of his will hadn't sent her into one of her temper tantrums that rivaled those of their aunt Celeste. Which reminded him . . .

"Have you heard from our infamous aunt lately? Daddy told me he ran into Aunt Celeste in Georgia. She was on the arm of some carpetbagger lawyer from Massachusetts. Told him they were going to be married. Will that make him husband number three or four? I've lost count."

"I heard from her all right. This will be husband number three. She sent me a long letter, dripping with sentimentality recently. She gets that way every time she falls in love. She went overboard this time though, telling me how much she loved me, and that she wanted me to know that she was not my aunt, but my *mother*."

Colt almost choked over that news. "What?"

"Oh, Colt, it comes as no surprise to me. I've known that for ever so long. Little Bit is much too nice a person to have given birth to me. Don't tell me you never suspected?"

"Of course, I never suspected. Are you sure of this? Did you ask Mother if it was true?"

"I didn't have the heart. She's kept it a secret all these years. Let her go to the grave thinking she's protected me from the awful truth."

Shaking his head, Colt said, "I can't believe you never told me. How could you have kept it to yourself? I thought we were closer than that."

Susan's face softened. "I didn't want you to know because we *were* so close. I adored having you as my brother. Next to Mommy and Daddy, you're the best thing that's ever happened to me."

"My cousin? I don't believe I could ever get used to that."

"Well, that's just fine with me. You just go on thinking of me as your sister. That's the way I want it. Let's not breathe a word of this to anyone. It'll be our little secret."

"Secrets, dear wife?"

Susan swiveled in her seat to face her husband. Her voice took on an arrogant tone when she answered him. "You'd be surprised to find out just how many secrets I keep from you, Brent, darlin'."

"Actually, my dear, I don't give a damn about your petty little secrets." Turning his gaze to Colt, he continued. "You're here rather early. Couldn't wait to tell my wife about our little confrontation at Destiny's, I see."

Ignoring Brent, Colt started to leave. Taking Susan's hands in his, he pulled her to her feet and hugged her. "Sue, you'll always be my big sister. Remember that. No matter what happens, we're still family."

Susan hugged him back, clinging to him for a long moment. She couldn't explain it, but she suddenly feared the secure little circle of her family was about to be breached. Blinking back tears, she decided that was utter nonsense. She loved only three people in this world, Little Bit, Gary, and Colt, and they were all doing just fine.

Feeling more optimistic than she had in a long, long time, Destiny dressed very carefully, wanting to look her best for Colt when she told him her news. Lily Tiger laced her into a pretty cream-colored cotton gown overlaid with ecru crocheted lace that she had never worn before. Gazing into the mirror, she decided it was the perfect choice.

In a festive mood, she impulsively took her last remaining zirconia off the silver chain and wore it on her finger, and for luck, tied the Seminole medicine bag to the pale pink sash around her waist. After the warrior's very timely intervention last night, she felt comforted in knowing that his leather pouch was close by.

Leaving the cocoonlike safety of her little home, she ventured out to greet the new day. The weather was perfect, cool and dry, exactly as she liked it, the sun just warm enough to keep her from feeling chilled. The perfect beginning of a new life. Her new life, and the one that grew inside her.

It was an omen, this perfect day. A sign that she should tell Colt about the child they had created with their lovemaking. He had a right to know. Even though it was too early to know for sure, she could at least tell him why she suspected she was pregnant.

She was more convinced than ever that their impulsive lovemaking on the rocking chair was nature's way of making sure she conceived when she was fertile. For some unfathomable reason, it was important to her that he should know that right away.

Walking up to the main house, she headed straight for the kitchen, and let Lily talk her into a hearty breakfast. Faith and Paul were still abed, but that was to be expected. After all, this was their honeymoon. But Hank and Jim were there, wolfing down a breakfast twice the size of hers.

Lily Tiger was in a talkative mood and entertained Destiny with a description of the old sugar mill ruins she had found on a ride over to see Colt's housekeeper Maybelle. It seemed the two were becoming fast friends.

Hunt joined them, looking bleary-eyed and tired, and Destiny knew he hadn't got much sleep watching over her. She would be glad when this nightmare was over and everyone could go back to leading a normal life. Ha! That was a laugh. There was nothing normal about the crazy life she led, waiting moment by moment to be swept back in time.

"Morning, Hunt. I'm surprised to see you up so early."

Hunt sank into a chair at the table, and held his head in his hands. "I thought you'd still be abed, too."

"Too fine a day for that," she answered cheerfully.

He answered with a deep groan.

Feeling devilish, she teased him with, "Thought I'd go for a nice long ride this morning. It will help pass the time while I wait for Colt to return. Want to come?"

Hunt lifted his eyes, staring at her with a scowl. "You don't want to be going for a ride today."

Lily Tiger tittered behind her hand. She knew Mister Hunt didn't have any choice but to go along.

"Yes, I do. I'm going for a ride, but if you'd rather not, that's all right with me. I'll just go off by myself."

Hunt groaned louder.

Destiny had a hard time keeping from laughing. She knew good and well he wouldn't let her go off by herself.

"Just where were you thinking of riding to?"

"Oh, I thought I'd ride out to the ruins of the old sugar mill. Lily told me they aren't far from here." Hmm, that wasn't a bad idea. She had just been teasing Lily about riding out there, but decided she really would like to go. She was curious to find out if the ruins were the same ones she had written about in *One Shining Moment*. "Sure you don't want to come along?"

Hunt glared at her. "You damn well know I don't have a choice. I'm telling you I'll be mighty glad when you and Colt get hitched, so I can go back to leading my own life, in my own damn way."

"My, my, that's a long speech for you, Hunt."

Jim spoke up then, eager to please his new mistress. "Mistuh Hunt, why don't yo' get some sleep. Hank and me can ride with Miss Destiny."

Pushing his chair back, Hunt rose, and stretched his arms. "Thanks, boys, but it's my duty to watch over her."

"Hank? Jim? I think that's a marvelous idea. Hunt, go

back to bed. You're going to need to be rested for the afternoon I've got planned."

On the verge of giving in, he looked over the decorative gown she wore and said, "You planning on riding in that flimsy outfit?"

"Haven't you ever heard of riding sidesaddle?"

That was too much for Hunt. He laughed heartily, startling Lily. "I didn't think you had. I've never known you to ride like a lady. Somethin's gotten into you today. What is it, Destiny, what's so different about you today?"

"I bet if you tried real hard, you'd figure it out," she said with a twinkle in her voice that matched the sparkle in her eyes.

Shaking his head, Hunt decided she was one hell of an unpredictable woman. "All right. You win. You're much too frisky for me this mornin'. I won't be any good for you if I don't get some rest. You boys take real good care of her, you hear? And if I hear any complaints from the lady, you'll wish you'd never been born."

Jim grinned from ear to ear. "I'll jus' saddle Mornin' Star for Miss Destiny. She's a nice gentle mare. Used to belong to Miss Susan till Mr. Langford bought her."

"Used to belong?" Destiny asked curiously. "Why did Susan sell her?"

"Mornin' Star ain't fancy enough fo' Miss Susan. Not since her daddy up and bought Colt Scarlet Lady for his birthday. You see, Scarlet Lady done come from Belle Meade, in Tennessee. Dat's where de finest horses are bred."

"Umm. I've known women like that. Unhappy, unless they have the very best of everything. Can't stand it when someone has a more expensive car, or . . ."

Jim and Hank looked at each other with a puzzled expression. "Car? Is dat some new kind of carriage?"

Destiny laughed out loud. "Actually, it is."

In a short while, they were cantering down a beautiful

narrow road overhung with a canopy of giant live oaks. It looked like the entrance to Tara, in *Gone With The Wind,* but instead, it led into the ruins of the old sugarmill. Destiny was in awe of the wild beauty, juxtaposed against the stark brick towers of half torn-down walls.

They were indeed the same ruins she had written about in her book. "It's really very beautiful here. And so tranquil. Is it part of Colt's property or mine?"

Hank was very happy he could be of help to Miss Destiny. "Colt's. He bought it when it came up for auction. Folks thought he be crazy."

"Crazy? Oh, no, he wasn't crazy. It's the most beautiful spot I think I've ever seen in Florida. I'm so glad he bought it."

Hank answered proudly, "Would yo' like to stay awhile and e'splore it? There's a old well through the woods over there, and over in dat direction . . ."

"Guys, would you mind terribly if I stayed here by myself? I've got a lot of thinking to do, and this is the perfect place for it."

"No, ma'am," the two men answered simultaneously. "We can't do dat."

"Please? I'll be fine. You can still stand guard over me, just farther away. I'd really like to be alone to contemplate. You see, I've got some very special news to tell Colt, and I want to figure out just how I should do that."

Hank was about to give in to her, she thought, smiling sweetly at him, but Jim jabbed him in the ribs with his elbow, saying, "Nothin' doin', ma'am. Hunt Farley would nail our hides to da stable wall, if anything was to happen when yo' was in our care."

Destiny gave in. What had she been thinking of? There was a killer loose out there somewhere. It would be stupid to take a chance. She had a new life to think about.

Tying Morning Star to a tree, she strolled through the ruins, engrossed in the quiet beauty that surrounded her. It was just what she needed. Peace. Tranquillity. She hadn't had either in a long, long time. At least, it seemed a long time. But she would have it again soon, once she found the answer to her dilemma.

A gentle breeze blew through her hair, and she sighed and hugged herself, happy to be at such a lovely spot. Spying a clump of resurrection fern growing on an old oak, she reached up and broke off a handful of it. How poetic that this fern should grow in the ruins. What a potent symbol of faith that life could go on, would go on, no matter what.

She would wear it for good luck. It was the perfect reminder that love could be everlasting. She decided, right there and then, that as long as she had a sprig of resurrection fern on her, she would not fear losing Colt.

Opening the Seminole medicine bag, she placed it inside. It nestled in amongst the other powerful medicine the former owner had carefully chosen. Closing the bag, her ring caught the rays of sun and sparkled like a star-filled sky.

Attracted by the beautiful play of light, she stared into the depths of the shimmering stone and saw the image of the Seminole warrior take shape within it.

The warrior gazed into her eyes with a sad smile.

She blinked in surprise and when her eyes opened again, he was gone.

My! Her supernatural powers seemed to be getting stronger all the time. She wondered if it were possible to conjure him up without the aid of the medicine bag, and decided this would be a good time to put it to a test.

Glancing over at her two companions, she saw they were oblivious to her strange behavior, too busy playing poker on a stack of bricks they used as a table.

It was just as well. They probably already suspected she was a little crazy. Especially after her speech to them about possibly disappearing one day.

Strolling down a narrow path, she found herself standing by an ancient well made from coquina rock. It was in terrible condition, with deep crevices marring the low, flat surface. It certainly didn't look like any well she had ever seen.

Untying the medicine bag from her sash, she hid it in one of the deep crevices. It was a perfect hiding place, safe from wandering animals, or curious humans. Now she would be free to test her psychic abilities.

Feeling suddenly tired, she walked back down the path to the ruins and sat on the lush, grass-carpeted floor, in the very center of the ruined structure.

The almost eerie stillness that surrounded her had a very calming effect on her. Breathing deeply of the fresh, clean smell of the woods, she relaxed to the point of almost falling asleep, readying herself for using her psychic powers.

But her lack of sleep last night was taking its toll on her. She was having a hard time staying awake. Lying on her back, she stared up at the canopy of trees, watching the mesmerizing play of soft sunlight through the swaying branches. It was like looking at a living kaleidoscope.

Almost in a dream state, she changed her mind about trying to conjure up the Seminole warrior. It would be much more worthwhile trying to use her increasing psychic powers to bring Colt to her so that she could tell him she was going to fight for their love.

Never before had she ever seriously tried using whatever psychic abilities she had. There was no reason to. But then she had never been in love before. Why not? Why not use the natural talent she had been born with? She wanted Colt. Wanted to be with him in this wonderful place that another set of lovers, Shining Dawn and Blade, had enjoyed so many years before.

Drifting in and out of consciousness as she watched the changing pattern of light and greenery, she concentrated on his image, sending a message for him to come to her.

Come . . .

Come to me.

Her focus was so strong that when she fell asleep, she was still calling to him from the realm of her dreams.

In the lawyer's office, Colt felt a sudden urgent need to leave. To go to Destiny right away. With a flourish of his hand, he signed his name to his new will, then shook hands with the lawyer. "Thanks, Cedric. I feel a lot better now, knowing my greedy brother-in-law can't get his hands on my property."

"How did Susan take the news?"

Come to me.

Colt blinked his eyes. He could have sworn he heard Destiny calling to him inside his head. What was going on? "Ah, what were you saying? Oh, yeah, Susan took the news better than I expected."

"Well, knowing your sister, you're lucky you got away from her without a few more scratches on your face."

Colt caressed the scabbed-over injury to his face and grinned. "You're right about that."

Come . . .

There it was again. "Well, I'll be on my way now. I need to see a certain young lady right away. Oh, by the way, I'm glad you suggested keeping my will here in your safe. If anything should happen to me . . ."

"Nothing is going to happen to you. I've got a good feeling about that. A good feeling. You'll be around for a long time. Long enough to see me buried, I'm sure."

Colt gave him a funny look.

"Just an expression, son. Just an expression." Slapping Colt on the back, he led him over to the door and ushered him out with a jovial goodbye. Cedric was free now to go over to the Widow Peabody's and indulge himself in the pork pie she promised to make for him.

Humming a new tune he had heard at the Wayside Tavern, he put on his jacket and was about to leave when he remembered Colt's will. Picking it up, he headed for the safe. Bending on one knee he started to open the metal vault when he heard the door to his office open.

That's odd. Folks generally knocked before entering.

Glancing up, the last thing he saw was the flash of the knife blade as it descended on his throat.

Twenty-two

Riding back to River's Edge Colt tried to tell himself his compulsion to be with Destiny was no more than a natural desire to be with the woman he loved. But, knowing how gifted she was with second sight, he couldn't help wondering if she was in some kind of danger, and calling out to him.

A few weeks ago, he would have thought that a crazy notion, but then, a few weeks ago, he was unaware of a lot of important things. Spurring Big Red on, his easy canter turned to a wild gallop as he raced down the road. He needed to get to Destiny as fast as he could.

He told himself that was foolish, that she was safe with Hunt watching over her, but he needed to see that for himself. She hadn't been safe last night, despite Hunt's presence.

Coming to the path that led to the old sugar mill, something told him to head down it, but he fought the compulsion and continued on the road toward River's Edge. But the farther away he traveled from the rustic path, the more uneasy he began to feel. Big Red felt it, too. The animal whinnied restlessly, and his usual smooth gait turned to frantic, uneven steps.

Confused, Colt tried to reason with his head instead of his heart, telling himself he was turning into a superstitious old woman, but the urge to turn down that path became so strong that he knew it had to be for a powerful reason.

Pulling on the left rein, he turned his horse back toward the path to the ruins.

He was learning to listen to his heart more and more when it came to Destiny. She was much too complicated a soul to listen to with his head alone. Smiling to himself, he thought, after all this, if she wasn't at the ruins, he was going to feel mighty foolish.

He couldn't help thinking about all the ways Destiny had changed his life since she had come to him in the middle of an erotic dream. He was still reeling from it all. But he wouldn't change a moment of it. She was the most exciting thing that had ever happened to him, and he couldn't imagine life without her.

Starting down the path, he knew instantly he had made the right decision. His insides were a lot calmer now and Big Red reverted back to his smooth gait.

When the ruins came into view, he saw Hank and Jim, and that threw him for a moment. He had expected to see Hunt with Destiny. An uneasy feeling swept over him. Where was she?

With a sweeping glance around the ruins, his heart stood still when he saw her still form lying on the ground.

Dismounting, he strode quickly to her side, breathing in a sigh of relief when he saw that she was sleeping peacefully. For just a moment there, he had thought . . . But he didn't want to be reminded about what he had been thinking.

Walking over to the two men, he spoke to them quietly. "You all can go now. I'll watch over her. Thank you for keeping her safe."

Pleased that they had done a good job, the two men mounted their horses and rode off, tipping their hats to Colt when they passed by.

Breathing a whole lot better now, Colt walked back to the sleeping form. He started to sit beside her, but decided he was too nerved up to just sit and watch her sleep. Reaching his hands under her he swept her up into his arm.

Destiny felt herself being moved and opened her eyes to see the face that she loved so much. In a breathless voice, she said, "I knew you'd come to me." Then, circling his neck with her arms, she kissed him passionately.

Her kiss hardened him immediately. "You little minx, I wasn't imagining it. You deliberately called me to you. I thought you were in danger, when all along it was just a whim."

"It wasn't a whim, Colt. I needed you. I have something very important I need to talk to you about."

"Hmm, speaking about needs, I need something, too. I'm just wondering whose need we should indulge in first?"

"Mine, silly. Put me down. I didn't call you all the way out here to make love to me on the damp ground."

Colt tightened his hold on her. "I don't think so. I like the illusion of having mastery over you, even it it's just for a moment."

"Well, then, if you won't listen to reason, I guess I'll just go ahead and tell you my news. Just don't drop me when you hear it."

Colt started to laugh, but it was instantly quelled by Destiny's next words.

"I think I'm going to have your baby."

Every muscle in Colt's body turned to jelly.

Destiny tumbled out of his arms, landing on her feet. The only thing that saved her from landing on her bottom was the tight grip she had around his neck.

Still embracing him, she laughed. "I knew you were going to do that." Staring into his eyes, she said, "Well? What do you have to say for yourself?"

"Damn, woman. You took me by surprise. Give me a moment to think about it."

"Well, while you're thinking about that, here's something else to think about. I've decided you were right. Life is too precious to waste a single moment. I want to marry you. Even if that means we'll only be together a short while. I'll take whatever time I can get with you, Colt Mandrell."

Tears glutted Colt's eyes as he took her beautiful head in his hands and kissed her tenderly. His senses were flooded with emotion as everything she was saying sank in.

"Red, you don't know what that means to me, knowing you believe in our love enough to overcome your fears."

"Oh, I wouldn't go so far as to say they're completely gone. But that doesn't matter, because I've decided that between the two of us, we'll find the answer to traveling through time. Don't you see, once we know the way, we'll never have to fear it anymore. We'll have the power to keep it from happening."

Colt wasn't so sure they'd ever find the catalyst for traveling through time, but he wasn't about to tell her that. She was optimistic about their future together, that was all that mattered, right now.

"Tell me about the baby. Are you sure about it? When did it happen? Was it the first time we made love?"

"Oh, Colt, you're not going to believe this, but it happened just yesterday when we made love in the chair."

"Whoa there!" he said, holding her at arm's length. "Let's just take a couple of steps backward here. I don't know much about the subject, but I do know it would be impossible to know for sure that you're pregnant after only one day."

"But I do know. Don't you understand? We made love at such an inconvenient time, in such a hurried way, because it was the moment I was fertile."

"Honey, take my word for it, I had no way of knowing whether you were fertile or not. It was the last thing on my mind at that particular moment."

"I know that. But don't you see? Mother Nature did know. She made sure we were motivated at the right moment. Maybe, just maybe, women give off a certain smell, or an aura when they're fertile. I don't know. Whatever it is, it's nature's way of making sure we procreate."

Drawing her back into his arms, he hugged her tight. "Then plan on having a baby a year, 'cause I'm damned sure with both Mother Nature and you tempting me I won't have a chance in hell of resisting you."

"Then you're not upset about the baby?"

"Red, how can I be upset about such a wonderful living proof of the love between us?"

Taking her by the hand, Colt pulled her down to sit beside him on the grass. His arm snaked around her waist. "Just in case it didn't take yesterday, do you suppose we could try again today? If having a baby can make you believe in us, I want to make sure it becomes a reality."

"Oh, Colt. I thought you'd never ask."

His mouth descended on hers, cutting off any futher conversation, while his urgent hand sought the hem of her gown, hiking it up to bunch around her waist. Encountering bare skin, he realized with a jolt that she was naked underneath. That knowledge did short work at making him ready.

Groaning, he slid his hand down between her legs. Searching fingers found her hot, moist opening, and he caressed it slowly, exploring her in an unhurried way as he gazed into the face of the woman he loved so very much.

He wanted to make love leisurely, to enjoy her body to the fullest, and there was no reason why he couldn't. There was no need of hurrying. They had the rest of the day to be together.

Reading his mind, Destiny said, "Colt, you'd better stop. I don't want to come too soon. I want to indulge in lovemaking to the very last minute we can manage."

"Honey, it's all right. I'll stop in time."

His exploring fingers were making that highly unlikely. Pulling his hand away, she moved it up the safer territory of her breasts that strained even now against the lace material of her bodice.

Colt wasn't satisfied with that. Reaching behind her, he began to unlace her bodice.

Destiny obliged with a quickening of her breath. She wanted to feel Colt's hands on her bare skin, and she couldn't do that with clothing on.

He quickly had her undone, then pulled her gown and corset free as expertly as if he had been doing it a long time.

He had. But only in his mind.

Pushing her gently backward until she was lying down, he stood on his knees, staring down at the exquisite beauty of her body. This was his lover, his woman. God pity anyone who ever tried to come between them.

She shivered then, and thinking her cold, he covered her with his body. The touch of her under him was so exceedingly sweet he wondered what he had done to deserve such exquisite pleasure. Overcome with love, he took one perfectly formed breast in his mouth, sucking on the delicate pink nub that jutted out to greet him.

Destiny gasped, then pulled his head tight against her breast, her breathing becoming more and more ragged with each delicious pull on her breast. His mouth felt so good . . . so good . . . so good. Rolling her head from side to side, she reveled in the deep sensation that raked her body.

His mouth worked on her engorged nipple until it became so sensitive to his touch she thought she'd come right then and there. He must have known, for he suddenly moved to her other breast, wetting it with his tongue, circling and sucking on one nipple while his hand played with the other.

It was as if her breasts were the very center of the universe, for she could think of nothing else but the deep pleasure his mouth and fingers were giving her. Wanting to return the pleasure, and show how very much she loved him, she reached out to unbutton his pants. Pulling his manhood free, she caressed it with her fingertips. Colt made a little groaning noise and nuzzled his head deeper into her breast.

Destiny's fingers trailed down the length of his manhood, delighting in the hard velvet touch of him. She deliberately took her time, exploring where her fingers had never ventured before. Finding the hot, solid globes at the source of his hardness, she cupped them one by one in her hand. She thought about using her mouth on them the way Colt was using his mouth on her, but knew she wasn't bold enough.

That would have to wait until a time when she was brave enough to explore his body to the fullest, but oh, she was so eager to know all of him. Reluctantly, her fingers left the velvet balls and felt along the length of his manhood once more until she had the tip of it against her finger. Feeling a drop of wetness, she knew she had better be careful or their lovemaking would be suddenly shortened.

Colt almost lost it when she explored him so personally. Overcome with feelings that had to be released, he let go of her nipple and worked his way up to her mouth with little kisses paving the way. When he found her lips, so deliciously ripe and swollen, his tongue pushed inside, delving as deep as he could. But even that was not enough. He wanted, oh, God, he needed penetration.

Impatient to feel Colt's wonderful body against hers unhindered, Destiny unbuttoned his shirt, and hastily pulled it off him.

The Celtic cross dangled in front of her face.

The shock of seeing it jolted her for a moment, but then she relaxed, knowing that by itself, it had no power to take her from Colt. Laughing, she pulled it over his head.

Colt was jolted, too. He had forgotten he still had it on. He was going to give it to his mother for safekeeping when he went to town, but then didn't see her after all. Taking it from Destiny, he placed it on the ground, then, eager to continue their lovemaking, his head descended to hers. "Where were we?"

Destiny answered by reaching out for his manhood again. The touch of her hand overpowered him with an urgent rush of desire. He grasped her buttocks, pulled her cheeks apart, and then squeezed them together, delighting in the firm touch of them.

Destiny was rubbing his hardness against the moistness between her legs. The slippery touch of him against the front of her, combined with his hands moving over her backside drove her crazy with desire. Surely, he was reaching the end of his endurance, too? Surely, he would put her out of this sweet agony soon.

But Colt was having far too much enjoyment exploring her. That pleased her. She wanted him to delight in her body, to know her intimately, but was afraid she couldn't wait that long.

Colt sent one searching finger between the crevice of her buttocks, teasing her with tiny little jabs inside her, and the sensation of feeling him at two places at once drove her beyond endurance. Ohhhhh! She knew for sure she couldn't wait any longer now. Wet with desire, she felt herself opening up for him, making herself ready for his entry.

Colt didn't know how much longer he could keep from entering her, but the knowledge he was gaining of the erotic side of Destiny was too exciting to discontinue. He took little breaths to keep from coming, plunging his tongue deep into her mouth again to ease his need for penetration.

It was too much for Destiny. Feeling the erotic touch of him at three places at once sent her over the edge, and she maneuvered the tip of him inside her. Wild with desire, she moaned softly into his mouth. She wanted more. She wanted it all.

Giving in, he thrust into her mightily, closing his eyes

and his senses to everything but the woman under him. It felt so good to plunge into her silken cocoon. To feel her close around him, holding him tight.

The sensation of the three-pronged penetration was so overpowering that at that incredible moment, she would have done anything he asked of her, wanting to pleasure him as much as he was pleasuring her.

Still trying to prolong their lovemaking, Colt's arms wound round her, rolling her over until she was on top. She laughed playfully, pulling herself to a sitting position over him. Taking her breasts in his hands, he held them tight as he moved inside her.

Each delicious thrust sent deep, wonderful sensations rippling through her. She responded by undulating her body, timing her movements for the most impact. It felt so incredibly good that her mouth opened wide as if it, too, were being plundered. It might as well have been, for her whole body was caught up in the rapture, the need to complete the act.

Colt gazed at the beautiful sight before him, embedding the vision into his brain where he could remember it for all time. Her shapely form moved gracefully, caught against the background of lush green forest, and framed by the ombré-hued clay of the crumbling brick walls while overhead the sun sent ribbons of light to decorate her body.

Suddenly, Destiny cried out in tiny little gasps and he knew her time had come. Wanting her captive under him with his last ecstactic thrust inside her, he began to roll her over once again.

Destiny felt herself being moved, and gave in to his desire. Let him take her where he would. At this incredible moment, her body and soul were slave to his desire. Moving her arm out of the way as she was being turned, her hand brushed against the metal of the Celtic cross. Her ring hi against the pewter causing a little metallic sound to ring out.

In that one awful instant, which seemed to last a lifetime, the knowledge of what that sound meant penetrated her senses.

She had heard that sound before . . .

. . . just before she was carried through time.

As she felt her body dissolve and disappear, she thought *I know the answer now.*

Too late. Too late.

Colt's last thrust with her pinned underneath him brought him the rest of his needed release. But the joy of their lovemaking disappeared in a rush as he watched the woman he loved beyond reason vanish, swept away like the invisible breeze that tickled his naked body with cool fingers of air, then moved on.

She was gone. In the time it took to call out her name.

In shock, he raised up onto his knees, staring down at the spot that one moment ago had held the warm body of his lover. His hand brushed over the flattened grass, as if seeking some part of her that still could be touched. But there was not so much as a hair from her head to show him that she had ever been there.

She was gone.

No!

Not when they were so happy.

Not after all they had been through.

Not after they decided they would become husband and wife and live happily ever after.

Happily—ever—after.

A deep rage washed over him. Deeper than anything he had ever experienced before. Deeper than sorrow. Deeper than love. Deeper than the rapture he had felt in her arms.

His rage was so overpowering he thought he would perish in its wake. Raising his fists to the heavens, he shook them at the God who was so cold and unfeeling that he could tear her from his arms. And when the rage would not dissipate, he pounded on the earth until his fists were bloody and raw.

Twenty-three

December 1995

Drake McAmmon always slept late the day after a grueling trial ended. Today was no exception. The only difference was, he wasn't in his own home where be was free to indulge himself in such decadent behavior to his leisure. Here at his Aunt Lydia's he knew if he didn't get up soon, she would be knocking on the guest bedroom door, informing him in her no-nonsense way that his breakfast was getting cold.

He hated breakfast.

But he ate it anyway, knowing how upset his aunt would be if he didn't. Sighing deeply, he decided he was beginning to regret his decision to stay with her until a suitable companion could be found.

Suitable? That was a laugh. Lydia should have been the lawyer in the family. The questions she asked the dozen or so applicants for the position were designed to make them look bad no matter what they said.

For an old woman, distracted and worried over the disappearance of the writer Destiny Davidson, she was certainly capable of thinking very clearly.

It had been three months now. He was losing patience. It was time to put his foot down and force her to hire someone. Stretching energetically, he opened his eyes and stared up at the ceiling. Oh, well, he'd better get up.

He was about to roll out of bed when a low keening noise stopped him cold. He froze, feeling the mattress beneath him move as if someone had lain down beside him.

Almost afraid to look, he turned to face the other side of the bed, but of course, no one was there. What was going on?

And then . . .

Oh, God, then . . .

. . . the form of a woman took shape right before his eyes.

A very beautiful, very naked, very enticing woman.

Jumping out of bed as if the devil himself was after him, Drake stood staring down at her in amazement.

He knew immediately who she was and where she had come from, and that knowledge sent him reeling. His aunt had been telling him the truth all along. But if he hadn't seen it with his own eyes, he'd never have believed it.

Pulling himself together, he calmed down, knowing if he didn't he'd be in serious danger of a heart attack. As a lawyer, he thought he'd seen and heard just about everything, but this, this was truly incredible.

Regaining his senses, his thoughts turned to concern for Destiny. She lay there with her eyes closed, tossing her head as if she were in pain. Fearing she was, he called out softly, "There, there, it's all right." It sounded so trite, so awkward, even to him, but he was at a loss of what else to say.

Seeing no response, he suspected she didn't even hear him, or know he was there. Pondering what he should do, he decided that notifying his aunt of her return should be the first order of business.

Shaking his head in wonder, he tried to grasp the reality of time travel, knowing if he hadn't seen it with his own eyes, he would still be thinking his aunt had grown senile. He had to repeat over and over in his head that this was Destiny Davidson, a woman who had traveled through time. Annt Lydia had told him that every day since she had disappeared and now, the reality of that was finally sinking in.

He would have to accept it as fact now that he had witnessed it himself. How very fascinating!

Fascination was too mild a word for what he felt staring down at the exquisite beauty. Once he got over the shock of seeing her appear out of nowhere, he became all too aware that her nakedness was having a very profound effect on his body.

Funny thing, how fast the mind adapts to new ideas. Here was living proof that time travel was possible and all he could think of was the enticing female lying in his bed.

His eyes traveled over her form, enjoying the delectable view, until, sheepishly, he felt as if he were peeking through a keyhole.

The proper thing to do would be to cover up her nudity. He knew that. But . . . it took awhile before his body responded to that order. When his sense of decency finally kicked in, he covered her with the blanket, pulling it up so that only her head was visible.

Finding himself uncomfortably close to her, he had to fight the desire to kiss the sleeping beauty, and he tried to think of the last time he had been so sexually aroused. Damn. He had been spending too much time being a lawyer and not enough time being a man.

Slipping into his velour robe, he wrapped it tightly around himself and tied it, then went in search of his aunt. He found her in the kitchen cooking breakfast.

One look at Drake, and Lydia McAmmon knew something out of the ordinary had happened. His face was animated, instead of closed, his eyes shining bright with life, instead of being their usual dull, cynical blue. "Drake, what is it?"

Repressing the compulsion to giggle, he said, "Aunt Lydia, your little time traveler is back."

"Whatever do you mean? Drake, stop teasing, you know I don't like it when you do that."

"I'm not teasing. Come. See for yourself."

Aunt Lydia turned off the burner and wiped her hands on a tea towel, her heart thudding so hard it hurt. Following her nephew up the stairs to the guest bedroom she told herself, it can't be. Dear Lord, it mustn't be.

If Destiny were truly back it would mean that something had gone dreadfully wrong.

Filled with sorrow, Lydia gazed down at the sleeping, restless form. It was true. Poor little thing. Swallowing hard, she said, "Destiny, wake up, child."

The girl moaned and tossed her head.

"There's nothing to fear. You're with family. Open your eyes and look at me."

Her words had no effect. Destiny seemed to be in the midst of a bad dream that she couldn't waken from.

"What do you think is wrong, Aunt Lydia? Why doesn't she wake up?"

Ignoring her nephew, Lydia walked around to the side of the bed and reached down to shake Destiny's shoulders vigorously. "Wake up, child."

Still no reaction.

"Drake, call Benjamin. Tell him we need him immediately."

Lydia waited outside the bedroom door as her good friend Dr. Benjamin Sauter examined Destiny. This wasn't the first time he had come to her home in an emergency, and she was sure it wouldn't be the last. He came to visit every time she had a series of little strokes. But this was the first time he had been called to examine someone who had traveled through time.

Did she dare give him that information? No. How could

t help Destiny? It would only distract Ben from finding ut what was wrong with her.

When the doctor came out of the room, closing the door oftly behind him, Lydia crossed her fingers, hoping he'd ave good news.

"I've never seen anything like this. As far as I can see, here's not a thing wrong with her. No reason for her to be n a coma, and yet, there's no doubt in my mind that she s. If there was such a thing as self-induced coma, I'd say hat's what it was. But I wouldn't say that in front of my olleagues, they'd laugh me right out of town."

Staring into the tanned, wrinkled face of her old friend, ydia asked, "But what would cause her to do such a thing o herself?"

"My guess is she's experienced something too terrible or her mind to handle. So, she repressed her memory in rder to cope."

Lydia nodded her head knowingly. She knew of at least wo terrible things Destiny's mind might have a hard time andling, but she couldn't tell Ben what they were. He wouldn't believe her anyway. "How long will it last? What an we do to help her?"

"Your guess is as good as mine. Let's be optimistic. Say he'll come out of it soon. She has to, otherwise it would lefy the very laws of nature. Relax, Lydia, she's in no real langer. She's breathing fine and on her own. Everything lse is functioning as it should. To be on the safe side hough, I'll send my lab technicians over this morning to lo a series of tests on her. And, if you like, I'll assign a rivate nurse to care for her."

Putting his hand on her frail shoulder, he said, "I'll stop y again tomorrow to see how she's doing. Now, do you want to tell me who this young woman is, and how she appened to be in your house?"

"I'd like to tell you it's none of your business, but you'd adger me until I told you. Destiny is, uh, a distant relative

of mine." She smiled to herself thinking, *a very distan*
relative. A century's worth of distance. "She's been visitin
me."

After Ben left, Drake looked at his aunt with a question
ing gaze. "Aunt Lydia, I've never known you to keep any
thing from Ben. Why didn't you tell him about Destiny'
rather unusual talent for traveling through time?"

"I could ask you the same question. You know the answe
as well as I do. Ben is a no-nonsense man. He wouldn'
believe it for a second. You didn't believe it either, unti
you saw it with your own eyes."

"I guess you're right about that. I have no intentions o
telling anyone about this. It would ruin my credibility as
lawyer."

Wrapping an arm around his aunt, he said, "But you've
had a great deal of influence on me since I've been stayin
with you. Today, believe it or not, a hypnotist will be com
ing to my office to put a client of mine under."

"What in heaven's name for?"

"To see if under hypnosis, he can remember the detail
of a crime more accurately. A lot hinges on that."

"Why, Drake. I'm very pleased that you've become so
creative under my influence."

Laughing, Drake hugged his aunt. "You see what I mean'
I'll let you know how it goes. But, right now, I'd better ge
dressed."

"Oh, dear. I've forgotten all about your breakfast. Yo
just help yourself. I'm not leaving Destiny's side until sh
wakes up."

True to her word, Lydia sat by Destiny's bed until Ben'
people arrived, and then she insisted on staying in the roon
while they performed their tests. By now, Destiny had be
come more relaxed in her sleep, and Lydia was very happ
for that.

She winced when Destiny's blood was withdrawn into
tube, but knew it was for the best. But, oh, how it frightene

her to think that the poor child didn't even flinch when the needle pierced her skin. If she couldn't feel that . . .

When the tests were done, the nurse, Miss Kramer, took over. She fluffed her pillow, took her pulse, and blood pressure, then placed Destiny's limp arms back inside the covers. That's when she noticed the huge diamond ring on the patient's finger.

"That will have to come off, Miss McAmmon. She might injure herself."

"Oh, dear, are you sure? Destiny never removes her . . . rings." For the first time, Lydia realized that there was only one ring on Destiny's hand now. That was odd. What had happened to the other two?

"Yes, I'm very sure. I understand how you feel. But really, she won't even know it's gone, will she?" Miss Kramer gave her a sympathetic smile.

Lydia felt very foolish. Of course, she wouldn't know it was gone. Not if she couldn't feel needles piercing her skin. "Very well."

Reaching down, Miss Kramer tugged on the ring and began to pull it off.

Destiny's eyes sprang open. "What the hell do you think you're doing?"

The nurse gave out a screech and jumped back.

"Destiny! Oh, my darling girl, thank heavens you're all right."

Looking at Miss Lydia's startled face, Destiny said, "Of course I'm all right. What's all the fuss. Has something happened to you? Is that why the nurse is here?"

Miss Kramer and Lydia exchanged glances and Destiny came to the uneasy conclusion that the nurse was there for her, not Miss Lydia. "What is it? What's happened? Did I faint?"

The nurse recovered her composure. "Everything's fine. We were worried about you for a while when you couldn't wake up, but now that you're awake, we're all very happy."

"Couldn't wake up? Me? I've always been a light sleeper. I don't understand."

"Please," Miss Kramer said, in her professional nurse's voice. "There's absolutely nothing to worry about. I'm going to give the doctor a call right now. He'll want to know of your miraculous recovery. I'll be right back."

Left alone, Lydia and Destiny gazed into each other's faces silently for a long time. Then Lydia took it upon herself to break the ice. "My dear, there's so much I want to ask you. I can hardly wait to hear about your journey to the past."

Destiny gave Miss Lydia a wary glance. "What in the world are you talking about? What journey to the past? Oh, do you mean Shining Dawn's journal? I've finished reading it, you know. Found it to be very exciting. I just wish I knew what happened to her after the last entry she made."

"But, child, surely by now you know. Surely she must have told you all about it when you met her. What year did you find yourself in? I've been so very curious about that."

Understanding flooded Destiny's senses. Poor old thing. It finally happened. She's gone senile. "Miss Lydia, I want you to try and pull yourself together. You must understand this. I haven't gone anywhere, and certainly not to the past. So, of course, it would be impossible for me to have met Shining Dawn."

Hearing the nurse's footsteps outside in the hall, Lydia shushed Destiny with a finger over her mouth. "Let's not talk of this until after she's gone. It's a private family matter, after all."

Destiny couldn't help but be amused. Miss Lydia seemed so earnest. She was like a little girl playing pretend. "All right, Miss Lydia, we'll talk about it later."

Pushing the covers aside, Destiny climbed out of bed. At her feet were a pair of men's slippers, and a man's robe was flung over the back of a chair in the same spot she had put hers the night before. If that were not enough, the distinct aroma of expensive after-shave lotion hung in the air.

Uneasiness settled in the pit of her stomach like a coiled snake.

How could that be?

Staring into Miss Lydia's eyes, she saw the concern and knew that it had happened again.

She had lost a chunk of her life once again.

With her heart in her throat, she asked, "Miss Lydia, what day is it?"

Twenty-four

Lydia was faced with a dilemma. How much of the truth could she tell Destiny without causing the girl more trauma? If she told her today's date, it was sure to lead to questions that she wasn't prepared to answer right now. But what choice did she have? It wouldn't take Destiny very long to find out the date from some other source.

In fact, as soon as she walked downstairs, she'd see the Christmas tree out on the back porch and know it was no longer September. She was sorry now that she had let Drake talk her into having one. But he had insisted they celebrate Christmas, and she had compromised by consenting to put the tree out on the back porch. She had to admit she liked the idea of it facing the river where the boaters could see the lovely lights as they motored by.

Well, all right. She would tell her the date, but nothing more. Not until she was sure the poor child could accept the information without going into another coma. She didn't dare take the chance of that happening again. Oh, why wasn't Drake here now, when she needed him? He was used to being diplomatic with people. He'd know the best way to handle this delicate situation.

"Miss Lydia? I asked you what today's date was."

Trying to appear nonchalant, Lydia answered, "Why, it's December twenty-third. Why do you ask?" Watching with trepidation as Destiny reacted to the news, she was relieved to see only mild dismay. Perhaps she had a better handle on the situation than she first imagined.

Destiny mulled the disturbing information over in her mind. December twenty-third? Three months! All right, calm down. That's three months missing front her life as opposed to the first eight years that were still a barren landscape in her mind. Okay. She could handle three months. She didn't like it, but she could cope with that. She could . . .

A horrible thought suddenly hit her.

What if it wasn't just three montlts? What if it was a year and three months, or two years and three months?

In a shaky voice, she said, "Miss Lydia, please, oh, please tell me it's still 1995."

Miss Kramer entered the room in time to hear this. "Of course it's still 1995. You were only out a matter of hours. We've found no explanation for that kind of reaction, but perhaps the tests will point the way to our understanding."

"Tests? What tests?"

Oh, no, Lydia thought. The nurse is going to ruin everything. "Destiny, I had a good friend of mine, a doctor, come see you this morning. He arranged for a few little tests to be done. You see, we were quite concerned when we couldn't wake you."

Thinking Lydia was trying to cover up for her three months' lapse of memory for the benefit of the nurse, she was more than happy to go along with it. The fewer people who knew of her proclivity for losing her mind, the better. She had her reputation as a writer to think of.

"We'll have the results of the tests in a day or so, Miss Davidson. Meanwhile, you can relax. I just spoke to the doctor about your rapid recovery, and he feels certain we won't find anything terribly wrong with you. He did want me to ask you a few questions, though."

Lydia's nerves were about to unravel. Miss Kramer had no idea how close she was coming to causing a setback.

"I see no reason to have to question her now. You said yourself the doctor could find nothing wrong. That's very reassuring. So reassuring, in fact, that I believe we won't be needing you, after all. I want to thank you for coming out here on such short notice. Tell Ben that Destiny and I will be looking out for each other."

Destiny was surprised at Miss Lydia's abruptness. It wasn't like her. She was practically pushing the woman out the door. Even more surprising, Miss Kramer took it in stride, much to her relief, leaving after giving Lydia instructions to call the office if an emergency arose.

Confused and upset, Destiny tried to relax, but it was a near-impossible task knowing that another three months was missing from her life. What if she continued to lose precious time? What if the next time it happened she became irretrievably lost somewhere deep within her mind? It had to stop.

"Are you hungry, my dear?"

Coming out of the blue like that, Destiny had a hard time shifting gears to such a mundane subject. When the answer to that question finally registered on her brain, the answer, surprisingly, was yes. She was ravenously hungry. "Mmm, I'd love some of your wonderful crepes."

Miss Lydia's obvious relief made Destiny aware of how much the poor thing had been worrying over her. She wished she could keep from disturbing her anymore, but there were so many questions that needed to be asked, and Lydia was the only one who could answer them. The only one who could tell her what had been going on in her life for the past three months.

Lydia had to know. After all, it wasn't as if she had just upped and wandered off somewhere where Lydia couldn't see what happened. She was still here at the same place she had been when her mind went blank on her.

A sliver of ice crept up her spine, but she shrugged it off. She was just being silly. What could have happened to her here in the safety of Miss Lydia McAmmon's beautiful Victorian home?

By the time she finished dressing, Destiny had the shocking answer to that. When she went into the bathroom, she was horrified to discover she had recently had intercourse. The seminal fluid that snaked down her thigh was evidence of that.

Remembering the men's apparel in the bedroom, her heart sank. Had she been sharing the room—the bed—with a man?

Anger mixed with cold fear pierced her heart as she thought about her body being violated without her knowledge. It was monstrous to even think of. But, surely, surely, Miss Lydia would never have allowed such a thing to happen.

No. She wouldn't. There was no question of that. She couldn't have misread the woman that much. There had to be another answer. But what in God's name could it be?

She showered quickly, then dressed in jeans and a T-shirt, feeling strangely more comfortable than usual in them. What was this new awareness that permeated through her? For heaven's sake, you'd think she'd been stranded on a desert island for those three months. An island barren of modern clothing and modern conveniences.

She felt as though something very vital had changed inside her. It was as if she were adjusting to a whole new person. Running down the stairs to the kitchen, she decided she had to get to the bottom of this before she lost her mind worrying over it

Lydia heaped her plate with crepes and fruit, and Destiny's growling stomach decided the questions could wait until after breakfast.

Her unusual hunger surprised her. What was going on with her body? It seemed to be changing, too.

Opting for a glass of milk instead of coffee, Destiny surprised herself again. She had always started the day with a cup of coffee. Obviously, her eating habits had changed while she was out of her mind.

When breakfast was over, and the dishes stacked in the dishwasher, Destiny and Miss Lydia went outside to the porch. It was too nice a day to be cooped up in the house.

A delightful breeze was coming off the river, and it was the kind of perfect December day that reminded Destiny what she loved most about living in northern Florida. December had its share of cold days, but never for more than a couple of days at a time. That made the warm, balmy ones like today all the more appreciated.

The sight of the decorated tree on the porch threw her for a moment. It was a potent reminder of the time that had passed without her knowledge. Settling into a white wicker rocking chair, she began to rock, trying to settle her nerves.

A shadow passed through her mind, a half remembrance of something. But it was gone too quickly for her to grasp. She only knew it had something to do with . . . rocking . . . in a chair.

She felt a sudden tightening through her belly and below, and wondered what could have caused such a reaction. This was really weird.

Unexpectedly, she gazed down at her hand, and the heart-shaped stone glimmered back at her in magnificent innocence. If only it could talk.

She had already noticed two of her rings were missing when she dressed, and was just grateful that she still had her favorite ring.

The ring . . . There was something important she should know about the ring.

Frustrated, and angry with her amnesia, she turned her thoughts back to finding the man who had violated her. But, obviously, she couldn't offend Miss Lydia in the process. She would have to use some diplomacy. "Miss Lydia?

The men's clothing in my room . . . who do they belong to?"

"Why, to my nephew Drake." Then, realizing what could have motivated that question, Lydia answered very emphatically. "He moved in here with me, the day *after* you disappeared."

The relief she felt at knowing she had not shared her bed with a stranger was quickly forgotten as Miss Lydia's words sank in. Disappeared? She had disappeared? Trying to keep from panicking, she said, "What do you mean, disappeared? Did I just leave one day and not tell you where I was going? Or, dear God, was I kidnapped?" Terror coursed through her as she thought that could explain the sexual intercourse.

Oh, dear, Lydia thought. Now I've done it. Closing her eyes for a moment, she tried to decide just what she could say, and decided nothing less than the truth would satisfy Destiny now.

"I wish it had been that simple, my dear. The night you disappeared, I heard you cry out, and immediately went to your room thinking you were having an unpleasant dream. When I opened the door to your room . . . I don't know how to say this, you looked as if you were having a very erotic dream."

Destiny felt herself blush as the memory of that sensual dream came flooding back.

"Deciding you were in no need of being awakened at that, uh, particular moment, I started to close the door, when, lo and behold, you just plain disappeared before my eyes. Not even a puff of smoke to mark your passage."

That was the very last thing Destiny expected to hear. Had Miss Lydia's mind snapped? "People can't just disappear!"

"Don't you think I know that, my dear? And, of course, Drake told me the same thing. I almost didn't believe it myself, But, it did happen, and when Drake saw you appear like magic just this morning, why, I don't mind telling you

I felt vindicated. He never said so, but I just knew he thought I was senile or crazy." Lifting her head proudly, she said, "But I wasn't, and he knows that now."

Destiny's first thought was that the nephew Drake must be crazy, too. Maybe it ran in the family. But she knew better than that. Lydia McAmmon was as sane as she. There had to be another explanation. "Where is your nephew now? I want to hear his version of this. It's not that I don't believe you, or that I think you're growing senile, it's just . . ."

Lydia frowned. "Hmph, you don't have to try and explain it to me. I'm an old lady, therefore you can't trust my word. Well, let me tell you, young lady, there are countries in this world where age is still revered."

"Oh, Lydia, don't lay a guilt trip on me. I feel bad enough, already. It's my fault you've had to take on the awful burden of worrying over me. What's wrong with me anyway? Why do I keep losing chunks of time? If I disappeared as you say I did, where did I go? Do you know the answer to that?"

Lydia became very still, and Destiny got the distinct impression that she knew much more than she was willing to say. Was she just imagining it? How could she trust her instincts about anything anymore, when her brain was so unreliable?

"Lydia? What are you keeping from me? Please don't do this. I have a right to know what's been happening to me?"

"Child. I'm not at liberty to say anything right this moment. I have to look out for your best interests."

"But don't you see? The truth will be my salvation."

"Or your destruction. I can't take the chance that the truth might send you back into a coma. I shall confer with Drake. Until I do, it's useless to try and get me to talk. Mum's the word."

Lydia pursed her lips and made a motion with her fingers as if she were turning a key in a lock.

Knowing the futility of trying to get Lydia to talk, Destiny decided she could be patient just a little while longer. After all, she had waited a lifetime for the answer to her puzzling lapse of memory.

Walking over to Lydia's chair, she knelt in front of her and embraced her, hugging her tight. "All right. We'll do it your way."

Lydia gave out a satisfied little sound, and Destiny's heart went out to her. If what she said was true, the poor old woman had been through quite a lot.

A car pulled into the driveway then, and Destiny knew it must be Drake. At last, she would be meeting Lydia's mysterious nephew. She wondered if he resembled the dreamy man she had seen in the mirror.

The man in the mirror.

She had almost forgotten about him. That was odd. How could she forget someone that sexy? Then remembering the sensual dream she had about him, she decided she would be better off forgetting all about him. It was too depressing to long for someone who didn't really exist.

She watched with interest as the man emerged from his car. Seeing her, too, he started toward the porch, striding very fast. "You're awake! Wonderful."

Remembering he was a supposed witness to her rabbit-in-a-hat-type reappearance, she smiled up at him as he drew close. "I'm awake, and feeling mighty strange. Did I really appear very suddenly in your bed?"

He was on the way up the stairs now, and Destiny gazed into his wonderful blue eyes, and felt a shimmer of recognition. They reminded her of someone. But for the life of her she couldn't think who. Certainly not her dream lover. He had gray eyes.

"Absolutely floored me. I haven't recovered yet. Cut short my appointments so I could see how you were doing.

I must say, I never expected to see you up and around." Holding out his hand to her, his face was transposed into a friendly grin. "I'm Drake McAmmon, Lydia's nephew."

Smiling brightly, Destiny took his hand. "Hi, I'm Destiny Davidson, Lydia's . . . friend."

"That's putting it mildly. According to my aunt you're . . ." Catching his aunt's eye, he saw the warning signal and changed his words. "Uh, her very newest friend."

Destiny didn't miss the exchanged looks between Lydia and her nephew, but she kept it to herself. Obviously, she was going to have to be patient.

Lydia immediately changed the subject. "You are home early tonight, dear. Does that mean you didn't get a chance to see your client hypnotized?"

"To the contrary. I did, and it was very effective. The man was able to remember the registration number on a car. After that, it was just a matter of calling up the motor vehicle's registry and finding out the name of the car's owner."

"What's this all about, Drake? Your aunt told me you were a lawyer. What in the world do you have to do with a hypnotist?"

"Just one of the tools of the trade."

Gazing into his eyes, Destiny couldn't help but compare him to the man in her dream, and she was disappointed to find they looked nothing alike. Where her dream lover was fair, Drake was dark haired, the only thing remotely resembling him was Drake's tall, lean body. She had to admit though, Drake was very good-looking and certainly had a lot of sex appeal. But it was those gorgeous eyes that held her attention. She had seen eyes like that before, when she was just a child. A child . . . As fast as it had appeared to her, the memory was gone, slipping out of sight like a shy ghost, reluctant to be seen.

Drake saw the way she was looking at him and his heart started racing. It didn't help that he kept picturing her as she had been this morning. Lying lusciously naked in his bed. He was going to have a hard time keeping his hands to himself. Thank goodness, his aunt would be there to act as chaperone.

Because this sexy lady definitely needed one where he was concerned.

By the time night fell, Destiny was feeling very comfortable around Drake. He wasn't at all the stodgy, uptight lawyer she expected him to be. After helping Lydia up the stairs to her bedroom, he had taken her by the hand and led her over to the balcony library.

"I thought we could sit here awhile and talk."

From the look in his eyes, Destiny felt sure he wanted to do more than talk, but she decided she'd deal with that when the time came. Her comfort level was decreasing very rapidly, though, and in need of doing something, she walked over to the nearest bookcase, pretending to read the titles.

Drake made his way over to her, and his arm reached out to her. She froze for just a moment, until she realized he was reaching for a book on the shelf behind her.

"I've read this, you know."

Destiny looked at the book in his hand. She smiled at him. "Really?"

"Really. In fact, I've read all your books. Went out and bought them soon after you disappeared."

"And?"

"And I enjoyed them very much. Especially the sex scenes."

Heat rose to Destiny's face. "I knew you were going to say that."

"It's nothing to be embarrassed about, Destiny. You have a rare gift of being able to describe the act of love in a very human way."

"That's an odd way of putting it. I don't know whether I should be pleased or insulted."

"Be pleased," he answered huskily, his head moving enticingly close to hers. "You should be very proud of the way you can bring those scenes to life, make them seem so real, so honest, so . . ."

His face was just a breath away from hers now, and she knew if she didn't move, she was going to be kissed. She didn't move, and the next thing she knew, his lips were pressed against hers.

I'll always remember you.

She jerked away as if she'd been stung.

"Sorry, I know I shouldn't have done that. It's much too soon."

"No. It wasn't you. Really, it was just . . ."

"What is it, then?" he said, relieved that she hadn't been offended, "Did you remember something?"

"No. Yes. I could swear I heard a voice inside my head say, I'll always remember you. Isn't that strange?"

"Tell me more. Was it a man's voice or a woman's?"

Looking at him with a puzzled expression, she declared, "Actually, it was my own voice."

Twenty-five

December 1870

Bloodied and hurting, Colt rode to River's Edge in a haze, his only companion the lonely moon staring down at him mournfully.

She was gone.

Gone.

So quickly. So easily. As if she had never existed. As if what they had together had meant nothing. But it had. It had. It couldn't be over. The love they shared counted for something. Destiny couldn't have hurtled through time to be with him because of some frivolous cosmic mistake. Things just didn't happen like that. It would be too hard to bear.

Too hard to bear? What was he talking about? He already had too much to bear, knowing Destiny had finally made up her mind to share her life with him just before she was taken from him.

He remembered how determined and proud she was that she had made the decision to fight back. To find the secret to time travel so they could make sure it never happened again. How could she be taken from him after that? They were about to realize all their dreams. They were going to be so happy.

The last image he had of her haunted him now. *She had known.* At the last second she had known what was going

to happen to her. He had seen it on her face. But how di
she know? What had happened at that last second that mad
her realize it was going to happen?

But what haunted him most was the thought that if sh
had learned the secret of traveling through time why hadn'
she immediately returned to him? He tried to discard th
obvious answer. That she didn't want to come back. Bu
some demon inside him kept that awful thought alive.

Pulling hard on his reins, he stopped in front of the hitch
ing post outside the main house, and climbed out of th
saddle. Faith and Paul were standing on the porch lookin,
very worried. Of course they were. They must be wonderin,
where Destiny is.

The sight of the newly married couple with everythin,
to look forward to in their new life together made the trag
edy all the harder to take and he felt himself falling int
an abyss of deep remorse. On the verge of breaking dow
completely he raised his bloodied hands helplessly in fron
of him, crying, "She's gone."

That was the last thing he remembered until he wa
seated in the cozy little parlor and Paul was handing hin
a glass of whiskey. Faith stood by his side with big eyes
and he couldn't imagine what she must be thinking seein,
the blood on his hands.

Placing a heavy hand on Colt's shoulder, Paul spoke i
a low voice, "What happened?"

The large lump in Colt's throat made it difficult to talk
but he forced the words out, in need of sharing what hap
pened with his friends. "She vanished. She was in my arms
and she just vanished." His voice became a fervent cry a
he tried to make them understand. "I tried to hold onto her
I tried so hard. But it was impossible. There—was—noth
ing—left—to—hold—onto."

Paul and Faith exchanged worried glances.

"God knows, I can't blame you for not believing me, bu
I swear to you it's the truth."

Speaking in a subdued voice, Faith said, "We believe you, Colt. Destiny prepared us for this, but, oh, I never wanted to believe it could happen."

Her voice dissolved in a veil of tears and Paul took her into his arms to comfort her. His expression was grave as he gazed over her head to his best friend.

"Then she's told you she's from the future?" Colt asked. Seeing the incredulous looks on Paul's face, Colt realized she hadn't. In a bitter voice, he said, "I know. It seems incredible to me, too. But, unfortunately for me, I was privy to seeing it happen."

Rising to his feet, he started pacing the floor. "There has to be a way of bringing her back. There has to be. Oh, God, I've got to find a way. I can't lose her like this. I can't lose her and my baby."

Faith raised her tear-stained face, and gazed at Colt. "A baby? She was carrying your baby? Oh, Colt, I'm so sorry. I feel so helpless. What can I do?"

Realizing he was upsetting her, Colt pulled himself together. "Honey, just being here, listening, understanding what happened is a big help to me. I would have gone crazy if I couldn't talk about this to someone, and you and Paul are the only ones I can trust with this story." Walking over to the window, Colt stared out as he told them everything that had happened concluding with his fit of rage.

"And then, after I could take the pain no longer, I stopped beating the ground, telling myself that she would return at any moment. Don't you see, I had to believe that in order to go on living. I sat there, right on the spot where we had just made love so wondrously, waiting for her to come back to me.

"I don't know how much time passed before it dawned on me that it wasn't going to happen. By then, it was starting to get dark, and I . . . left."

Sudden resolve filled him, and he jumped out of the chair, frightening Faith. "I've got to go back. What if she comes back now, in the dark. She'll be so frightened. She'll . . ."

Paul grasped his arm. "Colt. Calm down. You're in no condition to go back out there. You need to rest. You've been through enough for one day."

"I have to go. Don't you see? I can't just sit around waiting, doing nothing. I have to go."

Knowing the futility of arguing with him, Paul answered quietly, "All right. You do that. But I'm coming with you. I'm not going to let you spend the night out there alone."

Colt took in a deep shuddering breath. "I'd appreciate the company, Paul. The thought of being out there alone . . . waiting."

Faith blinked back her tears. "I'll just pack a supper for the two of you, and find some blankets you can use as a bedroll."

In a short while the two men were riding away and Faith was trying to be brave. She would have to face the rest of her little family and tell them what had happened. She was grateful now that Destiny had prepared them for this, and it occurred to her how little she knew her friend.

But that didn't matter. She had come to love Destiny, and she hurt now every bit as much as if she had lost a dear sister. Like Colt, she wanted to believe that Destiny would return.

At the moment that Colt and Paul laid out their bedrolls and sat solemnly before the warm glow of a campfire, Penelope Peabody was opening the door to Cedric Farley's office.

She had waited patiently all day for him to return, getting angrier and angrier as the hours passed. But when it became very late, she had swallowed her pride and gone to his room, only to find he had not returned from the office.

Fearing something was terribly wrong, she made her way to the sheriff's home and told him her fears. She could tell

by his expression that he thought she was just being a typical worrisome female, but he agreed to accompany her.

Entering the masculine, wood-paneled office that
matched her distinguished-looking lover so much, she
smelled something that brought her to a halt.

It was the sickly, sweet smell of blood.

Twenty-six

December 1995

Drake didn't sleep at all that night. How could he? Finding out that traveling through time was possible had him completely unnerved. Instead, he prowled the library all night, thinking reading, pacing. Trying to come to terms with his own feelings about everything that had happened.

He was a lawyer, a hardheaded business-minded professional, and yet, damn it all, he had seen a woman materialize from the very air he breathed. How could he rationalize that? Where did that fit into his belief system?

Hell, he couldn't even begin to try and understand it. Watching it happen had been no different from sitting in front of a television set seeing Captain Picard being beamed aboard the starship Enterprise. But there was a difference. Destiny's amazing feat had been real.

It was awesome knowing there were so many unknown areas of the human psyche yet to explore. But, as for him, he was going to keep his newfound knowledge to himself. He had his career to think of. He wasn't about to risk it by telling anyone what he had seen.

When morning finally came, Drake followed his nose to the kitchen and greeted his aunt with a kiss on the cheek.

Lydia looked at him curiously. "My, my, you haven't kissed your old aunt since you were ten, and decided you were too old for that mushy stuff. What is it, Drake? I know you were up late last night. I heard you pacing the floor. Did you find the sofa in the library too uncomfortable to sleep on?"

"Not at all. You know very well I like everything about your library, including your ancient sofa. It's been my favorite place since I was seven and discovered the magic of books."

"Then, it must be Destiny's situation that has you so restless. Oh, dear. I don't know what to do about it. She has a right to know the whole truth, but I'm so afraid it will cause more harm than good."

"I'm not so sure of that. Yesterday she had a breakthrough. She remembered a phrase she had spoken to someone. I'll always remember you."

"I'll always remember you? How odd. I wonder who she could have said it to."

Drake had his own thoughts about that, but didn't like the conclusion he had come to. Obviously, Destiny had met someone very special when she journeyed to the past. But if he was so damn special, why had she forgotten him as soon as she returned to the present?

"You know, Drake, I'm very optimistic that she will eventually remember everything on her own. Maybe, with just a little encouragement . . . something will trigger . . . Oh, Drake, I've just had a thought. What if you drove her out to the sugar mill ruins, the one she wrote about in her book? It still stands exactly as she described it."

"I don't know about that."

"Oh, don't be that way. It's worth a try. She wouldn't have mentioned the ruins in her book if that beautiful site hadn't been important to her in some way. Take her there. But don't tell her why. See how she reacts. What do we have to lose?"

Hearing Destiny on the stairs, she put a finger over her mouth, whispering, "Mum's the word."

Destiny walked into the kitchen, and couldn't help noticing the conspiratorial air between Drake and Lydia. She wondered what they were up to, but decided she wouldn't push it. Miss Lydia could be very stubborn when she wanted. She'd just pretend she hadn't noticed and wait for one of them to break down and tell her what was going on. "It looks like we're in for another beautiful day."

"I was just telling Drake that very thing, and he commented that it would be the perfect time to drive out to the old sugar mill ruins for a picnic."

Destiny gave Drake a curious glance. "Have you been to them before, Drake?"

Frowning at his aunt, Drake answered, "Not for a long time. If you'd rather not go, I'm sure . . ."

"Oh, no, I'd love to go. I haven't been to them in a long time either. I love the idea of a picnic."

Lydia spoke up quickly. "Good. I'll go pack a nice lunch." She started out the door, just as the phone rang. "Don't answer that, Drake. It's probably your office calling and I don't want them to take you away from us."

Ignoring his aunt's request, Drake made his way to the phone and picked it up. "Drake McAmmon here."

A long silence followed, and Destiny gazed over at Drake, wondering what the conversation was about. One thing was sure, it involved her, because at one point, he looked over at her with a strange expression on his face. When he hung up the phone, Destiny waited anxiously for him to speak.

"Who was that, dear?" Miss Lydia said, sensing something was troubling Drake.

"Uh, it was Benjamin. He had the results of one of the tests on Destiny."

Destiny's heart sank. "What is it, Drake? What did the doctor find out?"

A tinge of pain crossed Drake's face when he blurted out, "You're pregnant."

Miss Lydia gasped, but Destiny was too frozen to say

anything. Pregnant? She couldn't be pregnant. There had to be a man in your life before you could get pregnant. Feeling her knees buckle under her, she started to collapse, but Drake quickly reached her in time and guided her to a chair.

"Oh, my, oh, my," Lydia exclaimed.

After everyone's nerves had been calmed, Destiny decided the drive to the ruins was exactly what she needed most. Maybe, in the serenity of the setting, she would be able to clear her head and decide what steps to take next. One thing was certain, she had an important decision to make.

She had always wanted a family of her own, but this, this was not the way she wanted to have one. Impregnated by an unknown man? Was there nothing about her life that was ordinary? Why was it so difficult for her to lead a normal life like anyone else?

The thought of carrying a child to term without any knowledge of who the father was, or the circumstances of its conception, had her mind reeling.

They rode to the ruins in silence, while Destiny tried to cope with the idea of being pregnant. Drake kept his thoughts to himself, and she was grateful for that. He was an assertive, outgoing male, but he was no fool. He knew when it was important to keep quiet.

When they arrived at the ruins, Drake parked the car and grabbed the picnic basket, asking her to carry the blanket. They made their way over to the ruins and were happy to discover they had the place to themselves. That wasn't unusual; not many people came to the old sugar mill, especially on a weekday like this.

Drinking in the eerie beauty of the place, Destiny felt the serenity sink into the very center of her being and relaxed, pushing everything out of her mind but the wonderful ambience of the place. She had always loved it here, and never so much as now, when her mind was in such turmoil.

Taking in a deep breath of fragrant air, she murmured, "Mmm, I'm glad we came. It's lovely, isn't it?"

Drake looked at her, and the depression he had been feeling since hearing of her pregnancy vanished. She was so beautiful, so full of life, it was impossible to be sad in her presence. "Yes, it is beautiful. And I can't think of anyone I'd rather share it with than you."

"That's . . . very generous of you, considering all the trouble I've caused you." Something strange was happening to Destiny, but she couldn't put her finger on it. Gazing around her, she felt an invisible force tug at her subconscious.

She closed her eyes as the feeling grew stronger, and began to sway back and forth. Fighting it, she snapped her eyes open and said, "Shall we sit here?"

Drake could see that the setting was having an effect on Destiny, and suddenly he had misgivings about being here. What if something happened because she was here? How would he handle it?

Destiny spread the blanket on the grass, and smoothed it out before sitting on a corner of it. Drake set the basket on the blanket, then sat down beside her. "You've been here before?"

"Yes. When I was writing *One Shining Moment.* I loved it at first sight, and immediately knew I wanted to include it in my book."

"Why was that?"

Destiny laughed. "Authors never know why some things strike them that way. At least, this author doesn't. I never analyze my writing. I guess I'm afraid I'll lose the creative spark that sets my work apart from any others."

"I don't think you have to worry about that." Drake covered her hand with his, but she quickly moved it out of his range. "Drake. Slow down. You're way ahead of me. I need time."

Time? But time was her enemy, wasn't it?

Where had that come from?

"You're right. I'm sorry. I realize there must be someone very special in your life already."

"So special I can't remember him? Doesn't that strike you as odd?"

"If it was anyone else, I'd say yes. But you? No. You've been through something extraordinary. Something no one else has had to cope with. It's no wonder your mind blocked it all out. But I'm confident there will be a happy conclusion to your story, and you'll live happily ever after."

Destiny's gaze was drawn to her heart-shaped ring. It sparkled brightly. *Happily ever after.* "I hope you're right. Because right now, I feel like a stranger to myself and I don't like it at all."

"Good. That means you're motivated to remember, aren't you? Okay, here's the game plan. We'll relax a little, eat our lunch, then stroll through the woods. Nothing like fresh country air to make a person think straight."

Gazing into his warm blue eyes, Destiny decided she liked Drake McAmmon very much. "Mmm, country air and good food." Opening the lid to the picnic basket, she murmured, "Hmm, I wonder what goodies your aunt packed for us, I'm fam . . ."

In shock, she stared at the Celtic cross lying in the basket.

"What is it, Destiny?"

Taking the cross in her hand, she felt a slight tingle. "What ever possessed your aunt to put this in here?"

Drake stared at the cross in her hand, barely able to breathe. "Here. Let me have that."

Destiny handed him the cross. "Touch of senility, do you suppose? Funny though, every time I touch it, I feel a tingle in my fingers. Do you feel it, too?"

Taking the cross from her, Drake breathed in a sigh of

relief. For a moment there, he had been afraid she would disappear. "I feel the coolness of the metal. Nothing more."

"That's really strange." Holding her hand out for it, she said, "Here, I'll put it back in the basket."

"No! That's all right. I'll just put it in my pocket. Safer there."

Destiny shrugged off the strange feeling that swept over her, and turned her attention to the picnic lunch. Lydia had packed thick ham sandwiches with Dijon mustard and mayo, and a thermos of iced tea. Famished, she made short work of the sandwich, trying to ignore the eerie sensation that worked its way through her body. But with every minute that passed, she found it growing stronger and stronger. It was strange, but she almost expected someone to step out from around the corner of one of the half-torn-down walls to confront her.

But who? Why? Had she been here some time in the three forgotten months? Is this where she had made love to the man who fathered the child she carried? That was a definite possibility, for sensual vibrations were coursing through her body, and handsome though he may be, they weren't for Drake.

She tried to listen to Drake as he told her about his childhood, but something kept drawing her eyes to the path that led to an old well. She had the urge to go to it, but told herself she was being foolish, and forced her attention back to Drake.

He was in the midst of telling her about his visits to the ruins when he was just a boy. "And I used to play hide-and-seek here with Lady, my dog. She was part lab, part German shepherd, the perfect pet for a boy. She followed me everywhere. My mom had only to look for the dog and she'd find the boy. Lady was so devoted, she'd sit right outside my friend's house while I visited, waiting patiently for me to come back out."

"How in the world did you play hide-and-seek with a dog?"

"It was easy. I'd just hide behind a tree when she was off chasing after a rabbit, or something, then call out to her to come and find me. She loved it. She'd sniff along the ground and in no time at all, she'd find me. I remember one time, I actually climbed a tree, thinking I'd fool her."

Gazing around the clearing, ringed with woods, he searched for the right tree. "That one over there, I think. I remember it had a clump of resurrection fern growing on it, and . . ." Drake stopped, seeing the stricken look on Destiny's face.

"What is it? Have you remembered something?"

"Yes . . . I think so. Resurrection fern. There's something about it. Something . . ." Standing up, Destiny started walking toward the path leading to the old coquina well.

"Where are you going?"

Shaking her head, she motioned with her hand for him to be silent, afraid she'd lose the memory that was forming in her mind. When she grew closer to her destination, her heart became constricted. What was it that had pulled her here?

Spying the rustic well, overgrown with grapevines and covered over with moss and shrubbery, she knelt beside it. Immediately, she started rooting through the crevices in search of . . . what? What was she looking for?

Drake caught up to her, and shouted, "Hey! I wouldn't go poking my hand around. Could be a water moccasin hiding in there."

Ignoring him, she shoved her hand deep into the largest crevice as far as she could, and felt something soft with her fingers. Grasping it firmly, she tugged on it, until it was finally dislodged.

Pulling it out of its nesting place, she stared down at the Indian medicine bag in astonishment. Instantly, the face of a Seminole warrior appeared before her, smiling at her with great joy. She blinked her eyes and when she opened them, he was gone.

"What do you have there?" Drake asked. "Let me see it."

Destiny held tight to it. "No. It belongs to me."

Drake knelt beside her. "What is it, Destiny? What's wrong?"

"Why, nothing. It's just, this medicine bag is very special. I remember putting a resurrection fern inside it, then hiding it here." Loosening the leather thong strings, she opened up the pouch and took out a perfectly preserved specimen of a fern frond. "See?" she said, triumphantly, happy that her memory had been true.

Knowing she had had a breakthrough, Drake placed his hands on her shoulders and in a demanding voice said, "When did you put the fern in the bag, Destiny? When?"

A sea of memories washed through Destiny's brain as she stared sightlessly at Drake. She was blind to everything but the face that gazed at her with such deep love showing in his gray eyes.

I'll always remember you.

"Colt, oh, Colt. I remember. I remember you."

And she did. She remembered everything. In the time it took one deep shuddering breath of air to purge through her body, it had all come back to her. Burying her face in her hands, she felt a myriad of emotions sweep over her. Untold relief, that she had her memory back. Frustration that she could ever have forgotten the man she loved so much, elation that Colt was the father of her unborn child.

But above all was the overpowering desire to be in Colt's arms once again.

Composing herself, she lifted her head and smiled at Drake. "Thank you for bringing me here. I remember it all now, and you can't imagine how wonderful it is to know that I'm not crazy."

Drake chucked her under the chin with his finger. "Never thought you were. Do you want to tell me about it?"

"Oh, yes. I have to tell someone. And you and Lydia are the only ones who could possibly understand."

Listening to her story, Drake felt a dull ache in his heart. It was just as his aunt thought. Destiny had traveled to the past, had met some of the characters from her book, and in the bargain had found the man of her dreams.

He heard it all, from the time she woke up naked in the hotel room, to the lovemaking at this poignant spot, when she discovered the answer to traveling through time, too late. His dream of winning her love crumbled and died like the ruins of the brick walls that surrounded them.

Putting a smile on his face for her benefit, he said, "That's quite a story. I can see that the love between you and Colt is a powerful thing. I envy you that kind of love, Destiny. Ah, Destiny. The name fits you, doesn't it? Shining Dawn must have been as psychic as you to give you such an appropriate name."

A strange look came over her, and he knew before she spoke that he had blurted out something she had no knowledge of. Damn.

"What are you talking about? What does Shining Dawn have to do with my name? I named myself Destiny the first day of my remembered life."

"I'm sorry, I thought . . . I was sure all of your memory had returned. Not just the past three months."

"Drake, you're scaring me. Do you know something about the missing years of my childhood?"

"Yes. So does my aunt. You see, she has the McAmmon family Bible. There was a yellowed newspaper clipping tucked inside."

A deep, gnawing anxiety came over her then. Trying to fight it, she answered, "Well, tell me what it said. What do you know about my childhood? Why didn't Lydia tell me what she knows?"

"She planned on telling you, but not until she was sure that you were the right one. You can't blame her for that."

"Right one? Drake, what are you talking about?"

Irritated with himself for his slip of the tongue, he said, impatiently, "Don't you think it's time you figured it out for yourself?"

"Damn you. Don't you think I want to? Eight years of my life are missing. Of course I want to remember."

"Then do it. For God sakes, do it. You've got all the information you need locked up in that head of yours."

Feeling suddenly restless and edgy, she covered her ears with her hands. "I don't want to talk about this anymore. I want to go to Colt now. I can't afford to lose any more precious time."

Holding out her hand, she demanded, "Give me the cross. He's waiting for me. I know he is. He must be out of his mind worrying whether I can ever find my way back."

Drake put his hand over his pocket, guarding its contents. "You can't leave yet. Not until you know the whole truth."

Destiny threw herself at Drake, trying to take his hand away from the pocket. "Stop saying that. I know the truth. You're just trying to trick me into staying here because you have feelings for me."

Pinning her arms to her sides, Drake shouted, "God knows, you're right about that. I don't want you to leave, but that's got nothing to do with this, and you know it. Destiny, stop fighting it. It's time. Time to become whole. Time to remember your mother!"

Twenty-seven

December 1870

Paul Proudhorse gazed down at his tormented friend, finally sleeping after a long, torturous night of anguish. And no wonder. Before falling asleep Colt had relayed an incredible story about Destiny. A story no sane man would believe. And yet . . . deep in his heart, he knew Colt spoke the truth. Destiny herself had warned them that she might disappear, and now he understood why.

Colt was convinced Destiny would return here to the same place she had disappeared from. But as the night progressed, and it became obvious to him that she would not, he became so despondent, Paul feared he would harm himself.

Now, at last, Colt slept in peace. He was glad his friend was safe from pain for a little while, at least. He'd be out for some time. Long enough, at least, for him to go home for a little while. He was hungry and sore after a night on the ground, and wanted to have breakfast with Faith. Just to be safe, though, he'd send Hunt to watch over Colt until he returned.

Mounting his horse, he rode down the path leading toward River's Edge, and the warm, beautiful woman who waited for him.

From the cover of a thicket of tangled grapevines, Brent Raiford watched as Paul rode away from the ruins. It was the moment he had been waiting for. Faith, in her innocence had told him no more than an hour ago where to find Colt and he knew a chance like this would not come along again.

The young newlywed, so ripe and luscious, had been out near the main road chasing after a piglet when he happened by, and he had almost—almost—decided to take her then, just as he had Judith Langford.

The bitch would never know how close she came to dying. The only thing that saved her was the casual mention of her husband and Colt spending the night at the ruins. That had put everything else right out of his mind. His need to take care of Colt was more important than indulging in the pleasure of the flesh.

How fortuitous that he had decided to ride out to River's Edge today. It never occurred to him he'd have the opportunity to get rid of him so easily. It would be so much safer out here, away from prying eyes. He'd get Colt out of the way before he found out about the lawyer's untimely death. More important, before he had a chance to draw up another will.

Watching from his hiding place until Paul was out of sight, he led his horse into the clearing. Then taking the rifle mounted on his saddle, he walked up to the sleeping man. Colt didn't so much as stir.

Nudging him under the chin with the rifle's barrel, he said softly, "Wake up, Colt. The angels are calling you."

Through a fog, Colt heard a distant voice and thought he was dreaming, but the touch of cold metal against his throat brought him quickly back to reality. Instantly alert, he opened his eyes and saw Brent standing over him.

"Uncomfortable feeling, isn't it? Having the barrel of a gun pressed to your throat."

Colt didn't answer. His mind was racing. Trying to evaluate the situation. Trying to figure out how he was going to get out of this alive.

"What's a matter, boy? No saliva to talk with?"

Keeping his voice calm, Colt answered, "What is it you want me to say, Brent? Take the rifle away from my head and we'll talk."

Brent laughed. "Talk? That's really good, boy. We're way past talking now, don't you think? I have to admit though, you've got balls. Most men would be shitting in their britches right about now. But wait just a little while. We'll see how brave you are after we've taken a little walk in the woods."

Colt took a quick, shallow breath. He had a reprieve. Brent wasn't going to kill him right now. He had a chance. "You sick bastard. It won't do you any good to kill me. You're too late. I already changed my will. Susan won't inherit a thing."

A wicked smile crossed Brent's face, and Colt's heart sank.

"You talkin' about the will Cedric Farley drew up, boy? Poor man, he died never knowing who slit his throat."

Colt closed his eyes as cold, sick fear swept over him.

"They've probably found him by now. Wish I could have been there when they did. But I had more important matters to attend to. Everything's turning out exactly as I planned. Thanks to your cooperation. If you hadn't decided to spend the night out here in the woods, I'd've had a real hard time getting my hands on you. You see, I want it to look like you were attacked by an animal while you slept in the woods. An accidental death. Can't afford for anyone to point their finger in my direction."

"Accident? It's going to be pretty hard to make my death look like an accident."

"You underestimate me, dear boy. That was your fatal mistake. It will be a long time before anyone finds you. By then, it'll be too late. The animals and insects will have done their work. There won't be enough left of you to bury. Now get up."

Colt didn't have any choice but to do what Brent said.

If he resisted, he'd be shot. That would spoil Brent's plans for making his death look like an accident, but it wouldn't be doing him a hell of a lot of good either. No. He'd go along with him for now, and hope a chance would come along for him to survive.

Before he knew it, Brent was slipping a noose around his neck, and pulling it tight. "Make any sudden moves, and I'll cut your air off. Understand? Now, get on your horse."

Colt mounted his horse, then rode as Brent commanded toward the deepness of the woods. After a while, it became too overgrown to ride through, and they had to dismount and continue on foot.

They walked for what seemed like hours before Brent was satisfied that they were far enough away from civilization. Pulling the rope tighter around Colt's neck to make sure he obeyed, he said, "Don't struggle, or you die."

Knowing he had no choice, Colt let his arms go slack at his side.

"All right. Take off your clothes."

Colt slowly removed his clothing, feeling more and more vulnerable as each piece was removed. His mind was racing, trying to think of a way to get out of this alive, but he was in an impossible situation.

When he was completely naked, Brent ordered him to stand with his back up against a tree, and then proceeded to tie him to it. The roughness of the rope cut into his bare skin, but he suffered the pain in silence.

In a moment, he was bound tightly from his waist to his neck, his arms pinned helplessly to his sides. He rejoiced that the rope wasn't long enough to tie around his legs, too. It might afford him a chance to defend himself.

Evidently Brent wasn't worried about that. In fact, he was acting as if he were invincible. But that was to the good. If he thought nothing could harm him, he wouldn't be on guard.

Brent finished tying him to the tree, then walked over to his horse and pulled out something that gleamed in the sunlight.

Colt's heart sank seeing the cruel blade of a long knife.

Close to panic, he struggled against the ropes, but it was useless. They were too tight, too strong.

Brent enjoyed seeing Colt squirm. It reinforced the feeling of power he craved so much. Holding the knife up for Colt to see, he grinned viciously, and started toward him.

Colt knew he would only have one chance. He had to wait until Brent was exactly the right distance away before making his move.

A little closer. That's right, just a little closer.

Yes, now!

Kicking up violently, he caught Brent on the chest.

Brent went sprawling backward, his hands flying out to try and break his fall. The knife went sailing through the air, landing harmlessly at the base of a tree.

Enraged, Brent climbed back to his feet, still staggering from the blow. Picking up his rifle, he swung the butt hard against Colt's head.

Colt's world turned from blinding white to blood red and then slowly to black.

Twenty-eight

December 1995

The drive back to Lydia's was a somber one. Destiny sat huddled in the corner of her seat, staring out the window like a lost child, afraid and wary of what she was about to face.

Drake wanted to reach out and comfort her, but he knew she was beyond all comforting now. The only thing that could help, at this point, would be to break through the barrier her mind had constructed and come to grips with the truth.

Parking the car in the driveway of his aunt's home, he walked around to the passenger side and opened the door for Destiny. She sat there dully, seemingly unaware that the car had stopped. He couldn't help wondering if this was the way her amnesia always started, distancing herself, withdrawing, until she no longer was aware of her surroundings. That settled it, as far as he was concerned. He was going to get help for her right away, whether she wanted it or not.

He escorted Destiny up the front stairs to the house. The door opened and his aunt came out, scowling at him when she saw the condition Destiny was in.

But he wasn't going to take the blame for this. "Don't look at me like that. You started this. You're the one who insisted we go to the ruins."

"What happened?"

Regretting his outburst, he lowered his voice. "She remembers the past three months now, and I practically had to use force to keep her from going back in time again. I'm calling Joe Alphonso right now."

"Do you really think your hypnotist friend can help her?"

"I have no idea. But anything is better than watching her drift away from us."

Destiny heard Lydia and Drake's words, but she was past comprehending anything but the fact that Colt was waiting for her to return to him. What must he be thinking? She couldn't bear for him to think she had abandoned him. She needed to see him, reassure him that nothing could keep them apart any longer.

Drake couldn't stop her. No one could stop her. She'd just wait until everyone was asleep, if she had to. Then take the Celtic cross from Drake.

But what about her mother?

Drake had told her she had all the information she needed to find out about her mother, but it was a lie. How could she believe that, when all her life she had longed to have a family? Ached because she had been separated from her parents at such a tender age.

She had gone to great lengths to find her mother. Had even hired detectives to find out who she was, who her family was, and where they were from. If they couldn't find her mother and father, then how dare Drake presume to think she hadn't tried hard enough.

She let Drake lead her to the parlor and sit her down on the velvet sofa, even let him wrap a blanket around her legs. What did it matter? In a few hours she'd be back in Colt's arms.

Glancing over at Miss Lydia, she saw the concerned look on her face, but that didn't matter either. There was no reason for her to be concerned. She'd understand that soon enough.

Seeing Drake make a phone call, she couldn't be bothered listening to what he had to say. It wasn't important. Nothing was important anymore, except being with Col Mandrell. After a while, she closed her eyes, envisioning his wonderful face, and that had a calming effect on her.

The doorbell rang, and she felt mildly irritated. She didn't want to be bothered with strangers right now.

Drake escorted a friendly faced man into the room. The man was dressed casually in golf shirt and pants. He shook her hand and told her his name was Joe Alphonso. She tried to avoid his gaze, hoping if she ignored him he'd go away, but his eyes demanded her attention, and too tired to resist, she gave in and focused on his face.

"Destiny, I want you to take a deep breath and relax. Will you do that for me?"

Destiny was annoyed at having her peace disturbed, but she nodded her head yes. Anything to help make him go away.

"Good. Now I want you to look into my eyes and tell me what you see."

Reluctantly, she lifted her gaze to his eyes, and saw that they were a rich brown with glints of gold. Nice eyes. Friendly eyes. Eyes that made her feel suddenly at ease. Staring deeper into them, she could see the reflection from the windows shining there, so clear she could almost see . . .

"What do you see, Destiny?"

Staring past the brown and gold, past the shimmering light. deep within the windows of his eyes, she said, "I see . . . myself."

"Excellent. Keep looking at yourself. Deeper and deeper. Deeper and deeper. See yourself getting younger . . . younger . . . You are nineteen . . . Eighteen . . . Seventeen . . ."

With every fiber of her being, she concentrated on his eyes, surprised to see her seventeen-year-old face staring back at her.

"Now you are twelve . . . eleven . . . ten."

Surprise turned to uneasiness as he counted down the years. She wanted him to stop, but she couldn't look away from his eyes. They held her captive with their warmth, their intense but loving gaze. She watched herself growing younger and younger, until the child that stared back at her had enormous sad eyes.

"You are eight years old."

Destiny saw herself at eight, so small and sickly looking, her large eyes staring out from a thin, wan face.

"Look, Destiny. Tell me where you are."

Destiny found herself drawn even deeper into his eyes. Was there no end to their depth? She moved her head slowly closer to the man's face to get a better look into his eyes. It was like gazing through a window into a dark room.

"Where are you Destiny?"

She struggled to see through the swirling darkness. "I'm . . . I'm in a small . . . cabin."

"What are you doing there?"

"Please. I don't want to be here."

"Destiny, it's all right. Tell me what you're doing."

"I'm . . . in a bed."

"Is there someone in the room with you?"

"I don't want to look. Please. I don't like it here."

"Destiny, I'm with you. I won't let anything harm you. Look around the room and tell me who you see, and then you can go."

"Promise?"

"I promise."

Reassured and eager to leave, she concentrated harder. In a moment, the dark room began to lighten and she saw that she was inside the room now, lying on the bed. She felt the softness of the mattress beneath her, heard the frantic pelting of rain against a tin roof, and something else . . . the labored sound of someone breathing heavily.

Turning her head to the left, she saw another bed. Saw

a woman large with child lying there, her face obscured by the form of another woman standing beside the bed attending her.

Something was very familiar about the dress the standing woman wore, and it came to her in a soft, feathery sensation that it was her mother's dress. She had seen it on her so many, many times.

She wasn't alone. Her mother was there with her.

But, of course, she was. Her mother was always there for her. In sudden need of comfort, she cried out, "Mommy."

Shining Dawn turned to look at her daughter.

A rush of love swept over Destiny as she gazed at the beloved face of her mother.

"Dee Dee, you're awake. I'm so glad. Are you feeling any better?"

Suddenly, Destiny became aware of a muted pain all over her body, pain that grew and grew until she thought she couldn't stand it any longer. "No, Mommy, I feel worse. Help me. Make me feel better."

Her mother sat on the edge of her bed, and comforted her by caressing her forehead. Her hand felt wonderfully cool against her fevered brow.

"I know, honey. I wish there was something more I could do for you, but . . ."

A low keening sound suddenly rent the air, turning into a heart-wrenching howling. "Mommy. The wolves. They're coming closer. I'm scared. I don't want them to get me."

Shining Dawn was at the point of exhaustion after caring for two people for endless hours. Gathering what remained of her dwindling strength she smoothed Destiny's hair from her face and in a weary voice murmured, "Shush, now, there's nothing to be afraid of. The wolves can't get you. The door is locked, and . . ."

Glancing up at the door, Shining Dawn's heart lurched. It wasn't locked. She forgot to lock it when she drew water.

from the well the last time. She started to go to the door, but Little Bit started screaming again.

"I have to push! Oh, God, I have to push!"

She had been pushing for such a long time now, growing weaker and weaker, until Shining Dawn feared she would not have the strength to push much longer. "I'm going to feel for the baby now. Perhaps it's time."

Little Bit reached for the bedpost behind her and held tight as the pain racked through her body. "I can't stand it anymore. I can't. I can't."

From her bed, Destiny watched the scene in growing horror, her own sickness forgotten for the moment, as she sensed the danger Little Bit was in. Looking at her mother's worried face confirmed that feeling.

The howling started up again, as one after another of the wolves joined in. Destiny wanted to hide under her mother's skirts as she had done when she was much younger. Panic filled her as she tried, but failed, to sit up. She was too weak. Where had all her strength gone?

It all came back to her then. Coming to the cabin with her mother and Little Bit. The fever coming on her so suddenly, stealing away all her strength, and now her very life. She knew she must be close to death, for though her mother tried very hard to hide it, Destiny saw the dull sadness in her eyes when she looked at her.

She wanted her mother. Wanted her to hold her, comfort her, but her mother had to care for Little Bit, too. Oh, why did Miss Little Bit have to have her baby now? It wasn't fair.

Destiny started to sob. "Mommy. Mommy. Mommy."

Little Bit's screams drowned out her voice, and the howling grew louder as the wolves heard the crying females just a few feet from where they waited impatiently just outside the door.

"Destiny Dawn McAmmon. Step your crying. You hear? Can't you see how busy I am? Miss Little Bit's baby is coming."

Destiny heard her mother speak her name and a strange feeling came over her. Her mother never called her that except when she was angry. She was always Destiny, or Dee Dee, but never Destiny Dawn. One more weak cry escaped her lips and then she became silent. Her mother had no time for her.

The wind was beating at the door now, like a stranger trying to force his way in, and Destiny turned her head to look, needing reassurance that the rickety weather-beaten door would hold. Her eyes opened wide with horror when she saw it wasn't locked. Her mother had lied. The wolves were going to get her.

Suddenly, a strange sensation crept over her, and she felt her body jerk involuntarily. What was happening to her?

Shining Dawn finished examining Little Bit and didn't know how she'd find the strength to go on. Little Bit was tighter than a drum. There was no way she was going to have this baby naturally. That left only one thing to do. Cut her open and take it. If she didn't both mother and child would die.

Holding back the urge to cry, Shining Dawn exclaimed, "I've got to cut you open. The baby's head is too large to pass through the opening. It's the only way. Do you understand? The only way."

Little Bit let out another long, drawn-out scream before she could answer. "Do it! I can't take it any longer. I'm growing too weak to push."

Forcing herself not to think about it, Shining Dawn picked up the large knife she was going to use to cut the baby's umbilical cord. Lifting Little Bit's nightgown up to her chest, she said, "God, give me the strength to do this."

Biting down on her lip, she made a large slice on Little Bit's stomach. A bloodcurdling scream rent the air, and then there was silence. Little Bit had fainted from the pain.

A strangled sound broke through to Shining Dawn's brain, and in a daze she looked over at the bed where her daughter

lay. She was jerking spasmodically, and turning blue. Dear
God. No!

What could she do? If she didn't take the baby this instant, if she didn't close Little Bit back up immediately, she
would surely die. But Destiny, dear God, if she didn't help
Destiny immediately, she would die, too.

The chorus of howling outside reached a frenzied cre-
scendo, and Shining Dawn wondered if the smell of Little
Bit's blood had reached their sensitive nostrils. But there
was no time to think about that. No time to do anything
but try to save . . .

Oh, God, she had no time to save both her daughter and
Little Bit and the baby.

She had to make a choice.

There was no time to waste. *Choose. Choose now.*

Two lives for one. She had to choose two lives for one.
She had no choice.

But how could she let her daughter die? "Great Spirit. I
call on you. Save my daughter." While she recited the
words, she was reaching into the bloody cavity to pull out
the child pulsating with life. As she struggled with it, she
continued her prayer.

"Great Spirit, you have always listened to my prayers. Listen now. Save my daughter. There is no time. It must be now."

From a great distance, Destiny heard her mother's
prayers, but she couldn't speak, couldn't breathe anymore.
Echoing her mother's words inside her head, she pleaded,
"Great Spirit, help me, I don't want to die."

Suddenly, a soft, velvety voice penetrated her senses,
speaking inside her head. "Live, then."

At the same time, the pounding wind broke through the
flimsy metal catch on the door, and it slammed open. Destiny could barely move her body, but she could move her
eyes, and she saw . . . she saw the gleaming eyes of a wolf
standing in the doorway.

The faint cry of a baby was the last thing she heard.

A thick, black void filled her head, and she had the sense of being carried on the swirling wind. When her vision returned, she was lying on the steps to Flagler Hospital and a soft breeze was whispering her name. "Destiny."

"Destiny?"

She heard the masculine voice and blinked her eyes. She wasn't eight years old anymore. A large sob shook her body. She remembered it all now. Dr. Davidson finding her there. Breathing life into her. Caring for her until she recovered from the fever.

Yes, she remembered it all. The Great Spirit had listened to her mother's prayer and carried her to the only place where she could be saved. *A twentieth-century hospital.*

How strange to realize that this was not the century she had been born to. That she was not a woman of the '90s, after all. At least, not the 1990s. She had been born in the nineteenth century to Shining Dawn and Blade. But what was even more astonishing was the knowledge that she had been swept forward in time at the exact moment of Colt's birth. The sound of his first cry still rang in her ears.

No wonder she found herself in Colt's bed when she was transported back to her own time. The bond they shared was even greater than she ever imagined. They both would surely have died, and Little Bit right along with them if not for her mother and the intervention of the Great Spirit.

A peace settled over her then, as everything fell into place. For the first time in her life she felt completely whole. Looking up at the concerned faces surrounding her, she smiled. "I remember it all. I'm Destiny Dawn McAmmon, and you, Miss Lydia, are my great-grandniece."

Destiny awoke the next morning, full of energy and anticipation. Tonight would be Christmas Eve, the most marvelous Christmas Eve she had ever had. For she would be returning to Colt and to her parents. She had wanted to go back last night, but Drake, lawyer that he was, had convinced her to wait until today. He was going to have papers drawn up so that he could act as executor of her estate when she was gone.

He was right. She would have royalties coming in on all the books she had written, and it would be foolish to let it sit in a bank. As her executor, he would be in a position to see that her profits were distributed to her heirs.

And there would be heirs. She was pregnant with Colt's child. That would change the future, if only just to add a few more Mandrells to the world in the course of a century and a half.

The only thing that spoiled her happiness was worrying about traveling through time. What if she couldn't return? But that would be too cruel. She mustn't even think of that. She had to go back to Colt. Had to see her mother and father again.

Hugging herself with joy, she started down the stairs dressed in her favorite pair of jeans and a comfy T-shirt. Shining Dawn and Blade. Her parents. No wonder she was able to write their story. She must have heard all their adventures related many times in the years she was with them.

Now she would have stories for them. Stories to tell her own children.

A thrill coursed through her as she realized for the first time she was actually going to be reunited with her parents. She would have everything she had ever wanted, a family and a wonderful man to love.

Making her way into the kitchen, she was surprised to see that Lydia wasn't there. Hmm. Don't tell me she overslept? No. That would be too out of character for her. She must be in the parlor.

Walking down the hall, she heard the murmur of voices, and something about them gave her pause. She stopped, and listened as the spoken words swirled around in her head.

"Oh, dear, do you really think we have to tell her about her parents' tragic death? She's suffered so much already."

"Aunt Lydia, we have no choice. She'll find out soon enough anyway. As soon as she returns to her own time she'll find out the truth. Better to prepare her now, when we can be here for her."

Destiny's stomach churned. What were they talking about? Stepping into the parlor, she confronted Drake. "Tell me about my parents' death. You needn't worry about me. I'll be fine. After all, everyone has to die. I can handle knowing they died after a long, happy life."

The looks that Drake and Lydia exchanged made it clear to Destiny that her parents would not live to a ripe old age.

"Tell me how they died. I have a right to know."

"My dear, dear, girl," Lydia said, "You've suffered so terribly already. I didn't want to have to tell you this, but Shining Dawn and Blade McAmmon died tragically in a fire at their cabin early Christmas morning, 1870."

The color drained from Destiny's face as Lydia's words registered on her brain. "How . . . How do you know?"

"I know because I have the McAmmon family Bible. A yellowed newspaper clipping of the tragedy was pressed between the pages."

Destiny shook her head in denial. Today was the twenty-fourth. They would die tomorrow.

Time was once again her enemy. For she knew that whatever day it was here, in the twentieth century, it would be that same day when she traveled back to the nineteteenth century. Same day. Same hour. Only the year would be different.

Pushing back the panic that clawed at her heart, at her very soul, she cried, "Give me the cross. I have to go back. Now! Don't you see, there's still time for me to stop it from happening? I have to. I can't have regained my memory of them only to lose them again so tragically."

"Oh, do you think you can," Lydia exclaimed joyously. "That would be so wonderful."

Drake wasn't so optimistic. "I have the cross right here, but, Destiny, I don't know if it's possible to change the events of the past."

"Don't tell me that. I'm living proof that it can be changed. I'm pregnant with Colt's child. That alone will change things."

"It won't change a thing if you never go back. Don't you see, if your child is born in this time, it can't change the past. I'm sorry to be the grinch here, but it's possible you'll never be able to return. It occurs to me that you could have been sent back here precisely so that you couldn't change history with your pregnancy. Think about it. You touched the cross at the ruins yesterday, and nothing happened."

"But I've already changed history. With two of my cubic zirconia rings. The widow Peabody was able to keep her home from being foreclosed, Faith and Paul were able to marry."

"Perhaps small changes such as that have no effect on the future. I think you'd better face the fact that you may never be able to go back."

"I don't believe that. I wasn't able to travel through time last night because the cubic zirconia on my ring didn't come in contact with the metal of the cross. That's how it's done. It will work. I know it will. Give me the damn papers to sign so I can get out of here."

While Drake fetched the papers, Destiny talked with Lydia. "I hate to leave you like this, but I know you understand. I have to go, not only to be with Colt, but to see my parents again. If I don't leave right now, there may not be enough time for me to get to the cabin in time to save them. I have no idea exactly where I'll be when I get back. It will be wherever Colt and the Celtic cross are at that moment. I just pray he isn't far from the McAmmon place or I may not make it to their home in time."

Lydia patted her hand, and smiled. "You will. I know you will. I'll miss you terribly, but I understand. I just wish I could meet your wonderful young man. He must be very special for you to love him so."

"Oh, he is."

"Here," Drake said, entering the room. "Sign these and you can be on your way. I just wish you had time to gather whatever you might need back there."

"Everything I need is already there, Drake. Thank you."

Hurriedly, she signed the papers, and then held her hand out for the cross. Drake placed it in her hand reluctantly, and she knew he didn't want her to go. Embracing him, she said, "Be happy for me, Drake."

Then turning to Lydia, she swallowed hard. "It's time to say goodbye." Large tears formed in Lydia's ancient eyes as she received her farewell embrace.

Stepping back, she gazed at her distant relatives for one last time, then raised her left hand and struck her fake diamond against the pewter cross.

The little metallic ringing sound rang out, but nothing happened.

She blinked her eyes in disbelief, then struck it again as panic flowed through her like a river run wild.

Still nothing.

She hit it again and again, trying different spots on the cross, different spots on the ring, but nothing worked. Had she been wrong? Was it possible she still didn't have the solution?

Oh, please, no. Her parents' lives depended on her knowing how to go back.

Twenty-nine

The room was silent except for the ticking of the ancient grandfather's clock that stood in the corner of Lydia's parlor. The steady rhythmic noise of it grew louder and louder in Destiny's head until she thought she would scream.

It was a taunting reminder that precious time was passing. Time that could never be reclaimed. Time needed to save her parents from a horrific death. If only she knew how.

But she did know how. What could have gone wrong? There had to be something she had overlooked. Considering how much her mind had absorbed in the past twenty-four hours, it was no wonder she hadn't had the time to sort it all out yet. But that was the catch, wasn't it? There was no time. She had to act now. "Lydia. Drake. Forgive me, but I need to be alone."

Seeing the concerned look on Lydia's face, Destiny smiled reassuringly. "Don't worry about me. I'll be fine. We McAmmon women come from strong stock. I'm just going to think things out in the quiet of my room."

Giving Lydia a quick hug, she left the parlor, and went up the stairs to her room. Throwing herself on the bed, she buried her head under the pillow to block out the world she so desperately wanted to leave.

The answer had to be hidden somewhere in her brain. Somewhere in the sequence of actions that had occurred each time she traveled through time. She knew that touching the cross with the stone of her ring was part of the answer. It caused a momentary psychic spark, like when she saw Colt in the mirror, or felt a tingle when she touched it. But it was clear that the touch of it alone could not propel her through time.

Then there were the erotic dreams about Colt. Making love in her dream was part of the answer, too. The owl had interrupted them the first time, but they had completed the act of making love on the second night. That was when her ring got caught in the pewter chain of his cross at the moment they both climaxed.

Climaxing? Was that the magical missing element that would make it happen again?

It had to be. Because she was pretty certain that their lovemaking had been ethereal rather than real, until that last incredible moment when they were joined together in ecstasy. That was the moment it had all become real. The moment she had been transported through time to be with him.

In a screwy sort of way it all made sense. There was certainly nothing unusual about dreaming. Nothing unusual about having a sex dream. People made love to strangers in their dreams all the time.

But Colt wasn't a stranger. She and Colt shared a very powerful bond. She had been propelled from his world at the moment he had entered it. That was the difference.

A shiver of excitement snaked up her spine. What happened the awful night Colt was born was the key to it all. And that powerful supernatural phenomenon at work that night was still at work now. She was sure of that.

Suddenly, a feeling of profound completeness nestled deep within her, and everything clicked into place. She knew she had hit upon the heart of it.

It was no accident that she had dreamed about Colt. She was meant to. She was sure of that now. And there was one more thing she was sure of. *She would go back to her own time.*

She was never supposed to stay in the twentieth century this long.

She would have been propelled right back after Dr. Davidson saved her life so many years ago, except that something unexpected happened. She had lost her memory. Her mind just couldn't cope with the trauma of being swept through time, the heartbreak of losing her parents, and it had closed down, leaving her in no condition to travel back to her own time.

Colt had been the only person who could bring her out of her self-imposed exile. He was the one who made it happen. If there was such a thing as destiny, then surely she and Colt were ordained to be together.

Somehow, Shining Dawn with her wonderful earthy connection to the Great Spirit must have had an inkling of what lay ahead for her daughter. That could be the reason her mother had named her Destiny, believing that what was fated, must be. She had given the Celtic cross to the infant Colt, knowing its past power, hoping it was the key to bringing her daughter back to her.

Destiny understood so much now. She was destined to go back to the time she had been born to. But there was no comfort in knowing that now. What if it didn't happen in time to save her parents? Then, suddenly, a chilling supposition entered her mind. What if her parents' dying was the price that had to be paid before she could go back in time? What if they had to be sacrificed before she could be with Colt again?

Why would she think such a horrible thing?

Great Spirit, don't let it be true.

She pushed that terrifying thought from her mind, knowing she must stay focused if she was going to be able to help them.

She had to meld her body with Colt's in order to be

transported back, and there was only one way she could do that.

In a dream.

But, even supposing that she could fall asleep, in the highly agitated state she was in, there was still no guarantee she would dream about him. It could be fatal to rely on the whim of a dream. By the time she got around to dreaming about Colt her parents could be dead.

She felt like screaming out her anguish. What good did it do to know the secret if she couldn't use it in time?

But . . . maybe, just maybe, she could.

If she used her psychic powers to join with him wouldn't that be the same as dreaming about him? It had worked when she deliberately drew him to her at the ruins.

Yeah. But they had been in the same century then.

Turning over on her back, she punched the pillow before putting it under her head. Stop thinking negative thoughts.

Shadowy movement from the window caught her attention and she stared at the muted greenery of the stately oaks gently moving in the breeze from the river. She watched them a long time, knowing that it helped her to relax her body. Knowing that it calmed . . . her mind.

Soothed . . . her . . . soul. . . .

When she had relaxed enough, she conjured up the image of Colt's magnificent face, and focused all her energy on him. She knew immediately that it was working, for his face was becoming brighter, clearer, until she was almost convinced she was looking at a flesh-and-blood man. She could make out every tiny wrinkle, every . . .

But what was that?

Gazing up at his left temple, she saw an ugly gash. Oh, Colt, what's happened to you? The sudden shock of seeing him like that almost broke her concentration. Calming herself, she took her mind off his poor wounded forehead and called out to him from deep within her psyche.

His head rolled a little, but his eyes were closed, and the

position of his head was odd. It was as if he were sleeping standing up. But why would he do that?

Something was wrong.

She willed him to open his eyes and look at her, but he didn't respond. Feeling the first stirring of panic, she pushed it back. She mustn't lose her concentration.

Colt. I love you.

I love you so much.

Hear me.

See me.

She saw him stir, and hope sprang in her heart. His head listed to the side, and she gasped, seeing the extent of his terrible wound.

Then he looked straight at her, as if he could see her, and she pushed everything out of her mind but the need to commune with him. She sent him her love, her heart, and her hope and she knew he received it, for he nodded his head in understanding.

She urged him to join his mind to hers. To join with her in the act of love, but something prevented him from doing so. For a moment, he seemed to fade away, but she called him back, telling him how much she needed him.

Staring into his eyes, she locked onto his gaze with all her might, and gave herself up to the mysterious power of her Celtic ancestors. In a moment she was in a deep trance, or sleep, she had no idea which, and she saw Colt standing under a tree, from a great distance.

She was joyous. She had only to make her way to him and the mating that would transport her to him could begin. Using her psychic powers was easier than she imagined, but then, hadn't she willed a part of her mind to sleep for many years blocking out the memory of her childhood? She was an old hand at using the powers of her brain.

She started toward him, but found it hard to move. It was as if she were waist deep in water, trying to push against the current. She closed her eyes hoping for deeper concentration and it must have worked for she moved with greater ease.

With eyes still closed, she felt herself drifting toward him through a misty darkness as she deliberately sent out to him erotic images of them joined together. She wanted him to be aroused and ready for their lovemaking. But he wasn't responding. Dear God, he could be seriously injured. Please no!

Panic nibbled at her and broke her concentration. She opened her eyes. She was standing right in front of him. Thank God! Amidst tears of joy, she cried, "Colt! Oh, Colt I was so afraid I'd never see you again."

She knew she wasn't truly with him yet, not in a physical sense, but oh, it felt so real. She could actually feel the spongy earth beneath her feet and smell the pungent smell of the woods. But her joy at being with him quickly vanished when she saw the shocking condition he was in. He was tied to a tree, naked but for the Celtic cross, his neck and shoulder caked with dried blood, his head slumped against his chest.

His injury was serious. But how serious she wasn't qualified to tell. Dear God, she couldn't lose him, too. She had to believe that she had come in time to save him as well as her parents.

No wonder he hadn't reached out for her. He was in no condition to. But if they didn't make love, right away, she would find herself back at Lydia's house, and she would lose everyone she loved.

Reaching out she lifted his head gently with her hands. "Colt, I'm here. Look at me, darling, I'm here."

Colt's eyes opened for just a second, then closed again, but he had a funny little crooked smile on his face now. He knew she was there. Thank goodness for that much. Perhaps he had nothing more than a mild concussion.

"Colt, baby, I need your cooperation. I really need it bad

f we don't make love, I can't stay. Do you understand? *We
have to make it real."*

Standing on her tiptoes, she rained little kisses on his
face.

Colt groaned, and opened his eyes again. "Redddd, you
pick the damnedest times to make love."

"Oh, Colt, thank goodness. I was so afraid for you. Did
you hear what I said? We have to make love to complete
the transformation. I know this isn't exactly the most appropriate time, but it has to be done now, or it will be too
late."

"Red, I'm always ready to make love to you. But not
right now. Brent could come back at any moment."

His voice was husky with weariness, and pain, but he
kept it up. She had to know the danger she was in. "He
was going to kill me, but changed his mind. Told me he
had things to do first. . . . Find you . . . bring you here
where he could torture and rape you in front of me."

Destiny shivered, picturing that horrible image. "Brent
did this to you? That bastard. That, that . . . Wait. I don't
understand. Why didn't he know I disappeared?"

"We kept it from everyone . . . hoping . . . praying
you'd come back. No one knew you were missing. Now,
get these damn ropes off me before he shows up."

"Ropes?" She had been so intent on reaching her goal,
she had forgotten about them. "Oh, Colt, I don't know what
to do. If we don't make love right now, I'll be sent back
to the twentieth century. We've got to take the chance. How
long has he been gone?"

"Don't know. I was unconscious for a while."

"Well, I can't back down. I have no choice. But, Colt,
I'm afraid if I take the time to untie you, I'll lose my concentration. It could break the psychic bond that's keeping
me here."

Understanding the situation they were in, Colt answered,
"Red, my love will hold you here. Just listen to my voice.

Concentrate on me, honey. I won't let you go. *I'll never le*
you go."

Her spirits lifted. She had forgotten that Colt's love fo
her was as powerful as hers for him. Together they coul
do it. Letting out a long, shuddering breath to relieve th
terrible tension, Destiny made her way behind the tree an
set about untying him.

All the while, she listened as Colt spoke to her of hi
love, of his admiration for her courage. Of his dreams fo
their future, the children they would have, and all the thing
they would do together as man and wife.

Every word he spoke strengthened her, strengthened th
invisible bond between them, helping her to stay focuse
while she worked on the knots. She knew how hard it mus
be for him to keep talking, hurting and weary as he mus
be, but he kept it up until the very moment he was free.

Without the support of the ropes Colt started slidin
down the tree trunk, but quickly righted himself. Destin
mustn't know how weak he felt. It wasn't over yet. The
had to complete the transformation before it was too late

As soon as she rounded the tree, he opened his arms fo
her and she stepped into them and buried her head in hi
shoulder. Stroking her back with his hand he soothed he
with his voice. "There's nothing to be afraid of anymore."

Destiny knew better. In his weakened condition he migh
not be able to make love. "Oh, Colt, what if you can't d
it?"

"Red, honey. I spent the night tied to that damn tree wit
nothing to do but think. What do you suppose I was think
ing about? What do you think kept me from going crazy
Delicious thoughts of you and I making love."

Nuzzling her neck with his nose and lips, he said, "I ha
a lot of time to think of all the ways we could make love
I even thought of how incredibly sensuous it would fee
sliding into you when you were large with my child. Stop
worrying. It will happen."

With each word he spoke, Destiny found herself becoming more and more ready to believe it could happen. But still in need of assurance, her hand found his manhood. He came instantly alive.

Sweet relief rolled over her. There was no doubt that he could do his part. But what about her? She was a bundle of nerves, and no wonder. Her parents' lives were at stake. How could she ever perform under such terrible pressure?

Seeing her anxiety, Colt knew that it was up to him to make it happen. Gathering his strength, he held her at arm's length composing his face to hide any trace of the terrible pain radiating in his head. "Red, I want to adore you with my eyes. Undress for me."

The beginning of hope winnowed through her heart. With Colt in charge some of the terrible pressure would be off her. With a slight smile, she began to undress.

Good to his word, his eyes adored her as she stepped out of her jeans and pulled off her T-shirt. She felt the heat of his gaze in the very center of her being and desire unfurled inside her.

How could she have doubted for a moment that she would be ready for him? She wanted him, desired him, as much as she ever had. It was the most natural thing in the world to mate with Colt. How could she have forgotten that for a moment?

Stepping into the protective circle of his arms, she offered up her mouth for him to take and his lips came down on hers softly, sweetly. She breathed him in, reveling in the taste and smell of his breath, the electric touch of skin on skin. Closing her eyes, she surrendered her body to him, as his hands feathered over her breasts, then down the curve of her back to cup her buttocks.

Before she realized what was happening, he was kneeling in front of her, his head buried between her legs. Her lips parted, as a rush of air escaped her lungs. "Oh!"

Colt knew that pleasuring her like this was the quickest

way to take her where she needed to go, and he sent his tongue searching for the delicate little pleasure bud that would bring her to him in physical form. She responded by spreading her legs apart, opening up for him, both physically and mentally. Grasping the top of his head, she pulled him up against her.

Weaving her fingers through Colt's hair, Destiny stroked his head in time to the rhythmic stroking of his tongue as it worked its magic and was soon lost in a world of deep, intense pleasure.

"Colt. Now. Now. Oh, please, now."

Colt slid back up her body and ravaged her mouth, lowering her to the ground with the pressure of his hands on her shoulders.

In haste, she reached for him and quickly guided him inside her. The wonderful sensation that rolled over her as she felt him sliding deeper and deeper within her was all that she remembered it to be. She was no longer participating in an act that must be performed out of necessity. Oh, no. It was a need to be united with the man she loved so much, the desire to be joined to him as lovers had throughout endless time.

She wriggled her pelvis, eager to feel every inch of him to the fullest, and Colt answered with a deep thrust that sent her halfway to heaven. Holding him tight within her, the lovemaking that she prayed would bring her to his world in body as well as spirit began.

Weariness and pain disappeared as Colt became totally absorbed in the need to mate with Destiny. In the desire to become one with her. Everything forgotten as he concentrated on showing her with his body how much he loved her.

Taking advantage of her parted lips, his tongue explored her mouth. She took it, greedily, sucking on it, and sinking her teeth into it with tiny little love bites.

Her actions sent him reeling and he stepped up his thrusting, riding her as if he were riding for his very life. And he was.

Plunging into her, again and again, he knew he had her in his thrall, knew that she would respond to his every move in just the way he wanted. That very soon, her lusty cries would unite them, and they would be together forever and a day.

He worked her with all the skill he could muster, all the deep, undying love stored in his heart, while at the same time, his finger plucked an erotic tune on the moist, slippery nub that would bring her release all the faster.

She was almost there.

Almost . . . there.

Destiny felt herself slip away, reaching that high, mountaintop temple of emotion where she needed to go, and gave herself up to it. It was happening. It was here. The moment of their total union. Then, remembering she had to touch her ring to the pewter cross, she reached up to take it in her hand as Colt's voice sang out his rapture. She heard the familiar sound of the cubic zirconia striking against the metal cross at the same moment her voice joined his in passion's song. The world around her exploded, then expanded into enormous brightness and vibrant colors.

She had succeeded. The transformation was complete. She was there in substance now as well as in ethereal form.

Holding tight to his neck, she began to sob, releasing all the anxiety, all the fear and strain until it disappeared in the wake of her great joy.

She was with Colt.

Nothing could ever separate them again.

Colt stared into the face he loved so much. "Are you truly here? Or am I still dreaming?"

She laughed, then pulled his head down, her lips seeking his in a soft kiss. "You were dreaming, but no longer. I'm really here. Oh, Colt, I've got so much to tell you, but there isn't any time right now. We've got to go to my mother and father before it's too late."

"Your mother and father are here? Don't tell me time traveling is a family trait."

While they dressed, she told him what she had learned and the awful knowledge that Shining Dawn and Blade would die if she didn't get to them soon.

Colt dressed quickly, resisting the impulse to take her in his arms. If what she said was true, they had no time to waste. Especially since he had no idea how long it would take to find their way out of the woods.

Destiny looked around eagerly for the path that would take them back to civilization, but there wasn't any to be seen. "Which way do we go?"

"Red, all I know for sure is Brent and I came from that direction."

He pointed toward the west. She knew it was the west because a faint orange glow permeated the woods from that direction. Sunset. Dear God, it couldn't be that late. It couldn't. How long had she been in a trance? "Oh, Colt, don't tell me we're lost?"

Panic caused her voice to escalate, scaring off a covey of partridge. The beating of their wings filled the air as they rose from their hiding place and flew toward the sun.

"I'm sorry. Oh, God, I'm sorry, but I wasn't thinking about where I was going, at the time. I was concentrating too hard on waiting for the right moment to escape from Brent."

"Then we're doomed. My mother and father will die."

Destiny covered her eyes with her hand, her heart aching with sorrow. She pictured her mother in her mind, the memory of her vivid now, after so many years of being suppressed. She saw her in all her glory, lithe, beautiful, and so very brave. She saw her father, too, so handsome and loving, so worthy of the name father.

And then—unbidden—another face flashed before her. The Seminole warrior. She had almost forgotten about her psychic friend.

But something was different about him this time. His face hovered in front of her a few moments, staring at her with great curiosity, then it moved away from her, as the image turned from his face to a full-bodied form. He came to a rest several feet from her, and raised his right hand, pointing toward the northwest. Her heart filled with joy as she realized he was pointing the way out of the wilderness. "Thank you," she shouted joyously.

Colt looked at her with a curious expression. "Honey, are you seeing things again?"

"Can't you see him, too?" she said pointing at the Seminole. How could he not see him? The warrior was dressed in the colorful clothing of his people, complete with egret plume in his paisley print turban.

"I don't see anything."

"It's my Seminole friend. He's showing us the way out of here. Just follow me. Don't you see? We're not lost anymore."

Colt wasn't about to argue with her. He knew enough about her second sight now to trust that what she said was true. But it still seemed strange following her through the woods on blind trust that they were going the right way. If she were wrong they could become too lost to ever make it to the McAmmon place in time.

The wound on his head was throbbing now, and his vision was blurred. He wanted to slow down, gather his strength, but for Destiny's sake, and for Shining Dawn and Blade's sake, he stepped up his pace even more.

It soon became deathly dark, but they continued on, bumping into unseen roots and holes, being scratched by the low-hanging branches of the trees. They were both panting for breath by now, trying to keep up their pace, but the darkness made that impossible. Still, it was amazing how able Destiny was to make her way through the woods.

Colt had no idea how many hours passed before they

saw the faint glow of a campfire in the dead of night, and knew they had made it out. They emerged at the old sugar mill ruins, and Bo and Hank and Jim were there, guns drawn, until they ascertained whether it was friend or foe staggering through the woods toward them.

At the first sight of the men, the Seminole's form faded away, until there was nothing left of him. Just before he disappeared, she saw him smile triumphantly at her, and wave goodbye. He knew what he had accomplished.

She waved back, then turned her attention to the welcome sight of the rustic men who ran up to greet her. By now she was sure it must be past midnight. Time was growing short. It would take at least another hour of hard riding to make it to her parents' cabin.

Colt explained things as best he could to the three men, then helped Destiny mount one of the men's horses. Bo would join them and Hank and Jim would walk back to River's Edge.

They rode down the main road because it was the closest one to travel on, and the easiest, affording an unobstructed ride. That was important in the terrible darkness of the night.

They rode on and on, for what seemed like a lifetime to Destiny, and knowing she might be holding them back, urged the men to ride ahead of her.

Colt gave her a look that told her he didn't want to leave her, but she shouted, "Please, we have a lifetime to be together. You must save my parents. I'll be fine."

With that, Colt spurred his horse forward and Bo joined him, and it didn't take them long to ride completely out of sight.

Destiny tried to ride faster, but she was not an accomplished horsewoman by any means. The faster she rode the harder time she had staying on the horse's back.

After a while, the darkness didn't seem so bad, and that lifted her spirits some, until she raised her head and saw an eerie glow through the thickness of the trees. At first, she thought it was the rising moon, but as she rode closer and closer, her heart began to ache. She knew what caused the bright glow.

"Oh, God, no."

She spurred her horse on, everything forgotten but the sight of the terrible orange fire that lit up the night sky. And then, a short distance from the burning house, she saw Colt riding toward her. He drew up to her, and grabbed her horse's bridle. "You don't want to go over there."

She knew that he was trying to protect her, but she couldn't accept that. Not now. Not when she needed to find her parents. "No. Let go of me. I've got to go to them. I've got to see them. They can't be in the fire. They can't. They can't."

She jabbed at the horse's ribs and it reared, knocking Colt's hand away. Seeing her chance, she rode toward the awful bright light.

Colt caught up to her a few hundred feet from the house and grabbed the bridle again. She screamed unintelligible words that made no sense, even to her.

Bo saw the struggle and came to Colt's assistance, pulling her off the horse and holding her close to his chest until Colt dismounted and took her in his arms. "Honey, I'm so sorry, we were too late. The house is an inferno. It's impossible to get to them."

Destiny turned her head to look at the house completely engulfed in flames, and a deep rage began to build inside her. "Noooo. You were supposed to save them. Why didn't you save them?"

Her fists pummeled at his chest, but Colt was oblivious to the pain. His heart hurt so much more. Destiny had lost her parents again, and he knew how much she suffered. Tears formed in his eyes and he began to weep.

The shock of seeing Colt in tears stopped her from continuing her assault. She felt his pain, and it was almost as unbearable as her own. Throwing herself into his arms, she cried, "Oh, Colt, forgive me."

Colt's arms wrapped around her, and she buried her face in his shoulder as the fire crackled and roared behind her.

Thirty

Colt pleaded with Destiny to leave, but she refused. She kept telling him over and over that her parents weren't inside, and he knew she would never have peace of mind until she knew the truth, terrible though it might be.

The buggy standing before the stable should have been proof enough that her parents had returned, but she refused to look at it. Nothing he said would ever convince her that her parents were dead.

He understood why she couldn't believe that. It would be too much to bear, remembering them, after all these years, only to lose them before she could be united with them. In her shoes, he doubted whether he would feel any different.

Holding her in the circle of his arms, they stood watching until the house was completely consumed, leaving a blackened shell where once a home had stood. Then, as night turned to day, Destiny walked to the edge of the burned out shell. He started to follow after her, not wanting her to face the horror alone, but when he tried to accompany her, something held him back. A dark, cloying fear engulfed him, and he couldn't move.

This was crazy. Why should he be so frightened? He had no answer to that. He only knew it was impossible for him to walk inside. "Bo, will you go with her. I . . . can't."

Bo looked at Colt in astonishment, surprised that he would let her see such a horrific sight, surprised, too, that he couldn't face it himself. Colt wasn't a coward. There had to be a powerful reason why he couldn't go. "What is it, Colt?"

Colt shook his head. "I don't know. I can't explain it, I just know I can't go in there."

Destiny heard nothing of their conversation. Intent on learning the truth, she walked inside, stepping carefully over the still smoldering embers. Thick smoke stung at her eyes, and clogged her throat, but she couldn't retreat. She had to see. She had to know. Covering her mouth and nose with the bottom of her shirt, she took another step inside.

She felt a hand on her shoulder, and glanced back to see Bo's grim face through the swiirling smoke that curled up toward the morning sky.

"Over there," he said.

Destiny stared in horror at the blackened remains. What she saw had very little resemblance to anything human, but as the knowledge of what she saw registered on her brain she knew that what she saw was the form of two beings entwined in each other's arms.

Tears scalded her eyes. "Oh, no, it can't be true. It can't be true. It's not them. I know it's not. Oh, please, let it be anyone but Mommy and Daddy. Anyone. *Anyone."*

Bo pulled on her arm, trying to steer her out of that terrible place, but she didn't budge. Fearing the shock was too much for her, he lifted her into his arms and carried her out into the sunlight. She didn't resist.

Watching Bo emerge from the wall of smoke, Colt's strange paralysis vanished and he made his way over to him, taking Destiny from his arms. The grave look on Bo's face told him all he needed to know. Destiny knew the truth now. She would have to accept her parents' death.

Staring at the devastation over Colt's shoulder as he carried her to her horse, Destiny saw the Seminole warrior. Angrily, she blocked out his image and he quickly faded away.

She didn't want to see him now.

Didn't want to be reminded of how hopeful she had been when he had led them out of the woods.

What good had it done? They were still too late to save her parents.

No! That wasn't true. They weren't dead. They weren't. God couldn't be that cruel.

Colt set her on her horse, and took the reins, and she knew he was looking after her. She was in no shape to guide the animal herself. She watched as he mounted his horse and started them moving toward the road. He looked terrible, and she knew he must be suffering, too. But she didn't care.

She didn't care about anything right now. Let him lead her horse. Let him do her thinking for her. She was past thinking. Past caring about anything but the cold, gnawing fear, that what she left behind had really been her parents. Blocking out the horrible image, she prayed, oh, please, no.

Blinded by tears, and the sting of smoke in her eyes, the wretched smell of it clogging her throat, she wondered if she would ever smell anything fresh and clean again.

It was just as well Colt had the reins of her horse, for she could barely see through her tears. Through the rage that came over her. Had it all been for nothing, her remembering? What was the point? Why couldn't she still be in blissful iguorance of who her parents were? Better that than knowing she would never see them again. Better that than feeling such tremendous pain.

The Indian's face came to her again, looking at her with great curiosity, but again she blocked it out of her mind. She couldn't deal with him right now. She didn't have time. Time? Dear God, would she never have the luxury of time again? Must it always be her enemy?

Fearing she would go mad if she didn't stop thinking about it, she wiped her eyes and looked up. They were in sight of River's Edge. That surprised her. She had been almost completely unaware of the miles that had passed. Taking in a deep, shuddering breath in anticipation of see-

ing Faith and Paul and having to tell them what had transpired, a huge sob shuddered through her body.

Colt glanced back at her, with concern showing in his
eyes. "Hold on, honey, you're almost home."

"Almost home." The words washed over her like a balm
and she suddenly felt better. Something inside of her told
her that all would be well when she reached the sanctity of
her home, and knowing how crazy that thought was she
wondered if she had finally gone completely insane. How
could anything be all right again?

And yet, the feeling became so strong inside her that she
started to believe.

She had been right all along.

Her parents didn't die in the fire. They couldn't have.
Not when she needed them to be alive so much. She felt
it so strongly she wanted to share it with Colt and blurted
out, "They're not dead, Colt. It wasn't them back there. I
know it now. They're waiting for me at my house. Hurry,
please, hurry, I want to be with them."

"Red. Stop that. You've got to accept the truth. Don't
torture yourself like this." But as he spoke, he stepped up
the pace of the horses, wanting to get her safely into her
house before she broke down completely.

Destiny thought he finally believed her, and she smiled
through her tears as they galloped up to the door to her
gazebo house. Her parents would be waiting for her inside.
Or maybe they were sitting out on the deck, enjoying the
peaceful view of the river. She would join them there and
everything would be all right.

Yes, everything was going to be all right. They were waiting for her. She knew they were.

She just knew they were.

Without waiting for Colt's help, she jumped off the horse
and started for the door, shouting, "Mommy, Daddy."

Colt caught up to her, and pulled her into his arms, crying
out, "Red, don't do this. Please don't do this to yourself.

They're not in there. You saw them back at the cabin. You know they're dead."

The door was flung open then, and a woman stepped out into the morning light, her tawny-colored hair shimmering, touched with gold from the bright sun, her face beaming with happiness.

Colt's arms went limp as he stared in surprise.

Destiny heard a soft voice call her name, and spun around to stare into the face of her mother.

Destiny blinked, afraid she was looking at an apparition. Then, in a dreamlike state, she stepped into Shining Dawn's arms, and for the first time in so many, many years felt the loving embrace of her mother.

Her mother lived. Breathed. Existed in the same time as she. And that was the most precious gift she would ever, ever have.

Tears of happiness streaked down her smudged face as she whispered reverently, "Mother!"

Taking her daughter's face in her hands, tears glistening in her eyes, Shining Dawn said softly, "Destiny Dawn, my beautiful little girl, I've ached to hold you for so long."

"Oh, Mother, I don't know what I'd have done if you weren't here. I was so afraid I would never see you again. I saw those poor burned bodies and thought they were you and Daddy's."

Shining Dawn looked past Destiny to Colt. "Bodies? What is she talking about, Colt?"

Trying to get over his astonishment at seeing Shining Dawn alive, Colt cleared his throat, then answered, "Your cabin burned to the ground. There were two bodies found in it. We—I—thought they were you and Blade." Then worry creased his face as he asked, "Where is he?"

Shining Dawn smiled reassuringly. "Safe and in good health. He and Johnny just returned from your place, Colt. I sent them over there looking for the two of you." Glancing up the path leading to the house, she pointed saying,

"They're coming now. Blade's been so worried. We were both worried when we found out you and Destiny had been lost in the woods."

Staring at her mother in surprise, Destiny said, "But how did you know?"

Hugging her tight, Shining Dawn answered, "Do you mean you really don't know yet? Say hello to your father and brother and I think the answer will become clear to you."

Holding tight to her mother, Destiny turned her head in time to see her father running up to her. He looked exactly as she remembered, tall, handsome, with vivid blue eyes that reminded her so much of Drake's. "Daddy!"

Blade folded her in his arms, and she smiled up to his beloved face. "Oh, Daddy, I've missed you so."

"Baby, I've missed you too, but I never gave up thinking that we would all be together again some day. And here you are." Blade McAmmon kissed his daughter's forehead, still streaked with soot, then held her an arm's distance away. "Let me look at you, sweetheart."

A deep masculine voice said, "Believe me, she looks much better with a clean face."

Destiny stared into the face of her Seminole warrior. "You! It's you!"

Holding his hand out to her, he said, "Hi, Destiny, I'm your brother, Johnny. It's about time we met in person, don't you think?"

Colt stared from Johnny to Destiny, then back again. "He's your Seminole warrior?" Laughing joyously, he put his arm around Johnny's shoulder. "All this time it's been your brother you've been seeing?"

Destiny felt the warmth of Johnny's hand course through her as she held tight to him. He was real. He was here. This was no hallucination. None of this was a hallucination. She had her family back. "Johnny. Thank you for being there when I needed you. Oh, boy, have I needed you. But it's over now, isn't it? We're all together. Nothing can separate us again."

"Amen to that," Colt said. "Shining Dawn. Blade. It hasn't been easy trying to pin your daughter down long enough to marry her, but with your permission, I mean to do that real soon."

A radiant Shining Dawn took Destiny by one hand and Colt by the other. "You won't find any objections from us, Colt. I've always known the two of you belonged together."

Destiny gazed from one beloved face to the next, happier than she ever dreamed she could be. Everyone whom she loved was within reach of her touch, surrounding her with their presence and their love and she felt blessed. Nothing bad could ever happen to her again.

"I can't believe you are all really here. There's only one way I could be any happier and that is to have Colt's parents here to share this wonderful reunion."

Colt suddenly shivered, and wondered why.

Was it because everything was just a little too perfect now?

Would there be a price to pay for Destiny's newfound happiness? That was silly. He was getting as superstitious as she was. Nothing would mar this day for her, or for him.

But he should have known better.

He should have realized that there was a price to pay for everything.

When Blade spoke, he immediately knew what that price was.

"Sweetheart, you'll have your wish very soon, I'm sure. Lily Tiger told me Little Bit and Gary rode out to our place yesterday to make it ready for our return. Can you imagine that? What a thoughtful gesture. She got our letter and knew we'd be home last night. She must be wondering what happened to us by now. She couldn't know that we came directly here to find you."

Destiny listened to her father through a deep, muted fog

as the truth swept through her like wildfire. In horror, her gaze fastened on Colt's ashen face. "Colt, oh, Colt, I'm so sorry."

Moving toward him, she reached out for him, wanting to embrace him, to soothe away the pain he must be feeling. But that wasn't to be. He backed away from her, his hands flailing helplessly in front of him as if warding off an evil entity. "Tell me it wasn't them you saw. Tell me it was anyone but them."

Colt's words ricocheted through her brain, and she remembered her fervent plea back at the fire, that it be anyone lying there but her parents. *Anyone. Anyone.*

But not Little Bit and Gary, not them.

She didn't mean for it to be them.

"Oh, no, what have I done? Oh, Colt, I never wanted it to be them."

Colt stared at her in horror, but he wasn't seeing her, he was seeing the terrible fire that had taken his parents from him. In the midst of the flames he saw Brent's face, laughing at him, taunting him. Rage consumed him. Blocking out Destiny's pleading voice, he leapt on his horse, and quickly rode away.

"Colt, no! Oh, no, don't go. Please don't leave me!" She tried to go after him but her father grabbed her arm. "What is it, sweetheart? What's wrong?"

"Oh, Daddy, there was a terrible fire at your cabin last night, Little Bit and Gary died in it."

"Sweet Jesus, Johnny saw the fire in his vision, but for some reason the image was blocked before he could see where it was. All he knew was you and Colt were unhurt."

Destiny watched with a heavy heart as Colt barreled down the road. She knew what he was feeling. Hadn't she just been through it herself, thinking her parents dead? But the difference was, that in her heart, she had believed they were still alive. Colt had no hope of that.

Her heart became suddenly constricted as she realized

what he was going to do. "Bo, you've got to stop him. He's going to kill Brent."

Bo had already come to the same conclusion and was mounting his horse. As he rode away he saw Paul emerging from the main house and shouted for him to follow him. They had to stop Colt before he could get to Brent. It wasn't that he wanted to protect Brent. No. The bastard deserved to die if he was the one who trapped the Mandrells inside the cabin and started the fire. He wanted to protect Colt. Let the law take care of Brent Raiford.

Destiny watched as the men rode after Colt, and felt a measure of hope that they could reach him, but still she couldn't just sit back and wait. "Daddy, I've got to go after him."

Understanding washed over Blade. He knew what Colt was going to do. "Let's go. Maybe by the time he gets to town, his anger will have cooled some. But if it doesn't, you're the only one who has a chance of talking him out of it."

Shining Dawn pulled herself from the deep grief she was feeling. Hugging Destiny tight, she said, "Come back to me safely. I don't want to lose you again"

"Oh, Mommy, we'll never be parted again. I can promise you that. When I get back we'll talk about your grandchild who will be born in a few months."

Holding her hand to her heart while the wonderful news swirled around in her brain, Shining Dawn watched as her daughter and her husband rode out of sight.

She didn't deserve such happiness. Not when she was feeling such guilt. If she hadn't written a letter telling Little Bit the date of her arrival, Little Bit and Gary would never have ridden out to the cabin. They'd still be alive.

Then another revelation hit her. If not for Johnny's special bond with his sister, he wouldn't have had the vision that let them know Destiny was back. She and Blade would have stayed at the cabin last night, and they, too, would have been killed.

But when Johnny told her and his father about his visions of Destiny, they had headed straight for her gazebo, anxious to be reunited with their daughter.

Would Colt ever forgive them for surviving when his parents had not?

With a heavy heart, she had the thought that this terrible tragedy had been a long time in the making. It started the night Colt was born, the very moment Destiny had been swept through time.

A shiver coursed through her, remembering the awful moment she had watched her daughter disappear before her eyes.

But what had kept her from falling apart then was the knowledge that the Great Spirit had taken her somewhere where she could be helped, and the hope that she would be returned to her some day.

If that scene hadn't been horrible enough, she had no sooner lost her daughter, when she heard the low, feral growl of a wolf and saw it standing in the doorway.

It stared up at her with such cold, bright eyes, she knew that it was about to leap at her, tear the baby from her arms. But, miraculously, it hadn't. Instead, it gave out a frightened whimper and backed out of the doorway like some domesticated dog being chastised by its master. And indeed, she was sure it had been, for surely the Great Spirit had once again intervened.

She had a lot to be thankful for, although she hadn't fully appreciated it until now, when her daughter was returned to her. The Great Spirit has sent Destiny to a place where she could be helped, had saved her and Colt from the jaws of the wolf.

In turn, hadn't she given Little Bit many more years to live than she would have had otherwise? She would have died the night Colt was born if not for what she had done. She would try and remember that whenever she felt sad about her death. But it was small comfort. Gary and Little Bit had been her greatest friends.

* * *

Riding toward town, Destiny couldn't help but think that time was once again an old enemy. If she didn't get to Colt in time, their lives together could be destroyed forever. Her anxiety increased with each mile that passed, and she knew her father felt it, too. "We'll make it in time, sweetheart."

Knowing her father was by her side made the ride tolerable, and when they finally arrived in town without so much as catching sight of Colt, or even Bo and Paul, they rode directly to Brent's house. That was the first place Colt would look for him.

Susan answered the door, looking perturbed. "Just what the hell is going on? Colt was here looking for Brent, and then Bo and Paul. Now you two. Will someone tell me what's going on, before I go mad?"

"Where did they go, Susan?" Blade asked softly, trying not to alarm her. "Did you tell Colt where Brent was?"

"Of course, I didn't. Do I look stupid? I could see the state he was in, and I wasn't about to let him get into any trouble with the law over the likes of Brent Raiford."

Destiny drew in a deep breath of relief. "Oh, Sue, thank you."

"Don't thank me, just tell me what kind of trouble Brent is in. I have a right to know."

Blade and Destiny exchanged looks, and Susan knew it had to be something very bad. "You're scaring me. What is it, Blade? What has Brent done?"

"Sue, I wish I had the time to tell you this gently, but there isn't any. Hon, Little Bit and Gary have been killed. Brent set fire to the McAmmon cabin thinking Shining Dawn and I were inside."

Susan's face contorted into a myriad of expressions as she tried to come to grips with what they were saying. "This has to be some terrible mistake. What would my parents be doing out at your place, Blade? Oh, God! Tell me it's some awful mistake. Tell me! Tell me!" She knew by the looks on their faces that there was no mistake and great sobs racked her body. "Oh, noooo, noooo."

Blade tried to embrace her, but Susan pulled away. "Don't touch me. If not for you they'd still be alive. Why did she have to go out there? Why did she have to be so good to everyone?"

Destiny's heart went out to Susan, but she forced herself to do what she must. "Susan, there's no time. Colt is out looking for Brent. He means to kill him. You've got to tell us where Brent is so we can prevent it."

Hatred glimmered in Susan's eyes like fire from the depths of hell. "Let the bastard die."

"You don't understand," Destiny cried, "Colt will go to jail. Do you want him to hang for killing Brent?"

Destiny's words penetrated through her wall of hatred, and she took a deep, shuddering breath. Colt mustn't suffer for killing Brent. He didn't have to. She'd kill the bastard herself. Wiping the tears from her eyes, she said very calmly, "It's all right. I sent Colt to Brent's bank. But of course, he won't find him there. Today is Christmas, the bank is closed."

"Where is he then?" Destiny tried to keep the panic from her voice, but it wasn't easy. So much was at stake.

"He's . . . out back, sitting down by the river."

Blade and Destiny started immediately for the back of the house. Susan didn't follow them. Instead, she went to the little cherry wood desk her father had made for her, and opened the drawer, taking out the pearl-handled revolver.

Without a moment of thought, she left her house and strode down the street purposefully. Brent wasn't down by the river. She had told them that to get them out of the way. She knew where he was. At his favorite saloon, laughing and drinking while her parents lay dead. Well, he wouldn't be laughing in a moment. No. He wouldn't be drinking either. But she would be. Drinking a toast over his dead body.

Thirty-one

Bitter disappointment ate at Colt's gut. Brent wasn't at the bank. Susan had lied to him. But he blamed himself for falling for her lie. He should have remembered what day it was. In all his worry, all his grief, he had forgotten that the world was celebrating Christmas today.

Standing in the middle of the town plaza, the very center of the ancient little town, Colt surveyed his surroundings with a steady gaze, searching the landscape for any sign of Brent Raiford. A group of peole dressed in medieval costumes were gathered at the gazebo singing Christmas carols for the throng of people on their way to the cathedral across the way. That seemed so very odd. How could everything go on as usual when his parents lay dead?

A hard lump formed in Colt's throat listening to the joyous songs until his throat ached from holding back his tears. His mother and father would never hear that beautiful music again.

Could Brent hear the music? Was he enjoying his Christmas morning? Feeling smug, thinking he had gotten rid of him in the woods? Thinking he had killed Shining Dawn and Blade in the fire? It galled him to think that Brent had one moment of pleasure believing he had accomplished his goal. But that meant it would be all the more sweet when he witnessed the total abject failure on Brent's face. When the bastard found out that he would die for nothing.

But it wouldn't be for nothing, would it? He would die

for killing his parents. His mother, sweet, loving, and so innocent. His father, brave, honorable, his friend, his idol. Oh, God, how could he bear the loss.

He knew now why he hadn't been able to enter the burned out cabin. Somewhere, deep inside of him, he must have sensed their death and wanted to reject it. Destiny wasn't the only one with paranormal powers, it seemed.

Destiny. He hated leaving her that way. But for just a moment, he had blamed her for his parents' death. He knew now that was unfair. On his ride into town, he had sorted out what had happened, and he knew his parents would have died whether Destiny was in his life or not.

But it was clear that her presence had changed the course of history. Because of her, Shining Dawn and Blade had not gone to their cabin, where they would have died along with his parents. Because of her they had traveled straight to River's Edge for a reunion with their daughter.

But, perhaps, even that wasn't true. Perhaps, even without Destiny here, they still would have gone to River's Edge. The yellowed newspaper article about the McAmmons' death was wrong, not because Destiny's presence had saved her parents, but because the charred bodies had been too badly burned to be identified properly. Once the truth was discovered, another newspaper article would have been written to clear that up.

His parents would have died, in either case. His mother's generous and loving spirit had sent her to the cabin. Sent her to her death. And by God, he'd see that Brent paid for that.

But where was the bastard? If not his home, if not the bank, where?

Where? He had to clear his head of grief and think clearly before Brent was warned. If Brent knew he was still alive he'd slink off somewhere to hide.

Had he done that already? Is that why he couldn't find him anywhere? No. It would be too cruel knowing that he lived while his parents were dead. If there was any justice in this world, he would pay for all the deaths. His parents, Judith Langford, and Cedric Farley.

Slowly pivoting in a circle, Colt faced in each direction, his eyes searching for Brent, his hand resting firmly on his gun holster, ready, waiting, while the world around him spun peacefully on its way, seemingly untouched by the death of his parents. But he knew that was unfair. The town would mourn for them once it knew of the murders. But that was not enough. Not nearly enough to ease his pain. Brent Raiford must die.

The chorus of voices began singing "Oh Come All Ye Faithful," and try as he might he couldn't block it from his mind. Then, unbidden, the lovely image of Destiny's face penetrated his hatred, filling his heart with love, and he knew, somewhere deep within, that if he killed Brent his future with Destiny would be forever ruined. He tried to push that thought away.

He wanted revenge.

He thirsted for it.

It would eat him up and destroy him if he couldn't have it.

But Destiny. Oh, God, Destiny. He wanted her more. He needed her more than he needed revenge. Dropping his hands to his side, he closed his eyes for a moment, and he came to a stop facing the direction of the cathedral. For her and his unborn child, he would not kill.

Gathering his willpower, all his strength to resist the urge to kill, he opened his eyes and saw his sister Susan walking determinedly toward the tavern across the road. She had a revolver in her hand. He knew immediately what she was going to do, and for the length of time it took to draw in a deep breath of air, he considered letting her accomplish her goal.

Brent could still die. But not by his hand. Susan would do it for him. Do it for herself. She deserved to have revenge, too.

Then reason took hold of him and he started running toward her, shouting her name. He couldn't let her ruin her life over Brent.

"Susan. No."

Susan never looked up. She walked into the tavern without a moment's hesitation. With his heart in his throat, he started running faster.

Suddenly, he was wrenched to a stop. Bo and Paul were tugging on his arms, keeping him from going to his sister.

"Colt," Paul said, "he's not worth it. Let the law handle it. We'll dance at his hanging."

Colt gazed at his friends with a glazed look. "You don't understand."

"We understand," Bo said, "But we can't let you, do it."

"Damn it, Let me go. Susan just went inside the tavern with a revolver."

"Colt!"

Hearing Destiny's anxious voice, Colt swiveled his head to look at her. She and Blade were running toward him. Her face was pale beneath the streaks of black that still painted her face, and he knew what she must be thinking. "Red. It's all right. I didn't kill him. I couldn't, knowing I would lose you and the baby."

Hearing the sincerity in his voice, Bo and Paul released their hold on their friend.

Destiny ran into his arms. "Oh, Colt, thank goodness for that. I was so afraid I was going to lose you. So afraid you would hate me now, thinking I was responsible for your parents' death."

Gazing into her sorrow-filled eyes, Colt murmured, "Hate you? I could never hate you. Honey, you're not responsible for their death. Brent is, and he's going to pay for it. But not by my hands."

Bo and Paul started for the tavern, shouting at Blade to go get the sheriff. They entered the saloon, and came to a halt. Susan was sitting calmly at a table with Brent, sipping at a drink. Bo decided Colt had been mistaken. It was obvious Susan had no intentions of killing Brent.

Paul thought otherwise. He had been raised with Susan and Colt, and he knew the way her mind worked. Gazing closely at her face, he saw that she was working hard at appearing calm.

The two men sized up the situation, and decided to play it by ear until the sheriff came. They couldn't take the chance on innocent bystanders getting hurt.

Brent felt the tension in the air, and looked up to see Colt's men. "What's going on, boys? Come join me and the missus, have a drink with us."

"Got something to celebrate?" Bo asked, almost nonchalantly.

Brent looked puzzled. "I've always got a reason to celebrate."

"Well, that's real good. I'd like to join you, but I guess I'll just wait until Colt comes along. Wouldn't want him to feel left out."

"Colt?" A sly smile played across Brent's face. "We're liable to have a long wait then. I heard he's been missing for a couple of days."

"You heard wrong, brother-in-law."

The glass of whiskey fell from Brent's grasp, smashing violently against the floor, a sharp splinter of glass cutting Brent on the ankle. He didn't feel it. He was too numb. Too intent on staring at the man he thought he had killed.

Rising from his chair slowly, Brent reached for his gun, stopping in midair when he felt something hard poking into his back. "Don't do it, Brent."

"Susan! What the hell are you doing."

"Put both your hands on the table, Brent. I want to see them."

Thinking Susan must be angry because Colt told her about the incident in the woods, he decided he was going to have to try and talk himself out of this one. "Seems I'm in a ticklish situation here. Why don't we just forget all about our little misunderstanding, Colt, and be friends again? After all, no harm done."

"No harm done?" Blade said, walking into the saloon in time to hear Brent's remark, Destiny at his side.

Brent's eyes blinked shut for a moment. This was crazy. Here was another man who was supposed to be dead. Next thing you know, Cedric Farley and Judith Langford would be walking through the door, too. How the hell had Blade escaped the fire? He had tied both doors shut and set fire to the windows to make sure the McAmmons couldn't get out.

"You bastard. You killed two of the nicest people in this town, and you say no harm done?"

Brent had no idea what Blade was talking about. But he didn't have time to worry about it. He had to figure out how he was going to get out of here alive. Susan was still his best hope for that.

"Darlin', you don't believe any of this, do you? It's ludicrous to think I would kill anyone. Why don't you take that gun out of my back?"

"Why, that's a real good idea, Brent. A real good idea." Standing up, Susan pointed her gun at the men. "Boys, I want you all to leave. I want to have a quiet little drink with my husband."

Destiny's heart ached for Susan. Ached for Colt. She knew what was about to happen and felt powerless to stop it.

Blade gave Susan a sympathetic look. "Sue. The sherriff is on his way. No need for you to do anything rash. He'll be here with his deputies in just a moment."

Blade kept his eyes on Brent the whole time he talked. So did Colt and Bo and Paul. But none of the men drew a gun. Too many innocent people in the place. They knew better than to force Brent into going for his gun.

Susan was the one to worry about. She had the hammer drawn back on her gun, and was now waving the weapon at everyone in the saloon.

"I said, leave. Everyone. I can't be responsible for what might happen if you don't get out of here immediately."

The sudden shuffling of chairs filled the air as everyone started filing out. Everyone but Bo, Paul, Blade, and Colt. They stood their ground, their eyes never wavering from Brent.

Destiny wanted to stay, too, but knew Colt would feel better knowing she was safe. But, oh, it was so hard to leave him and her father there. Saying a silent prayer, she walked outside to wait.

When the room was cleared, Susan pleaded with her brother. "Please, Colt, don't do this. Leave him to me. Take your friends and get out of here before someone gets hurt."

"Sue, I know what you want to do, and I don't blame you for a minute. I want the bastard dead, too. I want him dead so bad I almost blew my only chance for happiness with Destiny. But I won't do that. Not even for revenge. We're going to be married and, honey, I want to make sure you'll be at that wedding."

Susan smiled grimly. "I wouldn't count on that."

Brent felt a cold fear in the pit of his stomach, hearing those cold words. What the hell was Colt talking about? What was going on here? Why was Susan sounding so depressingly melancholy? There was something he wasn't understanding yet. Why would Susan want to kill him? She had no reason. No reason at all.

Susan pressed the gun against the back of Brent's head, and he almost peed his pants. "What . . ."

"You slimy bastard, you don't even know what this is about, do you? I've only loved three people in my whole life, and you've killed two of them. You're going to die for that."

Colt started for her, but she warned him away with a crazy look in her eyes. He knew if he proceeded any closer to her, she'd pull the trigger. "Sue, he's not worth it. He'll pay for our parents' death with his life."

Brent's eyes opened wide with fear then. Little Bit and

Gary? It had been them in the cabin? He thought when he saw the lantern light, the buggy, and the horse in the corral that Shining Dawn and Blade had returned. Hell, it was Little Bit who had mentioned to him that the McAmmons would be returning that day.

He felt a moment of deep regret. Little Bit had always been good to him. Had treated him like a son, not like the wretched woman who had given birth to him. The witch who had scorned him all his childhood, belittling him, making him feel less than human.

His mother. A sneer curled on his lips at the thought of her.

It was the last thought he ever had.

The shot sounded obscene in the confines of the tavern, echoing off the walls. But Brent Raiford never heard it. He lay dead on the floor at Susan's feet.

Destiny heard the awful sound and ran into the tavern afraid of what she would find. Colt was standing there, his arms wrapped protectively around his sister. And then her father was there, comforting her, and she knew that the horror was over, at last.

On a cool, crisp day, one month later, Destiny and Colt walked arm in arm out to the deck of her gazebo house. Destiny gazed out at the water, knowing that what she was about to do would assure that she would stay forever in her own time.

After today, she would have everything she had ever dreamed of. She would have her parents living nearby, and she would have the man she loved, without fear of ever being separated from him.

If not for Little Bit and Gary's death, she would have been ecstatically happy. And, oh, how that scared her. It was hard getting rid of old fears, but she was learning how.

Colt still mourned the loss of his parents greatly, but she

knew that her presence eased that pain somewhat. And at least, he didn't have to worry about the fate of his sister. After a quick hearing, it was decided that Susan had shot her husband to save Colt's life, and no one told the judge any different. She got off without so much as an overnight stay in the jail house and left right after Little Bit and Gary's funeral to visit with her aunt Celeste and her new Yankee husband.

"It's time . . . Destiny."

Colt's voice broke through her reverie.

Time. Her enemy no longer.

"I'm ready," she answered, taking her last remaining ring from her finger. She was going to miss her beautiful fake diamond. Capturing the rays of the sun, the stone shimmered with light, like a flame of hope, or the first star at night. Wasn't that the star you were supposed to wish upon?

A lump came to her throat as she remembered standing at this very spot when Colt's father asked her if she was a fairy godmother because she had granted two wishes. First to Penelope, and then to Faith and Paul. He told her she had one more wish to go, and he hoped it would be to make her son very happy.

Gazing up at Colt's face, smiling down at her despite the dull numbness of grief that haunted his eyes, she knew that last wish was about to be granted. Kissing her beautiful heart-shaped ring goodbye, she raised her arm over her head and threw it out over the river.

Colt's arms closed around her as they watch the ring arch over the water sending fairy dust sparkles of light into the air. It hit the water with a delicate little splash, then sank forever out of view.

Smiling up at Colt, she said, 'You're stuck with me now. I hope you're happy."

The fervent pressing of his lips against hers was all the answer she needed.

Dear Readers,

Just a few short years ago Zebra took a chance on an unpublished writer's first book and my career as an author began.

Since that magical day in 1992 when *Rosefire* appeared in bookstores all over the country, I've had four more books published. *A Love for All Time, Thorn of the Rose, One Shining Moment,* and now, *The Heart Remembers.*

I want to thank all you wonderful readers who have also taken a chance on a new writer, buying and reading my books. You've let me know, through your letters, just how much you enjoyed my stories. I want you to know how much I appreciate hearing from you.

Sandra Davidson
PO Box 3634
St. Augustine, FL 32085-3634